Nathanial Ghere

Natnanial

Forward¶

Rattler is the story about a boy who grows up in a family specializing in snake-wrangling and developing anti-venom for various hospitals, clinics and native Indian villages. This story is set in the present day (2017), but takes place in an alternate universe. The main difference is; society as a whole is still grounded in the old west. All of the fifty states still exist, however, there is no federal government; no president or congress; no United States of America. Each state is independent; including city and county governments. Slavery never existed, and all of the settlers who came to this land lived peacefully alongside the Indians (no Indian reservations). There were no wars over land or slavery; no Civil War; no World War I or World War II. Mainly because semi- and fully-automatic weapons have been outlawed; there are no weapons of mass destruction. People only own single-shot guns like pistols, shotguns and rifles. And since there is no army, the law is enforced by marshals, sheriffs, and deputies.¶

Mankind decided to focus most of its efforts to advance technologies in the medical field. Hospitals have x-rays, MRI's, ultra-sounds, and can perform all of the surgeries that our world can. Yet there are no computers, televisions, or internet; they only have land-line telephones (no cell phones), radios and newspapers. Every mode of transportation, other than bicycles, is steam-powered; steam-cycles, boats, trains, and horse-drawn carriages. There are no planes; and steam-boats are not capable of crossing the vast oceans. Life is simple in this world. Most families have small farms in conjunction with their regular jobs. Copper, silver and gold coins are only minted in Canada and are the world's currency; there are one, five, ten, twenty, and one hundred dollar coins in circulation. Many people barter goods and services instead of relying on money. As a whole, society is healthy and balanced; there are no drugs, but alcohol has never been a real problem (drunk driving and such).¶

For some, this universe appears to be a sort of utopia; one without many of our planet's problems. But peace and prosperity does not last forever, there are some who seek to conquer parts of the world. And it is all starting in Blackwater, Texas; at a company named Dead-Eye Inc. They are secretly developing automatic weapons to sell on the black market. Max and his son stumble into the middle of things while clearing out venomous snakes from the company's loading docks and discover the schematics for a Gatling gun (which is highly illegal). Max, along with his friends, Butch and Scotty, decide that something must be done. Since they lack the evidence to go to the authorities, they choose to get personally involved as their families have lived in Blackwater for many generations.¶

Join in the adventure when a samurai, ninjas, and a mysterious organization emerges from within the company. Max also seeks help from the Blackfoot Indian warriors to aid in the fight against the evil gun manufacturing company. Max and his friends face danger from all sides; who will emerge victorious? The mysterious figure from Japan?

Dead-Eye Inc., the largest company in all of Texas?
Or will Max, Butch, and Scotty find a way to bring
those responsible to justice?

A Special Thanks To:

My father, Michael, for helping me write my book;

My brother, Stravier, for helping with the illustrations;

My mother, Starlene, for taking my picture;

My hairstylist, Brooke, for cutting my hair for the photo;

And everyone else who believed in me.

CHAPTER I - The Boy¶

Max was just finishing up with the last copperhead. He had milked this particular snake at least a dozen times, but each time was different. This snake should not be so aggressive after several months on the ranch. Max only milked his snakes once every ten days; this ensured that they produced enough venom and stayed healthy. After capturing snakes from the wild, he would slowly change their diet so they would except warmed, dead mice. Feeding them live prey also put them at risk for injuries and disease, which could lead to death. He liked his snakes living long, healthy lives. That is how a snake wrangler makes a good living.¶

Max's son was sitting on the porch playing his

harmonica. The late morning sun's light was reflected in the small pond which laid about thirty yards from the front of the house. It was not really big enough to swim in, but there were always plenty of frogs and minnows to catch and release. The paperboy rode his bicycle up the dirt driveway and tossed the Daily Blackwater about twenty feet, landing almost perfectly at the boy's feet. "Nice playing, what song is that?" He looked up a little confused, "This ain't a song, it's a random tune." "Ain't a song?! What kind of grammar is that?" Max had just rounded the side of the house and heard his son's broken English. "Sorry dad. This isn't a song." His father always corrected him whenever he used words that did not exist.¶

"Morning sir. Nice day for catching snakes is it?" he said, popping the kickstand on his bike. The boy's father bent down to pick up the paper when the paperboy pointed out the headline. "How Ironic… 'Gunz a' Blazin' burns down. Ha ha ha! What a headline! I know it's not funny, but at least nobody died." Max had a concerned look on his face. The paper explained that the fire was caused by faulty electrical wiring, but he did not seem to think that was the case here. "Yeah, thank goodness." He said as he looked up. "Sir, it's collection day." "Oh, right." He fished twelve dollars out of his pocket and handed it to the boy. "Here, go give this to our friend." The boy gave the paperboy the money and he promptly shoved it in his bag, jumped back up on his bike, and took off down the driveway towards the road.¶

"Go grab the phone, son, I think I just heard it ring." He set his harmonica on the big rock by the front steps and headed into the house. Running through the dining room and into the kitchen, he grabbed the phone and answered, "The Golden Snake, Max's son speaking." He always referred to himself as 'Max's son' because his parents never named him. Some thought it odd, but that was how it had always been, so it did not seem so strange to him. "Hello, this is Mr. Wilson over at the Wilson Horse Ranch. Can you go get your father please?" The boy knew who Mr. Wilson was and happily had him hang on while he went to get him. "Dad, it's Mr. Wilson."¶ Max took the phone from his son's hands and held it up to his ear. "Good day Mr. Wilson, hope all is well." He knew there had to be a snake-related problem, but he did not want to come off as serious and all business-like. "Well Max, I wish this was just a social call but you know it's a snake if it isn't social." Mr. Wilson was terrified of snakes and sometimes imagined hearing rattles here and there, but this time he and his wife both saw it while they were grooming their horses outside the barn. "Can you come by sometime today or tomorrow… preferably today?" The trepidation in his voice was quite apparent. "I can definitely be there today. In fact, I just finished my milking and can get there in twenty minutes, just let me grab my gear." "Thanks Max, the wife and I can't get any work done having to tip-toe around the place. See ya' in twenty then." Hanging the phone up, he turned to his son; but before he got a word out, the boy took off out the door to fetch the bags from the shed. He thought maybe today he would let the boy take the lead on this job.¶

He quickly returned with two large bags filled with snake wrangling equipment, including two poles with slip-rope on the ends. Max's son was so excited, he loved the fact that he was the only eight-year-old he knew of that helped capture venomous snakes for a living. "Why are you bringing them to me? Go load 'em in the sidecar." He was so distracted by the thought of snake-wrangling, he forgot they still had to travel to the other ranch first. Placing the bags at his feet he immediately put on the motorcycle helmet, placed the two poles between his legs, and pulled the goggles down over his eyes. Not only did he get to help out his father on the job, but riding down the road in a steam-powered motorcycle's sidecar was always a thrill.¶

Quickly warming up the cycle, his father slipped it into gear and barreled off down the road towards the Wilson Ranch. As they approached the fence along the property, they slowed a bit and went off-road to the rear of the barn. He throttled down to decrease the noise as much as possible; he did not want to spook the animals. Slowing to a crawl, he spotted Mr. and Mrs. Wilson who were already waving to them from the side of the stables. "Over here Max!" cried Mrs. Wilson. They had known each other since before his son was born. They had all grown up in Blackwater, Texas, and had even attended the same school.¶

Parking at the corner of the stables, Max dismounted the motorcycle as his son climbed out of the sidecar. "I made some fresh lemonade for when you're finished." She exclaimed. "We last saw it crawling towards that space between the barn door and the drainage pipe. "Grab a pole, son. What's our first move?" The boy's jaw dropped open. "Are you for real, dad? I'm taking lead?" His father chuckled just a bit. "Sure, son… you're more than ready. Besides, it's obviously a common rattlesnake. There shouldn't be much of a surprise for us here. Basic barn and stable layout; they cleared the horses out; mid-day; sunny; very little shadow or glare. This is the perfect time." Looking down at the boy, he knew that this was going to be one of the most exciting days in his son's life, and one of Max's proudest.¶

Mrs. Wilson showed a little concern, "Is he going to be able to handle this Max?" She nervously ran her hands up to her mouth, almost as if she were going to start chewing on her fingernails. "He'll be find. He's only going to pin it down. Boy, you heard me right. After you pin it down, call for me and I'll bag it. You still get to lay out the plan. Go ahead." Even though his son would not get all the glory, he would still be the one in charge of capturing the snake. Putting on their protective gear, he told his dad to circle around the other side and make sure there were no other animals around the backside of the barn.¶

Heading to the site where the snake was last spotted, he bent down to inspect the ground. Small swirls and pathways, not seen by the untrained eye, laid out in front of him as plain as day. He knew it had probably gotten under the baseboards and into the barn out of the sun, probably lying between some rocks and hay. He swung around to the inside, exactly to were the trail had ended from the outside wall. There was just enough space for a young snake to slither along unnoticed to the end of the stall. The earth was soft and damp, perfect for going undetected by horse and humans. "Where, oh where are you little sneak? I'm a professional. You can't hide from me." He was a little cocky. There was no snake smarter than him. He'd be calling his dad any minute.¶

Looking directly at a roughly rounded stone near the corner, he immediately saw the twinkle in the snake's eye. Moving the rock very slowly, the rattle was almost instantaneously triggered. Not thinking, he flipped the rock aside, pinned the neck and grabbed the snake right behind the head. He held it up victoriously and yelled for his father. "Grab the bag dad, I got it!" His father was there in seconds. Holding the bag open, they quickly lowered it in tail first and flipping his wrist down as fast as he could, he let go of the head while his dad slipped the drawstring, closing the bag tight. "What the hell were you thinking boy?!" He was so angry right now, it took all he had not to grab his son by the scruff and toss him to the ground. "You could've gotten bit. What did I just tell you to do?!"¶

The Wilsons came running into the barn. "What happened?! Is everything alright?!" Mr. Wilson thought something awful must have happened with the snake and seemed to be rightly distraught. "It's okay Earl, my son just didn't follow my instructions. It could have been a lot worse than it is." "But, I thought you said he was in charge this time?" Earl did not really understand the severity of the situation. "I'm sorry dad! I didn't think, I just reacted!" It was true; it was almost like one long series of actions looped into one second. "It's not that bad, boy. I'm just… it's not really about that. I understand that sometimes this can happen. I didn't mean to come off so gruff. I would have done the same thing. Your instincts served you well." "What's all the…" Mrs. Wilson came in holding a tray of lemonade-filled glasses. "…is everything all right? Is anybody hurt?" "It's fine Susan." Her husband reassured her. "It just happened so fast. Everyone is safe. They caught that damn snake." He replied.¶

"Actually, my boy did it unassisted!" Max stated proudly. "I was just being an overprotective father." "No you weren't Max. I'd be surprised if you didn't act that way, your boy's only eight." They all sighed a little and turned their attention to the hero of the day. "What do ya' say there boy? You thirsty?" Earl walked over and handed him a tall glass of ice-cold lemonade. "Thank-you Mr. Wilson, I am a bit thirsty. I didn't mean to make everyone so worried. I won't do that again Dad, I promise." After taking a sip, he lowered his head a bit and looked at the ground. He knew he should have taken his time and handled that snake a little different, but his father was right to be proud of him; his instincts kicked in and it had all come so natural, like a duck to water.¶

After packing their things into the motorcycle, Max finished talking business with Mr. Wilson. Since it did not take long, and there were no out-of-pocket costs (except for round-trip fuel), he barely charged Mr. Wilson a thing. "Thanks for the lemonade Earl… Susan. I'll let this guy go when I head out to the Black-Foot tribe." He downed his drink and placed it back on the tray. "You don't need any more snakes then?" "Not at the present. I especially have plenty of these common rattlesnakes. Besides, this one looks a bit old. He's only got a couple of years left. Doubt he'll travel far after I turn him loose." Waving good-bye, he headed towards the bike and started it back up.¶

Heading home, he took a quick detour to The Rustic Forge to see his life-long friend, Butch, to pick up his belt buckle he had ordered a while back. He had submitted his own design for a one-of-a-kind buckle for his business. It was a golden rattlesnake, climbing up a fence post like a roll of barbed wired with the name of his ranch across the bottom. He did not usually spend his money on this sort of thing, but he looked at it as more of reward for all of his hard work. Once it was purchased, he would only wear it to impress high-priced clients as more of a PR piece to look more successful.¶

Looking down at the fuel-gauge, he pulled into the nearest coal station. Tossing a dollar worth of coal into the furnace-engine he paid the attendant and finished the trip to his friend's shop. Pulling into the parking lot, he secured the rattlesnake in a safety box Butch had personally installed by the front door. Having a snake-wrangling friend meant possible visits with venomous guests. Walking inside, his son made a bee-line to the sculpture case to look at all the different pre-ordered belt buckles, spurs and other knickknack that various customers had ordered but had not picked up yet.¶

    While Max waited for Butch to emerge from the back, he heard a familiar voice as the front door opened, triggering the bell overhead. "I saw that deposit outside. What kind did you catch this time?" Scotty was glad to see him after being particularly busy for the past two weeks. "I didn't catch anything. It was all my son's doing. He only needed me to hold the bag this time." Hearing his father say 'son's' caught his ear and he turned to see Mr. Daniels' wide grin, which he assumed meant he was in a good mood and might spare a quarter for the gumball machine. "Hey Mr. Daniels, how are you, sir?" Even if he did not give him any money for some gum, he was still glad to see his dad's friend. He looked to him as kind of like an uncle.¶

    "I am well." He always made it a point to try and use proper grammar when the boy was with his father. Max had a reputation for being a strict, hard-ass when it came to the English language. "Here's a quarter for the machine. I have something I need to talk to your dad about." The boy ran over to get his gum as Max and Scotty made eye contact. He probably wanted to discuss the fire that was in the headlines. "Did you get a chance to read today's paper yet?" "Yeah, our paperboy mentioned it when it delivered it earlier this morning. Said something about an electrical fire or something?" He had not had a chance to actually read the article, but anything that had anything to do about weapons, ammunition or other things relating to either of his two friends' businesses would peak their interests.¶

"It says that the recent storm had did unseen damage to the main wiring on the rear-side of the building. It's a shame, they employed a lot of people." "But they're insured right? I mean, how long will it take them to rebuild?" He did not get why Scotty appeared so doom and gloom about a seemingly temporary set-back. "Oh man, Dead-Eye Incorporated won't let a tragedy like this go to waste. They'll find something to keep them from rebuilding. Their lawyers will find a loophole, pay someone off, or outright bankrupt them." Scotty explained. Since he owned The Gunslinger, a gun and ammunition store handed down to him by his grandparents, he seemed to be suspicious of any and everything Dead-Eye Inc. did.¶

"Everything isn't a conspiracy Scotty." Butch stated as he walked out from the back room. "Unless there's a conspiracy about conspiracies." They all chuckled while he went behind the counter, opened up the case, and pulled out a toaster-sized box. Setting it on the counter, Scotty remarked, "How big of a belt buckle do you need, Hoss?" "My dad's doing it for the publicity." The boy popped up from behind a rack of magazines and proceeded to blow a bubble with his gum. "There's a little bit more to it than that son." His father replied. "It's for specific publicity. I'm not wearing it every day, only for my high-price client's benefits." Other than a few niceties for business appearance, Max and his son lived rather modestly. One would not know by looking at their house and ranch that he pulled in a six-digit annual income. Although everything was new, it was neither high-priced nor fancy; just practical and sturdy.¶

"Max, take a look at this. It took all of my skill to etch your designs into this buckle. Tell me if you at least like my product." He took the box and swung it around to open it. Pulling it out, he immediately noticed the intricate detailing on the snake's scales. Butch had made some of them stick out slightly enough to actually resemble barbed-wire. "This is beautiful, Butch. I like the way he wraps around and over the top with its mouth open. It kind of looks like he's defending that fence post." "Glad it's what you envisioned. I was afraid it might have had too much detail… you know, people having to stare at your crotch to take it all in." Butch had forgotten that the boy was within earshot and quickly apologized. "I mean, stooping over too long could hurt people's backs." And with that follow-up, Max's son was none the wiser at the adult humor.¶

"So Scotty, sales are probably going to go up sharply for a couple of months for both of us. 'Gunz 'a Blazin' won't be able to rebuild for at least that long. Sad, but nice." Butch redirected the awkward conversation. Attention was again turned back to the burning down of a competing business. These kinds of tragedies have upsides for some people, especially when there are no fatalities. "I'm not so sure this will be temporary." Scotty replied. "Besides, it's only a matter of time until smaller stores like ours might be targeted next." "Targeted," Max chimed in, "this was an electrical fire, not sabotage. There's not even an ongoing investigation regarding this incident." Max was not angry, he had just heard the same thing over and over again from his friend about such things.¶

"Dead-Eye Incorporated is somehow involved… it's got its stench all over it. The storm was just an excuse to pull something like this off and make it look like an accident. Besides, they were trying to buy them out all last year. Now, with bankruptcy an actual possibility, they can close the deal and redirect some major politics in this city." Although it sounded like paranoid conspiracies, it seemed a plausible scenario. Dead-Eye Inc. was not the most reputable company in Blackwater, but it appeared to be the most powerful.¶

"Hey, by the way Butch…" Max interjected. "I see you're fighting O'Malley on next Saturday's Fight Card. Any chance you can let the boy carry your water pail and towel?" His son perked up, Butch was the local, heavyweight amateur boxing champion; he often bragged to his friends that he was close buds with "The Champ." And he had lots of autographed memorabilia to prove it. "Mr. Young, that would be so awesome. And my dad said I could train with you if you'd let me. I could do chores in exchange and clean up after." His mind and mouth were both moving at a hundred miles an hour.¶

"Slow down boy. You don't need to promise me anything, your dad and I go way back. I'd be honored if you wanted to learn to box from me. You're like my nephew. I'll just need a little time to rest and heal afterwards. How about in four weeks?" Butch felt close to Max and his son, they were like a family to him. He had never married, and was not on the lookout for a wife, so the boy was the perfect fit for a young relative. "You don't have any 'other' fights around that time, do you Butch?" Scotty inquired. By "other" he meant the underground, bare knuckle, and extremely illegal fighting league. "No, I'm free and clear. I have enough on my plate right now. So I'm taking a break from those for a while." Butch widened his eyes and nodded slightly towards the boy. "What 'other' fights Mr. Young?" He asked. "Not really 'fight' fights, more like training." They were always saying things like this in front of Max's son without realizing it. It was probably due to the fact that he did not behave like a normal boy. He was a lot more mature for his age, had more responsibilities and was brought up without a lot of coddling.¶

As they were heading for the door, Max overheard several men talking about, who they described as, a "funny-looking" foreigner. "Yeah, this guy's wearing like some sorta' dress, or robe, or some weird combination. And get this, he has some strange language I ain't never heard of." The way these men talked; their grammar was atrocious. Each sentence was like nails on a chalkboard. Slang, made up words, double negatives... Max could not take it anymore. "Excuse me, gentlemen. I didn't mean to eavesdrop, but I overheard you say something about a foreigner?" He did not normally listen to other people's conversations, but these men were so loud; and using improper English had caught his attention. "Yeah mister, this guy's weird. Can't understand anything we say. Not that it matter's much. And he looks like he's homeless." One of them said. Then the other chimed in. "And he's got these swords hanging off his back. Like he's after someone. At least that's what I think."¶

Interesting, Max thought. Although it was legal to carry weapons in this state, most people carried guns; not many carried swords. "Did he seem aggressive, or like he might cause trouble?" He followed up to see if they had a little more information on the stranger. "No, he actually seemed overly polite. Didn't stare at ya' too long, bowed his head at ya' after he spoke. Or tried to speak to you, I should say. Kind of a nice fella. You should try to say hello to this guy, it's a riot."

"Thank you, I'll keep a look out for him." Max nodded as he again headed for the door. These guys seemed a little weary of people from out of town, but he did not think they would cause any real trouble for this foreigner. He hoped he would bump into this mysterious person from another land. It could be a good learning experience for his son. Maybe he could be of some help to him. It cannot be easy to be somewhere when the people around you do not understand what you are trying to say.¶

Unlocking the "hazardous snake" box, he removed the catch-bag carefully and walked it to the motorcycle. Placing it in, he and the boy quickly put on their helmets and climbed aboard. Max had decided to drop off the rattlesnake a few miles away from the Blackfoot Tribe. On the way there he passed several ranches and farms where the people recognized his bike and gave waves to him and his son. There were several clients out this way, but he did not have any business, nor enough time to stop by. Once he let the snake loose, he was going to see the chief and drop off some anti-venom to the tribe.¶

Finding a random dirt road, they detoured out into a sparsely wooded area and let the snake go by some medium-sized boulders with some nearby trees. Being mid-day, it slithered off towards some underbrush that had apparently gathered due to some strong winds. Heading back to the bike, he heard the sound of a common black-hawk soaring nearby. Looking about quickly, he spied one swooping towards the ground, probably after a desert cottontail. Setting off again, they were soon pulling into the main camp of the Blackfoot Tribe. They were greeted by several members who let them know their chief was expecting them and led them to his lodge.¶

"Good day, Chief White Cloud. I hope today has found you well. I have brought medicines for you and your people." Max handed a box of vials to the Chief's wife, along with some ground herbs from his garden. "Many thanks to you and your son." The Chief answered. "I have a gift for you and your young boy. But first, tell us of your latest adventures." The chief and his tribe were always eager to here of their exploits. There were not many white men who shared their animal kinship and connection with the earth; especially deadly snakes. "Well, sir." The boy started respectfully. "Can I tell him dad?" He asked politely. "Go ahead, son. It's your story to tell." The boy loved sharing anything he felt was an important achievement. "There I was, staring down this rattlesnake coiled around a rock inside the Wilson's barn. And without hesitation, I flipped the rock out of the way, pinned his neck, and grabbed the back of the snake's head and just like that… I had him. I caught a rattlesnake without even thinking. It was great." He kept his story short and simple. Too much detail might sound like bragging.¶

"I had a vision of this." The chief started talking seriously, but calmly. "Your son was holding a deadly viper above his head. Telling the Spirits, he is not afraid of the brother snake." His voice echoed through the lodge in a soothing tone. Looking around, Max saw that it was filled to capacity; and the door was open, with even more people gathered outside. "The spirits respect your family and your boy. You are in harmony with the earth. They know you have great respect for all creatures, and wish to help others." He continued with every ear peaked with interest. "The time has come for you to name your son. A name is a gift. And when it is given in a vision from the Great Spirits, it is a special and sacred gift." With that, the chief exhaled very slowly, then continued. "You boy will be known as 'Rattler.' For he will grow up to know all things about the snake, and how to heal when they strike. He will be a holy man, defending against those who would do harm to snakes and people." The chief seemed to become physically tired after giving these words. "It is time for you two to go. There are important things to come in your near future. Go with our blessings and the blessings of the Spirits."¶

Max had never charged for any of his medicines or supplies, so he felt honored when the chief had given him and his son this great gift; the gift of a name. There was great cheering and celebration throughout the tribe when news started spreading outside. By the time they gotten back to the motorcycle, they had been greeted and hugged by nearly everyone. The boy, now known as Rattler, was more excited than he had ever been about anything in his life.¶

"So, Rattler. Would you like to invite some friends over for dinner this weekend for a dinner party where you can announce this news?" His father took an instant liking to calling his son by an actual name instead of "boy" or "son" all the time. This burden had been lifted from him like a fifty-pound weight from around his neck. He had always felt a little guilty, deep down inside of himself for not naming his son. He and his wife had decided that they were not going to come up with one ahead of time, but name the child when they both saw him or her for the first time together. When she did not survive childbirth, he could not bring himself to do it alone. And now it was done. His son had a proper name, thanks to a kind Indian chief.¶

"How many friends can I invite? What about Mr. Young and Mr. Daniels? Can we have a cookout?" Again, his mind raced as fast as he could speak. "Can we have it at Crawling Water Lake? Will I get any presents?" "Slow down, son. I don't think this counts as a birthday." He replied. "I think a cookout at the lake would be the gift. We have all that extra chicken we can grill up." "So we can do it then?" He urged. "Yes, Rattler. We can have the cookout at the lake. Invite about twenty people."¶

When they stopped talking, he noticed an oddly dressed person walking down the sidewalk. Could it be? This might just be that stranger that had all the people, at least at the "Gunslinger," talking about. He quickly, but safely, pulled over to dismount the bike. Smiling and waving, he approached the man in as much of a non-threatening manner as possible. He was simply interested in meeting this foreigner in order to help if he could. As he walked towards him, he noticed the man starting to smile and slightly bow his head. He seemed to know Max did not mean any harm. As he held out his hand to the stranger, the man smiled and shook his hand. And then he said… "Hello."

CHAPTER II - Dead-Eye Inc.¶

Sitting in his corner office, overlooking the Blackwater River, Mr. Johnson was finishing up a business proposal with one of Dead-Eye Incorporated's biggest customers when his secretary, Miss Swans, entered the room. "Mr. Johnson, your brother Henry is here to see you. Should I send him in?" She smiled politely and silently waited for him to reply. "Yes, send him in immediately, I've been expecting him to drop by." He closed out the file and tidied his desktop area, reached into his bottom left drawer and pulled out a box of cigars. Clearing a spot towards the front, he placed it gently and flipped the lid open. "Care for a cigar, Henry?" He said as his brother strolled in, turning the box around so he could take one if he so desired. "Certainly, I think I earned it. Our latest numbers show that theft is at an all-time low." Henry was head of security at Dead-Eye Inc., the largest weapons and ammunition manufacturer in Blackwater; and indeed all of Texas.¶

"There's more cause for celebration than that. Our sales are going to jump slightly more in the next couple of months due to that gun-store fire." William leaned forward and lit his brother's cigar with his lighter that was made to look like one of the first shotgun shells his families' company produced over fifty years ago. "If only they were unable to rebuild. That share of the market could become permanent." His telephone rang suddenly and he set his lighter down on the desk and answered it quickly. "Yes I know the meeting is going to start in a few minutes. My brother and I are just about on our way down now. Have my chair moved back to the head of the table, I do believe there is going to be a presentation by Mr. Lucas on that new sniper rifle under development." The voice on the other end softly answered and hung up. "Let's go Henry, we don't want to be late."¶

Walking out of his office and closing the door after Henry, William turned to his secretary. "I'll be gone for at least two hours, Janet. Have housekeeping give my office a quick cleaning while I'm in the meeting." "I'll call them immediately, sir." She answered. The two brothers continued down the hallway towards the elevator. "So, Henry, have you heard anything on this new sniper rifle." William was always excited whenever he heard from Mr. Lucas. He was the executive in charge of research and development. With a team of engineers and designers; it was up to them to come up with new concepts for better weapons. "I haven't seen any drawings, but I've heard the range has been improved." His brother answered.¶

Upon entering the elevator, Henry pushed the button for floor twelve and the doors slowly closed in front of them. After a few moments of silence, the doors again opened and they stepped out into the hallway where they were immediately handed the meeting's agenda and a cold bottle of water. "Sorry gentlemen, but the meeting has been moved down the hall to the big room. I believe a demonstration will be given by Mr. Boyd." Replied the intern that handed them both the papers and bottled water. "Demonstration?" Said William. "In a board room? Shouldn't we downstairs on the safety range for this?" Mr. Johnson seemed agitated by the change of venue. "Relax, William." His brother injected. "I'm sure they won't be firing live rounds or anything. Probably just taking the weapon apart and they don't want to put it on the polished oak table in the main room." He actually had no idea what they were going to be doing, but disassembling a weapon to show all the patented parts sounded like a logical explanation.¶

Upon entering the room, the brothers looked around the table at all heads of department. There was Mr. Hughes, head of Ammunition Production; Mr. Boyd, Product Testing; Mr. Price, head of Manufacturing; Mr. Peterson, Human Resources Manager; Mr. Thompson, Shipping; Mr. Coleman, head of the Sales Department; Mr. Reed, Store Manager; Mr. Brooks, Accounts Receivable; and Mr. Fisher from Maintenance. Everyone was here except for Mr. Lucas, head of Research & Development. William noticed a vice-tipped sort of tripod at the foot of the long table, and a small piece of paper taped to the wall approximately fifty feet away. "What is this?" Mr. Johnson stated as he stalked up to the piece of paper. "I haven't a clue." Said Mr. Peterson. "Mr. Lucas simply came in about two minutes ago, taped it up there, and then left. We're all baffled."¶

Upon closer inspection. William saw that it was a picture of a two-inch tall man with a rifle slung over his shoulder. "How bizarre. Are we having a mini-demonstration of some sort?" He seemed bewildered by this strange set up. "Not at all." Said Mr. Lucas confidently as he strolled into the room. "It's actually a full-size demonstration." He was carrying the prototype of the company's new sniper rifle in his hands. He proceeded to the tripod and started attaching the weapon to the vice piece. "Excuse me Mr. Lucas." Mr. Boyd interjected. "But I'm in charge of product testing, and this is neither the time nor the place for such a test." He started to stand up in protest when Mr. Lucas turned around and continued. "Of course not, Mr. Boyd. We are not here to see this weapon fired. We are simply here to introduce a new feature the we can safely demonstrate with a completely unloaded rifle."¶

Mr. Boyd appeared confused by the statement and asked. "What feature, what are you talking about?" He started walking towards the tripod. "Uh-uh, Mr. Johnson gets to try it first." With that, he stepped back and motioned for the CEO to approach the rifle. "Simply aim at the paper while looking through this 'scope' that we attached to the rifle." William was intrigued; he immediately took aim at the piece of paper on the wall and was astonished to see a full-grown man aiming a rifle back at him. "Amazing," He proclaimed as he quickly raised his head to see the target at a distance before again looking back into the scope. "Do you see the little cross-hair symbol? Try aiming it directly at the man's head." Mr. Lucas asked excitedly.¶

Mr. Johnson was extremely impressed; which did not happen all that often. "What is the range of this weapon? And how accurate will it be with this device?" He could already see a market for such a rifle. Its applications would revolutionize the hunting industry. "We'll need a field test to determine that sir." Mr. Lucas replied. "That's where Mr. Boyd comes in. I'm sure the sniper rifle will take up all of your attention for at least the next week or so." He followed up confidently. "The next month." He said as he approached, taking off his glasses. "May I sir?" He asked. "But of course." Said Mr. Johnson, stepping aside. "Have a go of it. I've never seen anything like it."¶

After Mr. Boyd, and the rest of the executives took turns looking through the scope, they proceeded to gather back at the table in order to officially start the meeting. "I'm very impressed with you and your team Mr. Lucas. I see a raise in your future if it lives to what I've seen thus far." Mr. Johnson said as he flipped open the file in front of him. "Thank you, sir. We've been working on this project exclusively for the last seven months." Mr. White took the seat on the right-hand side of his brother and proceeded to takes notes. "First order of business is the discussion of the rather unfortunate destruction of our biggest rival, Gunz a' Blazin.' Are we in any kind of condition to actually steal any of their long-time customers?" Mr. Johnson wanted to get right to the heart of this issue before any other business was discussed."¶

Mr. Coleman already had reports printed for each member on the board. "I think you'll find this information quite helpful. With contacts already made, we estimate that we can take control of roughly thirty-five percent of their cliental within five weeks." He handed half of the copies to Mr. Peterson on his left, and the other half to Mr. Price on his right; they then proceeded to pass them along to the entire table. "Thirty-five percent? Is that the best we can do?" William thought they might be able to seize more than one third of their rival's business after such a tragedy. "Well, it's the most we can expect from a legal standpoint; however, if certain things happened that delayed Gunz a' Blazin' for another month or so, the percentage could jump up another ten to fifteen percent. But I consulted with our legal team and there isn't really anything we could do to slow them down without… should I say, 'bending the law.'" He seemed a little nervous bringing up legal vs. illegal practices whenever he was in a meeting. Being the head of sales, he sometimes road the thin line with what he, and his staff, could get away with in the company's dealings, but then again, this sort of thing had not happened since he came to work for Dead-Eye Inc.¶

Henry Johnson put down his pen and pad of paper and added. "We'll look more into that with some of our contacts downtown. We could possibly arrange for some 'unexpected' construction to happen along certain roads that would slow down the suppliers and make it more difficult for the workers to build. Maybe even stage a phony picket line or something to throw off their momentum." He was already contemplating some ideas in his head to make it extremely difficult for them to rebuild. "I'll discuss this with you later, Henry." William said, turning the page of the agenda. "I'm curious about this point here. There's something that has slowed shipping temporarily over the last two days. What's this all about?"¶

Mr. Thompson from shipping chimed in. "There seems to be an infestation of rattlesnakes that moved in rather quickly over the holiday weekend. Plus, two days previous there was a gap in shipping because it was the end of the fiscal year for several of our larger clients. That area hasn't seen a lot of foot traffic for a good week or so. I would dare say we left an ample window for the snakes to move in." Even though it was not his fault, Mr. Thompson felt he might still be blamed for the incident somehow. "Well." William started. "Just send in a team of exterminators to rid us of these pests." It was a simple situation with a simple solution. "Excuse me sir." Mr. Fisher from maintenance interrupted. "I believe I have a better solution to all of this." He cleared his throat and continued. "It would be more beneficial, and less expensive if we hired a snake-wrangler to simply come and collect the snakes."¶

Mr. Brooks interjected. "That will take much longer, and it will also delay our suppliers from delivering our raw materials that are due in two days." "I do believe the gentleman over at the Golden Snake is very efficient. If we call him immediately and let him know that the snakes would otherwise be killed, he would most likely come within the next couple of hours." Mr. Reed informed them. "Also." Mr. Fisher, again adding to the conversation. "It would give us two additional benefits. One; we would not have to use harsh pesticides or worry about any dead snakes being left behind to smell. Second; the snakes would be milked to produce anti-venom. That would be a good for free publicity. Dead-Eye Incorporated gives back to the community by allowing local snake-wranglers to create much needed medical supplies and research." "Would we make any money from the anti-venom?" Asked Mr. Johnson. "No sir. But you can't buy that kind of PR. If we had simply paid for an exterminator, we wouldn't make anything off of dead snakes. But this route would make us look more sympathetic, and gain some much needed press for our humanitarianism." Replied Mr. Fisher. William thought for a second. "I like it. You make the phone call. Mr. Peterson, set up for someone from The Daily Blackwater to cover the story. I should have thought of this. Good work Fisher."¶

"Mr. Reed, is everything ready for the new gun show next week?" Mr. Johnson asked. "Are there any surprises there? Would you be able to give a sneak peek for this new sniper rifle? I want something to go out to the public about this scope." He was very direct with these questions; this would be the perfect time to come out with a new modification for a weapon. "I need to get a hold of marketing and get some kind of flier or poster made." Mr. Reed responded. "We could also set up a range-like booth, kind of like what's set up in here. If people could look through the actual scope like we did, we would probably do very well with pre-orders." Everyone in the room started nodding their heads in agreement. "How many of those scopes do we have?" Asked William. "We only have two." Replied Mr. Lucas. "But we could make up a couple more. Exactly when is the gun show? When would you need them by?" "Friday, May fourth is the gun show. I would thereby need them the day before… so at least seven days, six would be better though. I want to be sure I have the perfect display the day before."¶

"There shouldn't be a problem with that." "I need to test this thoroughly before we can get an actual production date." Mr. Boyd interrupted. "I would caution that we not push this 'scope' accessory too hard." He added. "Relax Mr. Boyd." Said Mr. Johnson. "We can make the availability date much further out. I simply want the general public abuzz for the next few months. Every hunter in Texas will want one of these. And as far as I'm aware of, no other company has anything remotely like this in the works. Am I correct in that statement Mr. Lucas?" He asked. "Correct sir." Came a reply. "So, simply give me an estimate of how long you would need to test this product to work out all the bugs." "I would say at least eight weeks." Mr. Boyd replied. "Okay, eight weeks for product testing. How many would you then be able to produce in an eight-week period, Mr. Price?" "That would depend on the resources needed. But I would assume we would be able to produce at least several hundred within a month's time."¶

"Several hundred would be a good number to introduce to the masses. We would be able to get an idea of how many more we would need to produce by Christmas. It would take at least eight to ten weeks to set up a new line of production. So if it would take at least sixteen weeks to get 'several hundred' manufactured and made available for sell, all we would have to do is project a release date for eighteen weeks. That gives us two weeks to play with. And if we can't get these scopes to market by Mid-August, then we've got a problem!" William drove his point home with a light pounding of his fist down onto the table. "Now, who's in charge of marketing?" To which his brother replied. "There is no one currently 'in charge' of marketing at the moment. Our last executive took a job in Cleveland, Ohio when his wife's mother became ill."¶

Mr. Peterson from Human Resources quickly spoke up. "We have several interviews lined up over the next two days, we'll have that spot filled by the end of the week. I will take all of this information and make sure the new executive has all available data in which to launch an ad campaign." This was not a good time to be without a head of marketing. A new campaign would be vital for a new invention of this potential to become a cornerstone in the market. "Now, if this thing succeeds, we need to postpone Gunz' a Blazin' from returning to the market until we have at least produced the first wave of scopes. They could find themselves with so few remaining customers, we could buy them out and have a new manufacturing facility for new year's line. That would be perfect."¶

"Well, if there is no other business?" Looking around the table, nobody appeared to have anything to say. "Then that's meeting adjourned. Mr. Coleman, I have something for you in my office. Meet me there in ten minutes." "I'll be on my way after a quick trip to the washroom sir." With that, everyone shook hands and dispersed. Passing several employees in the hallway, Mr. Johnson decided a trip up the stairs for some additional exercise was in order. Plus, he needed to stretch his legs a bit after sitting most of the day. Pushing the door leading to the stairwell, his brother Henry following him in. "Brother, a word." "But of course." "You're going to give Mr. Coleman the letter I assume?" "That's exactly what I had in mind." William retorted. "I feel you might be rushing things a bit. Mr. Armament has only come on board six months ago. I hope you know what you're doing." "I do know what I'm doing, Henry. You need to remember the goal here. And I have complete faith in your abilities to handle the situation should it go south. You haven't let me down yet." William reached the top step and proceeded to open the door leading to the fourteenth floor. "Excuse me, I do wish to beat Mr. Coleman to my office."¶

Walking past his secretary, Mr. Johnson had her hold all calls. This was a delicate, but important meeting with the head of the sales department. He did not want to be disturbed for the next few minutes while he went over the details with his rising star. Sitting back behind his desk, he pulled out an envelope and waited for Mr. Coleman's arrival.¶

Within two minutes, his secretary knocked on the door, entered, and informed him that his employee was waiting eagerly in the seating area outside of his office. "Send him in. I will require your services afterwards to draft up some letters to various heads of department." "Yes, sir." She answered. Turning towards the waiting area she stated. "Mr. Johnson will see you now." As she held the door open, Mr. Coleman walked through, thanking her. As soon as she closed the door, Mr. Johnson asked him to have a seat.¶

Sitting down, Mr. Coleman became a little uneasy as he waited for his boss to speak. "How long have you been with us Mr. Coleman?" Quickly, and quietly, he cleared his throat and answered. "Almost two years, sir." He waited for a response. William slowly turned his chair and gazed out of the window at the Blackwater River and did not speak for nearly a minute. "Twenty-two and a half months. Mr. Coleman. And in that time you managed to excel at your position without putting in much overtime. That also I'm impressed with." He stood and walked over to the window and opened it slightly. "Thank you, sir. I try not to work too much. A solid work schedule helps me keep enough time for recreation. I feel a good balance between work and a healthy social life is important for an overall satisfaction of one's career." He did not want to come off as smug or conceited.¶

"I agree. However, how would you like to elevate your social life with a larger salary and a lot more perks?" He did not turn to look at him, but continued to stare out over the river at the rest of the city. "I'm grateful for whatever you pay me, sir. I'm just not sure about what you're offering." He was slightly confused by what Mr. Johnson was saying. He was the head of sales and there was no higher position for him at the company for someone with his level of skills and knowledge. "I'm offering you more of a stake in the company. A way to expand upon your understanding on how things work… how should I say this… outside of what most employees are aware of." He then turned to face Mr. Coleman. "Would you care for a cigar?" He swayed his open hand towards his desk, motioning at the box on the edge. "No thank you, sir. I don't smoke. But my interest is peeked by your offer. I'd like more details."¶

Strolling back over to his desk, he picked up the envelop and proceeded to hand it to him slowly while he continued talking. "There will be a meeting with certain members of my staff. The details of when and where are in this envelope." Mr. Coleman took it and placed it in his suit's inside pocket. "Tell no one of this. We operate above certain procedures and traditional ways of doing business." He was slowly sitting back down into his chair as he continued. "Some might say what we do might be considered unorthodox, and slightly unethical. But we prefer to call it aggressive and motivated. Consider what I am saying before you open that letter. If you do not show up to that meeting. I'll assume you are not interested and you can continue to work for Dead-Eye Incorporated as you currently do, with no hard feelings." He lit a cigar of his own and took a couple of puffs.¶

"Understood sir." He was starting to feel rather uncomfortable with the situation. It appeared so 'cloak and dagger.' He was hoping there were no illegal activities involved with this proposal. "Is there anything else you can tell me before I read this letter, sir?" He said nervously. "Nothing but this. Regardless of your decision, shred the letter after you've read it. I will not ever speak of this meeting with you again. Now you can return to work. Have Miss Swans come in here on your way out."¶

Walking down the hall, Mr. Coleman was

unnerved by what had just transpired. He was certain that whatever offer was being made here, it was not quite on the up and up. If he refused to take part, he would surely be fired. He decided to wait until he had gotten home, have a drink, and then read the offer. He spotted Mr. Johnson's brother, Henry, standing by the elevators. "Hello, sir. I just finished a quick meeting with your brother." Henry turned and smiled at him. "I'm aware of what you and my brother had discussed. You'd do well not to say anything about it to me, or anyone else. I hope to see you at the meeting." With that, Mr. Johnson turned and entered the elevator. "Are you going up or down Mr. Coleman?"¶

Mr. Coleman stood there for a second before answering. "I'm actually going to take the stairs for a little exercise." "Suit yourself. Good day." After the exchange, the elevator doors closed and the whirs of the mechanical gears could be heard behind them. Now Mr. Coleman really felt strange. He was not sure what was going on here, but he was becoming more and more reluctant about even opening the envelope at this point.¶

After talking the stairs, he saw several of his fellow salesmen standing around the water cooler down the hall from his office. "Afternoon Mr. Coleman. How did the meeting go?" One of them asked. "It went fine. We're going to have a new gun to sale. I don't have all the specs yet, but we should have enough information about it by the gun show next week." The murmurs between several people got his attention. "I know, I know. We'll get more details when they print us out the FACTs sheet, listing all the features and when it will be projected for the open market." He explained. "What about any leaked details?" Someone in the back asked loudly. "I was informed that we can leak some information to our top one hundred clients over the phone before the gun show. But we need to ask them not to spread this information to casual acquaintances, we don't want rumors to spread to our competitors. I'll send memos to those included on the list. If anybody needs me, I'll be in my office." With that, most of the small crowd returned to their desks.¶

Closing the door behind him, Mr. Coleman finished completing his sales sheets, typed out the memos, handed them to his secretary, and started packing his personal supplies for the trip home. He only had one briefcase and a small backpack. He walked out into the parking lot and proceeded to strap them down to the back of his mountain bike. He was one of the few executives at Dead-Eye Inc. who did not own a motorcycle. His money went towards an active social life and a nice ranch-style house. He was not married and had quite a nest-egg saved up for when he met the right woman and was ready to settle down and start a family.¶

Pedaling out of the parking lot, he proceeded over the bridge and took off towards home. Passing several stretches of open land and trees, he arrived at what he liked to refer to as , Casa de Coleman. It was an older looking, log-cabin style of a ranch house set on twelve acres. He was not much of a farmer, but he had tried a couple of times to grow a small garden but was only able to grow several types of beans and some lettuce with any success. He put his bike in the small garage and continued inside. He checked his phone and saw that there were several messages, but decided he would check them later.¶

Walking to the bar, he poured himself a class of scotch and sat down on his comfortable sofa. After taking a couple of sips, he then put on a record and started listening to some light country music while he continued to contemplate reading the letter. He felt like his entire future relied on whether or not he agreed with what he would find written on the paper inside this envelope. Taking a deep breathe, he reached for the letter opener. Pulling out the folded piece of paper, he rotated his neck to crack it a little, looked down, and began to read.¶

Dead-Eye Inc. HQ, Top Floor, immediately following the gun show.¶

This was peculiar; he was sure there would have been a little more to it than this. What was all that talk by Mr. Johnson about opportunity? He was somewhat disappointed. It was actually just a 'when & where' note. How was he supposed to make this important of a decision with what little information he had? He did not feel comfortable accepting an offer with such a cryptic method of delivery. He was sure that if he felt this way now; whatever information they would share with him at this meeting would make him feel even less comfortable. How much money was there to be had? What perks would he be offered? Would it all be worth it in the end? He had no idea. And if he had no idea, he was not about to find out. His mind was made up. He went over to his home office and placed the paper in the shredder. He would simply ignore the invitation and go about his life as though the offer was never given.

CHAPTER III - A Samurai Named Ronin

Although Max and the foreigner could not communicate by traditional means, he was able to convince the samurai to come to their ranch for a hot meal. He drove his steam-cycle slow enough for the stranger to follow on foot. They were less than two miles from the ranch, so the samurai should not tire out from such a short jog. Besides, it was apparent that this man traveled on foot for most (if not all) of his life.

It took them less than fifteen minutes to complete the journey home. Parking his bike in the garage, he and Rattler put away their equipment and met their guest at the foot of the stairs leading up to their front porch. Max motioned for him to follow. "Come inside. You must be tired and hungry." He was pleased to have company and hoped he would not be offended by anything he or Rattler did during his visit. The samurai walked up the stairs, took off his shoes, bowed his head, and walked into their house.¶

As he walked in, the samurai looked around and smiled as he noticed the modest furniture and clean environment. Too many times has he been in the presence of royalty and the wealthy. He had always thought of how wasteful it was for people in high authority to purchase such lavish things while their subjects would often times go without food and/or shelter. He vowed never again to serve a master with such morals. The samurai started to wonder where he would end up in this new land when his host spoke up.¶

"Would you like something to drink?" He turned and saw that Max was motioning with his hand like he was drinking from a cup. The samurai smiled and nodded. As his host walked to the cupboard to retrieve a glass, Max turned and pointed to himself. "My name is Max… Max." The samurai repeated. "Hello… Max." He repeated what he assumed was an introduction. "My name is Ronin." He again bowed his head slightly and smiled. "Hello Ronin." Said Rattler. Making a gesture similar to what his father had done, he added. "That's a cool name. My name is Rattler." "Hello Rattler." Said the samurai, bowing yet again. Max and Rattler both bowed, hoping to show the same level of respect by the customs of their visitor. Max walked over and handed the samurai his glass of water.¶

"We're having chicken with rice and salad for dinner." He did not really know why he was telling him this, he was sure he would not understand what he was saying; but it was better to continue talking any way to avoid the awkward silence. Besides, this is probably the only way this man would start to understand any spoken English. "Rattler, guide – what was it again – Ronin? Guide Ronin to the dining room and let him sit down. I'll start dinner while you set the table." He watched as his son gently took the samurai by the arm and led him to the next room. He would never have guessed that today would bring a dinner guest from a distant land.¶

He took out the ingredients for the chicken and rice meal while Rattler starting hauling silverware, plates, cups, and napkins to the table. "Pick out whatever vegetables you would like in your salad and make sure you include as many different colors as possible for better nutrition." He and his son were very careful to eat extra healthy to maximize their physical fitness. He was not sure if their guest would require any special dietary needs. It was decided not to use any uncommon herbs or spices in this meal so Ronin could choose to season it as he saw fit. He would chop the vegetables for the salad slightly on the larger side so he could pick any off if he did not like them. Although, guests typically do not complain too much about the food; so he decided to spread the vegetables out on a large plate so Ronin could assemble his own salad. "Do you think there are any vegetables Ronin might not like dad?" His son was thinking the same thing as he entered the kitchen with a small basket with celery, carrots, radishes, peppers, onion, a few sprouts, and a tomato.¶

Suddenly the telephone rang. "Do you want to get that, son? I've already started dicing up the chicken." He rinsed the knife and set it down before washing his hands. "Sure dad." He said, glancing into the dining room to see Ronin's reaction to a ringing telephone. But he had apparently heard a phone ring before because he did not seem to react at all. "Hello, The Golden Snake, Rattler speaking." He had looked forward to answering the phone and introducing himself with his new name since they left the Blackfoot Tribe.¶

"Hello, is this the owner?" Came the voice over the line. "No sir. If you'll hang on a minute, I'll get my father." He had always tried to speak as politely as he could whenever he answered the phone as it was most often for the family's business. "Tell him it's Mr. Fisher from Dead-Eye Incorporated calling with an important job." His voice sounded a little gruff, but not rude. "Yes sir." Replied Rattler, placing the phone down onto the counter. "Dad, there's a gentleman on the phone from Dead-Eye Incorporated. He says his name's Mr. Fisher and it's an important job." Max finished drying his hands and walked over to the phone.¶

"Hello, The Golden Snake, Max speaking." The voice on the other end replied. "Good afternoon sir. This is Mr. Fisher of Dead-Eye Incorporated. I understand that you remove deadly rattlesnakes from properties with a strict 'no-kill' policy, is that true?" To which Max answered. "Yes sir. Depending on the species, I either keep them on my ranch for milking, or I turn them loose miles outside of the city. It also depends on how old the snakes are. I only keep younger, healthy snakes." "How much do you charge for your services, Max?" Mr. Fisher asked. "It depends on how many snakes I actually have to remove. But I don't charge nearly what licensed exterminators do. Again, I usually keep some of the snakes to produce my own anti-venom. Snake venom plays a key role in medical science. Besides anti-venom, it can be used in other medicines. Therefore, that is where I make most of my income. So I usually only charge enough to pay for fuel for their relocation, and a nominal fee for my time."¶

"Very good. I was hoping to hear something along those lines. Not that we can't afford whatever you charge, we want to make sure the community appreciates what we're trying to do here... not harm the snakes, only remove them. Speaking of which, do you mind if we have someone from the paper present? We're hoping to show the public we're helping a local business and the medical field with this." He waited for Max to reply. "I don't have a problem speaking to the press. However, if they could remain outside until I am finished. I'd wouldn't mind an interview once all the snakes have been wrangled and secured. I just don't want anybody present on the actual job. Of course you'd understand any safety issues Mr. Fisher?" "Of course Max. How soon can you come? We're at 1200 W. Texas Ave." "All I have to do is grab my equipment and fire up my bike. I can be there in about twenty minutes." "I'll personally meet you at the south entrance. We'll cut through the main building to the loading docks. If you need additional personnel with transportation of the reptiles, I have plenty of dock workers available when you are finished." "Thank-you. Let's see how many there actually are. See you in twenty minutes then."¶

As he hung up the phone, he suddenly realized the situation he was in. He had completely blanked on the fact he had a stranger who did not even speak

English as a guest expecting dinner. He had to think for a minute. Should he leave his son here? Should he leave Ronin by himself? Could he make him understand why he had to leave? "Rattler, come here a minute. We have a job to do immediately. I'm trying to think of what we should do regarding our guest here." He was not sure why he was asking for his son's opinion. "Dad, I think if we are friendly enough to invite him for dinner, we should trust him enough to leave him alone for a while. I don't see why he would steal anything from us. Where would he even go?" There was logic and wisdom in what his son had just said. "Very well, son. I agree. Let's hurry. You go gather the equipment and stoke up the steam-cycle. I'll try to explain the best I can to Ronin."¶

Walking back to the dining room, Ronin had stood up as if he knew something was going on. He simply smiled and walked to the front door. "No, no Ronin. You stay here. He acted out as best he could that they were leaving, but would soon return. He pointed to himself; opened the front door and motioned outside; then showed Ronin his watch and circled the numbers with his finger; motioned back into the house and pointed to the floor as he shut the door. Holding the samurai's arm and gently guiding him to the couch he added. "You stay here and relax until we return." As he motioned with his open hand to have a seat. Ronin replied. "Okay." As he sat down and folded his hands in his lap.¶

He did not like leaving the kitchen haphazard but Max had no choice, he grabbed his gear and met his son out by the bike. Rattler had already gone to get the snake wrangling equipment. What was he forgetting? Oh yeah; he put some extra coal into the furnace on the bike and let it stay idle while he ran back inside to grab his new belt buckle. Meeting with the press was a good time as any to wear something extra fancy to get his brand out there. Taking it out of the box, it looked even cooler than it did at the shop. With a little more darkness, what light did hit the surface made it seem to have a shaded kind of sparkle to it; if that were how he would describe it. Heading towards the door for the second time, he glanced into the living room and saw that Ronin was kneeling on the floor with his hands clasped together on his knees. He appeared to be meditating, but it almost looked as if he were praying. He smiled as he closed the door behind him.¶

Getting to the bike, Rattler was already buckled into the sidecar with all the equipment organized for the trip. Hopping onto the driver's seat, Max slipped it into gear and headed down the driveway. Looking down in Rattler's lap, he quickly counted at least a dozen burlap sacks that they used to put the snakes in. He had not really given it that much thought, but how many snakes were there actually going to be at the loading docks of such a large company? If there were not enough sacks for each snake, he would have to double up. He did not want to have to tell the press that he would have to take a second trip unless it were absolutely necessary. But then again, the health and well-being of the snakes were his top priority.¶

As they drove down Central Street, he started thinking of what he was going to say to the reporter. He would probably mention that medical research shows that certain malignant tumors could be treated by medication made from snake venom. And other medicines could extend treatments for stroke victims. He liked sharing his passion for snakes with anyone who would listen. His family had always had a kinship with these misunderstood reptiles, and he did not like those who would kill or even harm snakes out of ignorance and fear.¶

Looking up ahead, he saw the gates come down as he heard the familiar ding-ding sounds emanating from the nearby tower structure. The railroad company employed workers at every point where a public road crossed the tracks. The man, or woman, would use binoculars and look up and down the tracks every couple of minutes in order to see any oncoming trains. When one was spotted, he or she would lower the gate and ring a large bell nearby; what folks came to know as "train sheds." He decided to take a left on Wood Avenue and take the

Law Bridge over the train. Most people did the same when traveling from this direction.¶

Upon arriving at Dead-Eye Inc., he spotted Mr. Fisher waving him down by the main gate, which was being opened by two employees. Once inside, they immediately closed it behind him. He parked in the nearest vacant spot and dismounted the bike. His son climbed out and started handing him the equipment. "Hello, Max. I'm Mr. Fisher. If you follow me, we'll head straight there. The main hallways we'll be traveling will be vacant for the next two hours. As ordered by Mr. Johnson." This man seemed very professional and was also polite and soft-spoken. "That's not necessary. Once, the snakes are secured in the bags, there's no danger to anyone." "I understand, but the CEO likes to minimize any risks whatsoever. He's a man of routine, and always has a certain way of doing things. One could almost predict how he would handle any situation based on past experience."¶

He continued to talk as they made their way inside the main building. "As I mentioned on the phone, there will be a reporter from The Daily Blackwater here to interview you once you've completed rounding up the snakes. He'll be setting up over there." Said Mr. Fisher, pointing to an area off to the side of the information desk by a large bay window. "You'll be posing for a picture with one of the snakes by that tree outside the window

49

afterwards, if that's okay?" It almost seemed like an order instead of a question. But with it being such a large, important client; he did not see any reason to decline the request. "Sure, no problem. What sort of pose were you thinking?" He inquired. "There's a lady down in public relations who's a huge fan of yours. She was hoping you'd be willing to take a photograph of the actual milking process. She's going to clip the article and place it in one of her scrap books. I like her idea immensely, it'll make for an excellent story." With that, he opened the door to the next section of the building.¶

"I usually don't like to milk a snake right after capture. But if I find one that seems the right age, and it's very healthy, I would be willing to make an exception. After all, you said it's for an excellent story, and I agree." Max smiled at his son who was getting more and more excited as this little scene unfolded. "Could my son, Rattler, be in the photo as well. Perhaps holding some piece of equipment or something?" The boy's eyes grew even larger when he heard this. "Your son's name is Rattler? How did you decide on that name?" Mr. fisher seemed genuinely interested in the story. "It was given to him by the Indian Chief of the Blackfoot tribe east of here. He was told by the great spirits that my son would be a great advocate for snakes as he grows into a man. I couldn't be prouder." He again smiled as he looked at his son who was now walking with his head held higher, and his chest pushed out.¶

"I think having your son in the photo is a great idea. It shows that you're a family owned business. That's even better." Mr. Fisher pointed to the exit to the loading docks as they rounded the last corner. "And perfect timing… here we are. Now, when you are finished, ring the bell right outside that door and I'll let you back in. I'll be waiting here with a gentleman from maintenance with a multi-shelved cart for you to transport the snakes safely back to the lobby." "Wait a minute, where exactly are the snakes hiding?" Max asked. "Oh, I'm sorry. I was told that it would be obvious when you walk to the edge of the first loading dock. We were informed that there are at least six. Do you require any thing before I go to maintenance?" He asked. "No, I have all I need here, thank-you." He cautiously opened the door and held it open with his foot as his son passed him and stood just outside. "Good luck Max. And good luck Rattler." Said Mr. Fisher as the door slowly swung shut.¶

"Be careful, Rattler. I'll go to the end of the dock and look around first. If I see anything, I'll signal for you to come. Leave everything here by the door." Slowly, and as quietly as he could, Max walked to the edge of the loading dock and looked down. They were no snakes there. He scanned back and forth all along the wall; they were not along there either. He peered out and scanned the concrete area… nothing. Then he spotted a pile of old wooden pallets that had toppled over near a fence. That was probably what Mr. Fisher had meant by obvious. "Well, son. I think that pile of pallets is our best bet. Come on, we'll jump down here."¶

Once on the ground, Max and Rattler quietly made their way to the toppled pile of old, worn-out pallets. The angle of the sun made it easier to guess where the snakes would most likely be hiding. Scanning the ground around it did not show much in the way of tracks due to the lack of soil, grass, or leaves. Max began hooking the pallet that had fallen the furthest away from the main pile. He pulled it about twenty feet and placed it flat on the cement. He repeated this pattern and soon had half a dozen pallets stacked straight up. It would probably be a good idea to only stack them six high so another collapse would not occur.¶

Upon pulling on the fourteenth pallet, he heard a familiar rattle emanating from the rest of the half-broken pallets. "Careful son. I'll start clearing away from the other side. If any come out, you back away and call for me. Got it?" "Yes sir. But I think I see one from here." Max looked in the general direction of where Rattler was pointing and caught a glimpse of movement. "I do believe there is one right under that cross-section right there." He said, pointing to what appeared to be a perfect triangle of wood. Rattler readied his snag-rope and positioned himself to the left of his father. "I only hear one." He said. But no sooner did he utter those words than a second, third, and even a fourth distinct rattle could be heard. "Holy cow. There's at least five in there, dad. What are we gonna do?"¶

Max thought for a minute. "Let's go break-up a couple of those older-looking pallets and lay some out on each side in a line. It'll funnel them towards the loading dock wall and we can trap them between the two of us." Max wasn't sure if this plan would work exactly how he envisioned it, but if he could separate them, it would make it easier if anything.¶

After breaking apart several pallets, they had a descent track going. The "walls" were stacked three high so the snakes would probably not try to climb over them, but follow along towards where he wanted them to go. It was just a matter of whether or not they would all travel in the same direction; after all, there were only two ways to go once they reached the wall. Now it was just a matter of dwindling down their hiding spot by removing the rest of the pile.¶

After removing a larger, still intact pallet, two ridge-nose rattlesnakes crawled out several feet and coiled up near one of their homemade boarders. "Get in between the walls and stand about ten feet away Rattler. Sway your stick a little to distract them. When we're ready, I'll count to three and we'll try to snag them at the same time. Once we have them, pull back a ways and I'll secure the one I caught. Then I'll secure the one you caught." Rattler nodded to indicate that he understood. "One.. two... three!" Within seconds, they both looped the nylon rope rigs around their own snake and closed it enough to incapacitate them without any injuries or undo stress.¶

"Good job, son. Now slowly back up so that they're a good ten feet apart. I'll secure mine." He grabbed the snake quickly behind the head and forced it into the burlap sack he had secured at his hip. Once tied, he followed the stick down his son's rig and secured that snake in the same fashion. "I'll set our supplies over here. You go place these two rascals on top of the loading docks where he first jumped down." "Yes sir." Replied Rattler as his father handed him both sacks. He made sure to hold them out to the sides and tried not to jostle them too much as he walked. After gently placing them up on the docks, he returned and picked up his rig and waited for further instructions. This was an exciting outing. He had never been on a job as important as this before.¶

After rounding up the other three rattlesnakes from the fallen stack of pallets, Max spotted a twisted ball of black, yellow and red scales amongst the smashed wood. Could he be this lucky? Carefully getting a closer look, his hopes became a reality as he recognized the color patterns of one… two… three western coral snakes. Hopefully they were nice and healthy; he needed plenty of this species of venomous snake on his ranch. Their venom output was potent, but did not yield much from such a small venom pouch. He had two dozen at home who did not even come close to providing enough to meet demands.¶

"Rattler! Get three more pouches, we've got western corals over here!" Looking over at the boy running with more supplies, he motioned with his hands to toss him a rig. Turning back to the snakes, they started to separate. Moving as fast as they could, they managed to wrangle two of them; but not before the third could get a hefty distance away. Securing the snakes and transporting them to the others on the dock, Max chased after the one who was slithering towards the corner of the building. Man, this one is fast, he thought. It was as if it knew where it was going and bee-lined it through a large crack in the cement.¶

"Dang it!" Shouted Max as he stopped short of the hole in the wall. Looking around frantically, he spotted a door nearby with a glass window. He checked to see if he could open it, but it was locked. Without hesitation he picked up a rock and smashed the glass. Max was more concerned with preventing someone inside from getting bit by the venomous western coral than he was about property damage.

Besides, a company as big as Dead-Eye Inc. would obviously be insured. Entering the building, he noticed it was very different from the areas in which he had walked. It appeared to be an indoor firing ranch with a rather large work area. Checking along the inside of the wall where he had last saw the snake, he spied what appeared to be a ventilation duct along the baseboard.¶

Taking out his rig, he cautiously bent down and removed a small ventilation guard covering. Without warning, the coral snake sprang out, almost simultaneously, and struck Max in the forearm through his shirt. Having nothing to lose at this point, he simply grabbed the snake at the midsection and tossed it into the bag and tied it shut. He immediately sat down and started focusing on his breathing. Normally someone who was just bitten by a deadly western coral snake would immediately need to go to the hospital for treatment. But due to a family secret, Max was going to be okay. Since the days of his great- great- great-, he actually had no idea how far back it went; a very distant grandfather who had founded the business started a series of very minute injections of snake venom into his own body with the hopes of becoming venom-tolerant over time. And after many generations, it had worked. Max was practically immune to twenty of the most common, venomous snakes within a five-hundred-mile radius of The Golden Snake Ranch.¶

 After several minutes of controlled breathing, Max slowly stood up and checked his wound. There was barely any swelling and the bleeding had already stopped. Flexing and stretching fingers and wrist, he shook it off and started for the door. But something on a nearby table caught his eye. Walking over and looking at an interesting drawing revealed that it was a schematic for, what appeared to be, a fully automatic mini-gun. Picking it up he noted some interesting details about the trigger mechanism and firing pin. He took out a pad of paper and pencil and quickly drew a copy. Hearing talking just outside a different door than the one he had entered, he slid the drawing into his back pocket and hid behind some boxes stacked in the corner and pulled a nearby tarp down over his entire body. Lucky for him he had chased a coral snake into the building, or the rattling sound would give his hiding spot away.¶

 He heard several men enter the room, talk for a couple of minutes, and then leave again, shutting the door behind themselves rather loudly. He slowly peered out from underneath the tarp, and seeing no one, headed back over to the table. The schematics were gone. Looking down at the floor, he saw several spent rounds from what he had guessed, were from a prototype of the mini-gun depicted in the drawing. He pocketed a couple of the shells and exited the door back into the bright sun. Rounding the corner towards the shipping yard, he ran right into Henry Johnson, the CEO's brother.¶

"Hello Max. I was wondering where you had wondered off to." Henry said politely, staring him right in the eyes. "I had to act fast to catch this guy!" He answered quickly, holding up the sack containing the snake. "It's a western coral snake, not one I could let get away. If there's an issue with the broken window, we can discuss it with your brother." Max had tried not to sound rattled, but with what he had just seen, he wanted to get out off of Dead-Eye Inc.'s property as soon as possible.¶

"I'll get maintenance here for repairs immediately. Mr. Fisher is ready for you inside by the loading docks." With that, Mr. Johnson entered the door and called for a maintenance crew over his walkie-talkie. Max hustled over to his son and went to the door and rang the bell. The door swung open and he and his son loaded the all eight snakes onto the cart. They went directly to the reporter and gave a quick interview, and after a couple of quick photos, they headed for home. Max did not say much to his son on their return trip, his mind was racing with what he had just witnessed.¶

Arriving back at the ranch, he and Rattler took care of their new arrivals in the barn. They would keep all eight snakes for milking. In fact, he would probably retire a couple of his older ridge-nose rattlesnakes to the wild in the morning. Stowing the rest of their gear, they returned to the house. He had almost forgotten that he still needed to prepare dinner for their guest. But when they walked into the house, the table was already set. In fact, the food was also prepared and there was no sign of a mess. Ronin must have cooked dinner and cleaned while they were gone. The samurai was standing by the table; he had been merely waiting for their return.

CHAPTER IV - New Troubles¶

After finishing their chicken dinner, Max turned to his son. "I feel we're in an interesting situation here. We should try to see if Ronin has a place to stay." Rattler nodded in agreement and started clearing the table. Looking the samurai in the eye, Max wondered how he could make the foreigner understand that he would be welcomed to stay with them on their rather large ranch. "Would you like to stay with us for a while?" He said, pointing to Ronin and then pointing to the floor with both hands. He then folded his hands and tilted his head, imitating sleeping on a pillow. Ronin then replied. "Yes. I will stay… but I work." Max had never heard him verbalize this much before. "Do you understand English?" He asked. "I work for you in return." He replied. At least he understood enough to get his point.¶

Max stood up and pushed his chair in. "Follow me Ronin. I'll show you to the guest room." As he took his plate to the sink, he noticed Ronin doing the same. "You'll fit in here nicely. We could use an extra hand around here. Would you like to learn English? I could teach you as well as any tutor." He hoped Ronin would be able to handle some of the everyday duties that came with life on their ranch. "Being a samurai probably means you have very good reflexes. I would love to see a demonstration of your swordsmanship. Perhaps you could teach me and my boy how to use one properly." He knew this man did not understand him; but he would love to learn the ways of the samurai for the personal defense of his family.¶

Coming to the doorway of the guest room, he opened the door and turned on the light. Not having anybody stay with them for quite some time, it was just as he remembered it. A queen-size bed with matching nightstands on either side; as well as a dresser and chest at the foot. Looking into the mirror above the desk, Ronin held his hand up to his face and ran his finger down a small scar on his face. Max was curious as to how he had managed that. Probably in a great battle or something; at least that is what he would like to imagine.¶

Walking over to the bed, he turned the bedspread and sheet down to reveal two pillows. "This is a bed... bed." He tried not to sound condescending while at the same time trying to build Ronin's vocabulary. "Bed." Ronin repeated. He turned and sat down on the bed with a curious look on his face. "Slept on floor for a long time." He appeared to be very grateful for something to sleep on other than a hard surface. "Would you like to take a bath?" Max pretended to wash himself on his chest and under his arms with imaginary soap, hoping to make his guest understand the question. Sniffing his armpit, Ronin made a face and replied by nodding his head. Max let out a little chuckle, which made Ronin smile and laugh as well.¶

"What's so funny dad?" Added Rattler as he entered the room with a stack of clean clothes, folded neatly in his arms. "Here's some of your clothes that I've noticed you haven't worn for a while." Looking around the room, Ronin seemed to let down his guard and showed an emotion that could only be described as extremely grateful. He seemed to be on the verge of crying if not for the continued laughter. He stood up, bowed and again thanked them as he placed his two swords on the desk. "Well, follow me." Said Rattler as walked out of the room. He grabbed a towel and a wash cloth from the linen closet as he led Ronin down the hall to the bathroom. "Do you know how to run a bath?" Not sure if he would understand him, he proceeded to place the plug in the drain and turn on the water.¶

Putting one of his hands under the running water, Ronin could not believe that warm water was coming from the faucet. He had never bathed in a tub before, let alone indoors. He used to take his daily bathes in the stream near his master's palace for as long as he could remember before coming to this land. Since his departure, he had bathed as often as he could whenever he came across a remote, and clean, lake or stream; which had not been for at least four days. "I'll be outside if you need anything." Max said as he knocked on the bathroom door while closing it, indicating that he would knock before entering.¶

After his bath, Ronin went straight to bed. Max and Rattler had a dish of ice cream at the kitchen table as they talked about the day's events. Although he did not say anything, Rattler knew something was bothering his father, and it had nothing to do with their new guest. "Is everything okay Dad?" Max did not respond at first. "It's nothing, just some business I have yet to do with Scotty and Butch tomorrow." He did not want to burden his son with the events that had taken place at Dead-Eye Inc., but he had to tell his two best friends about the illegal activities going on that the large corporation. He was not sure if Mr. Johnson had believed his story; it was all so nerve-racking.¶

"What's Ronin going to do around here?" Rattler asked his father. "Oh, I suppose he'll cook and clean a little." Max had to admit that that chicken dinner was just as good as, if not better than, what he would have prepared. "Maybe we could teach him snake-wrangling." "Hold on son, we don't even know how long he'll be staying. I'm not expecting him to learn any of that too soon. Let's wait and see what he's willing to do. I'd be happy if he would train us in weapon use, it never hurts to learn new self-defense techniques." Max did not want to appear nervous about getting mixed up with any kind of trouble, but he wanted to make sure his son would be safe should anything happen. "I think hunting with a sword would kick ass dad." He rarely swore, but he knew 'kick ass' would not make his father angry. "It actually would." He said. "A samurai sword would be better than using a knife if your gun ran out of bullets. I wonder what kind of action Ronin has seen in his life." They both pondered that question awhile before turning in for the night.¶

Upon waking, Max looked and found that Ronin was not in his room. Checking around the house, he did not see the samurai anywhere. He went to the kitchen and started fixing breakfast for the three of them; hopefully. "Rattler! Would you like bacon or sausage with your eggs this morning?" He listened down the hall and smiled to himself as he heard the familiar sounds of his son's feet hitting his bedroom floor as he yelled back. "If we can have biscuits, I'd like sausage!" Throwing on his clothes for the day, he quickly met his dad in the kitchen. "Where's Ronin?" He inquired. "I haven't seen him. Perhaps he went outside for some fresh, morning air. Would you like to go check?" Max asked. "Sure dad." He answered as he headed for the front door.¶

Walking out onto the porch, he noticed Ronin carrying what appeared to be a couple of medium-sized branches towards a pile near barn. Walking over, he greeted the samurai. "Good morning Ronin.

My dad's making us breakfast." He looked and saw that Ronin had apparently been picking up yard waste and stacking it in a large pile by their burn pit. "Thanks Ronin. We've been a little busy lately and haven't gotten around to cleaning the yard for a few days." He smiled as he motioned for him to follow him back into the house for breakfast. "Hope you like what we're having." Rattler was curious as to what Ronin usually ate for breakfast.¶

Sitting down at the table, Rattler explained that their guest must have gotten up very early and starting cleaning up around the ranch. "He's got a pretty decent pile of old tree branches stacked and ready to burn." Rattler said before scooping some eggs into his mouth. "Yeah, we had that pretty big storm about a week ago and it knocked a good number of branches down. Probably for the best. Storms typically knock down weak, dead branches anyway." Max placed his sausage between a biscuit that he tore in half in order to make a sandwich. "What would you like me do today?" Ronin asked before talking a drink of orange juice. He had rarely had such a treat as freshly squeezed fruit juice and savored every mouthful.¶

"Well, Ronin. Just help Rattler today with chores." He replied as he patted his son on the shoulder. "I have business in town, not to mention setting a few rattlesnakes free back into the wild." Max had always rotated out older snakes whenever he obtained younger, healthier specimens; not that any of his snakes were unhealthy. But, he tried to only keep snakes in captivity for as short of period as he could, while still ensuring that he acquired plenty of venom before they were released.¶

"Dad, what should I do if he freaks out about all the snakes in the barn?" Rattler had brought up a good point. Would Ronin come close to understanding what they actually did for a living? Did they make anti-venom in his country? "I guess we'll give him a tour before I leave. I want to at least try to make him feel at ease with what we do. He seems to understand better when we act things out. Perhaps I can draw some pictures showing what we do." That was actually a good idea, he thought. "I'll try to teach him a little English over the next couple of days as well." Max finished his egg and sausage biscuit and drank his juice before taking his dishes to the sink.¶

Though he might not have understood their purpose, Ronin appeared to be okay with all of the snakes living on the ranch and went about helping Rattler with his chores. He did whatever was asked of him to the best of his ability and seemed to even take joy in his labor. Although he had only been here less than a day, Max was willing to let him stay as long as he wanted.¶

After about two hours of work, Max decided it was time to deliver the "retired" snakes before heading out to meet with Butch and Scotty. He gave Rattler some last-minute instructions and started up his bike. His stomach was in knots just thinking about a fully-automatic weapon being produced. What was their end game? Who would be in the market for such weapons? He hoped his friends might have some ideas. He barreled off down the road as fast as was legally possible and was soon miles outside of town in a spot where he typically let his once captive snakes go home.¶

After releasing the three ridge-nose rattlesnakes, he stowed the bags in the sidecar and headed towards Butch's shop. Taking the back road, he was there in less than twenty minutes. The sunshine and fresh air helped his mood a little before he pulled into the parking lot. The store seemed a little busier than usual; he hoped his friend would have some spare time over the next hour or two. They could not simply go to the police with no real evidence. Something had to be done.¶

Walking in the front door, the place was even more packed than the bikes outside would have suggested. He jumped behind the counter and helped Butch serve his customers for about half an hour until it died down enough for them to talk. "We need to call Scotty to meet us here on his lunch break. I've got some interesting news you'll both want to hear." With that, Max walked over to the phone and began dialing. "I had a feeling. You don't usually stop by without your boy." Butch added. "Hello Scotty. Can you swing by The Rustic Forge on you lunch break? Good, it's very important we all talk. See you then, bye." Max hung up the phone and started helping Butch with his inventory while they waited.¶

It wasn't too long before Scotty arrived on his lunch break. They closed the shop and went into the back room. "I have some grave news concerning that job I did for Dead-Eye Incorporated yesterday. But first I do have some good news before we get to that. Plus, some other news…" His head seemed to be pulling his attention span in several different directions and there appeared to be no way to put them in any logical order other than good news to worst. He cleared his throat and began to speak. "On the brighter side, Chief White Cloud gave my son a name… Rattler." His two closest friends were overwhelmed with joy that his son finally had a name. And although Max was not the one to give it to him, they were still thrilled for the two. "Rattler, that's pretty neat considering your guy's line of work." Butch remarked. "And your boy must be excited as well." Added Scotty. Both were impressed at the uniqueness of it all.¶

"We also ran into that stranger everyone in town's been talking about. Turns out he's a samurai who traveled here all the way from Japan. Apparently something happened between him and his former master." He continued as Scotty and Butch listened intently. "His name is Ronin, and he's going to be staying with us for a while." Butch jumped in. "How long do you think?" Then before Max could answer, Scotty added. "Does he speak English? How do you all communicate?" "I don't know how long. He speaks and understands some English. And we act out explanations like charades, and we also communicate by drawing pictures. Slow down guys, there's a lot more to talk about here. More about Ronin later. What I really need to show you two is this!" With that statement he pulled his crude drawing from his pocket.¶

Unfolding it and placing it onto a nearby table he continued. "This is a replica of an actual schematic that I found by accident in an indoor testing range while I was after a coral snake that had gotten into another area of their headquarters downtown. They're plans for a fully automatic mini-gun. What are we going to do? We can't even go to the authorities!" Max hands started to tremble slightly as he placed them under his belt at his sides. "How did you manage to copy this down?" Butch asked. "And how did you manage not to get caught?" Scotty added, both with shocked looks on their faces. "I almost did... twice. I didn't really think about it at the time. I merely copied it as best I could and got out of there as fast as possible." They continued to stare at the blueprints for the highly illegal weapon.¶

"What about your boy? Excuse me… Rattler. Where was he?" They almost asked in unison. "Luckily he was outside and around by their loading docks. The CEO's brother almost caught me red-handed as I left the building. He was very suspicious of the situation, but I told him I was in there after that snake and I think he believed me." Fiddling around with his hands he remembered another detail. "Oh yeah." He almost shouted. "I also found these," He fished the spent shells he managed to grab on his way out. "They must already have a prototype. These look like no other shells I've seen. And they were strewn all over the floor by the table where I found the schematics. Again, what should we do?"¶

They were all silent for what seemed like at least ten minutes before Scotty finally spoke up. "I think we need to develop our own 'answer' to their weapon. I have an idea for what I like to call an assault rifle." He stood up straight and stretched his arms out to the side as if he were finally telling a long, lost secret. "I never thought we were actually going to ever make it. I simply have had this idea for an automatic weapon in the back of my mind. You know, sort of a 'I could make this, but never would' kind of a thing." He shrugged his shoulders and waited for one of his friends to response.¶

"Well, Scotty. I guess it all comes down to

what we're all willing to do. Do we try to ignore the problem?" Butch said. "Of course not." Max interrupted. "Then we have to either try to gather real evidence, or actually go in and try to steal the prototype." Butch walked over to a desk in the corner of the room. "If we're planning on breaking the law. We better make damn sure that we can protect ourselves." He opened a drawer and pulled out some schematics of his own. "I've been working on a new type of armor plating that can move and act like snake skin. It might help us if we get into the kind of trouble I'm thinking we might get into."¶

Max took a look at the designs his friend had made. "I think we should make both of these items and test them to make sure they work. Then, if we find ourselves in a situation where we have no alternative, we use them. I have no qualms about leveling the playing field." His friends nodded in agreement. "I'll draw up the plans for the assault rifle by this weekend. Do we want to meet at your ranch Max?" "I'm sure we can do that. Perhaps our guest will be willing to meet some of my friends. Then he can keep Rattler entertained while we discuss this further." Max shook both their hands and headed for the door. He had to come up with a plan to break into Dead-Eye Inc.'s headquarters.¶

On his way home, he stopped by the hospital to see how much anti-venom they wanted to order for the following month. After that, he made another stop at a family whose boy was treated for a snake bite earlier in the week to check on his progress. He was all about visiting with those he had helped with his snake-wrangling business as a way of keeping his personal motivations high. His family had always been in it to help people, and not just to make good money. Once he got back home, it was time for a late lunch.¶

Entering the kitchen, Ronin and Rattler were both already preparing soup and sandwiches. "What's all this now?" Max said, looking into the pot of boiling liquid on the stove-top. "Ronin is making a vegetable soup and I'm making sandwiches with the leftover chicken and salad." Rattler answered while he grabbed some mayonnaise and started slathering it all over a slice of bread. "Is good to eat plenty of vegetables." Ronin spoke as he stirred the pot of soup with a wooden spoon. "Is very good." He seemed to be very educated on nutrition and did manage to speak quite a bit of English, even if he did not understand when other people spoke to him. "I'm impressed Ronin. Thank you."¶

Once at the table, Max asked their guest a question. "Would you like to learn some more English this afternoon?" He made a book with his hands, opened it, pretended to write on his left hand with an imaginary pencil, and then moved his fingertips to his mouth and moved them away to indicate writing and speaking. Ronin seemed to understand and nodded his head. "I like to learn." It was settled. They would spend the next hour eating and learning more about each other as Max taught Ronin some basic English skills.¶

Once they were done with lunch and lessons, they returned to working on the ranch as a three-man team. They finished burning all the loose yard waste, mowed the property, and edged the driveway. Max left to milk the snakes that were on the day's schedule; and after feeding and watering them all, it was time for supper. Rattler tried to teach Ronin how to play cards as his father prepared pork chops, potatoes, green beans, a side salad, and some dinner rolls. It had been a long day, and he was looking forward to a hot shower and an early bedtime. He needed to think of a way to get back into that lab and locate where they were hiding the mini-gun. After all, he had to find time to learn their security practices in order to make it on and off their property without being caught. It would have to take place on a Sunday when they were closed and no one would be working except for guards. He would also need to keep his son and guest occupied while he was gone.¶

"Dad! What's the plan for tomorrow?" Rattler repeated after his father failed to answer him the first time. "Sorry, son. My mind was wondering.

What was that?" His son asked him again. "What are we doing tomorrow? Are there any jobs that I can come along and help you with?" Rattler had already finished his vegetables and was working on his last little piece of pork and a small bit of dinner roll. "I don't have any jobs scheduled for the next three days, so that makes it smooth sailing. I need to make some deliveries on Thursday, but other than that, we're just going to focus on caring for the snakes and giving the barn an extra good cleaning." His father finished his last bite of food and took his dishes to the sink. "It will be too cold to going swimming at the party, be we could do a little fishing." Max mentioned before taking his last bite of dinner. "If you'd like to play cards or something with Ronin… I'm going to turn in a little early tonight." Max took a quick shower and crawled into bed.¶

As Ronin and his son kept themselves entertained quietly in the dining room, Max was thinking of the upcoming break-in of Dead-Eye Inc. He had to find another entry point other than the door he broke into on the job. He did not want any undo suspicion to fall his way. What could he do? He could make it seem like a rival company trying to steal their technology. Make it look like industrial espionage, that would work. If he threw suspicion onto say, Gunz a' Blazin' for instance, that could work. They would be in a position where they might seem desperate enough to need new ideas in the wake of their factory burning down. Enough to try a break-in of a rival company. If they were suspected of the trespassing, but were not responsible, that would simply mean wasted time for any investigations that would result.¶

He, Butch and Scotty should attend next week's gun show in order to gather some intel and the layout of the buildings, perhaps distract security enough to find him his entry point. But what would they do after getting the schematics and the prototype? Would they hide them? Would they try to turn them over to the authorities? How could they prove it was all Dead-Eye Inc.'s doing? They were, after all, the hub of this city. They would need a lot of damning evidence to convince anybody that there were illegal activities going on at the one company that was considered a pillar of society.

CHAPTER V - The Apprentice¶

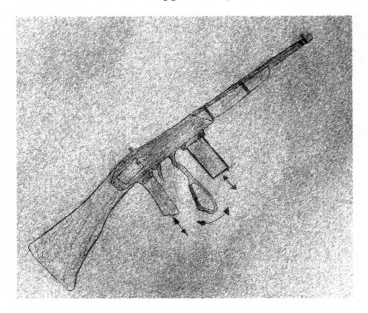

The sun beamed down on the wet grass behind the barn on The Golden Snake Ranch. A sheathed sword sits atop a nearby tree stump as Ronin practices a series of defensive fighting techniques with his personal sword, The Wind Sword. He always rose early and practiced his skills before starting his day. Today was especially pleasing to the samurai, although he did not have a new master, he had found a place to stay; if only for a short while. He could not afford the luxury of settling down, not even this far away from his enemies. He looked over at the sword on the stump and then continued with his training.¶

After a very restful sleep, Max awoke and checked on his son and house guest before heading to the kitchen. His son was already getting dressed; and Ronin, again, was not in his room. It appeared Max would have to get used to this habit. Must be part of his samurai training, he thought as he gathered up the cookware and utensils to make breakfast. "Hey dad, let's see what Ronin's up to before we eat." "You go ahead. He's probably found some chore to do." He told his son. "I don't think he would leave without telling us. I think it's his way to do things as he sees fit. How do pancakes sound?" He already knew the answer. "I'd love pancakes. I'll be right back." With that, Rattler ran out the front door and started looking for Ronin.¶

It did not take the boy long to find the samurai behind the barn. As he rounded the corner, he stopped in awe at Ronin's elegant movements. Wisp-like sounds penetrated the air as the blade sliced through it. After a few more swings, Ronin stopped and faced the boy. He then smiled and bowed before sheathing his weapon. "Good morning Rattler." "Good morning Ronin. Have you ever had pancakes before?" He asked, smiling and walking up to him. "Pancakes before?" He mimicked, not knowing what the boy was talking about. He walked over to the edge of the woods and broke a low-lying branch from a tree. He removed all the leaves and smaller branches from the main branch and bent it over his leg and broke off the tip.¶

He handed the sword-sized piece of wood over to Rattler and moved his right hand along one side as if to tell the boy to whittle it into a blade. "Cool." He replied, taking a pocketknife out of his pants. He started cutting into the branch and taking off chunks at a time as the samurai watched. It took Rattler less than ten minutes to turn the branch into a mock sword. Ronin then pulled his sword and sliced a long, thin cut into another nearby tree. He then peeled off a couple of long strips of bark and lashed it around the base of the stick in order to create a make-shift hilt. He then handed the finished product back to Rattler and motioned for him to hold it up. Once Rattler did that, Ronin pulled his blade and slowly swung it towards the boy. Once Rattler raised his sword to block, he realized that this was his first lesson.¶

After several minutes of pretend combat, Max found the two engaged in a fake fight and simply observed for a while. He was grateful for what Ronin was doing. He did not even need to ask him to teach his son, he simply took it upon himself to do so. When they finished, they all returned to the house for pancakes and sausage. It was Ronin's first experience with syrup, and seemed to enjoy it immensely. Once they finished eating, they did their daily routine of chores and ate lunch. Once again,

Max had to run into town and inform them of his plan for the upcoming gun show.¶

    After a couple of deliveries of anti-venom, he soon found himself back at The Rustic Forge parking lot. Dan, Butch's apprentice, was standing outside smoking some pure tobacco in a homemade pipe by the tree next to the building. "Are you even old enough for that?" Asked Max, walking towards the main entrance. "I'm nineteen, sir." He replied politely. "I know, Dan. I'm just razzing you a bit. Smells nice, did you get that from the Blackfoot tribe? I heard they finished drying out their latest crop." "Yes it is. I usually buy from them when I can." Max opened the front door and walked over to the counter. He rang the bell and waited for his friend to come from the forge out back.¶

    Once Butch came to the register, Max asked for an order form and a pencil. "Sure, what's it going to be this time? Cuff-links?" He pulled out the pad of order forms and peeled off a sheet. "Nothing like that. I got a special challenge for you this time… swords." His friend showed his excitement by sketching out his own ideas on another order form. "Are you guys going to be training with, what was his name again… Ronin?" "He already started training Rattler this morning before breakfast. I tell you, it was amazing to see firsthand. But we really need to talk." Max said finishing up his little sketch drawing. "Should we call Scotty?" Asked Butch.

"No need right now. I figured we would discuss my plan in more detail tomorrow night at the ranch over dinner, unless you've got a date or something?" "Sure, I've got nothing planned, wise guy."¶

"Here you go. This is the basic idea of what I want. Nothing fancy. Just put our initials on the blade near the handle." "What were they training with this morning?" Butch asked. "Rattler whittled a sword out of a small tree branch. It looks decent for training purposes, but if we're going to be serious about this, we'll need the real thing. How long do you think it'll take to finish?" He inquired. "I'm starting on that armor, and with my other orders, I'd say about two weeks." Butch handed him his own doodle of a sword handle featuring the same emblem as the one from his belt buckle; but instead of a fence post, the handle itself was what the snake was wrapped around. "Hey, this would be great. Kind of makes a running theme. How much is this going to run me?" "Not what you'd think. Especially after my friend discount."¶

After talking a few more minutes, Dan came back in and took over the register while Butch walked Max back out to his bike. "At least tell me a quick summary of your plan before you go." "We're going to attend the gun show and coordinate an entry point for me to break in. I'm going to spend this Sunday night studying their security protocols, and then do the deed next Sunday night.

We gotta' act quick on this. I'm going to Scotty's and talk to him about a couple of other things. Let's say 6:00pm for dinner." Max said as he donned his helmet and mounted his bike. "That's sounds good. Hey, what are we having?" "Don't know yet. It'll be good though." With that, he backed up, pulled out of the parking lot, and headed across town to his other friend's shop.¶

Since it was not that busy, he pulled right up to the front door of the Gunslinger over on Statehouse Avenue. "Afternoon Scotty." Max called to his friend as he entered his store. "Do you have a minute?" He asked. Looking around his shop and not seeing anyone, he jokingly answered. "Not right now, I'm swamped." He chuckled a little and proceeded to pull out a piece of graph paper from behind the counter. "Actually, I just got off the phone with Butch, so I've been expecting you. Here, look at this." He unfolded a drawing of the assault rifle he had mentioned to them at their last meeting. "Hey, should we be looking at this right now." Max said in a hushed tone, looking around suspiciously. "Don't worry, it's just a simple, generic rifle design. But check this out."¶

Scotty walked over and locked the front door, flipping the sign around to read "Closed," he returned to the counter. He pulled out another sheet of paper from underneath the cash register; except this one was thin and white. He carefully placed it over the graph paper and an altogether new weapon came into view. "Check it out now." Scotty exclaimed. Max took a long hard look at the design before commenting. "You know I don't know as much about guns as you do. So give me a rundown of how it works." Scotty put both papers away and went and reopened the front door. "The secondary sear disengages when the bolt closes into battery. And seeing as the trigger is still being presses, the gun fires and keeps firing until the trigger is released." Max looked a little confessed. "Basically, it will allow you to merely hold down the trigger and fire a continual stream of bullets."¶

"How many bullets will you be able to fire?" Max asked. "Depends on what we want. But I'd say we could fire up to thirty before we would have to reload." Scotty answered. He made a hush, hush gesture as a gentleman entered the store. After the transaction, Max inquired if Scotty would be able to come over for dinner. "Butch will be able to make six o'clock. How about it?" "That sounds alright. Hey, I almost forgot, I got a job for you. I mean, a customer came in earlier this morning and was complaining about a snake problem. I mentioned your name and line of work and got you a referral. It's right here." Scotty opened the register and lifted the cash drawer, revealing a piece of paper. "Here we go, The Royal Treat Bakery, 928 W Lumber Avenue. Here's the number. Make sure to ask for

Peggy." Max reached for his friend's phone. "May I?" "Go ahead." He dialed the number and after a few seconds, a young lady answered. "Hello, Royal Treat Bakery, Peggy speaking, how may I help you?"¶

After a short conversation, Max headed out the door with the information he needed. A quick trip home to gather his things and he would be at the bakery in less than half an hour. He was told it was definitely a rattlesnake because they had heard it. Once more, an employee was nearly bitten. He was hoping for a more, rare species as always, but he tried never to get too anxious about it. Since it was located in a busy area of town, and there would be lots of pedestrians nearby, he would do this job solo. Not that Rattler was not professional, he would simply be tempted to take greater risks with an audience; especially if there were any cute girls around. Although he was only eight, Rattler was already becoming a good-looking, young man.¶

He pulled into the driveway and gathered his supplies from the barn. He called for Rattler and Ronin; they were in the back cleaning around the snake enclosures. He simply told them he would be on a job and should return in about an hour. Things were getting done rather quickly with Ronin here, even with the extra time spent training. Max had a nice feeling of contentment as he continued to the bakery. Although there was some road construction going on a mile from his destination, he did not lose much time. Pulling into the business's driveway in the back, he grabbed his gear and knocked on the delivery entrance door. A few seconds went by and a young lady answered. "Hello, you must be Max. I'm Silvia, Peggy's serving a customer right now, but you can follow me."¶

Walking down a service hall, she led him around a corner and through the main service area. One wall was lined with ovens; another with sinks and counter-tops. There were several stainless steel prep tables. Once through to the front, he greeted and shook hands with Peggy, the owner. "Thank you for coming on such short notice." "It's no problem ma'am." Max said. "Can you give me any kind of description of the snake?" He asked. "Well yes. I got a pretty good look at it in the storage room. I don't know where it got in from, but it's hiding behind a couple of my large sacks of flour. It's very light brownish gray, with dark brown bands or rings, or whatever you call it." She was not very knowledgeable about snakes and so she gave as good of a description as she could. "Sounds like a typical rattler to me. Let's get to your storage room and I'll get him out of there. Or her." He smiled as she took off her apron and hung it on a hook by the doorway.¶

Winding through several rooms and shorter hallways, they ended up outside the storage room.

Rattler

There was a typical wooden door, with an extra
wired door locked on the outside; kind of like a
front door/screen door combination one would see
on a house. She unlocked the outer wired door. "I'll
leave the metal door unlocked, just close the other
one behind you or my staff will freak out on me. I'll
be down the hall around the corner, I've got a thing
about snakes." She made a funny, half-scared facial
expression that let him know she was serious. "Just
so you can sound smart, the Latin term is
'Ophidiophobia.' But that's an irrational fear of
snakes. It's actually healthy to fear dangerous,
venomous snakes." He hoped he was coming off as
friendly and not too businesslike. "Thank you,
that's good to know. I always like to sound extra
smart to people." "Before I head in, whereabouts
did you last see it? In a specific corner or area?" He
asked. "Far left corner. Good luck, I'm outta'
here."¶

Entering quickly, he shut the door behind
himself and scanned the room. It was approximately
twenty feet by forty feet, with shelving lined
completely along each wall, with several pallets full
of various bags and containers in the middle. He
carefully made his way between two large barrels of
what appeared to be… he did not know, and he was
not very interested in reading the labels. He was
much more focused on the floor and any dark areas
where the snake could be. He tapped along the base

of the pallets and the plastic buckets on the bottom shelves out in front of him in hopes of urging the snake to make itself known with a defensive rattle. And as soon as he reached the last pallet near the back left corner, he triggered what he was looking for. Sure enough, it was a black-tailed rattlesnake coiled between two large sacks of wheat flour.¶

Max pulled out his pin-stick that has a rounded tip hook on the end that he often used to pull snakes out of a small, hard-to-get spaces in order to get into a position where he could then use the outside of the hook to pin the snake down behind the head. Since there was not a whole lot of open space in this stock room, he pulled it as far out as he could, but still keeping a safe distance between himself and the rattler. "Rattler;" his son was now named after a deadly viper. He still wondered exactly what kind of vision the Indian Chief had had which led to this title. Max considered it as much of a title as a name, as if his son had somehow earned the respect of the Blackfoot elder.¶

The snake seemed to purposely travel with the hook and lunge at him as soon as it was out in the open. Max was able to dodge further back down the little hallway that was formed between the shelves and the pallets. He dipped a little and placed the hook perfectly behind the rattlesnake's head. Taking a quick breath, he snatched it up and stood straight to examine it for a few seconds. Inspecting for injuries, he did not see any and so placed the snake into a burlap sack and tied it off. Max then gave the room another once over and found the spot where the black-tail had gotten in. Stuffing an extra burlap sack into the hole, it would at least prevent another one from getting in until they had time to make repairs.¶

Exiting the storage room, he called for Peggy and she peered from around the corner. "Did you get it?" She asked nervously. "I sure did. I also found where he got in and put a temporary blockade in place until you can get it fixed." After he showed her the spot from inside the storage room, as well as walking outside to find where the repairs should be made, they returned inside the shop to the counter. Walking over to the cash register, Peggy pushed the no sale button, causing it to make a "ka-ching" sound and slide open. "How much do I owe you?" She inquired. "I actually don't need to charge you anything. I have a healthy specimen here that I will be able to milk and make anti-venom. Besides, I'm helping a local business and you're going to need money to get that wall fixed."¶

"But I still need to repay you somehow for your time. I insist." "Well, I do have guests coming over for dinner tomorrow night…" Peggy interrupted with a smile and said. "No problem. How many people?" "Five adults and a child." He answered. "What kind of cake would you like? I have a book that you can choose from." She walked down to the other end of the counter and opened a binder filled with beautiful cake designs. "I know. You pick. Whatever kind would be easiest. My friends and I are not picky." Peggy closed the binder. "Perfect. There's an idea for a cake I've been wanting to try, but so far, I have yet to make it for a client. So here's my chance." "Sounds good." Said Max as they shook hands good-bye.¶

Once he arrived back at the ranch, the rest of the day went smoothly. The snake milking schedule ran like clockwork. He would wait a few days, as he typically did with new members of their family, before milking the black-tailed rattlesnake. It was a little strange that he and his son looked at these reptiles as "family" more so than property. Perhaps that was one of the reasons why the Indian Chief gave him the name Rattler. Growing up, the idea of showing the utmost respect for snakes was taught to him by both his father and his grandfather. He had seen a few snake wrangling businesses that did not have that same attitude. They were more interested in the money than the overall health and well-being of their snakes; and it showed. Currently there were no other anti-venom producing companies in Blackwater.¶

The following morning, as soon as the sun rose

into the Texas sky, the three immediately went to work in order to get things done well before dinner. The plan was to make a dinner that would stretch out over time so that their discussion, however serious it was, would not bring down everybody's spirits. They wanted to have a good time as well. He would start the meal with cheese and crackers. Then a nice soup would be brought out, accompanied with a light salad. The main course would include a small rack of ribs, served with dinner rolls and steamed broccoli. They would finish the evening with whatever cake Peggy made for them with tea and milk. Max was especially looking forward to the cake. The bakery owner seemed as though she was going to make it extra special, and he was curious as to how well it would taste. The fact was that he and his son had not had cake in quite a while. They usually had fruit for dessert, with the occasional bowl of vanilla ice cream here or there.¶

It was about three o'clock when they finished all their chores and he rewarded Rattler and Ronin with some fresh-squeezed lemonade. "If you two would be willing to set the table and gather what we need for the salad, I'll run and get the cake from the bakery." No sooner did he make the request than his son started gathering plates and dinnerware. "Can I boil a few eggs to top the salad with dad?" He asked. "Sure son. Anything you want for the salad, just place it on the counter." Ronin was placing napkins at each place setting as Max walked through the dining room. "There will be six of us for dinner." He proclaimed as he held up six fingers. "Six." Ronin repeated as he nodded his head. The samurai seemed to be picking up simple English words fairly easily. Max knew he was going to be an excellent language student.¶

It seemed mere minutes before he was already parking and walking into the bakery he had just visited the day before. Peggy was behind the counter ringing up a customer with a cake made to look like a prairie landscape; it was very elegant. He knew that if that cake was for a paying customer, his must be a work of art. She had told him on the phone that it would be ready by now. "Hello Max. I'm so excited to see what you think of my creation. I already took a picture of it in the back for my binder. I was hoping to get one with you for my scrapbook. I like to take pictures of any new cake with the first customer who gets it, it makes it more personal and keeps a record of my career as a baker artist." She walked from behind the counter and again shook hands with him.¶

"That's fine. I actually like my picture taken. Where's the cake?" He asked. "It's right here on display. Not to toot my own horn, but I've gotten a lot of compliments on it in the past hour and a half since I brought it out." She walked over to a glass-covered table that she often used to show off her nicer cakes right before the customer came in to pick it up. "It's gorgeous." He commented as he turned and realized the cake was for him. "It caught my eye as soon as I walked in, but I didn't think you would create such an elaborate piece just for me and my guest." He was really stunned at the details in something that could actually be eaten. The cake consisted of a small patch of earth with a round cactus with pink flowers adorning it.¶

"I've seen this cactus before on a trip to Mexico." Max commented. "You have a good eye. This is a *mammillaria backebergiana*, it's native to Mexico. I bought a painting of some of these growing on a cliff from a local merchant on vacation last year. It's a dark chocolate cake with mint frosting. I kept it simple." "Simple? This looks like it took a lot of work. How did you get all these spines to look so real?" He asked. "It's a family secret. But basically I use homemade rock candy with a special process I like to use. They're edible, but I'd take them off and eat 'em separately." She opened the case and took the cake over to the counter where she had a box already open and ready to receive it. Closing and taping it shut, she slid a business card into the side. "I hope I'm not being too forward. I put my home number on the back if you'd like to have a cup of coffee sometime." She handed him the box and smiled.¶

"Thanks, I might take you up on your offer

early next week." Max was not used to a lot of flirtation from women. He was oblivious to it most of the time. He had not really considered a relationship with another woman after his wife had died. Besides, he had other things to worry about. "Thanks for the cake." "Thanks for getting that snake." He secured the cake in the sidecar and returned home. He put the cake on the coffee table in the living room and proceeded to the kitchen to prepare dinner. And with the help of Ronin and his son, the work went by quick as the doorbell rang to indicate the first guest's arrival.¶

"Hello Scotty, Jill, welcome. We have cheese and crackers while we're waiting." Max led them into the living room. No sooner did they sit down than the doorbell rang again. "I didn't see Butch when we pulled up." Said Jill as she placed a piece of cheddar onto a cracker. "I'll get dad." Rattler ran to the door and flung it open. "Hey, Uncle Butch. Come check out the cake dad brought home." Butch had no choice but to follow him into the kitchen to see the cake made to look like a cactus. After some chit-chat, the guests all made their way into the dining room for soup and salad. Plans were discussed for Max to go on a stake-out to learn security schedules. Sunday night. Scotty, being a business man, would mingle at the gun show and try to learn anything he could about any existing "black market" in the city. Butch would gather intelligence on new black-smithing techniques while keeping major vendors and security guards distracted.¶

Jill was going to babysit Rattler by having him spend the night. Max tried to communicate to Ronin that he would be out of town on business while he staked out Dead-Eye Inc. Finishing dinner and the excellent mint-chocolate cake, the friends all said goodbye for the night and each had his or her role to play in this intricate plan. The next ten days would be interesting to say the least.

CHAPTER VI - A Cookout¶

Max woke up slightly after Ronin had gone out to train; he wanted to get a head start on milking the snakes before making his deliveries. Letting Rattler sleep a while longer, he gathered his equipment and headed for the barn. Taking a quick inventory, he started milking the Mojave rattlesnakes first. Since it was considered by the known world as having the most potent venom of all rattlesnakes, he wanted to be fresh and focused. Since he had nearly forty snakes to milk that morning, he liked to save the less dangerous snakes for last; just in case his reflexes slowed over time. Once he had finished with the last of the common rattlers, he returned to the house to find Ronin and his son making ham and eggs with toast and juice for breakfast.¶

"Is everything on schedule for the cookout this afternoon dad?" Rattler asked as he started setting the table. "Everyone we invited said they would be there. I've already finished milking the snakes on today's schedule, so I'll be running errands while you do your chores." Max replied as he walked over and sat down in his usual spot. "If you're done before I get back, go ahead and gather our fishing gear and put it on the front porch. I'll drop you off at the lake so you and your guests can do a little fishing while I come back for Ronin and the food." He placed a napkin on his lap and waited for his breakfast. He was looking forward to not only celebrating his son's gift of a name with all his friends, but also to introducing Ronin to those who had not met him yet.¶

After a hardy meal, Max packed his anti-venom and a few other supplies and headed for town. He pulled into the side lot and parked his motorcycle near the main entrance. Walking into the bakery he found Peggy behind the counter waiting on an elderly woman ordering a cake for her husband for his retirement party. He waited patiently for several minutes until there was a lapse in business before approaching her. "Hello Peggy, I don't want to take up too much of your time. I just wanted to drop this off really quick." Max said as he walked up to her and handed her an envelope. "What's this?" Asked Peggy as she flipped it over and started to open it. "Oh it's just a thank-you card for the cake, everyone enjoyed it very much." He smiled as she stopped and placed it into her front apron pocket instead. "I was hoping we could get a cup of coffee together sometime this weekend if you're not too busy." Asked Peggy, wiping some flour off of her cheek.¶

Max had not even considered dating since his wife had died, but saw this as an opportunity. "Well if you're not busy this evening, we're having a cookout at Crawling Water Lake if you'd like to come." He hoped it was not too "last minute" for her. "I'd love to. I get off at four. What time and what should I bring?" "Oh, you don't have to bring anything. We've planned this earlier this week and we have all of the refreshments covered. Just bring yourself and a healthy appetite." Max was so excited she could make it. He just hoped Rattler would not be too upset with the idea. "We're going to start grilling about five and probably wrap up before ten. So anytime between then would be fine. We're having all kinds of meats: chicken, ribs, burgers, etc. But we're also having salads and fresh fruit."¶

Max had not talked to many women as of late, and felt as if he were rambling on a bit, so he paused, took a deep breath, and waited for her to talk. "Sounds great. You said you've planned it earlier this week, is it a special occasion?" She asked. "It's a long story. I'll tell you all about it when you get there." A bell rang as the front door opened. Several business women approached the counter and one of them started filling out an order form while the others looked at the cakes in the display case. "Well, I'll let you get back to work; and I have other errands to run." He turned to leave as the women started inquiring about a catering job. "See you at five." She said as the front door started to close behind him.¶

Max had several more stops to make before heading home. First he dropped of some anti-venom to Neighborhood Health Care, the local free clinic.

Then he stopped at a couple of small country doctors who still made home visits to farmers and low-income families. The Golden Snake supplied any non-profit, or near non-profit, business that helped people injured from snake bites. His family had always felt as though it were their civic duty to do so. And with a modest lifestyle, his family had plenty of money to help others with free medicines and research. Taking the quickest and least busy routes, Max was done within a couple of hours, most of his time was taken up by legal paperwork in order to keep records of which batch went to whom in hopes of tracking more successful medicines with specific patients.¶

*¶

Two man in a dark, business-like work suits walked onto the construction site of Gunz a' Blazin', one with a clipboard full of various documents and forms, the other with a toolbox. "Where's our truck?!" Shouted the foreman looking up from a worktable where blueprints for the new facility laid. "I don't know anything about a truck. I'm here to inspect the ground pipes to see if everything is up to code before you continue with any foundation work." "Another one. We just had one this morning about property lines. What the hell's going on with this crap." The foreman was visibly upset under the stress of rebuilding, or the attempt of rebuilding.

"I've had it up to here with all of these issues." He added, slamming his helmet to the ground. "Temper, temper." Said the inspector as he walked over to the large hole in the ground as his assistant started taking measurements.¶

"How does the city expect us to finish on time with all of these inspections and permit application delays?!" He reached down and picked his helmet back up and placed it firmly on his head. "Chief!" Shouted a workman. "Found out what happened to our truck!" The foreman looked over his shoulder. "Out with it. Where's the damn truck!" "They started road construction on Wood Avenue, so they're detouring up Central Street. With traffic, it'll be about 40 minutes!" There was dead silence for about ten seconds. "That's it! Someone get me Ron on the phone. We can't afford to pay overtime to workers just standing around and not working!" He stormed over to the on-site trailer, walked up the stairs, went inside, and slammed the door behind him. The door immediately opened again. "Until then, everyone clean up the site and run maintenance on the equipment. And somebody make sure we pass inspection."¶

*¶

The sounds of wood striking metal made loud clacking noises that emanated from behind the barn. Ronin and Rattler had been training every morning since the samurai's arrival. Max had even made an inexpensive fence to mark the area where spectators could stand far enough from the action to observe from a point of safety. He also had plans to till up the dirt, pull weeds, and replace the grass with a mixture of tiny pebbles and wood chips so it would take on the appearance of a small arena and eliminate the need to mow. Rattler lunged at his teacher, who easily stepped aside and lightly swatted his backside with the flat edge of his sword. "No! Slash side to side, or up and down. Keep distance from larger foe." Ronin explained with a firm, but kind voice. Rattler returned to his starting position, brushed a little sweat from his brow, and raised his sword for another melee. Ronin had never took on a pupil before, but from what he saw from others, no student as young as this boy had ever taken training so seriously; nor showed such tenacity.¶

Even though the sound of the steam-cycle coming up the driveway could be heard from the training area, Rattler did not lose his focus. They continued combat several more minutes before they stopped for a rest. Heading back to the house, Ronin stowed their training equipment on the porch as Max finished putting his paperwork away in the filing cabinet near the milking station. "Dad, we're all finished with our chores and sword practice, should I load the fishing gear in the sidecar?"

Rattler shouted as he ran towards his father; he shielded his eyes from the sun with his left hand. The sun was shining brightly in the Texas sky, and it was getting particularly hot for late April.¶

"Go ahead, son." Max answered. "I'm going to jump in the shower before we head out." He started thinking of a way of explaining the arrival of an unknown woman to the cookout held in Rattler's honor. Should he explain now; at the lake; or when she showed up? Max kept going over the conversation in his head. It was not that she was going to replace Rattler's mother, he just met her. She was only a friend at this point so why worry so much. He entered the house and went about gathering up a towel, washcloth and clean clothes before heading to the bathroom.¶

After he stepped out onto the slightly wet floor, he decided to wait until she showed up to the lake to introduce her as the person who had made that delicious chocolate mint cactus cake and downplay it for the moment. He finished drying his hair and got dressed. Yes, that would be best. If he did not make such a big deal about it in front of his friends and son, they would be less likely to assume they might be officially dating; which was actually the truth. Max did not really know Peggy's intentions after all. He would just let what happen... happen. There was no rush.¶

As soon as he had walked out the front door,

Rattler climbed the front steps holding both of their helmets. "Ready to go, dad." His son had a humongous smile on his face as going fishing was one of his favorite things to do. And getting to have freshly grilled chicken for supper was the icing on the cake. "I sure am, son." Max replied, grabbing his helmet from the boy's hand and strolling across the yard to the bike. "Why don't you do the honors of starting her up." The words barely left his lips as Rattler threw on his helmet and proceeded to load in more coal and start the engine. The steam-cycle hummed like a miniaturized train as it vibrated on its three wheels.¶

There were three fishing poles, a net and a large tackle box in the foot of the sidecar. Max had not given it much thought, but this was probably Ronin's first experience learning to fish with a rod and reel. The samurai seemed to get along so well with Rattler; he would probably let the boy teach him how to fish while he focused on grilling the food and setting the picnic tables. As soon as Rattler climbed into the sidecar and fastened his seat belt, Max slipped it into gear and they were heading out of the driveway and down Picket Avenue on their way to Crawling Water Lake.¶

Upon arriving at the picnic area, they found only a few other families enjoying the grounds and lakefront. A couple of people were out in boats, but most we lined along the docks with their fishing poles at the ready. "Butch should be here any minute, son. So let's get you set up under that tree over there so you can rest in the shade until he arrives." They were close enough to the water, so Max could leave the steam-cycle's engine running as they unloaded all of the fishing equipment. "Do you think Ronin has ever been fishing, dad?" Rattler asked as he carried the net and tackle box down to the lake. "I'm sure he has in a way. But I don't think they use rod and reels like we do. Technologies can differ depending on what state or country you're from. I don't really know, it's possible though." Max leaned the fishing poles against the tree in a way that they would not fall over. "I hope he likes to fish." Rattler added. "I hope he does do." His father replied back.¶

As soon as he turned around, Max spotted Butch walking towards them carrying a fishing pole in one hand and a medium-sized cooler in the other. He walked up to greet him and ask if it would be okay to leave Rattler with him for the next half an hour so he could return home to get Ronin and the food. "It's no problem, I came to do some serious fishing and relaxation before tomorrow night's fight with O'Malley. I'm predicting a first-round KO by the way." "You always predict a first-round KO." Said Rattler as he walked up to the two men. "Here let me get that for you Uncle Butch." He added as he reached for the cooler's handle. "okay, but be careful, it's awfully heavy." Rattler smiled as he took the full weight. It was awfully heavy, but he did not want to let them know that. "I've got big muscles. Ronin and I have been training hard, so I've been doing extra push-ups, pull-ups and sit-ups." Butch smiled at him and added. "You need to start lifting more weights if you want to get real muscles."¶

After a short conversation, the two friends shook hands and went different directions. Butch and Rattler went down to the shade under the big oak tree, and Max returned to the ranch to get Ronin and the food for the cookout. Pulling down the driveway, he found Ronin waiting at the foot of the front porch steps with the food neatly packed in burlap sacks. He bowed as usual as a simple greeting, picked up the sacks and headed towards the cycle. The samurai had never actually ridden in any type of vehicle before, so it took several minutes to get him seated and buckled in properly. But once he was in the sidecar with a helmet on, he began to relax and seemed to enjoy the twelve-minute ride back to the lake.¶

Seeing his father park the bike with Ronin, Rattler came running up in anticipation of fishing with his new teacher. After helping to carry the food over next to a vacant grill by a couple of picnic tables, Rattler took Ronin by the sleeve and led him down to where Butch was already fishing. He had not caught anything since his arrival, but he was enjoying the peace and quiet, as well as some conversation with young Rattler. The samurai seemed puzzled by the fishing poles and instead walked over to the woods, pulled out a dagger, and hacked down a low-lying branch from a sturdy tree. He then stripped off the bark and carved one end to a point. He walked back over to where Butch and Rattler were fishing and proceeded to wade out into the water to spear himself a fish.¶

"Never saw someone fish like that." Remarked Butch as he reeled in his line. "I'll watch you for a while and see how you make out. I won't be able to catch anything anyway with someone splashing around." Butch was not angry with Ronin, he took it as an opportunity to sit under the tree and watch someone else try their luck at catching. Rattler ran over to the woods and quickly returned with his own stick and whittled one end with his pocketknife so he could join in the fun and sport of spear fishing.¶

It took only ten minutes for Max to get a decent fire going on the public grill. He had just laid down a couple pieces of chicken when Dan strolled up and set a bag of food on the picnic table. "Hello, Max." He said politely. "Do you need any help with anything before I head down to join the gang?" "I've got everything handled right now. What's in the bag?" Max asked. "I just brought some different kinds of chips and some apples. If you're all set then, I'd like to get a line in the water before we eat." Max patted him on the shoulder and told him to have fun as he turned and walked towards Butch and the others.¶

An hour went by before Scotty and Jill arrived on foot. They had their niece, Daisy, with them. Max was happy they made it in time for his second batch of chicken and ribs, he had not seen Daisy in over a year and she must have grown at least two inches since then. "Welcome, hope you guys are hungry. You're just in time for chicken and ribs." They placed a couple of bags and containers on the picnic table as Rattler, Butch, Dan, and Ronin walked up after failing to catch or spear a single fish for the past sixty-some minutes. "No luck yet, dad. But Ronin and I have come awfully close a few times. We'll be snacking on blue gill before we leave, I know it." He placed his spear on the ground and took a seat at the table. Ronin and the others smiled in defeat as they too sat down for some supper.¶

They were just about to eat when Rattler looked up and noticed a woman walking towards them with a big white box. "Max?!" She shouted. "Max?! Is that you?!" She repeated. Max stood up and turned around. It was Peggy. "Yeah, right over here! That makes everyone!" He yelled. "Dad, who is that?" Asked Rattler. "I'll make introductions as soon as she gets to the table." In a few seconds, Peggy arrived and placed the box at the end of one of the picnic tables. There was barely any room with all of the food. Both were nearly overflowing with various salads, chips, drinks, and platters mounded with grill meats; along with fresh fruits and watermelon.¶

"Everyone, this is Peggy. I removed a rattlesnake from her bakery and she was the one who made that incredible cake we had last night." Max explained. "It was the least I could do. He refused to charge me, and so I lent my culinary baking skills to say thank-you. I'm glad to hear you all enjoyed it." "What's in the box, ma'am?" Rattler asked politely. "Son, be patient. I want to introduce everyone before we continue." After she had met Butch, Scotty, Jill, Dan, Daisy, Ronin, and his son, Rattler, she opened to box to reveal various pastries. "Peggy, you didn't have to bring anything. You're our guest." Max said sincerely. "Oh it's not a big deal." She replied. "It was extra from the bakery and a few items from a canceled order. I usually just give stuff like this away to my employees at the end of the day. I don't resell any products that may go stale. I won't have any food go to waste if I can help it. Please, enjoy."¶

After grace was said, everyone began to dig into all of the delicious food. Butch put down his drumstick and asked. "Daisy, how old are you now, you look like you've been growing quicker than a weed?" Daisy swallowed a bite of her salad. "I'm twelve, Uncle Butch." Even though they were not actually related, almost every child who knew him called him Uncle Butch. "Twelve already? Why, you're almost old even to vote." He teased. "Pass the potato salad please." Asked Jill. Max finished what little food he had left on his plate, cleaned the grill, and started the story of how Rattler got his name.¶

"Most of you already know this, but my wife passed away during childbirth." He did not want to shock Peggy with this information right of the bat, but it was necessary to the storyline. "I never did name my boy because Beth and I were going to name him together when he was born." He started to tear up just a bit, but not enough to actually start to cry. Choking it back, he continued. "I always referred to him as either son, or boy. I know, not the greatest plan. But I was a little lost for a while." Everyone listened intently as the story unfolded during the meal. "He wrangled his first snake, unassisted, two Mondays ago at the Wilson Ranch. And when we visited the Blackfoot Tribe later that afternoon, Chief White Cloud had told us he had a vision. And he bestowed on my brave young boy the name, Rattler." The tearfulness had finally left his eyes and a broad smile began to appear. "He had seen my boy growing into a strong young man and achieving great things and helping people. And that is all I've ever wanted for my son. So raise your drinks… and let's give a cheerful toast to my boy, Rattler!"¶

A big roar went up in their picnic area, enough to make a lot of people fishing turn and take notice. It was not every day that someone got to celebrate the honor of being given the gift of a name from the chief of the Blackfoot Tribe. It was a time of fellowship and rejoicing for all of his family and friends. They continued eating until almost all of the food was gone. "Not many leftovers to have to take home." Commented Jill as she started clearing away empty plates and cups from the tables. "Let me help Aunt Jill." Said Daisy as she threw some napkins into a nearby trash can.¶

Max turned to Peggy and kind of shrugged his shoulders. "Sorry about all of that. I hope it wasn't to overwhelming or emotional for you." "There's no need to apologize. I feel honored to have shared this moment with you and your family. I'm just glad all of my donuts and stuff were eaten. Saves me the trouble of dropping them off at my sister's place later." Max did not really know what to say next. Sensing a little shyness, Peggy started talking. "Do you have an extra pole? I haven't been fishing in a long time." She and Max both smiled. "You can share mine." Max added, picking his pole from the ground next to where he was sitting. "Do you like lures or live bait?"¶

"I've got one!" Shouted Butch. "I've got one!" Everyone turned to see him reeling like crazy. He had always used an extra strong line so he could muscle whatever fish he caught with his powerful arms. He reeled and pulled, reeled and pulled. And in no time flat, hauled in what appeared to be a sixteen-pound, large-mouth bass. Holding it up in his left hand he removed the hook as everyone around started clapping. "Should we eat him, or should I let him go?" He shouted. There were mixed reviews from the small crowd that had gathered, but since Butch was stuffed from the cookout, he decided to let the fellow go. So giving him a small stroke down its back, he placed him gently back into the water.¶

No sooner did he release the fish, then a stick flew ten feet in front of him. "I apologize." Said Ronin, walking over to retrieve his homemade spear. The samurai picked it from the water, revealing a two-pound, bluegill wiggling near the tip. Ronin quickly pulled the spear from the fish and drove it through its head to end its suffering. He then waded ashore and proceeded to skin and gut it before walking over to the grill. Max was already starting another small fire. They were mostly full, but grilled fish would make a nice, midnight snack later.¶

Max and Peggy fished together a little distance

away from everyone else so they could talk a little more. Before they knew it, an hour had passed. As conversations slowed and the sun started to go down, everyone started saying their goodbyes. The finished cleaning the picnic area and packed their things. Max walked Peggy back to her bicycle. He thought about asking her on an actual date, but he decided to call her sometime over the weekend instead. "Dad, would it be okay if Ronin and I walked home?" It was quite a trek, but since they were so diligent about finishing their chores, Max decided to say yes. "Could you load everything into the sidecar then, please?" "Already done." Rattler answered. "But what if I'd have said no?" "Then I would have just taken stuff back out." Smart boy, he thought. "okay, you guys be careful and I'll see you at home."

CHAPTER VII - The Gun Show

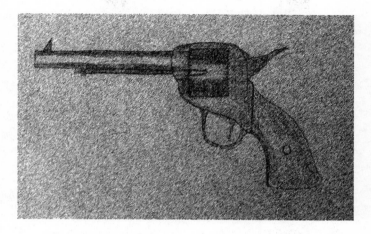

Waking up, Max was not as surprised by the actions of his guest. Ronin had already prepped the kitchen, cleaned the dining and living room tables, swept the floor, and taken out the garbage. He decided right then and there that he would do something special for the samurai. Max cooked the three of them a special breakfast and did what little chores needed to be done and left for town. What he really wanted to do was to drive around Dead-Eye Inc.'s headquarters a few times and decide on a spot for the stakeout Sunday night.

After two laps, he spotted the perfect location; a patch of grass by the Blackwater river bridge where people sometimes fished. If anyone questioned him, he could simply say that he enjoyed the peace and quiet of nighttime fishing and was using his binoculars to look at any wildlife that wondered into town making noises. He would bring along a small cooler of tea and snacks to further his story. Notes could be jotted down in a small notebook that would be kept in his jacket's breast pocket for quick access. Although it could be a little dangerous, he was excited at the prospect of being somewhat of a hero by taking down those responsible for the illegal activities.¶

Once home, he gave Ronin another short English lesson and then they all went behind the barn where Max watched as his son learned more about using a sword. He could hardly wait until Butch finished their swords. How would they compare to Ronin's? He was also curious if Ronin knew anything about actually making swords, or did he merely know how to use them. "Merely how to use them," that was not the term he had meant. He saw how well the samurai utilized the deadly weapon, and if he and Rattler could learn ten percent of what he taught them, he would be more than satisfied.¶

After about an hour of training, they retired back to the house for some sun tea. He asked if Ronin knew how to brew hot tea, and he thought by how he replied that he did. As they were getting ready to prepare for dinner, Rattler asked his father if it was time for their weekly injections. It had nearly slipped Max's mind. "Of course, we always do so right before bedtime." He replied. "I know,

but with Ronin staying here, did we need to change
our routine? Do you think he'd know what we're
doing?" His son did make a good point. What
would a foreigner think if he saw a father and son
inject themselves with some strange substance
before going to bed? "I think we'll go to the barn
and do it out there from now on. I wouldn't want to
upset our guest with our unique ritual." His family
had always referred as the injections as a ritual.¶

After a dinner of pork steaks, salad and mixed
berries with almonds, everyone prepared for bed.
After brushing their teeth, Max and Rattler took a
trip to the barn. Getting into the refrigerator, Max
took out two small vials with minute amounts of
this week's snake venom… the Grand Canyon
rattlesnake. After injecting himself, Max injected
his son and put him to bed. Though someone who
was not familiar with their ritual might be worried,
Rattler was already born with some resistance to
snake venom. He started giving his son injections of
snake venom since he was three years old. Max
would stay up all night monitoring his son's vital
signs and made sure he was safe. But after five
years, it was no longer necessary. His son's immune
system had become very strong over the last half
decade, and he was extra careful with the doses.¶

As the Sunday sun rose, Max made sure to
pack everything Rattler would need to spend the
night at Scotty and Jill's house before he made

breakfast. His son was already gathering the ingredients for homemade biscuits. They typically had biscuits and gravy on Sundays and spent the day playing board games and cards after their chores. Sometimes they would go over to Butch's or Scotty's for lunch, or invite them to their place. Sunday had always revolved around spending time with friends and family. They worked hard all week, so it was literally their day of rest. But rest would have to wait, this week was going to be very busy.¶

After breakfast, Max placed some drinks and trail mix into his cooler and set it to the right of the front door. He put the suitcase for Rattler, with his clothes and personal hygiene items, on the other side. He took Ronin into the living room and tried to explain that he was welcome to stay while they were gone. "I'll be gone overnight." He said as he drew a picture of himself and his son walking away from the house with Ronin on the front porch. He quickly drew another one depicting Ronin on a bed sleeping with a moon outside the window. Then, he drew a third picture showing the house with Ronin on the front porch with himself and Rattler walking back. "You're welcome to eat whatever we have. Just clean up after yourself. Now I have to get a lot of extra work done today in order to clear as much of my schedule for tomorrow as I can." Since he was going to be up all night, he needed time on Monday to take a nap.¶

"Let me check your arm son." Max told Rattler. "Any swelling or discomfort?" He did not really know why he was going through this routine at this point. His son would have told him if his arm hurt or showed any discoloration at breakfast. But it still showed his son that he loved him and was concerned nonetheless. "No. I feel great. Ready to take on the world today. And I can't wait to go over to Mr. and Mrs. Daniels. They're making pizza!" Rattler was anxious to get to his chores because he was told he could go over as soon as they were done. "Come on Ronin. I'm ready to go." He and the samurai always seemed to be on the same page whenever they headed out the door to start each day.¶

It did not take the three of them very long to complete all of the day's chores. In fact, they worked so efficiently, they were done by lunch time. As an extra reward, Max threw together his famous fruit salad. It had strawberries, blueberries, raspberries, almonds, and his homemade orange sauce. Since they had plenty of time on their hands before the Daniels would be expecting them, Ronin spent an extra hour training the boy behind the barn. They had gotten into a routine of stretching and doing what Ronin referred to as a "kata." It seemed to be an imaginary fight with invisible opponents. There were several katas that he was teaching Rattler, and his son was memorizing the steps rather quickly.¶

After they finished, Max insisted that Rattler take a bath before heading over to spend the night. "You don't want to be all sweaty and stinky when you get there." "I guess not." Came the response from his son. "I'll grab a towel and hop in the tub." Running his bath, he washed himself from head to toe and got into his favorite outfit. Grabbing his favorite pillow and blanket, he headed for the living room to wait for his dad. "Well, we'll see you tomorrow Ronin." He shook the samurai's hand and the two headed for the door. Rattler packed his things into the sidecar and put on his helmet. After climbing in, Max handed him his small cooler and he fired up the bike and headed towards his friend's house.¶

Within minutes they were pulling down the long driveway that led to Scotty's home behind his family-owned gun shop, The Gunslinger. Rattler could hardly wait for the steam-cycle to stop and practically jumped out while it was still moving. Their dog, Shana, spotted them from the porch and came running and barking. Rattler loved dogs but his father would not let him have one until his tenth birthday. It was a tradition in his family for children to get their first pet when they turned ten years old. Shana was a lab-mix with a beautiful brown coat. Rattler's plan was to find his tennis ball and play fetch until he tired him out; then they could sit on the porch swing while he petted him. It was going to be a fun afternoon.¶

Max grabbed his son's things from the sidecar and strolled up towards the front door just as Scotty and Jill came out onto the porch. Jill had made some sun tea and cut up some fresh vegetables with ranch dip for them to enjoy. Sitting down at a patio table, Scotty asked Max to remind him of the details of his plan again. "I'd be happy to stop by sometime during the night and help you in any way I can." He explained. "I'm not sure what you could do. I suppose if you stopped and I needed a second spot staked out… but I think two people with binoculars that close to their headquarters might raise suspicion with security if we're spotted. No, I think I'll be fine." He concluded. "Besides, if I need to, I can switch locations for a short time. And if I'm 'caught,' I'll simply explain that I saw a coyote or wild boar wondering around while I was fishing and went to check it out."¶

"That sounds reasonable." Scotty added. "I just wish there was more we could do to help. You shouldn't be the only one taking all the risks. We're your friends." Max was touched by his Scotty's words. "Keeping Rattler safe is enough help. But if you'd like, swing by the ranch before you turn in and see if Ronin is doing all right. I don't think he'll be a bother. He seems rather good with the whole self-discipline thing. I can never wake up before he does." It was true, Ronin appeared to not need very much sleep. He rose before the sun and went outside to train and clean the grounds while Max and Rattler slept; it was his way.¶

"Well, I'd better get going. I want to set up early and make it look like I'm doing a little fishing before the sun starts to go down. I'll be taking notes of everything I see. Security routes; time; different guards; whatever I notice." He took a sip of tea and a couple of pieces of celery from the tray. "I do hope you're careful Max." Jill added. "I don't want to see you get into trouble, or worse, hurt." "I'm not going to be doing anything illegal. Not tonight any way. Besides, the worse they could do is call the authorities about 'suspicious activities.' Night fishing is not a crime, and I'll be on public property. It'll be fine." He was almost reassuring himself as he spoke. Max was nervous about the prospect of eventually breaking into their headquarters. There was really no other way of exposing what they were doing without having actual, physical evidence of the crime.¶

"Well, I'm really going now. Wish me luck." He finished his last bit of tea, thanked his hosts, and returned to his bike. "Bye son, you behave for Mr. and Mrs. Daniels now." Max drove his steam-cycle down to the Blackwater River and set it on its kickstand fifty yards from the bridge in a patch of dirt people normally used for parking. Walking to the familiar, grassy clearing, he put down his cooler and pulled out his tackle box. Placing his fishing pole into a holder, he did not even bother putting any lures or bait, or even a hook on it. Max made it look like he was passively fishing while relaxing and eating. He had a small pocketknife in his pocket, so if anyone came close enough, or he felt like he was being watched, he could simply make it appear that he has lost his hook and lure to a snag. He pulled out his notebook and a pencil and wrote down the time. 4:00pm.¶

After several hours, he had noticed three guards; they all walked in different patterns, but their timing made sure that their paths crossed. He would need to keep track all night, but so far he had their patterns down to a couple of minutes. After a quick snack and something to drink, he decided to walk down the river a ways and check out the employee's parking lot and count how many vehicles there were. It was now 7:00pm and he was curious as to when the shift change was going to occur. Counting all the vehicles, most of which were bikes, he found that there were only sixteen. He actually had no idea how many guards were inside, but he guessed around a dozen or more. He had not really given enough thought of what he was going to do once he got inside the facility; he had been more preoccupied with where and how he was going to enter.¶

He spent the next hour nonchalantly circling the entire facility and made a crude drawing of all the different sections of the building. It took several sheets paper to map out everything in a grid-like pattern. Max was going to make a better copy of it when he got home. Once he knew the door or window that he needed to enter, he would mark it on the map, and make another drawing of the interior during the gun show so he could sync up how to get to what appeared to be their testing lab.¶

Checking the parking lot for a second time, it appeared that the shift change would take place at 8:00pm. After all of the vehicles were either parked, or gone; he counted only eight. That was interesting. He had not noticed anyone walking towards the main entrance from anywhere except from the parking lot. Could the number of people guarding the facility only be eight people? He did not notice if anyone rode of the back of another person's bike, or in a passenger seat. He returned to his spot to continue taking notes. He needed more information.¶

Upon reaching midnight, there were still three guards walking pretty much the same patterns as the ones before; their timing was a little different, but close enough for him to be within a couple of minutes. The next five hours went by without incident, and his notes showed a distinct pattern of when and where each guard would most likely be at any given moment. He had to make a decision of where he was going to make his entry before the sun came up. And he had the perfect location. There was a door by what appeared to be a maintenance shed on the opposite side of the loading docks from where he and Rattler had exited the main building. Hopefully, he would be able to take that same hallway once he got inside and simply go the opposite direction to reach the lab.¶

Writing down his last bit of information, he packed up and returned home for a couple hours of sleep before he would have to go and get his son after breakfast. Leaving his cooler and fishing equipment on the porch, he slid into bed and quickly fell asleep.¶

*¶

The sun rose into the Texas sky, casting a long shadow on the headquarters of Dead-Eye Inc. It was Saturday, and the gun show was a mere five hours away. Mr. Lucas and Mr. Boyd were both in the convention area seeing to the details regarding the unveiling of the company's newest product, the sniper scope. "Keep those curtains closed, we don't want anyone seeing what's in here. Mr. Johnson will be furious if word gets out before his big announcement during his speech." Mr. Lucas shouted. "Set the podium right there. And make sure the velvet rope is precisely twenty away from the product." He barked. Tensions were high among the employees scurrying around, making sure everything was set up to the CEO's standards.¶

After all the last-minute details were finished, it was time for security to open the doors to the general public. In mere minutes, the main hall was flooded with hundreds of gun enthusiasts, all wanting to get a look at the many different rifles, shotguns, handguns, and accessories available for purchase. But nothing grabbed their attention more than several security guards standing in front of the curtained-off booth behind a velvet rope. When asked, they were told that only photographers were able to stand directly behind it during Mr. Johnson's speech. Everyone else would have to stand behind them. The announcement would take place an hour before the gun show ended, ensuring lengthy stays for anyone wanting a good spot to observe.¶

Max, Scotty and Butch walked into the main entrance and split up. Each had a specific job to do; Scotty headed towards vendor registration in order to see what big players might be in attendance; Butch walked into the main area and looked for manufacturing demonstrations; and Max asked the guest information desk for the locations of all the nearby bathrooms. It was his intention to be familiar in case he had to duck into one, or use it as an excuse if questioned by employees or security.¶

Walking over to the registration table, Scotty recognized one of the executives from Gunz a' Balzin', Ron Edwards. "Hey, Ron. How's the rebuilding of your factory coming along? Smooth, I hope." He stated. "Not really, there's all kinds of construction delays going on. The main road is under maintenance all of a sudden. It's a mess right now." Scotty could tell by the expression on Ron's face that things were way worse than he could imagine. "Well, I hope the insurance helps out at least." Replied Scott, not really knowing what else to say. "That's even giving us problems. Our papers are all in order, but there's still a delay on our payment. Something about our deductible, I need more details from accounting. Besides, we're so into debt with lenders, we're barely going to break even before we can reopen for business. The last week has been a nightmare." Ron said good-bye and headed for a meeting with some distributors while Scotty continued to mingle.¶

As soon as Butch made his way to the nearest demonstration on hand-gun barrels, he was recognized by some boxing fans. "Hey, it's the champ!" Someone yelled above the voice of the demonstrator. People immediately started crowding around asking for autographs. "Settle down, we're all here for the gun show. I never turn down autographs after a bout, so I'll be giving out around nine thirty tonight." Butch stated. "But the fight's at nine." Someone added. "I realize that, it's not going past the second round, and more likely the first." The group of people circling the champ erupted in applause and laughter. "You get 'em champ. No one comes to our town and pushes you around." Another fan added. After the cheers died down, everyone's attention went back towards the demonstration.¶

Max was surprised to get a map of most of the main building showing all the restrooms from a girl at the welcome desk. It was not that surprising; most people would not be trying to break into the corporate headquarters, so Dead-Eye Inc. was more than happy to distribute them to guests. The brochure included a drawing of the main hall that he and Rattler had headed down the week before, but not the end by the loading docks. He could not locate the section of the building where he had originally found the schematics on this paper; so he simply needed a couple of small pieces of notebook paper to complete a more elaborate map.¶

Looking around carefully, as if he were looking for someone, he noticed the double doors to the main hall were not being guarded by anyone. In fact, there seemed to be a group tour organizing by the large bay window overlooking the tree where he and Rattler had their picture taken for the newspaper. Max had not bothered to purchase a copy of the paper because the entire situation made him uneasy. It was a relief that Rattler seemed to have forgotten all about it, at least for now.¶

Walking over to a table, he discovered that there was still a couple of slots for a tour of the facility. This would be perfect, he could tag along and take notes like he was a simple tourist. He just had to register and blend in with everyone else in the group. Registration was free and so in a couple of minutes, one of the staff members handed him a name tag to attach to his shirt. Max planned to use the same method of creating his map by using a grid that matched up when each piece of paper was aligned, so he could put different pieces in different pockets and not draw attention to what he was doing. If someone asked what any given piece was, he would simply say that it was a quick sketch of where the group stopped last before he went to the restroom in case he got separated.¶

Staying towards the back of the group, Max made sketch after sketch of each section of the building they toured. He tried his best to act like an interested tourist by asking the occasional question so as not to look suspicious. When they finally headed down the main hallway towards the loading docks, he made note that he would be unable to use this way as an exit as the double doors would be blocked by a reinforced, locked metal gate. Ideally he would be able to exit the point at which he entered, but he needed a secondary escape point should something go wrong. Rounding a corner, he spotted just what he was looking for; an office with a window overlooking a familiar maintenance shed.¶

"And this is one of the many testing areas we have here at Dead-Eye Inc. Of course we can't actually see any testing today because everyone is at the gun show, and there aren't any scheduled for the next two weeks." The guide motioned to the large room and then continued walking. Max jotted down some lines and approximate measurements, this was probably the room he was looking for. He had no idea the tour would actually take him right past where he needed to break into. He decided to wait a minute or two to ask about a restroom break. He needed to make sure all his data lined up. The entry point, testing room, and secondary exit were looking possible.¶

It was at that moment that he thought he spotted Mr. Johnson coming down the hallway towards the group. He quickly turned his attention to the art piece on the wall that the guide was talking about and stood near a tall woman and leaned close and asked her opinion. When she started talking, he stepped around to her other side and nodded. This allowed him to keep his back towards the man, even if it was not who he thought it was. After the man disappeared down a long hall, he raised his hand and asked where the nearest men's room was. As they would be here for another minute or two, she pointed towards a short hallway opposite the one they had entered.¶

Walking into the restroom, Max actually had to go. After washing his hands, he exited and found that the hallway was empty. Cautiously walking over to the door to the testing area, he jotted down some measurements and stuffed them into one of his pockets. He could not help but try the door handle, and to his amazement, it was actually unlocked. With his adrenaline racing, his instincts took over and he quickly slipped inside. Looking around, there did not appear to be anyone in the room. He ran over to the table and scanned the entire area. Max unexpectedly found the set of blueprints folded neatly in the second drawer of the very same table as before; he flattened them and stuffed them under his shirt and zipped his coat halfway up.¶

Heading back to the door, he caught a glimmer of something metallic under another work station, half covered with a tarp. Pressing his luck, he ran over and peaked underneath... could it be!? It appeared to be the prototype from the blueprints. He could not believe it! Without hesitation, he pulled it out from under the table and grabbed a nearby sledgehammer. With a couple of mighty swings, he destroyed the weapon. He grabbed a couple of small pieces that had broken off in hopes of foiling any attempt at repairs. Max then realized the severity of his situation and made a dash for the exit. Slipping back out the door, he bee-lined it back to the men's room. He splashed some water onto his face and looked into the mirror. What had just happened.¶

Collecting his thoughts and emotions, Max had no choice but to casually walk back out of the restroom and look for the tour group. It was fortunate that there was a lot of talking coming from the people and he found them quite easily around the corner, apparently coming back towards the place where the piece of art hung on the wall. He was able to inconspicuously rejoin the group as no one appeared to have entered the testing area. The tour wrapped up within ten minutes and he found himself back at the gun show. His head was starting to spin as if he had been drinking. Max needed to find his friends and get the hell out of there.

CHAPTER VIII - Plan of Action¶

Mr. Bull proceeded to bang his gavel onto the table in order to call the meeting of The Black Bull Society to order. "It's apparent to me that Mr. Coleman is not going to show. What a shame too, he would have been a great asset to our operation." Mr. Bull set his gavel down and opened a folder in front of him. "Do we know what his plans for the weekend are?" He added. Mr. White then spoke up. "He will be spending it at home, probably listening to music on his record player and unwinding from his busy week." He wrote this information in his file and continued speaking. "Take care of him during tonight's boxing match. We will all have alibis for the investigation." Mr. Bull spoke as though it were just another point of business on the agenda. "Are you sure he'll be alone?" Mr. Armament interjected. "Of course I am" Replied Mr. White. "Are you questioning my knowledge of the situation?" Mr. Armament seemed startled. "Of course not, sir. I'm merely nervous at the timing of all of this."¶

Looking around the table, Mr. Bull waited to see if there would be any other questions before continuing with the meeting. Seeing none, he continued. "What are the projected costs for full scale production Mr. Cobble?" To which Mr. Cobble replied. "Well below expectations. It will be very profitable; the problems lie with keeping it a secret from the employees. We have designed three phony weapons that share components so when shipped together, can be reassembled as the fully automatic Gatling gun we designed." "Then what exactly is the problem then?" He asked. "With projected sales, how do we explain the fact that no one will be seeing the phony weapons being used by anyone?" "That is a very good point. But we can solve that problem, by only shipping them to far away states and keep the actual destination of the weapons off the books. Would that be possible Mr. Civilized?" "That should not be a problem sir. I have adequate resources at my disposal to ensure those weapons would stay quite untraceable."¶

"Very good. Now onto the next point. Mr. Richards, how are the problems with jamming problems coming?" Mr. Richards opened the folder in front of him and looked for some numbers. "It appears we are coming closer to our goal." "Well what exactly does that mean? I need specifics!" Mr. Bull shouted, banging his fist down on the table. "Forgive me sir." He responded. "This is the first, fully automatic weapon ever made; we can't make more progress without sufficient testing data." With that, all eyes turned to Mr. Experiment. "We feel the design of the weapon is the main problem." He said softly. "There's nothing wrong with my design." Rebutted Mr. Richards. "Well the fact that it is so big, and that it needs a second person to carry the ammo clip, or should I say box, makes it difficult to keep it aligned with the firing mechanism."¶

Tempers flared as the discussion over making the weapon smaller continued. Mr. Bull realized that the problem would not be solved as soon as he would have liked. "As long as we can train teams of three to become proficient with the weapon; we can still show off the Gatling gun and demonstrate how well it can work. Besides, it is not our job to use the weapons in the field, it is our customer's job to train their own people." Everyone knew the market for a fully automatic weapon was extremely high, even if it did take two people to operate. The third person was needed to explain the details of what was being shown during the demo. "I totally agree sir." Added Mr. Richards. "So in a year or two, when we are able to solve the size issue, we can introduce a new and improved weapon that will be in even higher demand." The issue matter was settled and the meeting wrapped up with only a few minor details left to iron out.¶

Immediately following the meeting, Mr. White arranged a meeting with one of his top assassins outside a coffee shop two miles from Mr. Coleman's estate. "I want absolutely no evidence left behind. We want to make it look as though he simply 'moved.' We're going with the angle that he left our company for another job somewhere on the east coast." "Consider is done. And thank you for trusting me with this assignment." Mr. White handed him an envelope with the address and photo of the victim and a significant amount of cash. The man looked inside, closed it, and placed it in his inside, jacket pocket. "You'll get the other half of your payment in three months, assuming the police don't investigate." "Thank you, sir." With their conversation over, the two parted ways.¶

*¶

The three friends filed into The Rustic Forge; Butch locked the door behind them and they continued downstairs for an emergency meeting following the gun show. Max was visibly shaken up after what had just transpired merely twenty minutes ago. "I didn't get a chance to complete my assignment. I still had several people to talk to..." Scotty started to say before Max blurted out. "I already completed our main goal!" He then pulled out the schematics from one pocket, and the piece of the prototype from another. "Holy crap!" Butch said, grabbing the broken piece of Gatling gun. "How did you manage to get these?" Added Scotty, grabbing the schematics and giving them a once over.¶

"I wasn't planning on getting this lucky. The door to the testing area was unlocked, I had the opportunity, and there was no one around so..."

The three merely exchanged looks of shock and disbelief at how this whole ordeal had turned out. What would their next move be? There was nothing but silence for several minutes before Max finally spoke. "We can't go to the police yet." "Why not?" Asked Butch. "You got the schematics and that piece right there." "No, he's right." Scotty interjected. "Those schematics could have been drawn by anyone. And that gun piece… it can't be traced to any particular weapon." Butch seemed annoyed. "What do we do then?"¶

No one seemed to have an immediate solution to their predicament. "What about your assault rifle?" Asked Max. "What about it? How's that going to help us collect more evidence against Dead-Eye?" "We can't just rely on the authorities right now. We've got to do more!" Max said. "This might not be their only prototype. What if they have other schematics? We need to have a weapon to counter whatever they have." Scotty added. "What if they find out what you've done?" "What he's done?" Said Butch. "What we've done! We're in this together. We've always had each others' back, and that includes family."¶

Scotty suddenly got a worried look on his face. "What about tonight? Butch still has his bout. We've got Daisy for the weekend, do we still go to the fight? Should we cancel our plans?" His voice was starting to crack at this point. Max tried to reassure his friend. "No, no. We mustn't panic. If we don't show, some of our friends and business associates would notice." Butch also confirmed what Max had just said. "He's right. We act no different. It'll look suspicious if the champ's two best friends aren't at the match. But I should forge the parts and assemble our own prototype of the assault rifle just in case they do figure it out."¶

Max still felt like Scotty was right to be concerned about his wife and niece. "Tell you what Scotty, have Jill and Daisy come over to our place tonight. Ronin and Rattler can fix dinner. In fact, have Daisy stay the night so she can spend more time with Rattler. They haven't had much time together for months. It would be good for everyone." Max said. "Then on Sunday we can all meet somewhere for lunch and discuss the matter further and make a plan." It was settled, the three would do what they had just discussed, and hopefully they would know what to next by Sunday afternoon.¶

*¶

The sports arena was starting to fill in with very early spectators as the doors opened and employees started taking tickets. A line formed at the concession stand with most people purchasing beer and pretzels. The top executives from Dead-Eye Inc. arrived to their box seats with wine and various hors d'oeuvres waiting. William, Henry and Mr. Lucas sat in the front, with Mr. Hughes, Mr. Price, Mr. Boyd, and Mr. Peterson sitting directly behind them. They made small talk for a while until Mr. Edwards from Gunz a' Blazin' suddenly approached them.¶

"Hello gentlemen, I suppose congratulations are in order." He said in a recognizable tone. "Just what are you implying, Ron?" Asked Henry. "I'm sure you have no idea about the troubles we've been having with the rebuilding. I wouldn't be surprised if you weren't directly responsible. You surely have all the right connections and personnel." Henry stood to his feet. "I hope you're not accusing our upstanding corporation of any unethical behaviors. That sort of thing could become actionable." He stated. "It's no fault of ours if you're having troubles with deliveries and timetables." He added. "Speaking of deliveries." Ron interrupted. "Convenient how this sudden road construction on Lumber Avenue started a block past your shipping yard. It doesn't affect your delivery schedule, only ours."¶

"We didn't come here to discuss your flailing business." Said William. "We're here to enjoy the fight. And I assume you're here to do the same. So, if you don't mind, we were enjoying some pre-fight conversation... I have a lot of money riding on a first-round knockout." Henry sat back down as his brother's words had apparently convinced the scorned executive to move along. The anticipation of the night's match was starting to become more and more evident as the noise levels started to rise. The fight was scheduled to begin in two hours, but the seats were already nearly half-filled.¶

*¶

Scotty, Jill and Daisy pedaled up the driveway of The Golden Snake just as Ronin and Rattler were completing their training for the day. Daisy jumped off of her and bike and ran to meet them as they rounded the barn drenched in sweat. "Can I see your sword, Mr. Ronin?" She asked excitedly. Ronin pulled his sword from it sheath and lowered it slowly in front of her so she could take a good look at it. "May I?" She asked, slowly reaching out her hand with her pointer finger extended. "Use caution." He warned. "Sharp." She touched the side of the blade and could see various straight lines and nicks as this sword had seen many battles. "Very cool." She said, returning her hand to her side.¶

Scotty and Jill parked their bikes next to the porch as Jill began unhooking a small bag from the front basket. "What's that?" Asked Max, as he walked out the front door and down the stairs. "Just some ingredients for a special dessert I'm going to whip up for the children tonight. I figured since they're cooking the meal, I would bake some cookies." She opened the bag so Max could see some chocolate chips and brown sugar. "Could you save one for me?" He begged. "Sure, I have enough here to make two dozen." She replied, closing the bag back up.¶

Max tugged Scotty by the sleeve. "We'd better head out, Butch needs help our taping his gloves and keeping him company before the fight. Why he gets ready so early, just to pace around for an hour is beyond me." They both nodded at each other in silent agreement as they headed for Max's bike. Scotty loved riding in the sidecar any chance he got. He had thought about buying his own steam-cycle, but selling guns and pistols for a living did not give him a lot of exercise; so riding his bicycle all over town to deliver firearms to his customers in person gave him a good workout and kept him physically fit.¶

It took them about twenty minutes to make their way to Kelly Arena on Rambling Avenue. Once they were cleared by security, they entered the locker room where Butch was anxiously awaiting their arrival with his gloves and tape laid out on a table. "Right on time. Let's do this so I can get my walking in." He said, raising his fists. Max and Scotty each took a glove and proceeded to fit them snugly over his bear-like hands; which is how the local media liked to describe them. After taping them securely, the trio began the ritual of pacing around and up and down the hallways of the entire locker room. Butch continuously shrugged his shoulders, shook his arms about, and moved his head side to side to relax his neck muscles. He was ready for O'Malley, no doubt about it.¶

As the minutes ticked by and the anticipation mounted, the lights grew dim and the announcer climbed into the ring and walked to the middle. The roars of the crowd soon died down just as the introductions were being spoken. "In this corner, hailing all the way from Boston, Massachusetts, standing 6'1", and weighing in at 240 pounds, with a record of twenty-nine and two, twenty by knock-out, wearing green trunks, O'Malley the Mangler!" There were a few cheers, but mostly boos from the audience. The local favorite was waiting to enter the ring from the locker room, and there was almost dead silence as the announcer continued.¶

"Entering the arena now, from right here in Blackwater, Texas, standing 6' 2", and weighing in at 255 pounds, the undefeated champion with thirty-five wins, thirty-two by knock-out, twenty-two in the very first round, wearing black trunks, 'The Blacksmith with two Hammers,' Butch Young!" He barely got the words out as the crowd erupted with cheers and applause. It took nearly a full minute before the noise quieted down so they could continue. The two men met in the center of the ring as the referee went over the rules. As Butch and O'Malley went to their separate corners, the cheers again echoed through the arena.¶

*¶

The sounds of soft jazz emanated from a record player in the corner of the living room in the ranch-style house overlooking the Texas landscape. Mr. Coleman was behind the minibar pouring himself a belt of scotch. As he rounded the sofa to sit down and read a good book, he thought he saw a shadow pass by a corner out on the patio. He walked over and looked through the sliding glass door and saw empty chairs sat around a table and a nearby fire pit; nothing. Turing back towards the living room, he felt a hard thud on the top of his head and everything went black. The record finished playing its music and nothing but static could be heard for several minutes as the assassin stood over the unconscious body of the former Dead-Eye executive.¶

*¶

DING – DING. The crowd exploded as the two boxers met in the center of the ring for round one. O'Malley threw a couple of jabs and Butch circled to his left. He calmed banged his gloves together as he moved his head side to side waiting for an opportunity. His opponent led with a right uppercut which Butch easily dodged. He following with a mighty swing to the ribs. O'Malley hunched forward a bit, obviously in a great deal of pain. Butch did not let up. He let loose with an equally strong hook with his left to the very same area which O'Malley was unable to defend. CRUNCH. Medical reports would later confirm that the champ had fractured two of his ribs. By the expression on the face of the challenger, Butch knew the fight was over.¶

The champ released a flurry of shots to the face, since O'Malley was guarding his midsection with lowered gloves. Stumbling backwards a few paces, Butch closed in and chopped the man down with a crossing right blow, sending the would-be contender straight to the canvas. The ringside was rushed by photographers, snapping picture after picture as the referee counted to ten. The flashes continued as Butch raised his hands in victory to the cheers of the fans. "And the champion has done it again!" Cried the announcer. "His first-round knockout prediction has come to fruition in front of this capacity crowd!"¶

As William was celebrating his winning a substantial amount of money bet on this fight, a messenger delivered a hand-written note from security. Opening the envelope and unfolding the paper within, he scanned over the information. He quickly folded it back up and stuffed it into his jacket pocket, leaned over and pulled his brother by the arm. "There's been an incident at headquarters.

We need to go, now!" The team of executives gathered their things quickly and headed to the horse-drawn carriage that awaited them by the exit. Once inside, the CEO informed his staff that Research and Development had been broken into.¶

*¶

As Daisy and Rattler sat at the kitchen table playing board games, Jill was taking the last batch of homemade, chocolate-chip cookies from the oven and placing them on a cooling rack. Ronin had gone outside and was taking a late-night stroll around the ranch to meditate and reflect on his new life in Texas. He picked an apple from a tree and took his first bite when he heard a soft rustling sound coming from the large oak amid the small orchard. He placed the apple into the folds inside his kimono. Drawing his sword from its sheath, he immediately took a defensive stance. His instincts proved to be correct, as a ninja leaped down to the ground, and rushed towards him.¶

The attacker's sword reflected the light of the full moon as it sliced through the air, nearly ripping the samurai's sleeve. The sound of steel clashing did not carry far enough to reach the house. The children played and ate cookies safely as Ronin defended himself against this would be assassin. "You don't have to do this!" He said in Japanese. His opponent did not speak, he simply kept attacking in hopes of separating the samurai's head from his body. "This mystical sword does not belong in the hands of your master. He would simply use its power for his own evil purposes." He said as he deflected blow after blow of the ninja's sword. "This is your last chance to lower your weapon. Pursue me further and I will kill you!" Ronin stated firmly as he jumped back and raised his sword in defense.¶

The ninja laughed and closed in for a death strike. Unfortunately for him, the samurai knew he would not listen and was expecting this sudden attack. Ronin squatted slightly, lowered his katana to a horizontal angle, and lunged forward, slicing clean through his opponent's stomach. The ninja dropped his sword and fell to his knees, clutching the gaping wound. As his entrails started to slide out from his belly, Ronin stood up, twirled his blade around, and plunged it into the ninja's chest. "If you're willing to kill, you're willing to die." As blood gurgled from his throat, this was the last thing the ninja heard before he died.¶

*¶

The horses pulling the executives stopped at the gates of Dead-Eye Inc. as security officially checked them into the parking lot. William and Henry stepped out first and headed towards several men already standing by the front doors waiting to let them inside. The rest of them climbed out and hustled to catch up. Mr. Lucas and Mr. Hughes were out in front, with Mr. Boyd and Mr. Peterson bringing up the rear; Mr. Price was too intoxicated and remained in the carriage to be taken home once the situation was dealt with.¶

"Evening Mr. Johnson, Mr. Johnson." Said the ranking security guard as the two men approached. "Cut with the pleasantries and let's go right to the testing room." Said Henry walking past him and into the building. "When was this noticed? And why wasn't it noticed sooner?" He was almost shouting at this point. "I want the person, who evidently did not secure the area, fired immediately. How do you not lock the door when you leave?" Henry loosened his tie as they continued down the hall. It appeared as though he would beat the person responsible half to death.¶

Rounding the corner from the main hallway, there were no obvious signs that there was a break-in. "We think it was an inside job." Said the security guard chief. "We've combed over this entire area and cannot find any signs of a forced entry." "We know all of this already." William interrupted. "Do you have an estimated time of when it happened. Who made the discovery?" He asked. "I did, sir." Said the security standing behind them. He stepped forward and continued with an explanation of what had transpired earlier that evening. "When most of the interior lights were shut off for the night, we started using our flashlights to check each room through the door windows. When I checked this one, the flashlight reflected off those metal pieces on the floor by the table." He said, pointing to the broken prototype on the floor. "That's when I noticed the door was unlocked. I then called the chief. We checked with the personnel that had last used the testing facilities, and upon inspection, informed us of the missing schematics."

"Well isn't that just peachy. So it could have happened any time in the last four hours. We can't narrow it down more than that?" Henry barked. "I want every employee that worked today here within an hour!" "We'll get on that immediately sir." Answered the security chief. Snapping his fingers, the rest of the guards followed him back down the hallway. "What do you think, Henry?" Asked William. "Your instincts bring a suspect to mind?" "I think Gunz a' Blazin' could possibly be involved. Ron made a scene at the fight earlier. Perhaps he's directly linked to all of this. I'll look into at once." Henry turned and walked towards his office.

The CEO looked at the other four executives. "I want a list of anyone you think that might have had something to do with this incidence. We've got to act quickly before things start to unravel. I've got a very short list myself." He thought for a moment. "Mr. Peterson, are there any disgruntled employees that have been recently fired?" "Actually," Mr. Peterson started. "We haven't fired anyone in the last three months." "Anyone quit?" "Not any that I can think of right now. I'd have to check our records. I'll go gather a list of any employee that has quit or been fired in the last two years. That'll be a start." He said as he left for personnel. William looked at the remaining three men. "Someone go help Peterson sober up. He's not going home just yet."¶

*¶

Max shut down the steam-cycle as Scotty removed his helmet and started climbing out of the sidecar. He removed his own and secured them both in the compartment on the back. The two were still on a non-alcoholic buzz after seeing their friend defeat, what should have been a legitimate threat to his belt, the supposed 'Mangler' from Massachusetts. They walked up the front steps and through the door. "Rattler just finished washing up and is getting ready for bed." Jill explained. "Daisy is already clean and in her nightgown. She's brushing her hair and waiting for her uncle to wish her good-night." She was putting away the last of the dried dishes from the evening's meal and cookie baking. "There's half a dozen left on a plate by the refrigerator." She said as she started washing her hands. "How was the fight?"¶

"What fight, Butch destroyed O'Malley in less than a minute. What were the guys in Boston thinking when they sent this oaf?" Scotty said laughing as he reached for the plate of cookies. "It was a good fight. There were a few exhibition fights following the title match." Added Max. "It'll be a few weeks before they announce the next challenger. Until then, we only have the underground stuff to worry about." "I don't know why he risks injury with that bare knuckle nonsense." Said Jill. "Is it worth less money to take more risks?" "It's the only way he gets any actual training done. He didn't even get hit once tonight." Scotty explained.¶

"How did the two of you get along with Ronin this evening?" Asked Max, taking a large chocolate-chip cookie from the plate and biting off a piece. "He's a perfect gentleman." Jill started. "He did almost all of the cooking, helped Rattler set and clear the table, and even washed the dishes afterwards. Can he stay with us next weekend, maybe he'll rub off on Scotty?" She exclaimed. "Not likely, besides, I do cook on occasion." Scotty said in his own defense. As they continued talking, Max noticed Ronin walking down the hall to the bathroom with a folded towel and clean clothes in his arms. "Ronin, thank-you for all you did this evening. I appreciate it." Ronin smiled and continued on his short trip. "You're welcome, sir." He replied.¶

Entering the bathroom, Ronin thoroughly washed his entire body and inspected himself from head to toe for any injuries he might have received from the battle in the apple orchard. Seeing no signs of blood, swelling, or discoloration of the skin, he dried himself off and returned to his room. He folded his dirty kimono and placed it at the foot of the bed on the chest to be washed in the morning. It was then that he noticed a small tear in the left sleeve. the ninja managed to rip it after all.

CHAPTER IX - Plan Exposed¶

Mr. Johnson had come in extra early this Monday morning as it was not the typical start of a business week. He was awaiting his brother, Henry, to come to his office and bring the latest intelligence on the theft of the Gatling gun schematics. With the exception of the events on Saturday at the plant, all other plans had gone smoothly for the corporate giant. Gunz a' Blazin' was a mere month away from declaring bankruptcy; this issue with the prototype needed to be taken care of as soon as possible. If they did not get back on schedule by the end of the week, they could lose some very important and powerful clients in the process.¶

Since his secretary was not in at this hour, there was a knock at the door. Not waiting for an answer, Henry proceeded to open the door and enter the room. "I have all the information we were able to gather." He started. "I've already eliminated ninety percent of the people on this list. And security was able to eliminate all employees working on Saturday, and can account for their whereabouts during that four- to five-hour window when the schematics went missing." "What about the other ten percent?" William inquired. "They are either on vacation or traveling on business. I did however pull up our itinerary for the gun show and discovered that a tour group did pass by that area. But the guide did not notice anything out of the ordinary. The main problem lies with the fact that she, nor security, was aware that the door was unlocked." Henry finished talking as he took a seat opposite his brother.¶

"Guests were required to register. Have you started investigating anyone on that list yet?" "I already have the contact information for all but one of the visitors in that group." Henry answered. "All but one?" Asked William. "I'm assuming it's an alias." Henry countered. "This is the individual I suspect is responsible for the theft of the schematics and destruction of the prototype. And since we don't have any physical evidence at the scene, I will personally interview each relevant man or woman I feel may lead me to that individual." Henry said, once again standing up. "If there isn't anything else, I'll get to it." "There is one more thing, brother. Has Mr. Lucas been able to replicate his design on paper.?" Henry hesitated for a moment before he spoke. "He has some crude drawings that had first inspired his creation. But unfortunately, it will take some time to reproduce." "As soon as he steps foot inside the building, have him sent straight to my office." Ordered William.¶

*¶

Everything had gone like clockwork over the

weekend at The Golden Snake; Daisy and Rattler enjoyed time together with Ronin and Jill; Butch had won his fight; and they had apparently gotten away with stealing the plans, and destroying the prototype, to a highly dangerous and illegal, weapon. But Max knew he could not rest just yet. They would probably make new schematics and build a new prototype very soon. Something further needed to be done to ensure that that did not happen. He had contemplated the situation all morning during chores and was even distracted on a job during lunch. He was almost bitten by a rather large copperhead he had wrangled from the Blackwater River on a nearby farm. After the day's short work was finished, he headed to check on Max to see how things were coming along with the assault rifle.¶

Pulling into the parking lot, he noticed business was really booming. It did not surprise him much; business always rose dramatically for a few weeks after Butch had won a fight. A lot of people wondered why he even bothered to work as a blacksmith. He obviously earned enough money from boxing to live a comfortable life. But Max knew his friend very well. Butch was too intelligent and hardworking. He enjoyed creating weapons, accessories, and other works of art with different types of metal. Parking his bike, he entered the shop; and he was greeted by utter mayhem. Orders were being placed for all kinds of products. Belt buckles with "The Rustic Forge" elegantly etched onto the back were more valuable than any hand-written autograph.¶

Since he really needed his help, Max pitched in and helped Butch and Dan with whatever they needed. With an extra hand, Butch was able to close on time. Locking the door and turning the sign around to read "closed" from the outside, he turned and began talking. "I've finally finished them." Butch announced proudly. "I worked most of Sunday to give them an extra fine polish, but they're finished." "I've got to see them." Urged Max. "See what? What's finally finished?" Asked Dan. "The swords." Said Butch. "They're right in back."¶

The three of them proceeded to the back storage room where two expertly forged swords lay on the table, wrapped in a cloth. Max could barely contain himself as his friend unwrapped the larger one and handed it to him. "Try that for weight." He gripped it by the handle and slowly sliced through the air with its blade. "She's a beauty, Butch." He remarked. "Oh, and there's one more thing." Butch walked over to another table. "It's not ready yet, but I'm crafting two unique sheaths for these babies." Picking up the roughly tied together pieces, he continued. "When I'm finished, these sheaths will sharpen the blades every time they are pulled out, or placed back in." Max's jaw dropped slightly. "That's incredible!" "I thought you'd like that." He added.¶

Wrapping the swords back up in cloth, Butch placed them into a burlap sack and handed them gently to Max. "Thank-you, this means a lot to me, and it will mean a great deal to Rattler as well." Max said, shaking his friend's hand. "Speaking of which, I can start teaching Rattler how to box on Thursday." "But what about your bare knuckle fight on Tuesday night?" Max asked surprised. "There won't be one. After I demolished O'Malley in fifty-six seconds, the guy I was supposed to fight backed out. I don't have another fight scheduled for two more weeks." Butch grinned, he was flattered by how much fear he instilled in other fighters. "Rattler will be thrilled. He's been taking all his training very seriously. Head over after work and stay for dinner, Ronin and I will fix you something nice." Max said. "Nothing fancy, meat and potatoes will be just fine."¶

Saying their goodbyes, Butch locked up for the evening and headed to his office. Walking over to his drawing table, he sat down and pulled out a design that was already half finished and starting adding to it. It had snake-like scales and various clasps and hooks. He drew and defined his design for the next few hours. Finally completing his work, he placed it back into the drawer and turned off the lights. "I sure hope Max will be able to use my creation." He said aloud as he closed the door and headed upstairs to bed.¶

*¶

A couple of days had gone by in Blackwater, Max added two more snakes to his ranch; a healthy young rock rattlesnake and a very large western diamondback. Ronin was diligent with Rattler's training and the young boy had made real progress in only a few short weeks. Butch and Dan were very busy filling orders, but managed to complete their work on time. Scotty and Jill's gun store, The Gunslinger, managed to turn a fine profit following Dead-Eye's gun show. And Peggy was working overtime in order to make her date with Max on time at the end of the week. The Golden Snake seemed to be running smoothly despite the dark cloud hanging over the unsuspecting city.¶

Wednesday afternoon saw mild weather as Butch walked up the driveway. Of all of his friends, he was the only one who did not own a cycle of any kind. He preferred to walk or run everywhere he went. Although it took him longer, Butch made sure to make the time. Knocking on the front door, he was greeted by a very enthusiastic Rattler. "I finished all of my chores already, Uncle Butch." He said proudly. "I'm all ready to go." Rattler was anxious to show Butch the training area his father had built and updated over the last week and a half. "Let him come in a sit a while first." Max's voice suddenly came from the living room and spilled out onto the porch as he walked towards them from the kitchen.¶

Butch sat only for a short time, he was anxious to see how much Rattler wanted this training. He had known a lot of other children growing up who said they wanted to become a boxing champion, but very few would actually put the time in in order to make it happen. Rattler ran ahead, leading his adoptive uncle to the training area behind the barn. Rounding the corner, Butch was impressed by the layout. "This where you train with Ronin, then?" He asked, already knowing the answer, but wanting the boy to elaborate. "Yeah, it's an outside dojo, sort of." He bowed at its edge before entering the circle. "You have to stop and bow on the grass before you come in. It's a tradition in Japan." Butch bowed and walked over to the boy; and for the next two hours, he showed Rattler the basics of defense and had him practice over and over again.¶

Heading into the house, Ronin was already waiting by the door with small towels for them to wipe the sweat from their heads and faces, and a couple of glasses of cold water to quench their thirst. "Thank you, Ronin." Said Rattler. "Yes, thank you Mr. Ronin." Butch followed. "Rattler has been telling me all about your training sessions and how bad-ass you are." Ronin had a puzzled look on his face. "bad-ass?" "Don't worry, Ronin." Rattler explained. "It's a compliment. It means you're tough and know what you're doing. Enemies should fear you."¶

As soon as he heard the word 'enemy' came from the boy's lips, he had a flashback to that late evening in the orchard. After killing the would-be assassin, he dragged the ninja to the burn pit and buried the body underneath the brush. He then spent the following hour and a half, gathering fallen branches and other yard debris. He remembered getting up very early the next morning and burning all physical traces of the enemy that was sent after him. The remaining weapons, made of metal, were buried deep in the ground on the corner of the property behind some large rocks. And ever since then, he had debated on whether or not to tell Max about what had transpired on that fateful night.¶

"Ronin." Max repeated. "Are you joining us for dinner?" The samurai's mind had wondered so far, he did not hear his host the first time. "Yes." He answered, turning around and walking to the dining room. "I was thinking." "About what?" Asked Rattler. "A decision I must make, soon." He sat down at his usual place at the table and placed a napkin in his lap. "I hope you are deciding to stay longer." Max said, placing a large bowl of mashed potatoes next to the large pot roast. "We enjoy having you here." He added. "Yeah, don't leave." Pleaded Rattler, not knowing what the samurai was really contemplating. "No, no. I must speak with your father later." Ronin stated, lifting his hands and clasping them together. He was anticipating Max saying grace before they ate. It was not his custom to pray before a meal, but he honored and respected the family's traditions.¶

The four of them ate dinner and discussed general topics, including chores, snakes, training, and how business was going. It was during this part of the conversation that Ronin learned that Butch owned and operated his own forge. "I wondered who made Rattler's sword." The samurai stated. "Fine work. Could I help? I would work for a new blade. Mine was broken during a battle." Ronin's English was getting better every day. Rattler swallowed his mashed potatoes. "But your sword isn't broken." He said, confused. "My other sword, my wakizashi."¶

"Waki-what-she?" Butch repeated. They all listened intently as Ronin continued. "Use two swords. One longer, one shorter. Used together... daisho." He managed to find the right words. "Daisho? So one is for regular battle, and the other is for close-quarter fighting?" Butch asked. "Yes." Ronin replied. "Correct." The samurai finished eating and started clearing the used dishes from the table while everyone else finished their meal.¶

"What about that other sword?" Rattler inquired. "That is sacred nodachi. It is 'The Snake Blade.' That is a story for another time." Ronin stopped speaking and went about washing the dishes. Not wanting his son to press for more information, he looked at him, made the "shhh" gesture with his finger and nodded his head. Not in a mean way, just simply to imply to Rattler to let it go for now. The three of them finished their food and took their plates to the kitchen counter. It was then that Max came up with his idea to repay Ronin for all his kindness. "Rattler, stay and help Ronin with the dishes. I'm going to have a word with your uncle Max."¶

The two friends went into the living and took seats in the chair and couch on opposite sides of the coffee table. "How about letting Ronin make that replacement sword. I'll pay for whatever materials he might need." Max said. "I was thinking something similar." Butch started. "But I was thinking instead of charging for the materials, he might be able to teach me a thing or two about Japanese weapon making. Think of it. I'd be the only smith for miles around with such knowledge." He paused a moment. "Now I would actually be willing to pay him for his time. I don't want to take advantage of him or anything." Max held up his hand and spoke. "No, of course not. We don't either. He acts almost like a servant, but we treat him like one of the family at this point. He's so good with the boy, he cooks and cleans. He's even offered to train me a little bit as well. That samurai is the best thing to happen to our family."¶

Seeing his friend off, he tucked his son into bed and walked down the hall. Knocking on the door, he cracked it open a bit. "Are you decent?" He asked. "Come in." Answered Ronin. "I apologize. I have put your family in danger by being here." Max showed concern for the samurai. "The family, what happened, are you in some kind of trouble." Ronin explained in as much detail as his knowledge of the English language would allow. Max was sure he understood the situation. "It's not your fault, Ronin. You couldn't have known they would be able to find you here in Texas. How many more of these, what are they called? Ninjas? How many more will they send after you?" Ronin shook his head. "I do not know how many. They send a few at a time to track and go different places. I have not left the farm since I came here. I do not know how he found me."¶

The samurai started to pack his things before Max stood up to stop him. "It's okay, Ronin. I don't blame you for this. You can stay. We can work this out ourselves." He said. "You seem to be an honorable warrior who can defend himself. If you continue to train my son and me, we can help you. We are fighting evil within our own city, and you are doing the same." Max sat down and explained to Ronin everything that had happened with Dead-Eye Inc. Both men were trying to do the right thing to protect people, and during the next hour or so, they decided the right thing was to help each other.¶

*¶

After the rather short board meeting, several of the more important executives remained behind to speak with both William and Henry Johnson, including Mr. Lucas, Mr. Hughes, Mr. Boyd, Mr. Price, and Mr. Peterson. "So where are we at with the investigation?" Asked William. "We have the suspect list narrowed down to three people. But I do believe I know the culprit personally." Responded Henry. "That wrangler Max we hired, from The Golden Snake, was actually in that area the day he did that job for us." His brother started to get a look on his face. "The champ was at the gun show and they're friends." William thought for just a second. "How do you know for sure that they're friends?" He asked. "I noticed him at the fight, he was in the champ's corner." Henry answered. "They must be close, then." Added William. "Have Mr. White look into it." "Yes, sir."¶

"Lucas, how are the new schematics progressing?" Mr. Lucas cleared his throat. "It took me nearly a year to complete the first one. Starting over from scratch is giving me some problems."

"You're an engineer! It's your design! What's the problem?!" Mr. Johnson's voice was rising rather quickly; he was not a patient man. "Well, sir… that's what the schematics were for. I'm having troubles with some of the technical aspects, and…" William slammed his right fist down onto the table. "Don't give me any of that complicated jargon, give me specifics!" Mr. Lucas was obviously shaken a bit. "Sir, I just need some more time. If we had made copies of the originals.." William interrupted again. "Are you questioning my leadership?" "Not at all sir, but I…" "Extra copies means more opportunities for them to fall into the wrong hands, like what has happened this time." The room became quiet after that.¶

"On the brighter side." Mr. Price said, breaking the silence. "Gunz a' Blazin' has just filed for bankruptcy early this morning." "That is very good news, ahead of schedule in fact. What changed?" William asked. "It involved some allegations of arson from within the company, so they did not receive the full return on their insurance policy." Mr. Price had greased a few palms within the company to insure suspicion fell on Gunz a' Blazin' for fraud. "With them out of the way, our monopoly on the southwestern part of the state will be secured. Business should jump another fifteen to twenty percent in the next quarter alone." Mr. Johnson leaned back in his chair and pulled a cigar from his inside, jacket pocket.¶

As the meeting adjourned, everyone went about their business. Mr. Lucas returned to his office to tweak and finish the schematics, hidden within layers of other projects on his drawing table. Manufacturing continued on schedule to ensure the month's quotas were met. And Mr. White stepped off the elevator to the meeting room of the Black Bull Society, where one of his henchmen, Sawyer, was waiting by the door. "Come inside." Mr. White snapped. "I have an important assignment for you." Sitting down, he started rolling off a list of things he wanted him to do. Handing the gentleman, a small envelope, he continued. "I want you to investigate this man and look for the information contained within. If you should happen upon the schematics, retrieve them at all cost. But I don't want any assassinations if possible." On this point he was adamant. "We already have one person's death to cover up, we don't need the hassle of another."¶

Sawyer slipped the envelope into his pocket and stood up. "Consider it done, sir." The men shook hands as Mr. White headed back towards the elevator. The henchman took the back staircase and went straight to his steam-cycle, he quickly read over the list while his bike warmed up. He would proceed with the plan immediately and already had a few ideas on how to accomplish each step. Flipping up the kickstand with his foot, he pulled back on the throttle, turned out of the parking lot, and headed toward his destination.¶

*¶

Butch and Dan had managed to stay up on all the orders for the week and started closing up after an exhausting Thursday. "I've decided to close the shop tomorrow so we can enjoy a three-day weekend." Butch announced. "Sounds good to me, it's been a busy four days and I've been looking forward to getting some extra sleep this weekend." Dan said as he continued wiping down the counter and main display case. "You don't have any hot dates or other plans?" Butch asked. "Not this weekend. My girl knew I'd be extra busy for the next two weeks, so we didn't plan anything." He looked at his apprentice. "You know I kind of think of you as a son, so I'm going to give you some advice. Take that extra day and plan something special." He said, handing him his paycheck. "There's a bonus in here based on all this extra business we've been doing in addition to your regular salary." After Dan had looked at his check, he was almost at a loss for words. "This much, sir?" He stammered. "I haven't quite put any overtime in. Thank-you very much." He folded the check and placed it in his back pocket. "You work hard, Dan. You earned that bonus and don't think any different. Now get outta' here and I'll finish locking up."

"Thanks again." He said.¶

Turning the sign around and switching off the main lights, Butch put away the last of the cleaning supplies and completed the remaining paperwork before heading upstairs. He glanced out of the window and saw a lamppost fizzle out across the street. *Oh well*, he thought to himself, *I'll call the city and have maintenance come fix it in the morning.* He took a quick shower and headed for bed, it had been a very long day. As soon as his head hit the pillow, he drifted off to sleep.¶

Butch had only been asleep for about twenty minutes when he awoke to sounds coming from his downstairs office. Slipping on pants and a shirt from the chair next to his bed, he quietly sneaked down the stairs and peered around the corner. The lamp on his desk had been turned on. He crept closer and caught a glimpse of a man rifling through the drawers in his desk and drawing table. The only visible weapon Butch saw on the man was a knife strapped to his left boot. *So, a southpaw*, he thought. He had dealt with these types of people before. He stepped into the room to corner him and turned on the light. The man, obviously surprised, turned around and took a defensive stance.¶

Seeing Butch's six foot, 255-pound frame standing in the doorway, Sawyer immediately picked up the lamp and threw it as hard as he could directly at his head. Calmly leaning to the side to avoid being struck, he stood straight up and said. "You don't know who I am, do you?" He shrugged his shoulders and raised his fists. "I know you." The man said. "And you don't scare me." Reaching for his knife, Butch was on top of him before he could pull it from its sheath. It only took him a few seconds to knock the intruder out. He then proceeded to tie the man to a chair and call the local sheriff's office.¶

Within minutes, two deputies showed up at the front door to arrest the man and take him away. Butch decided not to call his friends about the incident until the following afternoon. They were all dealing with enough already and it was late. After making sure nothing was missing from his store and office, he started straightening up. It was then that he noticed the assault rifle schematics on top of his desk. He thought he had left them attached to his drawing table. Had he looked at them sitting at his desk while he ate his lunch. He could not remember.¶

He put schematics away and returned to bed. As he laid there tossing and turning after all of the excitement, he began to wonder if this was a mere break in. The man did not act like a simple thief, he seemed more confident. Did he know what the schematics were? Could this be linked to Dead-Eye Inc. somehow? Calling Max and Scotty first thing in the morning was the last thought that crossed his mind as he drifted off to sleep.¶

*¶

It was nine in the morning in Mr. White's office when the phone rang. Answering it, he was irritated to discover Sawyer had been arrested and was waiting to be bailed out. "How did this happen? You're supposed to be one of my top men!" He said angrily. "I didn't know Butch lived above his shop. He surprised me." The henchman replied in his own defense. "He does own the heavyweight championship belt. "I'll be there in twenty minutes. You better have some information for me when I arrive." Mr. White said in a very serious tone. "I do, sir. And I think you'll forgive me for being caught." Hanging up the phone, Mr. White opened the safe behind his desk, took out five thousand dollars in cash, and placed it in an envelope.¶

*¶

Butch had called both Max and Scotty immediately following his breakfast. They had all agreed to meet for lunch at the Bison Bar & Grill to discuss the possible connections of the previous night's break-in. "What can I get you fellows?" Asked the waitress. They all ordered coffee and the lunch special. She walked away to place the order when they began their discussion. "We need to be more careful." Said Butch. "I think he saw the schematics for the assault rifle." Max tried to calm his friend a little. "I told Ronin everything that's been going on and he's going to help us." He informed his friends of the assassination attempt on the samurai's life by the ninja. They continued to discuss their situation for the next two hours and had concluded that they needed to learn more about the intruder.¶

*¶

Mr. White entered the jailhouse and signed the visitor registration with an alias. Sitting down at a table with Sawyer, he began asking question. He learned that Butch, probably with some help from some friends, had designed a weapon that could be an answer to their own Gatling gun in a confrontational showdown. "When am I getting out of here?" Sawyer pleaded. "I can finish this assignment. Just give me another chance." "I'll fix everything immediately." Mr. White replied. The guards came and took the prisoner back to his cell. Mr. White looked around the room at the other inmates visiting various people. Spotting an obvious veteran of the justice system, he waited for his visitor to leave. Without the guards noticing, Mr. White walked past the man and slipped him an envelope. The convict stashed it in his pant leg and was eventually led back to his own cell. When it was safe to do so, the man open the envelope and

found the money and a small note, which read:
"Take care of Sawyer!"

CHAPTER X - Finished Project¶

It was mid-Monday morning when the sheriff showed up at the front gate of Dead-Eye Inc. Security quickly logged in the names of the law enforcement team and let them through. They were immediately escorted to Henry Johnson's office by the current chief on duty. Mr. Johnson met them at the elevator and guided them to one of the conference rooms where they could all sit and discuss the reason for their visit. "Sorry for the confusion, we are simply making an appearance for a very important citizen on the behave of one Nicholas Coleman." The sheriff stated. "May I ask who this 'important citizen' is?" Mr. White inquired. "It just seems a little odd that local authorities would be called for something of this nature." The sheriff continued. "All I can say is that a neighbor of Mr. Coleman is a city council member, and they had plans with Nicholas Sunday afternoon. They say he would not have missed this event as they were planned for a couple of months."¶

It was then that Mr. Peterson entered the room with one of the company's lawyers. "I've got everything you'll need to see right here." He said confidently as he handed a folder to one of the deputies before having a seat next to Mr. Johnson. "Mr. Coleman is no longer an employee of ours. He took a job on the east coast with another firm. We are in the process of procuring his property for future use by our top executives and visiting clients." As he explained more of the details, the sheriff looked over the documents in front of him and shook his head slightly. "I apologize for the intrusion. Everything seems in order here. Let me make a quick phone call and we'll let you all get back to work." Mr. Johnson's secretary led them to an adjacent room where they could use the telephone.¶

"That was a little nerve-racking." Said Mr. Peterson. "Mr. White's plans seemed to have had some unforeseen variables." He gave Henry a curious look. "There was no way of knowing Mr. Coleman had plans with one of our city's councilmen." Mr. Johnson retorted. "Besides, there will no investigation as long as all the proper documentation has been provided and notarized." They knew they had covered up every loose end possible. "They have no evidence of foul play whatsoever." Concluded Henry.¶

After a few tense minutes passed, the sheriff and his staff returned to the conference room. "The councilman is a little curious as to why Mr. Coleman would have left without telling anyone. He would have at least said good-bye to his neighbors." He stated. "I cannot speak for what Nicholas would or would not have done. He was excited about his new job and our offer for his land and property was quite generous." Countered Mr. Peterson. "I do a couple of more questions before I go." Stated the sheriff. "Do you have a phone number or address where Mr. Coleman can be reached." Mr. Johnson stood up slowly. "No I do not. I'm sorry you and your deputies were called out here for no reason. Since Nicholas was a model employee, he's leaving on very good terms. We wish him nothing but success." He paused for a second. "Perhaps Mr. Coleman had personal reasons for wanting a change, and has grown tired of his neighbors." He chuckled slightly. "Perhaps he did." Added the sheriff. "Good day gentlemen.¶

After the authorities left the premises, the documents were placed into Mr. Peterson's wall safe and the executives returned to work. Everything had worked out as planned for the moment. They had maintenance personnel at Mr. Coleman's ranch house packing all his clothing and personal effects. The boxes were then loaded onto a moving van that, once miles outside of the city, would have them driven to a remote location and buried ten feet underground. Mr. Coleman would never be mentioned again, and a search for his replacement had already begun in human resources.¶

Max and Butch stopped by The Gunslinger

after closing The Rustic Forge earlier than usual. Walking into the shop, Scotty already was cashing out the till and had some information to share. "I found out from a frequent customer that Dead-Eye Inc. has a testing range out on Everyman Road. We should check it out one night and see if we can discover evidence that shows they've been testing illegal firearms." "We could meet over at my place around seven." Butch offered. "You might as well join us for supper." Said Max. "We've got a lot of stuff for sandwiches we need to use up. Besides, we should include Ronin in our plans from now on, I think he'll be a real asset to the team."¶

The three exited the building and started towards The Golden Snake. Max warmed up his steam-cycle, Scotty took off on his bike, and Butch started jogging. It took just under an hour for Butch to catch up with his friends. The table was already set as he entered the house. There were three kinds of bread, meats, cheeses, vegetables, and plenty of condiments spread out for everyone. Within minutes, they were all eating and discussing their next move. "I say we plan for Wednesday night." Started Butch. "I already have Dan there half the night doing inventory, the store will be in good hands while I'm gone." "I shouldn't have any problems with Jill." Added Scotty. "As long as we're just gathering information." Max thought a moment. "I should swing by tomorrow and check out whatever security they might have there. I know we're mostly going to stay back and observe through binoculars, but what if there's an opportunity to actually gain access to the test sight?" He asked.¶

"I will go, tonight." Stated Ronin. "I have the most experience and will not be seen." The samurai was finishing off his sandwich and started wiping his face with a napkin. "This is important and cannot wait. I will do this now." He stood up and started clearing dirty dishes. The rest of the table grew quiet as they finished their meal. They knew Ronin was the best equipped for this mission, so they did not argue. "I will at least accompany you to the facility on my way home." Said Scotty. "I'll describe everything you should be looking for on the way there... as best as I can." Ronin bowed he head slightly as a sign he understood. After they had put away what little leftovers there were, they were ready to go. Scotty pedaled slowly as the samurai ran beside his bicycle.¶

"Have you ever seen empty shells from a gun?" He asked. "Yes." Replied Ronin. "Try to count any piles you might find, and only take a couple. Describe everything you see." He continued to explain what to look for that might indicate a fully automatic weapon was used. "This could be anything from lines of bullet holes in targets, to patterns in the sand near the firing range. If you

come across any drawings, take them if you can."
He added. "You're very brave, Ronin. Not every
man would help in a situation that was this
potentially dangerous. Max was right, you're the
best thing that's happened to our family." Ronin
seemed unphased by his words, as the expression on
his face did not change as he continued to run. The
samurai appeared extremely focused on the task at
hand.¶

As his feet continued to strike the ground one
after the other, Ronin was reminded of his past. He
remembered quite well the long distances he was
required to run by his sensei. He would carry only
his swords while he wove through thick forests and
marshy undergrowth. The occasional animal would
become startled and run away as he continued for
miles past the dojo. His master wanted him trained
not only to serve as a royal protector, but be able to
survive in the wild if need be… and it had indeed
come to that. Ronin was forced to flee his master's
home to protect the sacred sword. The Texas sky
and countryside was very different from his native
Japan. For one, it was much hotter here, he found
himself bathing twice as much as he had grown
accustomed too.¶

Scotty turned to say something to Ronin when
he noticed he had stopped running and was looking
into the woods. Pedaling back to his companion, the
samurai held up his left hand, signaling Scotty to

stop where he was. He then pulled out his katana and took a defensive stance. "Someone or something is watching us." Ronin said softly. It was then that Scotty heard crackling noises from the tree line just off the road. Without warning, a small boar came barreling out onto the road. Scotty jumped off his bike as Ronin somersaulted out of its path. "Holy crap, that gave me a start!" He shouted, apparently out of breath. He stepped towards his bike and bent over to pick it back up off of the ground.¶

As soon as he grabbed onto the handlebars, a growl rose from a nearby outcropping. Scotty had just started to lift his bike when a cougar jumped down from its hiding spot and ran directly towards him. He lifted his bike to his chest with both hands, using it like a shield as the large cat leaped towards his throat. Time seemed to speed up, Scotty did not even remember falling into the dirt; but the cougar was on top of the bike struggling to get through the spokes of the wheel, trying to get at him. He could tell by the thick foam dripping from the cat's mouth that it definitely had rabies. Scotty did not remember getting scratched, nor did he feel as if he were bitten.¶

Before he could even think of how to defend himself, Ronin came in from the side and plunged his sword through the cougar's rib-cage and lifted it from the bike, freeing Scotty to scramble to his feet.

Flinging the injured cat to the ground, the samurai raised his katana and swiftly slit its throat, nearly taking the head off. He then lowered his weapon and checked them both for injuries. Seeing no breaks in their skin, it was safe to say they were not infected. They quickly buried the carcass and continued towards their destination. Both men were a little shaken by the experience, but no worse for wear.¶

Within an hour they reached the testing range, which appeared to be guarded by two individuals armed with pistols. Getting to a good vantage point, the two men discussed their next plan of action. "Should I distract one of them while you go in?" Scotty asked. "I wasn't expecting more than one guard. I thought the remote location would mean less security." "Leave this to me." Was the only thing that Ronin said as he tucked his weapons to his side and took off towards the perimeter. Approaching the fence, he rolled into a crouching position in the shadows. Looking above the bushes, he quickly scanned for the guards. Noticing their pattern of walking, he devised a way to incapacitate each one before they knew what was going on, in case they could trigger some kind of alarm.¶

In an instant, Ronin scaled the fence, using his loose clothing to protect him from the barbed wire that lined the top. He approached the first guard from behind and rendered him unconscious within seconds. Dragging him into a dark space between a shack and the walkway, he tucked him safely between two crates. He then made his way towards the second guard, making sure to stay out of the light and not make a sound. Ronin managed to take care of this guard in the same manner as the first. Dragging him to a nearby ditch, he made sure the man was safe and still breathing before returning to Scotty.¶

"How did you do that?" Scotty asked. "Was that some kind of martial arts sleeper hold?" Not quite knowing what he was saying, Ronin tugged at his arm and waved for him to follow. Coming to the front gate, they found it secured with a chain and padlock. "Good, there doesn't appear to be an alarm." Scotty said, scanning the area around the hinges and ground. "We simply needs the guard's keys." Ronin pulled a set from the folds in his garments. "Here are keys." He said, handing them to Scotty. After they entered the gate, Scotty decided to chain and lock the gate from the inside, in case other guards showed up for a shift change or something.¶

"You go check the target area." Scotty said, pointing towards the shot-up wooden planks down the range. "I'll go check out that little office trailer by the fence over there." The two men split up and went about finding any evidence they could find of illegal weapons. Entering the trailer, Scotty went directly to the only filing cabinet by a desk. Searching through several files, he did not find anything suspicious, only details of test results for Dead-Eye's top selling rifles and shotguns. Checking the other drawers, Scotty found nothing incriminating; perhaps such details were kept at their headquarters. Closing the last file, he turned to leave when something shiny caught his eye. He leaned down and picked up a memo that must have missed the trash can near the water cooler, it had a paper clip attached to it. "Must have fallen off a file folder." He thought to himself.¶

Semi-Successful testing of rapid-fire prototype.¶
Noise level extremely high, prone to jamming on occasion.¶
Continue to modify to avoid these problems.¶

- Mr. Bull¶

Tucking the memo into his pants pocket, Scotty decided it was time to check on Ronin, there was not much else to be done from inside the trailer. He peered out the blinds to check if everything was clear. Jogging down the range, he came upon the samurai examining a wooden target. "Any luck, Ronin?" He inquired. Ronin pointed to the splintered wood that lay all around the area. "Is this anything?" He asked. Scotty took a moment and ran his hands across what was left of an apparently human-shaped target. "There doesn't appear to be a typical grouping of bullet holes in the wood." He started. "If looks as if there were at least fifty or more shots fired at this target. Unless several men fired at the same time and were extremely accurate, I'd say they were testing a fully automatic weapon here, and fairly recent." A chill went up Scotty's spine as he thought back to that afternoon when Max showed him the schematics.

This was getting too real, what can be done against the biggest gun manufacturer in all of Texas, and perhaps the West. "What's the purpose of a fully-automatic weapon?" Scotty softly asked Ronin, not expecting an answer. "War." Said Ronin. Scotty raised his eyebrows, he had not that about that. If Dead-Eye Inc. was developing such a weapon, there must be demand for it. Regular shotguns and rifle were used for personal protection and hunting. A fully automatic Gatling gun would be used to take down multiple targets. Something had to be done immediately -before things progressed further. "We need to take action, Ronin!" Scotty said with a raspy voice. He had become extremely frightened and angry at the same time. "What do we do?" Asked Ronin. "First, let's take care of those guards."

Scotty and Ronin bound the two guards with rope, covered their heads with burlap sacks and moved them outside of the facility. It took nearly forty minutes for them to arrange things to carry out their last-minute plan. Stacking crates around the trailer, they were going to set fire to the main points of the facility; this would at least slow down their activities and could send a strong message that someone is aware of what they are doing. This would only be a temporary solution to the much bigger problem, they needed more time to gather information and evidence to stop those responsible. Once the last bit of kindling was in place, they set it ablaze.¶

It took only five minutes for the trailer, maintenance shed, and the storage bunker to become completely engulfed in flames. They kept quite a distance only to ensure that the fire would not spread. Once they started to hear shouting coming from the other side of the range, they decided to split up and return to their respective houses. They did not bother with good-byes or handshakes; they simply left. Scotty knew his way around the city and would be able to get home within twenty minutes. He did not know how long it would take Ronin, so he would call Max an hour later (and every ten minutes after that) until the samurai made it home safely.¶

*¶

The Black Bull Society was just starting its monthly meeting when Mr. White hurriedly entered the room. "It's extremely rare to see you arrive at a meeting so late, Mr. White." Mr. Bull said, looking at his pocket watch. "I hope your news justifies your tardiness." Mr. White flung a dossier on the table in front of where he was about to sit. "I think you'll be more than pleased. My team and I have pooled our resources, spoke with our many contacts and followed every lead." He started. "We've discovered those responsible for setting the fire and destroying our testing site. And, they're the same people responsible for the theft of the schematics and destruction of the prototype as well." The room fell silent as everyone around the table realized the gravity of Mr. White's statement.¶

"What does all of this mean?" Asked Mr. Cobble. "It means…" Answered Mr. White. "…they don't have enough information to go to the authorities. They are trying to stop our efforts themselves." After a couple of chuckles, Mr. Bull slammed his fist on the table before standing up. "You think this is funny?! Just because they don't have enough on us just yet, they have managed to get to our most prized possession and cost this company hundreds of thousands of dollars!" The laughter stopped faster than it started. "If they could do more, they would cost us millions. I'm not going to underestimate anyone at this point. You and your men bring me their ringleader, and let them know how serious their actions were."¶

The meeting was adjourned early after this information was brought forward. The urgency in Mr. Bull's voice was enough to get the wheels turning and a second meeting was quickly rescheduled. Mr. White had done a thorough investigation of Max, Scotty, and Butch, and had already come up with a plan of action. He anticipated Mr. Bull's wishes and deployed several of his best henchmen immediately.¶

*¶

Butch's right cross connected with his opponent's jaw, sending the man sprawling backwards. He managed to slowly scramble back to his feet. The roar of the crowd echoed throughout the basement of the abandoned factory. This was the chosen location for this month's underground, bare-knuckle tournament. Butch was favored to win against local tough man, Matt Sanbul. Although Matt was taller and heavier, he was not as in shape as Butch, who not only had arms like tree trunks, but had learned long ago that cardio was just as important as strength and skill. The challenger was gassing quickly. Butch had drawn this fight out to show would-be contenders that he could go the distance with any man, and not just rely on knock-out power to finish a fight.¶

Sanbul mounted one last attack; he rushed at Butch with his arms open wide, hoping to grab hold and take him down to the ground for a defensive stand to catch his breath. But Butch saw this attempt coming from a mile away. He ducked just enough to get at Matt's waist, and using his forward momentum against him, flipped the large man up into the air and onto his back. The cheers went up as the champ spun around and proceeded to put the challenger into a head-lock, to which he quickly tapped out. Having nothing left, Sanbul fell to the floor gasping for breath as Butch released his hold. The referee ran up to Butch and raised his hand to indicate him as the winner. Max and Scotty started collecting their winnings from the foolish gamblers who were dumb enough to bet against them. All-in-all, they made about twenty-six hundred dollars.¶

Seeing this incredible feat of strength, the last man in the tournament, who has just won his match, decided that second place was good enough. Forfeiting the final fight, Butch was named May's bare-knuckle champion and collected his prize money. Rattler was a little disappointed that the tournament was over, but soon realized that a much healthier Butch would be able to train him much sooner. The four of them left and traveled to the Bison Bar & Grill for late-night burger and fries. Since Max and Scotty won so much money, they split the bill as Butch managed to down nearly six pounds of chicken wings. The friends ate their fill, then traveled their separate ways home.¶

As Max and Rattler pulled into their driveway, they were greeted by Ronin, who motioned for them to follow him. He led them behind the house, where a man, bound and gagged was sitting on the ground, leaning against the back porch. "Rattler, go in the house!" Max said firmly. "But dad…" "I said now!" He almost shouted. Rattler quickly ran inside and up to his room, leaving the two men with the stranger. "What happened while we were gone?" He asked Ronin. Ronin seemed to choose his words very carefully. "He was trying to get in the barn. I stopped him. He can fight some." Was the samurai's response. "Not well enough I see. I think I'll drive him to the police station myself. Help me load him into the sidecar." The two of them managed to safely secure the bound man into the steam-cycle. "Make sure Rattler takes a shower and goes to bed while I'm gone." Ronin bowed and entered the house.¶

During the ten-minute drive, the man tried to talk through the gag, but Max simply ignored him. He would not be drawn into a conversation with someone who had trespassed on his property. He instinctively knew that someone at Dead-Eye Inc. suspected him and his friends of being behind the attacks on the company. Max tried not to let his anger get the best of him, he would simply drop this guy off at the authorities and return home to take care of his son. He would visit his friends first thing athanial Ghere

in the morning to discuss what they should do next. He pulled into a parking space and walked into the station.¶

"I have a trespasser in my side-car." He announced to the officer behind the front desk. "A trespasser? What happened?" The policeman asked as he stood up from his chair. "I returned home from a late dinner with my boy and some friends, and a hired hand who lives at my ranch subdued him while he was trying to break into my barn. I have a lot of expensive equipment in there." He opened the front door and showed him to his steam-cycle. Pulling the man out onto his feet, the policeman led him into the jailhouse and put him in a cell before taking Max back to his desk to file a report. Max was anxious to get back home and so explained as best as he could what had transpired.¶

After nearly forty minutes, Max was free to go. He took a copy of the official report and made his way home. Rattler was already asleep, and Ronin was finishing his shower and bedtime meditation routine as Max climbed into bed. He would clean up first thing in the morning, it had been a long day and he needed as much rest as he could get.¶

*¶

"It's obvious Aaron has failed his mission and won't be joining us." Said Mr. White as he looked around the circle of men standing by the loading docks. "It doesn't matter though; we have enough information to move forward with a plan I like to call 'Operation Thorn.'" It involves kidnapping four people, and finding out exactly what they know. We then apply pressure and threats to ensure their silence. If we suspect further investigation from these individuals, then one of them will come up missing... permanently." He glanced around the circle once again, mentally deciding on who would be responsible for collecting each target. "I will take care of the mysterious foreigner myself. And the final list will be posted through regular channels later tonight."¶

Mr. White broke up the meeting and returned to his office. He wanted to get all the details down as soon as possible. It took him nearly two hours to complete the fine points of the plan and place them into the corresponding envelopes. He delivered the orders to everyone's door personally and called it a night.

CHAPTER XI - Fleeing¶

Several weeks came and went, Rattler was excelling at sword fighting, and Butch had managed to teach him the solid basics of boxing. The Golden Snake saw a couple of new snakes finding their way into the barn for milking, and several others being retired back into the wild. Among the new arrivals was a four-foot Harlequin Coral, rather big for the species. Max had a couple more dates with Peggy, growing slightly more serious. And Scotty managed to snag more business now that Gunz A' Blazin' was officially closed for good. The three friends had decided to keep a much lower profile since the fire. They had not come up with any new ideas in which to cripple the illegal activities of Dead Eye Inc.¶

Ronin was at The Rustic Forge, sharing his knowledge to create a new battle sword to replace the one he had lost during his escape from Japan. Butch was excited at learning the intricacies of forging the unique 'nodachi' blade. Since Ronin did not speak throughout the entire process, Butch merely observed closely each hammer strike he made. It took nearly six hours to complete the sword. "That was spectacular." He commented as Ronin returned the tools to the work table. "I hope the materials I provided were sufficient. I know you probably used specific metals back in your homeland." Wiping his brow with a cloth, Ronin bowed and thanked Butch for the use of his forge. "I will return for the nodachi in two days. If you have any questions before I go... I will try to answer." Butch could not think of anything right off hand, but would probably have a couple by the time he returned for the sword.¶

Seeing the samurai off and locking up for the evening, Butch went upstairs to make himself supper. Being a of with simple tastes, he cooked up some homemade beef stew with biscuits on the side. Sitting down in his favorite chair, he turned on the radio and listened to the local news. They made mention of the ongoing investigation of the Dead-Eye Inc. testing range fire, as well as Gunz A' Blazin's attempt to restart their business from the ground up. Without enough investors, their efforts were futile. "Could the two events be linked somehow?" Said the reporter in a rather convincing voice. "Nope!" Said Butch as he took another bite of beef, potato and carrots. It was then that he heard noises coming from his shop downstairs. "Not again." He thought as he set his bowl down on the coffee table and stood to his feet.¶

Walking to his shop as quietly as he could, he unlocked the door and slid inside. Even with the lights off, he could make out four figures in the near-darkness. "I think you gentlemen are in the wrong place." The nearest intruder turned around and came at him; swinging wildly, Butch easily ducked the hay-maker and followed up with a solid blow to his midsection. He could tell by the cracking sound and the man's yell that he had broken a rib or two. Pushing him to the floor, he headed towards the next attacker, determined to take each one out as quickly as possible. Butch managed to reach the second man just as he was pulling out a gun. Knocking the weapon from his hand with a back-fist, he proceeded to crack the man across his jaw and drop him to the floor.¶

It was then that the lights came on and he found himself face to face with the remaining three men with guns already drawn and pointing straight at him. "So… five on one and you guys still need guns. Cowards!" Butch stood up straight and snapped his head to the side, making a cracking sound. "Alright, who's next?" He already knew the men were not going to shoot him, but were simply hoping he would give up at the sight of their weapons. He had dealt with thugs like these before and knew how they operated. Butch continued to talk to them as he made his way to the cash register. "I'm assuming you want money and…" THUD! Butch fell to the floor as Mr. White delivered a precise blow to the back of his head. "And that's how it's done." He said in a condescending tone. "He was almost to his shotgun behind the counter. This is exactly why I came along. Tie him up, gag him, and put this bag over his head." He tossed a small sack to his nearest henchman and slipped his pistol back into its holster inside his jacket; he then leaned over and turned the lights back out.¶

After Butch was bound and gagged, they pulled him outside and loaded him into the sidecar of Mr. White's steam-cycle. "You have thirty minutes to comb over his shop and find anything useful. I'll expect all of you back at the storage facility in forty-five minutes." Mr. White drove off into the night as the men went back inside to continue their search. Everything was going as planned for the moment.¶

*¶

Ronin was walking down the sidewalk and was about halfway home when he heard shouting emanating from behind the general store. Running up to the edge of the building, he peered around the corner. There was a young woman, perhaps in her early twenties, being harassed by several men. It was apparent by the way they carried themselves that they were most likely drunk. Stepping from the shadows, Ronin simply said. "Let her go." The men were startled, but did not let go of the young woman. "Beat it, stranger!" One of them shouted. Taking a closer look, they noticed Ronin had drawn his sword. "Let her go." He repeated calmly. Their leader threw a whiskey bottle at his head, but he simply sidestepped to his left to dodge the projectile.

"This is last warning. Let her go."¶

It was clear that being intoxicated had given these men false courage; pulling knives, two of them advanced on the samurai. Ronin let out a war cray and, spinning around, sliced through each man's hat in one fluid motion. Stunned by a blade flying that close to their heads, he easily followed through with elbow strikes, knocking the knives out of their hands and onto the ground. He finished his attack by swiftly kicking each man in the chest, sending them sprawling into the dirt. Ronin re-sheathed his sword and walked towards their leader, still holding the woman by her arm.¶

The man pulled a pistol from its holster and took aim at the samurai. "Gun beats sword!" He exclaimed with confidence. But before he could pull the trigger, he felt a sharp pain in his shoulder. The would-be attacker uncontrollably dropped the weapon from his right hand and reached for his shoulder with his left. There was a small handle sticking out from a fresh wound. Pulling the small dagger from his shoulder, he looked up, only to see a fist make impact with his face before going unconscious.¶

"Thank you whoever you are!" The woman said, gasping for breath as she tried to collect herself. "I dread to think what they would have done to me if you hadn't showed up." Ronin wiped the blood off the dagger before returning it under his clothing. "I will walk you home." He stated, helping her to pick up her bag. "I live about a half mile that way." She said, pointing down a side street. Within fifteen minutes, the samurai watched as she safely entered her home and shut the door. Ronin decided to jog the rest of the way to shake off the unpleasantness of the incident. Feeling the cool crisp air running through his hair, he sprinted up the driveway and onto the front porch.¶

As he entered the dining room, he noticed Max had left him a plate of food on the table. He quickly ate his supper and cleared off the table before heading to bed. He felt a sense of pride from helping the young woman against would-be attackers, but also felt somewhat guilty for missing dinner with Max and Rattler. He might share his little adventure with Max during breakfast, but for now he welcomed some much-needed rest.¶

*¶

Butch awoke to a throbbing headache. Opening his eyes, things were merely a blur. After several minutes ticked by, his surroundings came into focus, but he did not recognize where he was; nor did he know how much time had passed since… last night? Three men had broken into his forge. Or was it four? Feeling the back of his head, there was a huge lump left by whomever had managed to knock him unconscious. Sitting up straight, he realized he was sitting on a bed in a prison-like cell. It was part of a larger room, but the cell was only about ten feet by ten feet. There were bars on one wall, and the cell contained the bed he was sitting on, a toilet with a sink, and a small table with a chair nearby. "What the hell is going on?!" He thought to himself.¶

"He's awake!" The shout echoed through the room beyond Butch's cell. The sound pierced through his ears and wreaked havoc and pain inside his head. "Whomever caused this situation was in big trouble." He thought. "Who's there?" Butch asked softly as he stood to his feet. "Why have I been brought to this place?" Anger began to wash over his body and penetrate his muscles; which somehow eased his headache. "You'll know soon enough." Came a reply from an unseen captor. Butch stretched and rolled his arms at the shoulder while leaning his head side to side, loosening the muscles in his neck, similarly to what he did before a boxing match. Only this time, he was sure his opponent would be armed.¶

"My name is Mr. Bull." Came the reply. "And we are very interested in your particular knowledge and set of skills." An average sized man stepped into view wearing a black hood with eye slits cut into it. "We know you were involved with the Dead Eye Inc. fire that occurred weeks back. But, we aren't here to seek revenge. No! In fact, I'm here to offer you a chance to make up for your misdeeds…

and the misdeeds of your friends." Butch remained silent for a few seconds. It was obvious that he could not lie at this point. Whomever this hooded person was, it was clear that he had done his homework. "I knew about the fire. But I was not there when it happened, so I can't really…" "I already know who was directly responsible for the actual fire. I'm not here he to try and get you to rat on your friends. I simply want to find out what you know specifically about the prototype and schematics." The lights seemed to dim slightly as Mr. Bull stepped closer to the bars and awaited a response from his prisoner.¶

"I don't know where the schematics are." Butch exclaimed. "I don't think I made myself clear." Said Mr. Bull. "I'm not interested in recovering the schematics for our Gatling gun, I'm asking about *your* schematics. The ones for an assault rifle." Butch's eyes widened as he realized that Mr. Bull knew much more about their activities then he had first thought. "Our Gatling gun has had some… let's say size and reliability issues. I'm keen to see if your design might be an improvement on our concept." Mr. Bull began to stroll back and forth in front of the bars as though he were waiting for something else to happen.¶

"I'm not telling you anything. Do you think for one moment that you frighten me?" Butch said in a lowered tone. "You know who I am, and you know what my friends and I are capable of. It's only a matter of time before you have no choice but to let me go. I'm too famous in this town to go missing for very long." There was a confidence in Butch's voice that Mr. Bull did not expect. Even though he was clearly at their mercy, he did not show any outward signs of fear. "I'm not expecting you to spill your guts to me because you are afraid." He stopped pacing and turned to face his prisoner. "But I do think you'll come around eventually when your God-nephew's life might be threatened."¶

Butch lunged at the bars and tried reaching at Mr. Bull's throat. But Mr. Bull was standing mere inches from his grasp. "That is precisely why you are in there, and I am out here. So, you see, it's only a matter of time before you have no choice but to give me what I want." That was the last thing Mr. Bull said as he turned and walked out of sight. Butch heard murmuring before the sound of a door slammed shut. He sat back down on the bed and thought long and hard about his next move.¶

*¶

Ronin walked purposefully through the parking lot of The Rustic Forge towards the main entrance. Dan had just unlocked the front door and was flipping the sign around to 'Open.' "Hello, Mr. Ronin sir." Dan was not sure if Ronin was his first name or last, but the samurai never corrected him so he kept greeting him as Mr. Ronin. "Hello." He replied. "Is Mr. Young here." Dan furled his eyebrows a bit. "I'll have to check his upstairs apartment. It's not unusual for him to sleep in a little on Mondays. Sometimes I open the store for business before he comes down. Is there anything I can help you with?" He inquired. Ronin nodded his head. "I'm here for my nodachi, it is a samurai's battle sword." "Oh yes, Butch did tell me something about you crafting a sword on Friday before we closed. Come on inside, I'll go check to see if he's come down yet." Ronin made his way to the forge as Dan walked upstairs to knock on Butch's apartment door.¶

Ronin retrieved his sword. Since he was in a wide-opened space, he gave it a couple of slices through the air to get a feel for the newly forged weapon. I barely made a sound as it swung gracefully around the samurai. He returned to the store just as Dan reached the bottom step and walked in from the rear. "He's not answering his door. It's not like him to simple not be here." Dan said with some uncertainty. "He would have told me if he had business elsewhere, or at least left a note by the register." Walking over to the counter, Ronin began looking on the floor. "Does anything look like it is missing?" The samurai ran his finger from the counter top down to the carpet. "I'll take a quick inventory, but everything seems to be where we left them."¶

Seeing a small drop of what could be blood, Ronin continued to scan the floor and followed a tiny trail to the back exit. Once he stepped over onto the tile floor of the storage room, he found slight trails of scuff marks. "Here Dan." The samurai pointed to the floor. "Someone was dragged through here." Dan checked the back door… it was unlocked! "Now I'm freaked out. What happened here?" The two exchanged glances before Ronin began speaking again. "I think he was taken from this place." Dan shook his head. "I don't see anyone getting the jump on Butch in his own shop, there would be more signs of a struggle. He wouldn't have gone so quietly." He again looked at the scuff marks on the floor. "Last time someone tried to rob this place, Butch made sure they needed stitches to remind them how bad of an idea it was."¶

Ronin knew Butch would have put up a good fight, even against several opponents. "Someone trained was here. Mr. Young did not see it coming. There is blood by the counter." Showing Dan the spot on the floor where Butch was most likely knocked unconscious, he called the police right away. Sensing that Butch was taken by professionals, Ronin immediately said goodbye and headed for the front door. "I must go, now!" Dan waved knowingly as the door shut behind him. Ronin sprinted down the street, focusing on his breathing. He needed to get back to The Golden Snake as fast as he could; Max and Rattler's lives might depend on it.¶

In less than half an hour, Ronin found himself running up the driveway shouting for Max. "Over here, Ronin, I was just finishing up milking the last snake for today." Max said, places his work gloves into his back pocket. "Why are you so worked up?" Ronin started looking around frantically. "Where is Rattler?" There was desperation in the tone of his voice. "He's in the house finishing up his chores. He's really looking forward to your next lesson." Before he could get another word out, the samurai sprinted towards the house. Max followed right behind him. "What's going on? Is something wrong?" Once inside, Ronin found the boy drying and putting away the breakfast dishes. "We need to go see your friend right now!" "Slow down Ronin, what happened to you?"¶

Catching his breath, Ronin laid out the details of exactly what had transpired earlier that morning. He also confessed how a ninja assassin had tried to get the sacred Snake blade weeks before. "I'm sure your intentions to protect the family were honorable, but I don't think these two things have anything to do with each other." Max assured him. "I think someone at Dead Eye Inc. figured out who was behind the espionage. But I do think we should call Scotty right away. Max picked up the phone and dialed, but the line was busy. Rattler, go warm up the bike. Ronin, do you know how to get to The Gunslinger from here?" "Yes sir" He nodded. "I will go now." Bowing, Ronin turned and started jogging towards Scotty's gun store. Rattler ran outside and stocked the steam cycle with coal and started it up.¶

*¶

Scotty was in the middle of a sale when he spied Ronin through a window walking towards the front entrance. He gave the customer his change and thanked him for his patronage. The samurai held the door open for the man, who thanked him on his way out. "Good day, sir." He said as he turned and headed down the sidewalk on foot. Scotty said hello to Ronin and motioned for him to come inside. "You here alone? What can I do for you Ronin?" Scotty said in a normal tone. "Should I lock up?" He then whispered. "Max and Rattler will be here soon." He answered, walking over to a display rack. Ronin appreciated guns and how they worked, but he would never own one himself. In mere minutes, Max pulled up with Rattler in the side car.¶

Scotty waved them in and proceeded to lock the door and turn the sign to read 'Closed.' "Ronin told me very little, I do hope everything is alright with Butch. What's our next move.?" Scotty was visibly shaken up. He was worried that their actions might have serious consequences outside of the law. "I'm going to run over to The Rustic Forge and retrieve the assault rifle and check to see if there's any word on Butch from Dan. You all head up to Scotty's." Max continued. "I'll meet you over there in half an hour." Scotty finished his paperwork, locked the money in his safe, and locked up. Max had made it to Butch's shop about the same time as everyone else walked up onto Scotty and Jill's porch.¶

"Hey, Dan." Max called out as he walked through the front door. "I need to talk to you when you get a chance." There were only a couple of customers wondering the shop looking at various gun holsters and belts. "Actually, I was just about to close up here and give you a call." He replied. "The police said they would have to wait twenty-four hours before they could investigate Butch's disappearance. Said he's an adult and all that nonsense stuff about how he could just be hungover somewhere or something like that." Dan informed the two men in the store that they would need to make any purchases soon as he was closing early for the day. After they bought what they came for, they both left.¶

"I need to get a rifle from the storage closet." Max went into the back with Dan in tow. "Is there anything I should know, or be doing?" He asked. Max fetched the assault rifle (which looked like any other rifle) and replied to Dan. "Scotty, Ronin and I are looking into the whole situation ourselves. The less you know, the better." Dan started to speak. "But…" Max cut him off. "There are serious things going on right now that you need not get mixed up in. I will tell you this… in the back of the safe, there are papers in an envelope marked 'Dan.' If you don't hear from Butch within thirty days, take them downtown to legal aid and ask for Tom, he'll know what to do." Dan had a puzzled look on his face as Max jumped on his bike and headed back to Scotty's house.¶

As he approached the driveway next to The Gunslinger that led up to his friend's house, he noticed a man in a suit hanging around the front door of the shop on the sidewalk. As Max pulled in, the man started walking slowly towards him. Looking in the rear-view mirror, he saw the man rounding the corner and following him up the driveway. Max had a bad feeling about the situation and pulled his steam-cycle into the grass and instinctively grabbed the assault rifle. Spinning around, he aimed the gun at the stranger. "Can I help you with something?" He said. "The Gunslinger's closed, and this is private property." The man was obviously caught off guard; instead of responding to Max's question, he reached for his gun. "Don't…" Max warned, clicking the fully automatic switch to semi-automatic.¶

Unfortunately, the man called Max's bluff by pulling out his pistol. ***BLAM*** Max had no choice but to drop him. Scotty witnessed the whole scene from the porch. He ran into his house and yelled for his wife. "Jill, grab a suitcase full of close! We're heading for the cabin." Having heard the gunshot, Jill did not stop to question her husband. Scotty ran over to the phone and called his lawyer. After a few rings, Mr. Ace answered. "Hello." "Tom, I don't have a lot of time here. The papers I had you draw up last week. File them as soon as possible. I'll call you as soon as I can once my wife and I are safely out of the city." He did not wait for a response as he hung up the phone and headed towards his bedroom.¶

Max came running up onto the porch and into the house. "Where's Rattler?" He shouted. His son was hiding behind the couch and sprung to his feet when he heard his name. "What happened dad?" He asked, but his father simply ran up and hugged him. Max started looking around the room. "Where's Ronin?" "Ronin went back to our house. He said he was going to wait there for our return. What's going on, dad?" Max did not know how to explain things to his son, so he tried to simplify things as best as he could. "Son, a man just pulled a gun on me. I shot him in self-defense, but there are going to be more bad men coming after me, Scotty, and your uncle Butch. We've got to get home and pack.

We're leaving Blackwater for a while." Not wanting to argue with his father, Rattler followed him back outside and jumped into the sidecar and put on his seat-belt. Max and Scotty exchanged a few words and then they were on their way home.¶

Within thirty minutes, Max and Rattler managed to pack the essentials for their trip. The plan was to get out of town for a few weeks and regroup before returning for their friend. Max would not rest until Butch was found. They had no leads, no clues of any kind, and they did not know for certain who was running the operation. Who was the man in charge? Was everything controlled by the executives at Dead Eye Inc.? They had no idea how much trouble they were actually in at this point.¶

"Dad! Dad! The barn is on fire!" Rattler shouted from the porch. Max ran outside to see the building that held all their valuable snakes slowly going up in smoke. "Get back in the house!" He shouted. As Rattler darted back into the house, two men appeared from behind the barn with shotguns and started firing at the front porch. Max dove under the wooden swing behind the short wall surrounding the porch. He collected himself and decided to switch the assault rifle to fully automatic.¶

Ronin sprang from behind the two men and quickly struck one of them down with a mighty blow from his two-handed nodachi, nearly slicing the would-be killer in two. The second man, hearing his partner's scream, turned around to see what had happened. But before he could aim his shotgun, Ronin separated both his hands from his arms; the shotgun fell to the ground. Spinning 180 degrees, he plunged the sword straight through the man's chest with a battle cry. Pulling the blade back out, the hand-less man fell face first into the grass.¶

Max scanned around looking for more intruders. Seeing no one, he proceeded to run over to the samurai. "Ronin, you're more than just a member of our family. And I know how bad things are getting very quickly. I need you to protect Rattler." The samurai sheathed his sword and bowed his head to indicate that he understood, as well as feeling honored that Max would feel this way about him. "We need to split up. Take Rattler with you and protect him. Go about a hundred miles south of here and set up camp. I'll join you as soon as I can when things get settled here. I need to make sure Scotty, Jill and Butch are out of harm's way." Max was so afraid his entire body was shaking.¶

Ronin put his hand on Max's shoulder to both steady his nerves, and to show that he knew how serious he was being. "I will guard your son's life with my own." Ronin ran into the house and took Rattler by the hand. "Come Rattler, your father wants us to get to safety. Grab your sword and follow me." Rattler, not showing any fear, retrieved his sword and followed the samurai out of the house and into the woods south of the ranch. Max grabbed some important items from the house and hopped onto his steam-cycle. He headed for the Blackfoot Indian tribe on the back roads, making sure he was not being followed.

CHAPTER XII - A New Life¶

Max rode steadily up the main entrance to the Blackfoot Indian campgrounds, and although they were not expecting him, they welcomed him with open arms as usual. He asked to speak with Chief White Cloud, and was guided to the elder's lodge where he was meeting with leaders from a nearby Sioux tribe. He waited until they were finished before approaching his long-time friend. He handed the chief's assistant a thick envelope containing one third of the assault rifle schematics and instructed them to hide it away until either he or Rattler returned for them. "I was expecting you. We will talk to the spirits and have them guide you, your son, and the foreigner out of harm's way." Began Chief White Cloud. "I have had another vision. Come, let us retire to my tee-pee so we can discuss these things."¶

They were ushered to the chief's private quarters and told that they would not be disturbed until they reemerged from their meeting. "Rattler will become the greatest warrior Texas has ever seen." The wise Indian spoke as he stirred a large pot of soup in the middle of the room. He quickly spooned some into two bowls and offered one to Max. "I have seen him battle with many different men who are bent on starting wars to gain power over those whom he protects." Max took a sip of the soup. It contained indigenous roots and vegetables which were harvested from the Blackfoot's fields.¶

"What does he do in these visions of yours?" Max asked eagerly. "He was learned to focus his gifts given to him by the snake spirits. The snake is not an enemy, but more of a misunderstood brother. That is why you, Max, are able to turn their venom into medicines.

Your brother, the snake, gave you that ability."
White Cloud sat back in his chair and took a
drink of soup from his bowl. Max looked a little
puzzled by the chief's words. "So what gift have
they given my son?" He waited patiently as the
chief continued drinking his soup. "He will
become more like the viper. Sensing his prey,
except Rattler will be able to sense his enemy.
That is all I can say, come, finish your soup my
friend."¶

Suddenly a young Blackfoot warrior came
inside. "Apologies, my chief. There are several
white men on steam-powered horses coming this
way. We have stopped the fire in the belly of our
friend's horse and have hidden it away." He
motioned for Max to follow him. "We will hide
you as well, until these men leave this place."
Max followed the young man and hid
underneath a corner of the main lodge. A small
shelter was dug out of the earth that could shield
several people from view. It was used whenever
there were innocents to protect from bounty
hunters and other crooked law men.¶

Chief White Cloud gathered several other
elders to meet with the strangers before they
could make it to the main lodge. "Hello my
friends, what can we do for you? We have lots of
vegetables for sale, as well as tobacco and

clothing." The big man spoke first. "We're not here to trade chief. We're looking for a guy named Max." He set down his kick-stand and dismounted the steam cycle. "He was last seen heading this way." The other two men also got down from their bikes. "The man you speak of has already gone away from here. He has business at the hospital where he delivers medicines." The chief replied. The three men started to walk towards them. A dozen warriors stepped between the men and the elders and stared them down. "We're not looking to start anything here." The big man said as he looked several warriors in the eye in an attempt to show that he was not afraid of them. But, with there being so many, it did not work. "We'll head on over to the hospital right now." He returned to his steam cycle and slipped it into gear. "Come on, there's no use wasting any more time here. Let's ride, boys." Within minutes, the steam from their cycles disappeared over the horizon.¶

After about twenty minutes, when they were sure the men would not return, they released Max from his hiding spot. "Thank you, Chief. I need to be more careful in the future, I had no idea they knew where I was headed. They must have many men watching us." He said, apologetic. "It is not your fault, Max. When evil is among us, there is almost nothing we can do to avoid confrontation." White Cloud said. "You must go and do what you need to do. We are on the same side. Your enemies are our enemies. Remember you have many friends here." The chief smiled as Max retrieved his bike and headed out. He thought he might start looking for clues back at The Golden Snake after the sun had gone down.¶

*¶

It was now day ten since Ronin and Rattler set out to reach the hundred-mile mark and set up camp. Rattler missed his father, but Ronin was fast becoming his respected teacher, and helped ease these temporary feelings of separation. Stopping by a large stream for a much-needed drink of water, Ronin scanned the area carefully. There was an ample supply of running water; a large field with few trees at the edges; and a small thicket of trees and bushes set at the bottom of rolling hills. This would be a perfect spot to make camp. It was also miles from any roads and a shelter could easily be made from surrounding resources.¶

"We should sleep here and gather our wits and strengths, for tomorrow we build." Ronin spoke to Rattler in the best English he could muster. Some of what he spoke was in Japanese, but Rattler had been slowly learning the language over the past months and could understand his teacher better than anyone. "okay, sensei. What should we do first?" Rattler was eager to learn anything he could from the samurai. The boy started looking at this whole ordeal as part of his overall training, rather than merely be afraid. Ronin smiled and motioned for him to sit. "Please, sit and rest a while first. We must relax and regain our energy before we do anything." Rattler had been so eager to please both his father and teacher, he did not realize how much his body was trying to tell him to slow down. Sitting in the grass, he noticed blisters on the bottom of his feet; and his shoulders starting to ache from carrying their supplies. He laid in a soft patch of clovers and promptly fell asleep. The trip had taken more of a toll than he had shown.¶

Nearly two hours passed by before Rattler woke from his nap. Ronin had meditated for twenty minutes to rejuvenate himself and was over halfway done with a humble shelter made with fallen branches from the nearby forest. Rattler stood up and stretched his weary muscles before joining Ronin in completing the make-shift hut. "We do not know how long your father will be. We must prepare ourselves for and extended stay." Ronin motioned for the boy to follow him to the top of the hill. "We will start a garden over there." He said, pointing to a field full of nothing but tall grass. "I have walked all around, the earth there is good for planting. We will catch fish and small game from the stream and forest." Rattler paid close attention to every detail his teacher laid out to him. "We must search and gather edible plants to put in our garden, but first we must eat." The two spent the remainder of the day collecting edible roots and herbs for a simple stew. It would not be the best tasting stew ever, but it would provide enough nutrition to repair their aching bodies.¶

*¶

Mr. White continued to question Butch while Mr. Bull was tending to other business. One of his henchmen entered with a folder and handed it to him. Flipping it open, he scanned a couple of pages and set it on the table next to him. "Well it appears that all of your friends have fled Blackwater. Doesn't look good for you." Butch looked up and met Mr. White's glare. "I would have done the same thing." He said with a smile. "They're going to make sure everyone is safe before coming for me. I'm sure they already have a plan." "They wouldn't need a plan if you would simply take the deal we're offering you." Mr. White was past irritated with his prisoner. "Join us and you'll be rewarded with riches. Do you even realize how valuable your assault rifle is?"¶

Butch sucked a mouthful of blood and saliva and spit it out onto the floor at Mr. White's feet. "We only designed it as a defensive weapon against your Gatling gun. And how is your new prototype coming along?" Mr. White stepped forward and punched Butch clean across his jaw. Butch let out a small moan. "I've been hit by opponents twice as hard as that in the ring. Do you expect me to comply to your threats?" He started laughing slightly. "We know what would happen if such a weapon were mass produced and sold." Mr. White punched him again. "I'm starting to enjoy punishing you. I'm almost hoping you don't break. I would love to kill you myself." He punched him again to emphasize his point.¶

"That's enough, White." Mr. Bull said, as he entered the room. "You should really try a different method of persuasion; you don't seem to be getting anywhere. Besides, I've seen plenty of his underground, bare knuckle fights, he has been hit harder than that." Mr. White stood up and wiped the blood from his hand with a handkerchief. "So what would you suggest?" He asked sarcastically. "I'm getting bored punishing this buffoon!" He threw the wadded-up handkerchief in Butch's face and turned to face his employer. "What would you like me to do next? We've already checked the records at the courthouse. If Max or the Daniels own any property outside of Blackwater, it's registered under an alias."¶

Mr. Bull grew tired of the whole situation. He turned around and pulled his hood off, revealing his face to him. "Mr. Bull, what are you doing?" Mr. White was astonished at his boldness. "It doesn't matter. He should know exactly who he'll be working for." "I'll never work for you. Innocent people will be hurt." Butch moved his head to one side, cracking his neck. "I'm giving you one week to come to your senses." Said Mr. Bull. "If you don't join us, you'll die. It's just that simple." He turned to one of Mr. White's associates. "Put him back in his cell. And get him cleaned up, he's supposed to be our guest." He turned and walked out of the room and Mr. White's goons took Butch under each arm and dragged him back to his cell.¶

*¶

Ronin and Rattler where settling into their new surroundings quite well. They traveled several miles to a small town and traded several hours of general labor for vegetable starter plants. They would grow a dozen different varieties of beans, peppers, tomatoes, root vegetables, and leafy greens. Although he was trained primarily as a samurai, Ronin was well versed in agriculture. Rattler knew quite a bit as well, so their garden should be fruitful. He and Ronin enjoyed farming and yard work. They both found it relaxing, as well as time for quiet meditation.¶

They managed to fill an entire half acre within a week. They also set spring traps to catch rabbits and squirrels; and rigged a primitive, but reliable, fish trap near the river's edge. It would be possible for the two to live here for quite a while. They had no idea how long it would take Max to find them, assuming nothing happened to him. "Sensei, are we going to train soon?" Rattler was anxious to get back to learning the ways of a samurai. "Be patient, my student. Once we are completely settled, we will return to your training." "How much more do we have to do?" Rattler asked. "Only a few more days. We need to learn the rhythm of the land." Rattler looked a little puzzled. "Rhythm of the land?"

Ronin took a seat on the ground, and Rattler followed suit. "The rhythm of the land simply means, the flow of nature. We need to learn where all of the predators and prey come and go from this place." Rattler looked at him with much interest. "We need to make sure we do not take more from the earth than we need. If we create a balance, we will be able to survive and flourish until we return home." Rattler nodded in agreement. "Come, my student, let's prepare our supper."¶

Checking their trap in the water, they found that they had managed to catch three trout. Ronin removed the largest, and let the other two go, unharmed. "We eat only what we must." The samurai cleaned the fish as Rattler started a modest fire near their shelter. "Can I season the fish?" He asked. "I've had trout before and I know the best spices to use." Ronin was eager to try his student's homemade recipe. Even though his travels had led to many a fish dinner, he never actually had trout before. The two sat and watched the sun set as they enjoyed a meal of fish and carrots together. Ronin had always wanted a son, and Rattler was fast becoming the next best thing.¶

*¶

Daisy stepped off the train inbound from Mt. Tenino; Dan stood on the platform with Tom Ace, Scotty and Butch's lawyer. "Welcome back to Blackwater, Daisy." Dan grabbed her luggage and they all headed for the carriage. "I'm so confused, I still don't understand what's going on. Your telegram said I was needed to sign some documents from my Uncle Scotty. But he never told me he was leaving town." She was convinced something was very wrong, but her parents insisted she take time off from school to handle family business. Their trip to the legal aid office took less than ten minutes, but it seemed much longer due to the uneasy silence.¶

The trio stepped down from the carriage, Tom tipped the driver before heading inside. "This might take a while, we have a lot to discuss. But don't worry, I have everything you two will need in my office." Tom informed them while turning the key to unlock the door. "Where's your secretary?" Asked Dan. "Since this is an intimate meeting, I gave her the afternoon off." The lock clicked open and they entered the consultation room. "Please, have a seat." Tom pulled out the chair for Daisy as Dan sat opposite her. "There's no proper way to begin here, so I'll just come out and say it. "Your Uncle Scotty and Aunt Jill have gone into hiding." Daisy's jaw dropped slightly and her eyes widen. "What?! Where?!" She demanded in a troubled tone. "To keep everyone involved safe, I'm not even privy to that information. All I can tell you is that your aunt and uncle initiated their executive will. As did Mr. Young."¶

Over the next two hours, Daisy and Dan each read details on how they would take over their respective business. In Daisy's case, there was a plan laid out for her to live in her aunt and uncle's house while attending school at the prestigious Blackwater Academy. "This doesn't seem real." Dan said. "I've only been an employee for a couple of years. I didn't know Butch put me in his will." "Butch told me that in the time you worked for him, he knew you were a trustworthy, hard-working young man." Mr. Ace reassured him. "But you needn't worry about the business aspect. You will be allotted an allowance, and I take care of the legal aspects. There are also partners that Butch did business with who will assist in an advisory capacity. And his personal accountant will manage the financials. Butch is a very rich man. The money he made at The Rustic Forge is a drop in the bucket compared to the money he made fighting."¶

"And what about my Uncle Scotty?" Daisy

inquired. "Surely he wasn't as rich as Butch."

"That's another situation altogether." Tom began.
"Since the gun shop was founded by his Great-
Great-Great Grandfather, the residence has long
been paid for. Whomever runs the store will live
in the house located at the rear of the property.
Again, I will manage the distribution of your
monthly allowance. The accountant will see that
all property taxes and tuition be paid in full and
on time. We have arranged for one of the
headmasters, a Mrs. Gentry, to reside in the
home with you until your eighteenth birthday, at
which time you will take full control of both the
house and the business. This all of course hinges
on you completing your education as scheduled.
But your Aunt Jill has no doubts in your
abilities." Daisy could not believe her ears. It
had always been her dream to go to work in the
family business, and within six years that dream
will become a reality.¶

The next couple of hours entailed in-depth
discussions, questions, and the signing of serious
legal papers. Once completed, Dan and Daisy
both walked out of the building and into new
lives. But each was concerned about the details
that led to these current events. They were both
being forced into responsibility, even if it were
in a positive way. "Miss Daisy." Dan began to

speak. "I know you don't know me all that well. But Butch and your Uncle Scotty were the best of friends. And I hope we can become close friends as well." Daisy could see that he was being sincere. "I agree. And you are more than welcome to stop by for dinner whenever you like." The two hugged for a moment and then went their separate ways. As Dan rounded the corner, he looked in the large envelope Mr. Ace had handed him on his way out. It was part of a schematic for some type of rifle.¶

*¶

Ronin and Rattler circled in various defensive stances, each waiting for the other to show the slightest lapse in concentration. They had been sparing now for nearly forty minutes. Their training entailed lots of cardio, so each session seemed to go on longer than the last. A dragonfly flew right in front of Rattler's face, and Ronin used that split second to disarm the boy with a spiraling swing of his katana. "No fair." Cried Rattler. "That bug distracted me, you cheated." Ronin gave him a stern look. "If the dragonfly flew in front of your face while you were in a real battle, would your enemy wait for you to refocus... no!" He told his pupil. "You do not make any excuses for a lack of focus.

Distractions can happen at any time." Even though Rattler was bested again by his teacher once again, he knew his words were true.¶

"Come." Said Ronin. "I will tell you a story." Rattler sheathed his own sword and walked beside his sensei and sat by the dwindling fire where they had lunch earlier. "What's the story about?" He asked softly. "It's about a great samurai warrior who wielded the Snake Blade in during a noble battle." Rattler perked up and listened closely to his teacher's words. "The great samurai warrior owned acres upon acres of pristine land; clean water, excellent soil for growing crops, and ore mines that produced quality metals to make weapons and armor. He had given some of his lands to the poor, so they could grow their own food, and raise their own livestock so they would no longer live in poverty. An opposing army of samurai attempted to take land that was given to these people. The rival Lord thought it was a waste of resources. He stated 'These people do not deserve such a gift. I will conquer and take this land for myself and become richer.' The great samurai warrior warned this Lord that he would defend the people with his mighty Snake Blade."¶

Rattler asked Ronin. "What's so special

about the Snake Blade?" Picking up some sand from near the fire, Ronin lifted his hand and let the grains fall between his fingers. "It is said that whomever wields the Snake Blade in battle cannot be defeated." He let the rest of the sand fall to the ground as he spoke. "The rival Lord did not believe the legend, and so he sent six samurai to kill the great warrior. These were no ordinary samurai; they were known as The Black-Hearted Six." Ronin stood up and dusted the sand from his hands before continuing with the story. "The great samurai met them on the hillside at the edge of his lands. He warned them to turn back and he would spare their lives. But The Black-Hearted Six merely laughed. 'How do you expect to defeat the six of us with just one weapon?' 'I will only say this once more. Turn back and be spared.' He said as he drew his sword from its sheath.¶

"Did they turn back?" Rattler could hardly contain his excitement. Ronin went on. "The Black-Hearted Six advanced on him, and one by one they were struck down. News traveled fast, and the great samurai warrior and his protected lands were not challenged again for six years. One year for each samurai he defeated." Rattler grabbed his sword and jumped to his feet. "That's how good I want to be. I want to defeat anyone who threatens the poor." Ronin smiled at his young student. "Remember Rattler, you need not kill someone in order to defeat them. The great samurai warrior only killed because he was outnumbered and they would have killed him. You can disarm someone as I did earlier to you. And sometimes that is enough to persuade an enemy to surrender to a superior warrior." Rattler took his teacher's words to heart as they returned to their training.¶

The covered horse carriage came to a stop miles outside Blackwater. Two men grabbed Butch from his seat and forced him outside and into the dirt. "Get him up!" Said Mr. White from inside the carriage. "Let's make this quick, we've got other things to attend to." Butch managed to sit up-right before his gag was removed. "You won't get away with this!" He shouted. "My friends will find out what you've done!" Mr. White looked intensely into Butch's eyes as he spoke. "You know, a lot of people have said that, and… the friends never seem to find out what we've done. I would personally like to be the one to kill you, but I promised my two best 'employees' the honor of dispatching the champ. It is a pity though; you would have made an excellent asset to our company."¶

The two henchmen pulled Butch to his feet and forced him towards a steep hill. One of them spoke. "Would you prefer to face us like a man on your feet? Or would you prefer a shot to the back of the head?" The two started laughing as they each loaded a single bullet in their guns. Butch did not answer, he simply looked over the edge of the hill and turned to face them. Mr. White was quite impressed. "Most people at least beg for mercy before we shoot them. But have it your way." The two men raised their guns and took aim at Butch's mid-section. "You should pray that you break your neck and die instantly on the way down." One of them said.¶

"On the count of three. One… two… three!" They both fired in unison right into Butch's gut. He first dropped to his knees, then grabbing his stomach, he plummeted over the cliff. It took nearly twenty seconds for his body to roll all the way down to the bottom. Mr. White exited the carriage and walked to the edge. Looking down, he saw Butch's lifeless body in a slowly dissipating cloud of dust. "Let's go boys." He said. "That wasn't as enjoyable as I thought it would be. He didn't even scream, how disappointing." The three of them returned to the carriage and soon were on their way back to town.

CHAPTER XIII - Ronin's Past¶

The sun was just beginning to rise over Kyoto, Japan, Ronin had risen early and was meditating near the temple. He opened his eyes and could see the shadows made by the many trees behind him. He finished focusing on his thoughts and rose to his feet. There was only about thirty to forty minutes before the morning's meeting with his master to discuss the day's business. Ronin pulled his katana from its sheath and began a difficult kata, a simulated fight routine against imaginary opponents meant to hone one's skill. After completing it several times, he returned his sword to its home and ran to the small palace where he found his master finishing his breakfast in the garden. Walking up slowly as to not disturb him, Ronin sat beside him and waited for him to speak.¶

Putting down a piece of fruit, his master blew across the top of a hot cup of tea before taking a sip. "Ronin," He began. "I have decided to start collecting contributions a day early this week because of the upcoming holiday." Instead of collecting taxes from the citizens dwelling in his land, Ronin's master collected five percent of all crops and livestock to feed himself, his samurai, and all the servants living in the palace.

He only collected a small tax from the business merchants who sold non-food goods at the market. His "kingdom" was not the richest in the land, but the people who lived within its boundaries were certainly the happiest and most loyal. "I will ride out immediately, unless there is anything else?" His master shook his head after sipping his tea. "No, there is nothing more for you to do today."¶

Saddling up his horse, Ronin headed for the servants' quarters at the other end of the palace grounds. "The master wishes us to collect contributions today, before the holiday weekend." Two men started hitching up the large wooden cart to their two-horse team. Most of what was to be collected would be packaged in burlap sacks, buckets and/or cages. The larger contributions, such as pigs and cows, would be delivered directly to the palace by either ranch hands or the owners themselves. Within ten minutes, they were ready to go. Ronin pulled out a small scroll, scanned over it quickly, then spoke. "We will start with the settlements to the west today." With a sharp whip of the reins, all three horses started trotting in unison.¶

After collecting wheat, rice, various vegetables, a dozen chickens, and some fruit, Ronin and the two servants found themselves on a long stretch of road to an outlying farm. This particular homestead was run by a single father with four daughters and a young son. As they approached, they saw several men harassing the family and their livestock. "Stay here!" Ronin told the servants. "Guard the cart. I will go see what is going on." He squeezed his legs together a couple of times and his horse bolted forward towards the farm.¶

Once he got within ear shot, one of the men shouted. "Look out, here comes somebody!" Ronin was not wearing his formal armor and gear, so from a distance, they probably did not recognize him as a samurai. The other men shoved the father and one of the daughters to the ground and pulled out knives. "You'll do well to move along stranger. We have business to discuss with these people." Ronin slowed his horse and dismounted in one fluid motion. "What business requires physical violence?" He asked. "Are you okay, sir, ma'am?" He walked towards the two as they were attempting to get to their feet. But the men shoved them back into the dirt with the business end of their boots. Now all three men started walking menacingly towards Ronin, with a fourth coming from behind the house.¶

The samurai quickly assessed these men as

best he could and decided not to pull his sword. "You are trespassing on my master's land. If you do not wish to be arrested, I suggest you leave from here and do not return." The four men laughed at his offer. "Let me see." Their leader began. "There are four of us, and only one of you. The way we see it, we also get a horse out of the deal." The would-be bandits advanced on Ronin. The samurai thought back to the wise words of his master. *"If you are willing to kill, you are willing to die. But, there are times when mercy can be shown, and you do not need to kill."* Taking a step towards the men, Ronin did not want the children to see men being kill. Like his master, he preferred being loved and respected by the people, instead of being feared.¶

He waited for the first attacker to lunge at him with his knife. In close-quarter combat, he was trained more for defense and countering. Disarming the bandit with little effort, his opponent quickly found himself face down in the grass. The remaining three men rushed him at the same time. Ronin took a low side stance and placed all his weight onto his right leg. He swung an open palm strike into the side of one of the bandit's knee. The man buckled; his momentum carried him over Ronin's head and into another bandit, sending them both sprawling to the ground.¶

The samurai stood to face the fourth attacker. Being somewhat hesitant after seeing his comrades bested, their leader swung defensively as he stepped forward to attack. Ronin sent a roundhouse kick which connected with the man's elbow. There was a loud cracking noise, which indicated a broken bone. The bandit leader let out a scream as he dropped his knife and grabbed his arm. Dropping to his knees, he begged for mercy. Two of the other bandits scrambled to their feet and took off running. The third was still rolling around on the ground, clutching his chest and breathing shallowly, it was obvious that he had the wind knocked out of him.¶

Ronin returned to his horse, wrote a quick letter, and attached it to the leg of a homing pigeon he kept in a small cage strapped to the back side of the saddle. "I have sent for a doctor and law enforcement to come." He then proceeded to bind both bandits around the ankles with some rope, then tied them to a corner fence post. Ronin then motioned for the servants to bring the cart up near the house. The farmer then loaded a bushel of apples and a bushel of pears. Two of his daughters came from the house with bowls full of freshly made won-ton soup for the samurai and his two traveling companions. The aroma quickly filled their nostrils; they thanked them for the soup and enjoyed every bite.¶

Ronin and the servants managed to finish over half of his master's lands; the cart was nearly overflowing with contributions. It was time to return to the palace and place the foods into their respective root cellars and storage bins near the kitchen. They would be able finish collecting the rest of the food by the middle of the afternoon the following day. The picked up their pace as they neared the palace as the sun set beyond the horizon. It was completely dark as they entered through the front gates. Ronin instructed the servants to store the food and take care of the horses while he cataloged the haul and reported in.¶

As the two servants began taking bags of various grains from the cart, Ronin notices the guard by the back entrance to the kitchen and dining room was not at his post. He stowed his paperwork in a saddle bag and ran stealthily over to the door. Turning the knob, he found that it was unlocked; which was unusual for this time of night. He motioned for the two men to come to him. "Stop what you are doing and return to your quarters." Ronin said with urgency. "Secure your doors and do not come out until I or a guard comes to give you the all clear." He did not want to alarm the servants too much, but he was always taught to give priority to safety above all else. Sometimes it is better to raise a false alarm than no alarm at all, especially if lives could be at risk.¶

Ronin placed his right palm on the handle of his katana; he slowly cracked the door open with his left. Looking across the floor, he saw one of the cooks face down in a small pool of blood. Pulling his sword, he crept into the kitchen in full defensive mode. He rushed as quickly and quietly as he could behind the counter and knelt to check on the servant. The cook was not breathing, and there was no pulse. Turning him onto his side, it was apparent that his throat was slashed very precisely. Ronin's instincts led him to only one conclusion… ninjas. At this point, it took all his samurai training to remain calm. His thoughts first went to his master; it was obvious someone wanted the Snake Blade.¶

Ronin had no idea when the siege first started, he could only assume his master would be in the great hall, waiting for his report. Keeping to the shadows, he made his way through the dining room and out into the greeting hall. There were several dead bodies, most of whom he recognized as palace staff. "Where are the guards?" He thought to himself as he continued to the great hall. Ronin did not have the time to retrieve his armor, he would have to rely on skill alone to defend his master and the sacred Snake Blade.¶

Peering into the large room through a cracked door, he saw that it was too late. His master had fallen, and there were five ninjas searching the entire area. Ronin knew that, in a palace this size, there would be many more assassins roaming the grounds looking for an item as valuable as the Snake Blade. At this point, he no longer cared who was after the sword; his priority was to secure the weapon and keep it from falling into enemy hands. His master had told him long ago that, in a situation such as this, the safety of the Snake Blade came before all else. Ronin was instructed to defend the sacred sword at all cost. Were it to find itself in the possession of the wrong leader, evil could easily spread across the entire country, and thousands would become enslaved or even killed. Ronin would not allow that to happen… not on his watch!¶

Running down the hallway that ran parallel to the kitchen, he rounded the corner slowly. The path to the nearest window was clear of enemies.

Climbing out onto the ledge, he flipped up onto the roof and made his way towards the stables. Reaching the edge of the roof, Ronin spied a ninja creeping along the wall. Reaching into one of his hidden pockets, he threw a kunai (a small Japanese throwing dagger) directly into the back of the ninja's skull, dropping him instantly. Scaling down the brick wall, he retrieved his small blade and dragged the body towards the stables and hid it beneath some hay.¶

Making his way inside, Ronin made absolutely sure no one had seen him enter the structure. Creeping to the far corner, he removed a few items from a medium size table that was bolted to a larger work bench. Twisting one of the legs, he then lifted it at an angle, revealing a secret passageway. Jumping down as quietly as he could, he closed it behind him. Since the palace grounds were overrun, he dared not light a torch. He made his way through the maze of tunnels by memory. Each corner had grooves carved into the stonework that only he and his master could decipher as a map. In complete darkness, it took him nearly an hour to navigate safely to his desired destination; a secret room beneath his master's bed chambers.¶

He could hear several ninjas with their leader speaking rather loudly from above. They had no idea where the Snake Blade was, nor did they have a clue how to activate the hidden staircase in the middle of the room. Ronin quickly retrieved the weapon, still wrapped in silk inside a bamboo case. He left the same way he entered, but took an alternate route that would lead him outside the palace walls. It took him over two hours, but he and the Snake Blade were safe. Climbing out of the tunnel far beyond the walls, he found himself in the woods beneath a strategically placed row of decorative hedges near the private temple.¶

He could hear shouts of alarm coming from the nearside of the stables; someone had discovered the body under the hay. He had gone unnoticed for over three hours, which proved to be enough time to complete his master's last, and most important, task. Ronin fetched his bow and a quiver of arrows from its storage just outside the temple. With the amount of activity going on near the front gate he had to hurry. He took aim at, who appeared to be, the leader of this clan. But holding for a few seconds, he stopped. He would have surely given away his position. Despite all his training, revenge was still on his mind. "Run, my friend!" Ronin heard his master's voice inside his head. Stowing his weapons beneath his robes, he ran. He would have to wait another day to avenge his master's death.¶

*¶

It took Ronin three months to make his way to the Kamchatka Peninsula. He first followed the less traveled trading routes used by farmers and lower-level merchants; these routes were not targeted by thieves because nothing of substantial value was ever hauled along the substandard paths. He then secured a wasen (a traditional Japanese boat), fishing gear, and several months' rations; which took nearly all the money he had. The samurai lived on the wasen for weeks, traveling along the Kuril Islands and arriving in Petropavlovsk-Kamchatsky. It was the biggest city on the peninsula, and housed over fifty percent of Kamchatka's population. In a city of over 180,000 people, he found work until he had saved up enough to continue to Alaska. His research over the last few months told him that Alaska was an independent state which lead to a country called Canada. Once there he would travel south where many other independent states lied.¶

Once restocked, he laid in a course across the open ocean for the Near Islands. With all his survival skills, and a bit of luck, he could make it there in just over eight days. He ate mostly rice and the occasional salmon he caught, along with citrus fruits to ward off scurvy. The weather was mostly kind, and he only experienced one minor storm that lasted a mere four hours. And when the sun rose on the eighth day, he finally spied land.¶

Following his arrival, he again restocked his wasen with supplies and continued to Canada. He traveled along the coastline and only went ashore to work and gather more supplies. Ronin managed to reach the Canadian border in just over a month and a week. It had been nearly twenty weeks before a lone ninja assassin caught up with him. Luckily he managed to lose him in a crowded fish market; Ronin had no desire to kill anyone in this country. The laws here were vastly different than from those in his homeland. He did not wish to go to jail anytime soon.¶

The months seemed to drag on as he made his way along the coastline; he traveled along Washington State, Oregon, and California. Once he made port in Santa Monica, he decided to sell his sea craft and head west. The next several weeks saw Ronin travel through the beautiful countryside of this new and foreign land. Although they looked slightly different, he hunted rabbit, deer, squirrel, and wild boar. Fresh red and white meats were a welcome change to fish and other seafood. Over the course of the next year, he managed to travel through Arizona, New Mexico, and into Texas. Heading into the next town to trade furs and dried meats, he looked up at the sign; even though he could not yet read this new language, he liked to look for letters and characters that seemed familiar. The sign read, "Welcome to Blackwater."¶

Walking down the side of the road, he came upon a stranger riding a peculiar machine. The man pulled over and dismounted what looked like a metal horse. Smiling and waving, he approached Ronin in a non-threatening manner. He smiled and bowed his head to the stranger; he could tell that he meant him no harm. The man held out his hand. Ronin recognized this gesture from his days trading at the fish markets all along the coast. He smiled and shook the stranger's hand and said... "Hello."¶

*¶

The sun hung low in the Texas sky, casting shadows across the parking lot of The Rustic Forge. Dan had been running the business for the last ten years. And although he was not as skilled as Butch, he was still successfully turning a tidy profit. "Ding, Ding." The front door rang out as a gentleman opened the door for a young lady. It was Daisy, now almost twenty-three, she was as beautiful as her mother. "Hello, Dan. I hope I'm not too early." She placed her purse on the counter and rummaged through it looking for a letter she had folded up. "You're never too early, Sis." Dan had come to calling her Sis instead of Daisy as they felt like family, and since he was nearly a decade older, he was a big brother of sorts.¶

"I received another correspondence from Uncle Scotty and Aunt Jill." Daisy said, opening the letter and handing it to Dan. "Where is this one from?" He inquired. As Scotty and Jill were still being pursued by hit-men tied to Dead-Eye Inc., they sent letters whenever they traveled. "This one came from Toluca, Mexico. Oh, I want to visit there one day." Daisy sighed. "From their letter, the scenery there is gorgeous." Dan took the letter and read through its entirety. "Sounds like they're doing well. But we've yet to hear anything about Butch." Daisy's mood changed abruptly. "Those A-holes downtown told me our last appeal to keep his missing persons case open was denied." She nearly cried, but managed to choke back the tears for the moment.¶

"We could always hire an investigator." He offered. "No." She replied. "I've been told by our lawyer that would be too expensive and most likely not get any results. He did however tell me we should put out a bounty on him." Dan looked puzzled. "But he's not wanted for any crimes." "Doesn't matter. A private citizen can put a bounty on someone for their safe return. The law would look at it as if we were tracking him down to collect a debt or other personal business. As long as we aren't hiring someone to harm him, it's fine." Daisy took out the lawyer's business card with a date and time written on the back and handed it to Dan. "We just need to decide on how much we're willing to pay."¶

Dan took the card and pondered a moment. "What if we find out he's... well... if he's...?" He did not want to finish his question out loud. "If he's dead." Daisy whispered softly. "We'd still pay the bounty. At least we'd know. And then we could reopen his missing persons case and get him justice. We owe him... you owe him that much." Dan looked away from Daisy's stare. "I know I owe him, a great deal. I'm just worried that whatever happened to him and your aunt and uncle, and Max and Rattler... Those people might start coming after us if we snoop too hard." He turned and met her gaze. "They love us and want to keep us safe. Would they want anything to happen to us because of all of this?" "I guess you're right, it's just…" "I know, Sis. We'll discuss this more over dinner." Dan turned out the lights and locked up. He and Daisy walked down the street to a small café just as the sun started to set.¶

*¶

"I now call this meeting of The Black Bull Society to order." Said Mr. Bull, lighting a cigar as Mr. Lucas stood to his feet. "The Gatling gun is finally finished. All preliminary tests have been done, and we've corrected the jamming error from the previous model." Mr. Lucas turned to Mr. Bull and smiled. "And it only took you nine and half years." Mr. Bull said sarcastically. "But the improvements don't end there. You don't need two men to operate this model." Sarcasm turned to astonishment. "How did your team manage that?" He asked. "Well, after many tests, we decided to on two different methods of transportation. First, it can be mounted inside a carriage or in a wagon."¶
Every member at the table quickly opened the file folders in front of them and looked at proposed sketches. "As you can see in the

drawings, one side of the carriage can swing open, revealing the Gatling gun mounted on a sturdy tripod. Or, if surprise isn't needed, it can simply be attached to the flatbed of almost any wagon capable of carrying the load." Mr. Bull started flipping through the next couple of pages. "And the second method of transportation?" "Page eight, sir." Said Mr. Lucas. "It can be mounted on wheels. This weapon takes the idea of a tripod, and makes it portable. And it takes only one man to operate."¶

Looking over the drawings, Mr. Hughes spoke up. "What about the ammunition for the portable option on wheels?" Mr. Lucas was ready for that question. "Half of the total ammunition is carried beneath the gun, and the other half is carried on the back of the operator. It only takes a few seconds to attach the belts before firing." "Question." Said Mr. White. "How many rounds can be fired in total, and how fast?" "As fast as 250 rounds per minute. Of course, nearby soldiers can also carry additional rounds."¶

Within thirty minutes, as the meeting came to an end, Mr. Bull had contemplated future sales in his head. He already made a mental list of over half a dozen clients who would be willing to pay top dollar for this technology.¶

*¶

Rattler had already returned from the river with some freshly caught spotted bass for lunch. Ronin gathered vegetables and herbs from their vast garden which now spanned over an entire acre of land. They had built a permanent hut for sleeping; a root cellar for storage; a combat arena; a workstation for preparing food; and a small fishery attached to the river to store caught fish. They were totally self-sufficient on their claimed property.¶

As the fish started frying over the fire, Ronin sat on the bench made from an old log and motioned for Rattler to sit as well. "The time has come for me to tell you more about the Snake Blade." Rattler had been waiting a long time for his master to share the lore behind the mysterious sword. Ronin had been protecting it for nearly twelve years now, and Rattler was about to learn the reasons why. "Last night I had a vivid dream about my journeys to this land, and it reminded me that I cannot continue on forever." Ronin had a look on his faced that expressed both seriousness and peacefulness as he continued. "It all started hundreds of years ago on my master's ancestors' land."¶

Rattler turned the fish over on the spit as the

story progressed. "Many people in Japan thought the lands they owned were magical. The waters that flowed throughout its borders were the purest anyone had ever collected. The fish caught from it were always large and healthy. The grains that grew were the tallest in all the lands. The fruits were sweeter than any other. Everything that grew, caught, or was eaten seemed better than anywhere else." Ronin stirred the coals in the fire while he spoke. "The mines yielded high quality ores, some of which were found nowhere but on the master's land. One day he commissioned a sword be made from three different ores by the most talented blacksmith in all Japan. It took several weeks to forge the metals just right. When completed, the sword was perfectly balanced. It was said it was also the sharpest ever made. And after a while, it began showing mystical properties."¶

"What kind of mystical properties?" Asked Rattler. "There weren't too many specifics about the blade, that's why it's so mysterious. Whomever wielded the sword was never defeated in battle. My master's ancestors were never challenged over border disputes or business dealings. Their family and all who dwell in their lands prospered for nearly two hundred years, until…" "Until The Black-

Hearted Six challenged them, right?" Ronin smiled at his student. "You remember that story, do you?" "That's one of your best stories ever, sensei. Was The Great Samurai your master?" He asked. "No, it was my master's grandfather. A rival Lord coveted his lands and wanted them for his own. Ever since his defeat, he probably plotted to once again challenge my master's house. I believe it was this rival Lord's descendants who hired the ninja assassins to kill my master and seize the Snake Blade. That is why I was forced to flee Japan with it."¶

They ate their lunch of fish and vegetables before Ronin stood up. "Come, you must train even harder today now that you know that the Snake Blade will someday fall under your protection." Rattler was eager to continue with his training. It seemed like he grew a little stronger and a little faster every day. Ronin had never had such a dedicated student. "Let's start with your swimming exercises." Rattler disrobed down to his underpants and waded out into the middle of the river. He began swimming against the current. "If you can stay ahead of that tree for an hour," Ronin said, pointing fifty feet downstream. "then I will cook supper for you tonight. But if you cannot, you will cook for me." Rattler smiled. "You're on, sensei." He began backstroking and looked up at the clouds to focus on his breathing. He was confident his teacher would be fixing venison stew for supper.

CHAPTER XIV - The Death¶

Rattler had just finished dragging a hundred-pound log around their entire property using a homemade rope and leather harness. It had taken him only thirty-five minutes; a new record. Throwing the rope from his shoulders, Rattler approached Ronin who was busy packing their knapsacks for their trip to visit the

Blackfoot to trade herbs and other items. They traveled to the tribe every three months to keep in touch and relay messages to Dan and Daisy. His father and Butch were both still missing, and although it had not been confirmed, Butch was presumed dead. Rattler was hoping that now that he had turned eighteen, something would be different on this journey near home.¶

"I packed smoked meats, fruits, nuts, and seeds. We need to get going right away." Ronin spoke with earnest. Although Rattler was quite winded, he did not complain for a rest; he never complained or spoke against his teacher... his master. "Will I get to join you in town this time?" He waited for a reply, but already had an idea of the answer. "We will see what Chief White Cloud has to say, first." Rattler often wondered why Ronin took the Chief's counsel instead of making his own decisions. Perhaps with age came wisdom, and the tribe's warriors knew more about what was going on in Blackwater than he and Ronin. "I'm ready sensei, let's go." They jogged at a steady pace for over an hour before stopping to rest.¶

Sitting in the shade, they took out a small snack and talked for a while. "Sensei, are you checking out the ranch this time?" Rattler asked. "I will speak to Dan and Daisy. They told me they would talk to their lawyer about the legal status of the property. I do not know how we could return to your old life. Those responsible for all that has happened know that Max had a son. If you return to claim and live on the ranch, your life would immediately be endangered." Ronin did not like sounding all doom and gloom, but the reality of the situation could not be ignored. "I was thinking of selling the property." Rattler replied. "I do not wish for my old life back. Even though my father and I lived very comfortably, I would prefer the life that I have now. We don't need the money, so I was thinking of giving it to the Blackfoot Tribe. They would use it to do good, charitable things with it."¶

Ronin was glad to hear those words come from his student's mouth, but he hoped he was not competing with Max for the boy's loyalty. "Your father was also a very charitable man. I hope that one day this will all be resolved and you can be reunited with him." Ronin did not know what else to say to the young man about what was going on, so he decided to focus on their journey. "I hope for that as well, sensei. I prefer training and defending innocent people to working on a ranch. If we ever fine my dad, I want him to come live with us on our farm."

Ronin could see how passionate Rattler was, but it was time to get going.¶

All of Rattler's extreme training and conditioning had been paying off. When they first traveled from The Golden Snake to where they lived now, it had taken ten days. But over the years they made the trip faster each time; and now they could make the hundred-mile journey in just under a week's time. As they approached the main entrance, they were met by a handful of young Blackfoot warrior scouts. They escorted them directly to the middle of camp where Chief White Cloud was awaiting their arrival.¶

"Welcome my friends. I am very eager to speak with you both. The spirits have revealed much to me in the past few days. They knew you would be coming and have told me a great many things about the near future." The Chief said with a smile. "Come, let us break bread together before we speak of such things." Several young maidens arrived with bowls of Indian corn soup and fry bread. After eating the delicious meal, they retired to a corner of the grounds. "We aren't going to your quarters?" Asked Rattler. "Today we need as much fresh air as we can get, a horrible storm is coming tonight." The trio walked through the fields to a little, out-of-the-way circle of logs with a small fire be attending to by a young Blackfoot maiden. She stood up, nodded politely, and left them alone.¶

"The spirits have told me a great many things concerning Rattler's destiny. He has become immune to brother snake's venom. He has been given another gift as well." Rattler listened contently. "What gift is that, sir?" "Patience young one, it will come to you when you need it most. You will also wield a weapon of great power one day soon as well." Ronin and Rattler made eye contact, and the sensei knew exactly what the chief had meant by that statement. The Snake Blade will once again be wielded by a great samurai warrior; one who is worthy to use it against evil.¶

"The spirits have also given me a warning about you, Mr. Ronin." Ronin paused for a second. "The spirits look over me as well? But I'm not from here." The wise Indian Chief merely smiled, and continued speaking. "The Great Spirits are concerned with all living creatures. It does not matter where you are from. They speak to anyone who is patient enough to listen." Chief White Cloud then looked serious for a moment. "They are warning you about a traveler from a distant land. He means to do you harm, and take something of great value." Ronin knew the mysterious clan of ninja assassins would not stop until the Snake Blade was in the hands of the person who hired them.¶

"Please stay the night here in our village. Tomorrow you can go to town to do what needs to be done. Rattler can train with our young warriors in the morning." As spoke, the chief rose to his feet and stretched. "I am growing tired, so I will turn in for the night. Come, let us return to the others, they are preparing a place for you to rest." Ronin and Rattler both thanked him for his hospitality and followed him back to the main part of the village. Even though the sun had not yet set over the horizon, Ronin and Rattler fell asleep after their long journey.¶

*¶

Ronin was already gone when Rattler awoke. "How does he do that?" He thought to himself. Although the ground was very wet, Rattler had managed to sleep through the storm. There were several young Blackfoot warriors waiting about twenty yards from his quest quarters. "We were going to start with a little target practice before we go hunting." Said one of the warriors. By the looks of him, Rattler guessed he was around his age, maybe a little older. Most of the warriors were teenagers, once they reached their twenties, they usually married and did not train with the younger, single men. Rattler grabbed his own bow and quiver from his knapsack and followed the others to the target range.¶

Once they arrived, they seemed to line up according to their age; oldest at the front. The first warrior approached the line, cocked his bow, waited several seconds, and then let the arrow fly. It hit a few inches from dead center and the rest of the warriors cheered. Several more took their turns but none came closer than the first. They waved for Rattler to take his turn. He approached the line, but before reaching it, he cocked and fired all in one fluid motion. His arrow hit dead center. He drew a second, cocked and fired again and grazed the first arrow and hit nearly dead center again. He then drew again, cocked and fired and hit between the first two arrows, nearly dead center for a third time. The rest of the warriors stared in awe of the feat they had just witnessed.¶

Rattler walked down range to retrieve his arrows and returned to the firing line. "What are we going to hunt today, I'm all warmed up." The other warriors cheered and laughed, patting Rattler on his shoulder. They were always impressed with his skill with the bow, as well as the sword. "We were thinking whitetail or mule deer. We need at least four to feed the village."

They all gathered their gear and headed out to the forest. They were all wondering who would take down the first deer.¶

*¶

Ronin arrived at Daisy's house and was waiting on the corner of the porch, He had already checked several locations to gather intelligence on how much Dead-Eye Inc. had progressed with their illegal activities. From the information he had pieced together over the past year, Dead-Eye had indeed managed to reproduce its Gatling gun that Max had destroyed ten years ago. But this newer weapon would probably be an improvement over the last one, given the time spent in its development.¶

Daisy came to the door and let Ronin inside. The first couple of visits, she was startled to find him on her porch so early. Be she was used to it as he needed to travel a few places before the sun rose. "How are you and Rattler doing?" Daisy asked, pouring him a glass of orange juice and sitting at the table. "We are doing well. Rattler trains much harder than I did at his age. He will soon surpass me in skill." "I've been meaning to tell you about The Golden Snake." Daisy said, taking a drink of her juice and continuing. "Our lawyer told me that the money

Max had placed in the bank to cover property taxes is almost gone. The county lowered them after the fire. But there is only enough left for about four months. What should we do?" Daisy did not really know why she was asking Ronin, he was not well educated in Texas laws regarding property taxes and such.¶

"Rattler wishes to sell the property and give all the money to the Blackfoot tribe to do with as they see fit." "Really, he doesn't want any of it. That property is his inheritance, assuming Max does not return to claim it." Daisy was puzzled as to why he felt this way. "I see you are concerned about this." Ronin responded. "He has grown to become self-reliant. We have been living off the land for the past decade. Rattler knows a great deal about growing crops. We also hunt and fish for our meat. Other than that, he spends most of the day training. He has grown very strong, and very fast. He only wishes to help those in need with his skill. One day soon we will return to stop Dead-Eye from achieving their goal of mass-producing a fully automatic weapon to sell on the black market."¶

Ronin stood and finished the last of his orange juice. "Thank you for the drink, but Rattler and I must return home. Chief White Cloud warned us about a threat and we must prepare for it." Daisy stood as well. "Is there anything I can do to help? Are there any supplies I can send with you?" "There is one thing you can do." Ronin replied. "We do not know how to sew, and most of our clothes are becoming worn out…" "Say no more." Said Daisy. "I still have Uncle Scotty's clothes in a steamer trunk upstairs. Take what you wish." Ronin followed her upstairs and took only four outfits; two for Rattler, and two for himself. "Thank you, these are sturdy clothes and should last us a while."¶

Ronin packed everything into his knapsack and returned to the Blackfoot Indian tribe. Rattler had returned around the same time, and a feast was underway in the center square. Several warriors killed two whitetail deer and one mule deer, but Rattler had taken down a wild boar. The boar came at a less experienced warrior, who froze as the tusked animal charged towards him. Rattler took it down from nearly fifty yards away, saving the young man's life. Within minutes, the large pig was on a spit over a roaring fire. The boy's parents thanked Rattler for his bravery and quick thinking. Ronin could not have been prouder of his pupil.¶

As soon as the mid-day meal ended, Ronin and Rattler set out for home. They did not eat too much at the feast, but took some of the meat with them. The two of them generally eat small portions of food every few hours, as their training kept them very active. *A full samurai is a slow samurai.* This was their motto, and they followed it religiously.¶

"Sensei." Rattler started to ask a question. "I would like to try something when we get closer to home. Could we take a little detour to that small canyon?" "What would you like to do?" His teacher asked. "I want to see if what Chief White Cloud said is true." He replied. Ronin had an idea of where this was going. "You mean to find a great basin rattlesnake and let it bite you?" "A smaller one, yes. I want to know for sure. My routine injections stopped years ago." Ronin agreed, and on their seventh day, they detoured south.¶

It only took Rattler about ten minutes to find the perfect specimen beneath a small outcropping of rocks. "I'll let him bite my left hand, that way I can still walk." He already had the snake cornered, and its rattle was shaking wildly. In a blink of an eye, the snake struck him on the meaty part of his hand, right between his pinkie and wrist. There was only a small amount of pain and blood. Ronin kept a close watch over the next several hours to see if he showed any signs of fatigue. They were only five hours away from home, if he were to show any signs, they had several vials of anti-venom stored in their root cellar in damp burlap sacks.¶

The rest of the day went as expected, Rattler showed no signs of any kind. There was absolutely no swelling; an average person could look at his hand and not even know he was bitten. Ronin and Rattler retrieved a small bass from their fishery and cooked it over fresh vegetables for supper. Turning in early, they slept soundly after talking a little more about the words of wisdom from the Indian chief.¶

*¶

The following day saw the two of them tending to their large garden, fishery, setting new snares, and reorganizing their root cellar. Training came and went, Rattler probably sweated off a couple of pounds, and they settled in around a warm fire for a late-night supper of BBQ squirrel, pine nuts, and mixed vegetables. "Tell me again about the process of making the Snake Blade, sensei." Rattler always liked to hear more about the weapon that would one day fall to him.¶

"When the miners stumbled across this unique, unknown metal ore deep in the mines, the tips of their pickaxes dented in and became dull." Ronin started his story of the making of the sword. "They had to find all of the edges and dig around it. Once removed from the earth, it was twice as big as a watermelon, and needed four men with ropes to life it into the cart. It was then taken to a special forge that needed to reach 3,500 degrees Fahrenheit. Since that is the highest a forge can burn, it took several blacksmiths to maintain such a temperature in order to create the sword with all three metals." Ronin stirred the fire and was about to continue when Rattler noticed a mostly yellow figure moving towards them on foot, with a little red and orange mixed in. "Sensei, someone is approaching from the north, he's about sixty, seventy yards away." Rattler stood up slowly to get a better look. Ronin looked in the same direction as Rattler. "I don't see anything, it's too dark."¶

"He's right there." Rattler said, pointing exactly where the man was crouching. "He just ducked behind a tree." Ronin strained to see, but still could not. "What does he look like, what kind of clothes is he wearing?" He asked. "I don't know, I only see a yellow and reddish figure." He answered. "This could be a highly skilled assassin, grab your things, we need to go... now!" "But sensei..." "I said grab your things!" Ronin almost shouted. It was unlike Rattler to question his teacher, but he did as he was told.¶

Ronin crept towards the tree where the would-be assassin was supposedly hiding. With his battle sword drawn he announced his presence. "I know you are there! Come out and identify yourself!" Without warning, a ninja leaped from the tree and landed behind Ronin. He was barely able to spin around and deflect the blow of a lightning fast katana. Several more followed, Ronin somehow knew this ninja was the assassin he had lost in the fish market all those years ago. It took all his skill to block each attack as he was forced back a step with each strike. He needed to turn the tides in his favor by going on offense, but the assassin was relentless in his attacks.¶

Nearing a boulder, Ronin knew he had to make a move, and make it fast. Once he was within reach, he shuffled back, placed the bottom of his left foot on the large rock and pushed out to the side of the ninja. He countered an expected thrust and swiveled his sword around, switching hand positions, and disarmed the ninja by flipping his sword up into the air. He lunged at the assassin's midsection, but his opponent was too fast. He jumped aside and squatted low to the ground, and as he stood back up, a fine smoky mist sprung from his hands, temporarily blinding the samurai. Ronin repeatedly swung in long, defensive arcs as he retreated backwards.¶

Suddenly, a shuriken plunged into his leg. He knew if he was going to survive this encounter, he had to make his way to the river. Taking only two seconds, Ronin reoriented himself and, knowing the entire area like the back of his hand, he turned and sprinted towards the water. He managed to reach the edge and splash a handful into his face before the ninja could retrieve his sword and catch up with him. Instead of being totally blind, everything was a blur; but it was just enough to be able to defend himself. He backed into the river as the ninja advanced. The water here would not go above his waist and soon he was emerging on the other side. The assassin, not wanting to get wet, took a running start and jumped the twenty feet to the other side. But it gave Ronin the opportunity to scoop up a handful of sand and fling it into the ninja's face.¶

With the playing field now leveled, the samurai had the chance to go on the offensive. Ronin shuffled forward, determined to drive the ninja back into the water before he could wipe the sand from his eyes. Feeling his back foot stepping into wet ground, the assassin cartwheeled to his left and flipped backwards several times, putting a little distance between them. Ronin turned and continued his attack, driving the ninja towards the edge of their campfire. With his vision slowly returning to normal, Ronin swung and slashed through the air to insure the ninja would not be able to come within striking distance.¶

The battle continued for several minutes, neither quite gaining the upper hand. But as time went on, the injury to his leg started to slow Ronin down ever so slightly. And on one of his defensive swings, the ninja's blade managed to slice him across his other leg. A couple more swings and the ninja went in for the kill. Their blades connected as Ronin held firm in a defensive stance. The assassin's blade slid the entire length to the hilt, and spinning completely around, plunged it into Ronin's back as he knelt by the fire. "NOOOoooo!" Shouted Rattler as Ronin fell face down in the dirt. The assassin looked up as a new combatant appeared on the other side of the dwindling fire.¶

"You think you are worthy to wield that sword, peon.?" The assassin stood up straight, seemingly unafraid of Rattler. "I mean to take that sword back with me to my employer. So, I suggest you give it to me." He threatened. "Hand it over now, and I will let you live." "If you are willing to kill." Rattler proclaimed as he pointed the Snake Blade at the ninja. "You are willing to die." The ninja cracked his neck. "So be it." He raised his weapon and leaped to attack.¶

Rattler raised the Snake Blade to deflect the blow. His mind was racing with what just took place, he needed to stay focused. If this man could defeat his teacher, what chance did he have. He did not wish to dwell on that, but instead, chose to think of the words of the great Indian chief, White Cloud. "You will also wield a weapon of great power one day…" Not only did those words give him courage, but he remembered that whomever wielded the sacred sword could not be defeated in battle. "Just because you possess the Snake Blade, doesn't mean you can't be destroyed." The assassin taunted. "You must also be a great warrior. And you are merely a boy. Your best chance of victory is lying face down in the dirt." Rattler knew the ninja was trying to make him loose focus. But he would not allow it, and his master's training would not allow it.¶

"You are not facing a mere boy, but a true samurai." Rattler proclaimed as he blocked blow after blow from the skilled ninja. "I have been training for over ten years by samurai and Blackfoot Indian for the sole purpose of defending this weapon from falling into the wrong hands." A smile came across Rattler's face as he spoke. Knowing that his words were true, he was at peace within himself; a decade of training had led to this confrontation. "You had never trained for someone like me." The assassin continued to try and play mind games with him, but it would prove useless as the fight went on.¶

The ninja pulled three shuriken from his clothing and aimed straight for Rattler's head, chest, and stomach in quick succession. He was astonished as this mere boy blocked all three with what appeared to be little effort. The Snake Blade simply moved faster than what seemed humanly possible in a blur of black, brown and orange. Not wanting to underestimate his opponent any further, the ninja doubled his efforts and let fly a series of attacks to gain some ground. He then pulled a second supply of dust and flung it near Rattler's face. Most of the cloud reached its target, but Rattler could still see the vivid colors of the assassin's body amidst the darkness. The ninja was stunned that he was still able to block strike after strike when any other opponent would have started swinging wildly after becoming mostly blind.¶

"How can you still see?" The ninja asked without thinking. "I can see your body heat signature." He answered. "There is no way for you to surprise me. I am much younger and much faster." Now it was Rattler's turn to taunt and unnerve the assassin. "I have been a trained assassin longer than you've been alive, boy!" The ninja continued his assault as they bantered back and forth. "But my master says that I train harder than any three students he has ever taught, so I'd say we're even." Rattler felt more comfortable as the fight went on, he spent much of his days training for stamina. Battles with Ronin sometimes lasted over an hour, and this one had barely reached three minutes. His master told him that ninjas used the art of surprise as their best weapon. Speed and accuracy was how they trained. Stretching the fight beyond ten, and even fifteen minutes, would surely discourage a ninja.¶

Since he had time on his side, Rattler continued to play defense to wear the assassin down. As the minutes ticked by, the ninja became more and more frustrated. He tried several times to deliver a death strike, but each time Rattler countered and sent the ninja scrambling to recover. With a flurry of long-arcing slices, the ninja tried once more to end the fight; Rattler took this opportunity to make a statement. He spun with the ninja's blade and continued in a circle, and bringing the Snake Blade around and upwards, sliced the ninja across the face. Jumping back and checking his wound, the assassin took a moment to regroup and think about his next move.¶

Rattler held his weapon up in defense. "Why are you even seeking the Snake Blade? Are you content on letting a ruthless man change the balance of power in your homeland over money?" The ninja thought about those words for a second. "It matters not whom has the power, as long as our clan is well-compensated for my work. What does it matter to you anyway?" He asked in a gruff voice. Rattler rolled his shoulders around, stretching a bit. "It mattered to my master, and so it matters to me." He said. "Do you believe the sword I wield is sacred?" He was not really expecting an answer.¶

"That sword is merely a symbolized trophy. Any leader that possesses it gains control over the masses as a true ruler." Rattler shook his head. "Should it not find itself in the right hands then?" The ninja seemed a little confused. "You think your fallen master was the right person to wield the sword?" Rattler lowered his sword slightly. "He never wielded the sword, he merely protected it." The ninja stood straight and let his own sword point to the earth. "Do you believe you, a foreigner, should become a ruler in Japan?" Rattler again shook his head. "I do not intend to be a ruler of anything. I only wield this blade because an Indian chief told me I would accomplish great things and defend those who could not defend themselves." Rattler paused a moment before continuing. "I will say this, I am wielding the sacred Snake Blade, and you cannot defeat me. So, there seems to be truth in the story, wouldn't you say?"¶

The ninja dropped his sword at his feet. "What would you have me do then? I am honor-bound to carry out my mission or die." Rattler cautiously sheathed the sword. "For a sacred weapon to be taken from someone worthy enough to wield it and given to someone who is not... where is the honor in that?" The assassin, for the first time in a long time, was at a loss for words. "Since you have failed, then I should kill you." Said Rattler. The ninja lowered his head. "But the memory of my teacher would be completely dishonored from such an act. He told me that it is sometimes better to show mercy than to kill. As much as it saddens me that he is now gone, it would be sadder if his death meant nothing."¶

The ninja and the young samurai talked for hours; shared stories of things that had transpired over the last several years, and came to an understanding that there was more to the plans of the Lord that hired his clan than simply owning a sacred weapon. There had been whispers up and down the coasts, from Japan and Russia, throughout Alaska and Canada, every state from Washington to Texas. An entirely new enemy had casted its shadow across both of their homes, and if someone did not stop it, lives for thousands of miles would be at risk. There is a secret organization known only as The Black Bull Society.¶

"A ruler possessing the Snake Blade and nearly infinite wealth, would be in a very good position to purchase all the illegal weapons produced at Dead-Eye Inc." Rattler stated. "You have seen a rifle before, haven't you?" "I have seen a rifle, very good for taking down wild game, but not as effective in taking down a ninja." "That is only true because it can only fire one bullet at a time. But how would a ninja fair against a rifle that could fire over a hundred bullets within seconds?" The ninja smiled oddly and laughed. "There is no such weapon in existence." "Yes, there is." Said Rattler. "My father is missing, his close friends are in hiding, and my Uncle was killed because they had evidence of such a weapon."¶

"If that is true, then the contract with my employer is hereby invalid." The ninja rose to his feet. "But I need to see with my own eyes this weapon you speak of. What do you suggest we do?" Rattler thought thoroughly for a minute. "Give me two weeks. If you come with me, I will get you the proof you seek." The two made a blood oath that evidence would be found within the two weeks, and a temporary truce would be upheld during that time. The ninja pondered long and hard over the consequences for his clan and his family if what Rattler had told him were true.

CHAPTER XV - A New Team¶

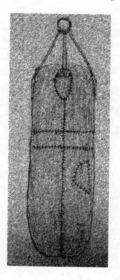

It was 2:00 a.m. in the morning when Rattler and Tsume, the ninja assassin, arrived in Blackwater. They were sticking to the shadows, and heading directly towards Dead-Eye Inc. Their plan was to break in and find enough evidence to convince Tsume of the plans to manufacture and distribute the illegal, fully automatic weapon. "And remember," Said Rattler. "Zero body count." The ninja agreed as they circled around the perimeter of the property to find the best place to enter.¶

As soon as Rattler saw the loading docks, he remembered something. "My father and I did a job here when I was about eight years old." He said. "Come to think of it, this is probably where he stumbled across that evidence. We'll enter here." Scaling the fence, they managed to avoid a guard with a lantern walking from around a corner. "There's a pipe running up that side of the building." Whispered Tsume. "We should get up to the roof, there's probably a way in up there." "That'll work." Replied Rattler. "As soon as that guard is around the next corner, we make our move." Within a minute, they had their opening. The ran swiftly across the yard and made it to the pipe unseen. "You go first." Tsume insisted. Rattler did not hesitate; he climbed the thirty-foot pipe in what seemed like seconds. Tsume followed closely behind, only not quite as fast. The ninja was impressed with the young man's skill.¶

Once on the roof, they looked around for any entrance that they would be able to squeeze through. Scanning for a few seconds, they spied a trap door, probably used by maintenance. They crept over and tried the latch. "It's locked!" Tsume announced. "I'll be right back." Replied Rattler. He ran back over to the pipe and slid back to the ground. After about two minutes, the ninja saw him climb back onto the roof with a six-foot metal pipe. Using a knife, they pried up the corner just enough to fit in the pipe. They both leaned on the exposed portion and managed to break the lock and gain entrance to the four by four shaft lined with a ladder leading to the bottom.¶

Reaching the ground floor leading to a maintenance tunnel, they found their way to the main part of the building overlooking several different offices. Peering into each window, Tsume quickly asked. "What exactly are we looking for?" "We need to find some kind of large room, large enough to test such a weapon. There's going to be work tables and machinery." Rattler came up to a corner of a t-shaped hallway. Looking both ways, he saw another guard heading their way. Rattler flashed a look at Tsume and held up a finger to his lips, signaling to be quiet. As the guard approached their position, the ninja flipped in front of him, taking him by surprise. The restrained assassin choked him just enough to render him unconscious.¶

"I was worried for a second there." Rattler said with relief. "I promised a zero-body count." "That's why it was only a second." They dragged him to a hall closet and sat him in the corner. They continued down the hallway and came upon a large window looking into, what seemed to be, a testing facility. "This looks like the place." Said Rattler. "But I'm assuming it's locked as well." Checking the handle, he was right. "Give me a second." Tsume pulled a small case from his gi and proceeded to pick the lock with the tools inside. Entering the room, they began a thorough search.¶

After ten minutes had gone by, Tsume managed to find a section of the wall that pivoted 180 degrees, revealing a secret panel. He looked at the drawing and called Rattler over. "I think I found something." Rattler looked closely at the schematics. "You certainly did. This is exactly what we're looking for." Tsume looked a little confused. "You have to tell to me what this is. I only see a gun. What makes it fully automatic?" Rattler tried his best to explain, he had not seen a weapon schematic in such a long time. "Basically this firing pin here is altered in such a way that if you hold down the trigger, it will keep firing… Wait a minute?!" Rattler looked very closely at what he was just explaining. "This isn't the Gatling Gun that my father discovered, this is something else. We need to take this."¶

They examined the entire panel, but it was

behind at least an inch of hard plastic. Without the proper tools, they would be unable to retrieve them. "What are we going to do?" Asked Tsume. "Well do you at least believe me now?" Rattler asked. "I would have to say that I do believe you, Rattler. I will help you stop this destructive company." Tsume had a very serious look on his face. "If this gun is an improvement from the one you told me about earlier, things are much more dire. We need to get out of here and come up with a plan to stop them." Rattler nodded his head in agreement. It frustrated them both, but they would have to leave without the schematics.¶

Running back the way they came, Rattler returned to the closet where they stashed the unconscious guard. "What are you doing?" Asked Tsume. "We need to tie up a loose end. A little trick Ronin told me about." Rattler pulled the guard into the middle of the hallway and gently laid him flat on the floor. "I usually use this to sterilize a wound." He said as he pulled out a flask of alcohol. "But it will be more useful this way." He poured it on the guard's mouth, neck and chest. "This way, whatever he tries to tell the other guards…" "I get it." Said Tsume. "They won't believe him because they'll think he's drunk. Good, now let's get out of here."¶

They returned to the maintenance tunnel and climbed back up the ladder. "Here, let's pry the door all the way off the hinges and put it over by that wall. It just might fool someone into thinking the storm ripped it off." After they completed their task, they returned to the pipe. Making sure there were no guards around, the scaled down and place the metal pipe back where Rattler found it. Climbing back over the fence, they ran into a nearby group of trees and waited a few minutes to make sure no one was about. They continued over to Daisy's house where they slept a couple of hours on her porch, out of sight. Rattler needed to reconnect with some old friends.¶

*¶

Once Daisy finished preparing breakfast for her guests, she had many questions for Rattler. "I have not seen you in over ten years. What have you been doing all of this time?" She sat at her place at the table and took a bite of her eggs. "I've been training and building a life for myself down south. Ronin visited every three months, didn't he tell you everything that's been going on over the years?" Daisy put her fork down. "Where is Ronin by the way? And who is this?" Rattler and Tsume exchanged glances before he continued. "Ronin passed away." Daisy covered her mouth with her napkin in shock. "This is Tsume, he is going to train me in the art of ninjitsu and help us in our battle to stop Dead-Eye Inc."¶

They talked a while and caught up on how they each were doing, but they ultimately decided to pay Dan a visit and discuss things further. They helped her wash, dry and put away the dishes before they left for the Rustic Forge. Walking down the street, Daisy noticed how much Rattler had grown. For one, he was now much taller than she was. And although he was only eighteen, his arms and chest were almost as big as she remembered Butch's being. Rattler noticed her looking at him. "A penny for your thoughts." Daisy turned away, blushing slightly. "I'm just shocked at how much you've grown. The last time I saw you was when you got your name from Chief White Cloud, remember?" Rattler smiled. "Oh, yeah. We ate grilled chicken, salad, and went fishing all afternoon." They both chuckled a little as they continued down the street.¶

Crossing the road and turning down Mutt Street, they noticed a couple of scruffy ranchers heading towards them, staring intently as they walked. "Outta the way, new-cower!" One of them said rudely as he purposely bumped his shoulder into Tsume as he walked past him. "Hey watch it, buddy! Where are your manners?" Rattler said, turning around to face off against the two men. But Tsume held up the back of his hand to Rattler's chest to discourage him from saying anything further. The two men laughed and continued on their way down the road. "Why didn't you stand up for yourself?" Rattler asked Tsume. "There was nothing to stand up for." He replied." Those were just words from buffoons. If I had wanted to fight them, I would have won easily. They did not appear to be of any threat, so what would be the point?" Rattler quickly apologized. "I guess I still have much to learn, at least with my attitude. I just don't like bullies."¶

Within a few minutes they arrived at their destination. The Rustic Forge was not that busy for that time of the day, so Dan closed a little early for lunch so they could talk. Heading to the back, Dan gathered some papers from the countertop and handed them to Daisy. "Here's the legal papers our lawyer managed to get from the sheriff's office. Our appeal to reopen the case was denied." "What was denied?" Asked Rattler. "They have officially stopped looking for Butch." Daisy answered, looking through the documents. "And they say there is not enough evidence to prove foul play of any kind, so they're simply closing the case." The anger welled up inside of Rattler. Uncle Butch, along with Ronin, was like a second father to him. He still incorporated the basic boxing techniques he was taught into his daily training routine.¶

Seeing a heavy punching bag hanging in the corner, Rattler walked over and threw a punch with all he had. A "clang" sound emanated from inside the bag. "I never noticed that sound before." Said Dan. He walked over and inspected the bag. Then he lifted it up slightly. "This seems much heavier than it should be. Grab that and let's unhook this from the top and put it on the table." "Why?" Asked Daisy. "Because I think there's actually something inside the bag." Rattler and Dan carried the bag over to the table and laid it on its side so they could unzip it. Feeling through the stuffing, they came across something metallic. The pulled it from the bag and discovered what appeared to be a trench coat made from metal scales, like that of a snake. "I think this was meant for your father, Max." Dan said. "Butch made this. He must have hid it inside the bag before all of that bad stuff went down."¶

Holding it up at the shoulders, Daisy

commented. "It looks like it will fit you, Rattler." Dan agreed. "You're his son, and you're taking up the cause. I think you deserve it the most anyway." Rattler tried it on. It seemed as if it were tailor-made just for him. "I don't like the shine of the metal, though." Added Daisy. "I could cover it with snake skin to make it look like a normal coat. That way you can wear it all the time and not draw attention to yourself." Rattler walked around in it and imagined wearing it in a fight. With Butch's exceptional black-smithing talents, it should protect him from quite a bit. Tsume walked up and inspected the craftsmanship. "This is very fine work." Dan chimed in. "Hey, this could be an opportunity for me to try something new. I could make you a matching wide-brim, fedora to go with it. Complete the outfit, so to speak." Rattler liked the idea of wearing armor into a battle, but before he could say anything, Tsume pulled a shuriken from his sleeve and threw it directly at Rattler's shoulder. It merely struck the metal scales and fell to the floor. "What the…" Said Rattler. "Very fine work." Tsume repeated.¶

"What is this made of?" Rattler asked Dan. "It doesn't feel very heavy." Dan examined the scales for a moment. "I believe it's titanium. I've seen Butch work with it before, but it's quite expensive. I have never used it because no one has ever requested it. But it has the best strength to weight ratio of any metal I know of." Rattler ran his hand down one of the sleeves. "It feels just like snake skin. He must have spent a lot of time on this. Is there any way to find out how much this metal would have cost him?" "I could tell you in a just a couple of minutes, but why?" Dan took the coat and folded it carefully as he walked over to the scale next to the main work table.¶

"I want to reinvest that amount back into The Rustic Forge so we can fight Dead-Eye." Rattler stated matter-of-factly. Weighing the coat, Dan scribbled some numbers on a piece of paper and did some quick math calculations. "For the metal alone, probably around four hundred dollars or so." Rattler thought for a moment. "How can I make that kind of money? I've been living a simple life for the past decade. We grow our own fruits and vegetables; catch and prepare our own meats; we were pretty much self-reliant in all areas of our lives." Saying the word 'were' aloud hit Rattler emotionally. He sat on a stool as if he had the wind knocked out of him. His master was gone, and although he had forgiven Tsume for his death, it still hurt.¶

"You don't owe me, or The Rustic Forge, anything. We're in this together because we're like family." Dan said. Daisy chimed in as well. "If you're that concerned with money, couldn't you just sell some of your crops?" Rattler shook his head. "We eat pretty much all that we grow, and we trade animal skins for what we need. Any excess we have goes to some of the poorer families about six miles away. We haven't used actual money in years." He stood up to stretch. "Well." Said Dan. "If you're that serious, they still have that underground, bare-knuckle fighting circuit…" "I don't want Rattler getting hurt over money." Daisy interrupted. "The money is not that important."¶

"It might not be that important for you. And I appreciate your concern." Rattler disagreed. "But the decision is ultimately mine. And besides, I would consider it part of my training. The bonus is I get paid. Where do I sign up?" He added, jokingly. "I know some people that promote the fights. I could probably get you a preliminary fight next Friday. If you win, you could easily clear a thousand dollars in your next fight. It all depends on how many fights you are willing to accept." Dan said. Daisy seemed worried. "How many fights? He only needs four or five hundred dollars." "We're going to need a lot more than that if we're going up against Dead-Eye Inc. We'll need weapons and supplies. I want to contribute more than just muscle." Although she and Dan were financially stable, Rattler was right. They all needed to pull together as a family to fight the large, corrupt corporation.¶

*¶

Mr. Bull picked up the phone and called one of his biggest clients about the appointment for the demonstration of their new weapon. "Hello Mr. Jackson, I'm calling to confirm your attendance at the BBS Testing Range next Sunday afternoon." The phone was silent for a few seconds. "You can assure complete anonymity for me and my company?" "I can assure you a lot of things. I just need to know that you will be there, and more importantly, you are still interested in purchasing our product." Again, the phone was silent for a few seconds. "I will be there with one of my… associates." Mr. Bull chuckled slightly. "Bring as many associates as you see fit, just be on time and be ready to place any orders. I think you'll find our product to surpass your expectations."¶

As soon as he hung up the phone, Mr. White knocked on his door. "Here's the part of the list you had me deal with. How many people are planning to attend our little reception?" Mr. Bull placed his burning cigar on the side of his ashtray. "Twelve in all, not including associates." He smiled. "And I sense a bit of fear in some of the attendees, that's good." Mr. White seemed amused by his statement. "Fear sells weapons, but too much fear might drive away business." "Nonsense!" Said Mr. Bull. "Fear means loyalty. And loyalty means the law won't be able to touch us." "If you subscribe to that school of thought, maybe. If there's nothing else, I have other business to attend to."¶

Heading to his office, he was stopped by the head guard who had some information for him. "Sir, do you have a moment? I need to talk to you about an incident with one of the guards." Mr. White seemed impatient. "Did someone fall asleep on the job? Fire him and replace him with someone more reliable." He continued walking down the hall, but the head guard kept talking. "No sir, it's nothing like that. He claims a man dressed entirely in black wearing a mask knocked him unconscious last night while he was patrolling his route inside the building." Mr. White stopped. "Do you believe him?" He asked. "Well, I smelled alcohol on his breath. But I've never seen him drink, and he's never gone to the bar with any of our employees, not that I'm aware of."¶

Mr. White looked around quickly and leaned closer to the head guard. "Don't alarm anyone, but gather a handful of men from maintenance and inspect every way possible to enter and exit the building just in case. We have important new weapons technology and I'll be damned if someone's going to swoop in and steal our hard work. Report back to me as soon as you're done with your sweep of the premises." Mr. White stepped into the elevator. "There hasn't been an incident like this since they dealt with The Golden Snake." He thought to himself as he hit the button while the doors began to close.¶

*¶

As they approached the Blackfoot Indian Tribe, Rattler spoke up. "Tsume, you wait here for a moment. I need to talk to Chief White Cloud before we head out. If you see anyone approach the entrance on steam-cycles, come and get me." Tsume nodded and Rattler headed for the village. He walked through the front gate and was immediately escorted to the Chief's quarters. "Nice to see you Chief White Cloud. I came to seek your guidance regarding recent events." "I already know of Ronin's fate regarding the stranger. The spirits are very wise concerning such things. And I feel as though this will help you in your journey." The chief reached under his bed and pulled out a small wooden box. "You have just turned eighteen recently. It is time for you to have this." "What is it?" Asked Rattler. "Your father told me to give it to you when you become a man, and I see a man standing before me now."¶

Rattler took the box and opened it. There was a scroll inside. Unrolling it he discovered what appeared to be a portion of a schematic for some kind of rifle. "This must have been what my father, Scotty and Uncle Butch were working on before they were forced to flee Blackwater." The tears started to well up in his eyes. "Worry not, Rattler. I happen to know your father is alive and well. Unfortunately, he is still in great danger. Things are worse than was once thought. He has not been able to contact you for fear that those searching for you mean to do you great harm." Rattler managed to clear his throat. "What has he told you exactly?" He asked. "I know it is hard to understand now, but your father will be able to answer all of your questions someday soon. The Great Spirits have told me you will be reunited with him when you need him most." Rattler broke down emotionally as the chief embraced him in a grandfatherly hug. "Go quickly, there are things in motion that will require your full attention. So, remember to stay focused." Rattler thanked him and left the village to get Tsume.¶

The two headed back to the settlement to harvest the remaining crops, dismantle the fishery, and take down all the snares. They planned to save enough food to travel back to Blackwater with and give away the rest. Rattler had trained so hard, the hundred-mile trip would take just under a week; with a day to harvest and take care of everything else, they could return to Daisy's house with two days to spare before the fight Dan would be scheduling for him. Whenever they stopped to rest, the ninja would share stealth techniques and defensive moves that samurai did not train in. The samurai was a mighty warrior, whereas the ninja would stick to the shadows. Although Rattler would not use these techniques for attacking, he would utilize them to sneak into places to gather evidence of illegal activities or to destroy illegal weapons. He also planned to learn ninjitsu from Tsume, giving him another fighting tool.¶

The harvesting went without a hitch, they ate fish for lunch and dinner, and the two rabbits they managed to trap would go to the needy families six miles away. They visited Ronin's grave and paid their respects. Tsume was extremely sorry for his blind faith to an obviously evil employer. Rattler knew in his heart that if Tsume could somehow exchange his life for Ronin's, he would. They went to bed just as the sun was setting so they could get an early start in the morning. Rattler always slept well after the long journey home. He would come to miss the simple life, but there was too much going on in Blackwater for him to ignore any longer. It was time for him to become the man his father and Ronin wanted him to become.¶

*¶

The return trip back to Blackwater took even less time than before; since they were eager to train and engage the enemy, neither Rattler nor the ninja were surprised. The six days went by quickly as they discussed many different training techniques for stealth, cardio, strength, and fighting. Rattler mostly trained with the sword or bow, he had little experience with going undetected like a ninja. "You sometimes need to get into the heads of those you wish to hide from." Tsume stated. "Take armed guards for example. They are constantly on the lookout

for intruders. But, they are focusing on things far away, like the perimeter, or a tree line.
Sometimes the easiest place to hide from a foe is close by. I have followed many a guard down a hallway, walking directly behind them. The key is silence. You must learn to move without making a sound." "So that's the ninja's greatest weapon, surprise?" Rattler asked. "One of them. The most important weapon of the ninja is his mind."¶

Once they arrived at Daisy's house, they noticed a couple of changes. She had completely rearranged the living room and removed all the decorations from the walls. "This is going to be both your bedroom and your dojo." Tsume was impressed that this young lady knew what a dojo was. "You are most gracious, and I am honored that you would share your home with someone like me. If there is anything I can do to help you maintain a clean house, I will be happy to do so." Tsume bowed slightly as he spoke. "Is this all necessary?" Asked Rattler. "I don't want you two training out in the yard where my neighbors could see. Rumors would spread and could eventually reach someone working at Dead-Eye Inc. Training indoors ensure complete privacy, and the living room is the biggest room in the house. So, it just makes sense." Daisy went into the kitchen to fix them both a couple of sandwiches and a bowl of soup.¶

Tsume and Rattler quickly unpacked, ate lunch, and trained for several hours before taking a break. "I've invited Dan for supper so we can discuss what our next move is going to be." Daisy said as she brought in a pitcher of lemonade. "I'm impressed at how long the two of you are able to train. But here, you need to re-hydrate." Handing each of them a glass, she set the tray on the dining room table. "He should be here around six o'clock. So, if you two could straighten up and take a shower before we eat, I would appreciate it." Rattler stowed his gear and gave Daisy a hand with the dishes in the kitchen. "It's kind of weird being indoors so much." He commented. Daisy continued to wash the dishes. "Didn't you and Ronin build a house on your property?" "Yes, but we only used it to sleep in. Or eat and relax if it was raining too heavily. Other than that, we were always outside. We tended to our garden; we maintained a small fishery; trapped and hunted wild game; but mostly we trained."¶

As they finished drying and put away the last of the dishes, Daisy finally asked the question she had been wanting to ask since they arrived two weeks ago. "What are we going to do about Butch's disappearance. The police are refusing to reopen his missing person's case." She sat down on her couch and continued. "Dan has an idea about hiring a bounty hunter, but our lawyer advised against it. I just want to find him, Rattler." She was nearly in tears. "Daisy, we'll look into it ourselves. Do we have access to his case file?" Daisy perked up a bit. "Mr. Ace, our lawyer should be able to get us a copy. Oh, thank-you Rattler." She wiped the last bit of tears from her eyes and went to the phone to call their lawyer.¶

*¶

A ninja made his way down the winding street. Looking at the nearest street sign, he found himself on the corner of Wood Ave. and Central St. He turned left and climbed up into a tree to avoid an oncoming group of people. Climbing into a neighboring tree, he made his way onto the roof of a small grocery market. Checking his map, he had to wait a few minutes for the foot traffic to clear. Running to the edge of the roof, the ninja flipped across a narrow gap to an adjacent clothing shop. Tsume's trail had led him to Blackwater, and he desperately needed to make contact with his fellow clan member. Don'yoku had already waited over ten

years for his prize, and his patience had just
about reached its end.

Chapter XVI - Bare-knuckle¶

Rattler, Dan and Daisy walked through the
noisy crowd on their way to Rattler's locker
room. Once there, Rattler changed into his shorts
and started shadow boxing facing the wall. Daisy
sat worried while Dan grabbed a bucket of ice.
"What's the ice for?" Asked Ratter as he turned
around and shook his hands by his sides. "I've
seen many trainers rub bags of ice on their
fighters before a bout and between rounds to
keep them from overheating." He replied.
"When your body starts to overheat, it can start
to shut down and slows your reflexes. Trust me,
I'll make a great corner man." Dan shoved a
couple of handfuls into a plastic bag and rubbed
it over Rattler's shoulders, chest and back.
Rattler shrugged and twiched a little from the
extremely cold ice.¶

"It's time!" Shouted one of the ringside
workers as he opened the door. "Your opponent
is John Duke, do you have any questions before
we head out?" Rattler looked at Dan, Dan looked
back at the worker. "None from us." Dan said.
Daisy spoke up. "I have a question. What are the
rules." She said. "What do you mean 'what are

the rules?' There's no biting, no kicking, and no eye-gouging, other than that…" Daisy still looked a little worried. "Are we good?" The worker said. Everybody nodded. "Alright then, let's go!" They all filed out the door and followed him to the ring.¶

The crowd started cheering as they approached; the announcer called out the names of the two fighters. "In this corner, weighing in at 240 pounds and standing 6'2", with a record of twelve and two, eight by way of knockout… John Duuuuuuke!" The crowd erupted. "What's the deal with this guy?" Asked Rattler. "He's a solid fighter who can take a punch." Stated Dan. "He'll come out fast and furious. Dodge his punches for about a minute or two to frustrate him. He should gas a little and you can unleash your hardest punches then. Just protect yourself at all times." "And in this corner, weighing in at 220 pounds and standing 6'4", making his debut… Raaaaattleeer!" The crowd cheered a little, but not as much as they had for Duke.¶

The referee motioned for Rattler to step into the ring, which was just a bunch of a gym mats arranged in a large square in the middle of the room. There was approximately two hundred people standing around the fighting area, most were waving cash around and placing bets.

Rattler was not used to this much noise, so he tried extra hard to remain calm and focused. He was very anxious to get this fight over quickly without sustaining any injuries. "Remember what I told you!" Shouted Dan. Rattler barely heard him over the roar of the crowd. "I remember!" He shouted back.¶

Both fighters met in the center of the ring for last minute instructions. "You both know the rules, follow them and we won't have any problems." The referee instructed them. "Good luck to both of you." Rattler and John both returned to their respective corners and waited for the bell. After a few seconds, the bell sounded. "Ding-Ding" John rushed towards Rattler and threw several hay-makers in an attempt to finish the new fighter early and add to his knockout record. Rattler easily dodge all of them and circled around the outside edge of the ring. John followed him, shuffling his feet as he pursued his opponent. Throwing several more punches, each of them missed their target as Rattler continued to dodge and weave.¶

Rattler avoided everything John was throwing at him by ducking, swaying side to side, and moving around the ring. After a minute and a half had gone by with no contact being made, the crowd started booing. "Oh you're just a pretty boy pussy, aren't ya?" John started taunting him. "You look tough, but you ain't got the skills." He threw a couple of jabs that Rattler easily dodged. Rattler refused to get drawn into an insult battle. He just continued to focus on his breathing and kept his eyes on his opponent. The two of them continued to circle each other as the crowd booed and started throwing garbage towards the ring.¶

Dan stepped to the edge of the mat and yelled so Rattler could hear him. "He's ready, drop him now!" Rattler heard the words shouted from his corner. He focused all his attention on John as he looked him in the eyes. It was just like Dan had told him earlier, he was beginning to gas. Rattler waited for him to throw a right hook, and after a couple of jabs, John threw a hard, right hook that seemed to go past Rattler in slow motion. It was exactly what he was waiting for. Rattler threw a hard body shot to John's ribs; he couldn't hear it, but he definitely felt it. His opponent hunched over a bit and covered his mid-section with both hands. The crowd stopped booing and started to cheer. Rattler had cracked John's ribs. Although he felt bad for him, he had to end the fight.¶

Rattler threw a fake punch at John's chest. This caused him to flinch and look up a bit.

Rattler threw his hardest punch and connected square across John's jaw, sending him flat on his back. The referee rushed over and started the count. But Dan could tell that the fight was already over. He started jumping up and down as the referee continued counting. "Seven – eight – nine – ten!" "Ding – ding" The crowd erupted even louder as Rattler raised his hands in victory. "At two minutes, five seconds of the very first round; the winner, by way of knockout... Raaaattleeer!" Rattler flexed a little for the crowd before walking back to his corner. "Let's get paid and go home." Daisy said; she was simply relieved the fight was over and he did not hurt.¶

After they had returned to the dressing room, Rattler took a quick shower and put his clothes back on. He had just stepped out into the hall when a man holding a small stack of bills approached him. "Here's four hundred dollars." He said. "If you want to sign up for a bout next week, I can guarantee you'll make twelve hundred." Rattler smiled. "Sure, we'll be here." Dan spoke up. "Only if you tell us who he's going to be fighting by Wednesday." The man did not even hesitate. "It's a deal!" They shook hands and he disappeared back the way he came.¶

"Why do we need to know who I'm going to fight beforehand?" Rattler asked. "I've been watching these underground fights for a long time." Dan answered. "If we know who you're facing by Wednesday, that will give us four days to train. I know just about every fighter in the league, so we'll be prepared ahead of time." Rattler thought for a second. "What if I fight someone new?" Dan chuckled. "After that fight, you'll be fighting someone much tougher. Twelve hundred dollars tougher." Daisy still felt uneasy. "I just don't want him to get in over his head. I would feel awful if he got injured." Dan tried to reassure her. "Are you kidding me!? John Duke was not an amateur, and Rattler ended him with only TWO punches! I think whomever Rattler fights next should be worried."¶

The three friends left through the back exit as a mysterious man in the shadows jotted down a few lines on a notepad. "Who gets a debut fight with John Duke and is able to finish him in the first round? And with only two punches?" He thought at he placed the notepad in his jacket pocket.¶

*¶

The weather was rather nice as Mr. Ace

walked down the sidewalk. He could see Daisy and her friends waiting on the doorsteps to his building from nearly a block away. They had made an appointment for nine o'clock in the morning and said it was rather urgent. "Good morning Miss Daniels, Mr. Wilder, and…?" "I'm Rattler." "Of course, Rattler. Your friends have told me quite a bit about you." Tom said. "I really like your name, and the story behind it." He took the keys from his pocket and, finding the right one, unlocked the front door. "Come in. From your message, you need my help."¶

They walked down the hall as Daisy filled him in on recent events. "My uncle talked about a secret stockpile of weapons somewhere outside of town, somewhere remote." Mr. Ace opened the door to his office. "You'll have to excuse the clutter; I gave my secretary the week off so she could visit her mother."¶

He walked over to one of his filing cabinets and opened the second drawer. "Every piece of property your uncle owned will be in this… where is it? Oh, yes. It will be in this file." He handed Daisy a folder containing various deeds and bills of sale. Flipping through them quickly, she singled one out. "What is this one here? I don't remember ever going here. And it seems like a small plot of land, only a half-acre." Tom looked it over. "This might just be it. I know he did not build anything on this property, at least nothing he wanted to draw attention too." "How can you tell all of that?" Asked Dan, looking over his shoulder. "If he were to have built something here, there would be a copy of the permit paper-clipped to the deed. I'm very thorough."¶

"The address is unfamiliar; how would we get there?" Asked Rattler. "Already ahead of you." Tom pulled a small map from his desk drawer. "The property is right here. It's approximately fifteen miles from your house, Daisy." He drew a circle around the lot with a pencil and handed it to her. "Thank you, Mr. Ace." She folded the map and placed it in her purse. "If we don't find what we're looking for here, we'll need to do some more research." Walking over to his secretary's desk, Tom picked up a very large case file. "And here's everything the police have on Butch's disappearance. Whatever help I can be, don't hesitate to call. I consider you all as family." He added. "Thank you for all your hard work." Daisy said, giving him a kiss on the cheek. Tom saw them to the door. As they left the building, the weather seemed to change on a dime. Dark clouds seemed to roll in out of nowhere. "I hope

this isn't an omen of things to come." Said
Rattler as they headed home.¶

*¶

It was about three o'clock in the afternoon
when the four of them arrived at the location
indicated on the map. Tsume had not attended
the meeting with their lawyer earlier because
they did not want to draw any attention to
themselves. "This looks like the place." Rattler
said, looking around. "There are definitely no
visible structures here. But my guess is there is
an underground bunker somewhere on the
property." "An underground bunker?" Daisy
asked. "That's what I'd do." Rattler remarked.
"Let's spread out and go over every inch." They
all followed his instructions and began a
thorough search of the area.¶

Within twenty minutes, Tsume shouted.
"Over here! I think I found something." They all
ran over to where the ninja was digging in the
dirt. "I don't see anything." Said Dan. "Look
around on the ground, there's nothing growing."
Tsume said. "It's the only spot of land with no
plants." "That makes since." Said Rattler. "What
makes since?" Added Daisy. "Well if I were to
have an underground bunker, I wouldn't want
anything growing on top of it. The root system

of any large plants could eventually damage the structure. Your uncle probably introduced chemicals or salt to make sure nothing would ever grow on top of it." After a couple of minutes had gone by, Dan found a handle. They only needed a few more minutes to clear the entire hatch of dirt and debris.¶

Once inside, they split up and each searched different rooms. Upon inspection of the entire bunker, Daisy found what appeared to be part of a schematic for a new rifle. "Look at this!" She cried out. Dan and Rattler both looked it over. "I think I have another part of this schematic." Said Dan. "And I have another." Said Rattler, excitedly. "I bet my father, Uncle Butch and Scotty each had a third of the master copy." "Those clever devils." Added Dan. "They insured that only we could bring them all together to build it." They all celebrated for a moment before Daisy spoke up. "I think I just heard some thunder. We should bunk down here tonight, instead of setting up tents outside." "Agreed." Said Rattler and Dan in unison. Tsume unfolded his bedroll and laid down. "Good idea."¶

*¶

The week had gone by without a hitch. Dan was busy acquiring the materials necessary to manufacture the new assault rifle. Daisy organized Rattler and Tsume's training, with more emphasize on Ratter's boxing regimen once they found out that he would be facing Holt Walker. They received the information about the match-up early Tuesday afternoon instead of Wednesday. Dan knew exactly who he was and drilled Rattler constantly about his strengths and weaknesses every couple of hours up until the fight.¶

Holt typically threw high arcing crosses with either hand. He did this so, in case he missed with his fists, he could follow through with an elbow to open cuts above the eyes. But, if Rattler was quick enough to dodge these attempts, Holt would leave his face wide open for a counter punch. His strengths however, were a different story. Holt could definitely take a punch as he had never been knocked out. But Dan was betting Rattler would be the first. He was so sure; he was placing two weeks' pay on the line.¶

Once they arrived in the locker room, news trickled down that Holt was only favored at three to one. These were the worst odds he's had in over twenty fights. Although this was only

Rattler's second fight, there were obviously those who felt he had a better chance than most. Rattler was enjoying earning easy money for something he had been training for every day for the last ten plus years. He had made a promise to himself, and to the memory of his fallen master, that he would stay humble as a professional fighter. He did not have to destroy his opponents, he just had to win. Breaking John's ribs last Saturday night was an accident, he would be more careful while fighting Holt.¶

"Time to go." Came the familiar voice from the doorway. "I'm ready." Rattler said. "I hope so, I've got twenty bucks on you myself." The worker added. "Let's go." They made the same walk down the hall to ringside, however this time the roar of the crowd was much, much louder. "In this corner, weighing in at 230 pounds and standing 6'1", with a record of twenty-two and three, eighteen by way of knockout... Hooooooooolt Walker!" The crowd erupted with cheers and applause. "And in this corner, weighing in at 220 pounds and standing 6'4", with a record of one win and zero losses, with his only win by way of first-round knockout... Raaaaattleeer!" The cheers got even louder. If one did not know any better, one would think Rattler was the favorite.¶

As he and his opponent met in the center of the ring for instructions, Holt began with the taunting. "I shouldn't even be fighting a nobody! Who do you think you are anyway?" Rattler listened to the referee and remained silent. He stared right back into Holt's eyes to let him know he could not be intimidated by any man. And, he wouldn't be drawn into a verbal match with him. Rattler would let his skills do his talking for him when the bell rang. Walking back to their corners, he decided he did not care much for Holt's attitude. One should not taunt another fighter, let alone one whose skill level you did not know much about. Likewise, Rattler had not faced this man in battle before, so he would respect his ability and never let his guard down for a second.¶

"Ding-ding" This time it was Rattler who rushed to the middle of the ring. His first fight gave him confidence, and he had learned that controlling the middle of the ring gave him both an offensive and defensive advantage. Holt, surprised at his aggressiveness, threw a few jabs to start the round. Rattler slapped them down with his open fists. This seemed to anger Holt, who then started throwing stronger shots to the body. One slipped through and hit Rattler right beneath his rib-cage. He had not been hit in a very long time. And the funny thing was; it did not hurt him. His abdomen was extremely muscular and Holt's fist seemed to just bounce off him. Feeling like this was something to exploit, Holt continued his attack to Rattler's midsection. But sensing a rhythm to his punching, Rattler kept slapping away punch after punch; which did nothing but frustrate Holt more and more.¶

It did not take long for Holt to throw his signature high-arching right cross at Rattler's head. But, because he had been training for this for the past four days, it was second nature for him to duck low and follow through with an uppercut to the jaw. He connected cleanly to Holt's chin, which sent him stumbling back a couple of steps. Although the crowd was cheering loader than it had all night, Rattler was so focused, he was barely aware of it. He continued walking towards his opponent to finish the fight. Holt managed to throw an off-balanced left hook, but Rattler caught his fist mid-air and threw his own right hook which again, landed cleanly on Holt's face, knocking him down. As the referee counted. "One-two-three-" Holt tried desperately to get to his feet. "Four-five-six-" But his efforts were futile, his legs were just too wobbly. "Seven-eight-nine-"

Holt fell face first onto the mat. "TEN!" "Ding-ding" The fight was over.¶

"At one minute, forty-five seconds of the very first round; the winner, by way of knockout... Raaaattleeer!" The crowd was stunned. He had managed to win his second fight in even less time than his first. Rattler repeated his muscle flexing performance and returned to his corner just as he had done in his previous fight. "Come on, let's go collect our winnings." Said Dan. Unlike the first bout, Dan had placed a significant bet on this one. With the $1,200 purse, their total winnings added to just over $3,000. Once Rattler had returned to his locker room to get dressed, the worker appeared quickly with a slip of paper.¶

Dan read it through, twice. "Holy cow! They're giving you a title shot already! There must be some bigwigs who just made a lot of money betting on you or something." He said. "I've never seen someone get a title shot this soon. It says they're going to call us in a couple days with the details. I'm thinking they're probably going to schedule it in the next few weeks. Strike while the iron's hot." "How big of a purse are we looking at with a title shot?" Asked Rattler. "If you win, thousands! Butch cleared nine grand his last fight, but he was the

champ." Dan shook his head as he continued.
"I'm guessing at least five or six. With that kind
of money...."¶

They waited for the next fight to begin
before once again heading out the back exit. And
like before, they were being watched by the
same mysterious figure lurking in the shadows
and jotting notes. Placing the notepad in his
pocket, the man walked inside and went to the
office. "Let me use your phone, please." He
asked. "Of course. Anything you need, sir." The
man in the office said, handing him the
telephone. Picking up the receiver, he dialed.
Within a few seconds, the phone picked and a
voice answered. "Hello." "Yes, let me speak to
Mr. White."¶

*¶

Sitting around the breakfast table, Tsume
and Rattler continued their conversation. "I've
taught you most of what I know how to teach,
you are a very quick learner." Tsume told Rattler
as he finished the rest of his eggs. "In fact, you
should be teaching me." Rattler finally nodded in
agreement. "I'm going to miss you for the next
year and a half." Daisy re-entered the room with
some fresh biscuits. "The next year and a half?"
She asked. "It will take that long?" She placed

the biscuits onto the nearly empty plate next to Dan.¶

"That's a generous estimation, it might take even longer for me to travel back to Japan for my daughter and return." Tsume said in a soft tone. "And there is a chance I may not return at all." "Don't say such awful things." Daisy said. "If you're half as tough as Rattler, you'll be back enjoying my homemade biscuits in no time." Finishing the last bit of orange juice, Tsume got up from the table and headed for the door, grabbing his bedroll off the floor. "Is this how it's going to be? Not even a proper good-bye?" Daisy walked over to Tsume and gave him a hug. "Come back safe, you hear me." He smiled and headed out into the Texas sun just as the phone began to ring.¶

"That's probably the call we've been waiting for." Said Dan, wiping his mouth with his napkin before running over to answer. "Hello. Yes, this is Mr. Wilder. Yeah, uh huh. Hey, Rattler, how soon are you willing to except a title match?" Rattler swallowed his milk before answering. "The sooner, the better." He replied. "Okay, then. He says as soon as you're willing to put him on the card. Okay. That'll work. Two weeks then. He's looking forward to it. Tell Mr. Prescott, Rattler will be ready." With that, Dan hung up the phone. "If you win, you'll clear $7,000. That's a record for a first-time champion." "And if he were to lose?" Asked Daisy. "He'll still get four grand and a shot at a rematch if he wins his next three after that." "If I lose?" Said Rattler. "Have more faith in me than that."¶

Daisy started gathering dirty dishes from the table. "Here, let me help you with those." Rattler began collecting empty glasses. "I only mean that you're fighting to earn extra money. If you lose, shouldn't we have enough? If you become champ, you'll have to keep fighting to defend your title, won't you?" She inquired. "Not necessarily." Interrupted Dan. "This is a title shot only. Unless he wants to remain champion, at which point he'd sign a contract with the office. But champs make quite a bit more…" "That's enough!" Said Daisy. "Fighting for a cause is one thing, fighting for money is another. After this fight, we should have plenty for what we want to accomplish. I won't have Rattler risking injuries for that. Win or lose, you'll retire." Dan and Rattler exchanged looks, and they agreed that arguing with Daisy would be a waste of time. "Win or lose, I'll retire."¶

*¶

Arriving at the underground fighting arena, Rattler and his friends were escorted to the VIP locker room. "We need a bucket of ice and some fresh towels." Dan asked the attendant by the door. "They should already be on the table as was instructed ahead of time, sir." Looking behind him, Dan saw the ice and towels were already there. "Sorry, probably should have checked first." "That's all right sir. Will there be anything else, gentlemen?" The attendant asked. "No, this will do nicely." Said Rattler. "How much time do we have?" "About twenty minutes." Dan closed the door and they began their prep work.¶

"Remember to keep moving to his left so he has a harder time connecting with his right hook. They don't call him 'Iron Fist' for nothing." Dan began icing Rattler with the large cubes instead of putting them in a bag first. "This way, the water that melts with soak into your boxing shorts, and it'll keep you cool longer. This won't be a first-round knock-out." Daisy shook her head. "Way to instill confidence in our fighter." "I'm just saying, he needs to think beyond the first round. Daisy could you give us a minute?" She stepped out in the hall for a moment.¶

"Look, I know what you told about your fight with Holt, but this is way different. You managed to knock him out with two punches, but Thorne actually broke his jaw. This guy isn't your typical fighter, if he connects enough times, you won't just feel them, you could lose." Rattler reassured him. "I never underestimate my opponent, no matter who it is." He shook his arms out a little. "That bit I do at the end isn't ego. Once I win the fight, I showboat for the crowd, to keep them betting on me. It's just fan service. Relax, this is my last fight." Rattler threw a few shadow punches as Daisy returned.¶

The minutes flew by when the attendant announced they needed to head to the ring. This time, however, they were led by security. "Fancy." Said Rattler as he was also given a robe to wear for a dramatic reveal of his muscles. He was also the first to the ring. "In this corner, weighing in at 220 pounds and standing 6'4", with a record of two wins and zero losses, both by way of first-round knockout... Raaaaattleeer!" By this time, he was used to the noise of the crowd, even though there were now over four-hundred packed inside. "And entering the ring now, the defending champion, weighing in at 245 pounds and standing 6'3½", with a record of twenty-eight and one, twenty-two by way of knockout... Thorne the 'Iron Fist' Preeeescoooott!"¶

As they met in the middle of the ring, neither man spoke during the last-minute instructions given by the referee. Rattler respected his opponent for not resorting to name-calling or insults. They returned to their corners for only a moment before the bell rang out. "Ding-ding" Both men ran full speed towards each other, but instead of throwing punches, or colliding, Rattler jumped and flipped over his opponent. Landing behind him, Rattler spun around. Seeing such a feat hushed the crowd temporarily as Thorne reoriented himself to what had just happened. Rattler did not let up, and took advantage of the situation by landing two straight punches directly to the face. That seemed to snap 'Iron Fist' back to reality. He immediately covered up and tried to counter. Rattler chose to dodge rather than slap the punches away, at least for now. Thirty seconds ticked by as Thorne viciously threw blow after blow at Rattler's head and body, alternately with quick lefts and rights, but nothing landed.¶

The crowd started cheering for Rattler, perhaps Thorne's popularity was on the decline. He pictured his Uncle Butch in his corner, standing alongside Dan and wondered what advice he would have given him at the start of the round. "Look out!" Screamed Dan. Rattler barely managed to avoid a hay-maker that could have ended the fight. Rattler had been daydreaming for a split second and dropped his guard. He knew what Ronin would have said. "If a dragonfly flew in front of your face, would your opponent give you a chance to recover? No!" Rattler unleashed a flurry of body shots to the champ's stomach, landing several and backing him up. He had to keep going before he could recover. Faking a right to the body, he instead threw a left hook to the side of his face. Butch had always told him to train to be ambidextrous. Before he could counter, Rattler threw a right, another left, and a right to the body. Thorne was not used to so much speed and power.¶

"Finish him!" Shouted Dan. "Yeah, finish him!" Shouted Daisy. Rattler did not let up, he landed blow after blow, to the head and to the body. Thorne could not defend himself. Rattler could sense this and stopped throwing punches. The crowd grew silent as the defending champ struggled to keep his feet. The referee stepped forward. "Continue fighting!" He ordered. Rattler was not going to throw another punch at the defenseless fighter. Instead, he pushed him enough to let gravity do the rest. Thorne Prescott crashed into the mat. The referee did not even bother to count. He signaled ringside. "Ding-ding" Rattler had just become the new, bare-knuckle champion.

Chapter XVII -Rattler's New Suit¶

Over a year had gone by and Dead-Eye Inc. expanded their company's business to include both Mexico and Canada. Their reputation for high-quality guns drew in many new clients. The Black Bull Society's efforts to sell the improved Gatling gun proved unsuccessful due to its bulkiness. Although they managed to sell a few hundred units, the scope that was projected never came to fruition. Rumors of its unreliability in the field was the main culprit for low sells. Even those who witnessed the highly secretive demonstration were weary of the complicated process of attaching a second belt of ammunition to maximize the benefits of the weapon. Mr. Bull did not take the lack of sales well; he demanded all manpower and resources be refocused on a better alternative to the Gatling gun. They needed to recruit new members into their organization as well.¶

Inside the secret meeting room, Mr. Bull was asking for the progress of what was to be called, a "machine gun." "Mr. Richards, what have the latest tests shown?" He was not in a very good mood, and was not going to handle any bad news well. "We have had a break through, however recent testing has shown that it will take some time to work out all of the bugs before we can proceed." Mr. Bull was about to say something, but Mr. Richards continued. "But, our patience will be rewarded. Instead of a belt of ammunition hanging out the side, we're developing something we like to call a "magazine." Mr. Richards did not want to give Mr. Bull a chance to get angry. "The magazine will hold thirty rounds, and can be changed very quickly, making it far superior to the Gatling gun." Mr. Bull interjected. "How quickly can it be changed?" Mr. Richards was anticipating this question. "A properly trained individual can swap out a magazine in well under ten seconds; the fasted time clocked in at just under six. And, the average time it takes for someone with no training is around fifteen to sixteen seconds. So, the more you use it, the faster you become."¶

Everyone looked at Mr. Bull for a reaction. "Will these machine guns cost significantly less than the Gatling gun? And, how easy will they be to manufacture?" The eyes at the table switched back to Mr. Richards. "So far, numbers indicate that we will be able to sell this weapon for about the same price as our most expensive hunting rifle models, or half of what the Gatling gun costs." Mr. Richards turned a page in his report file that laid out in front of him on the table. "As for the ease of production, we won't have to manufacture it in three separate pieces. If the average gun owner looked at one without the magazine, it would simply look like a normal rifle. The space for the magazine would be the only thing that would look different." "So?" Asked Mr. Bull. "So…" Replied Mr. Richards. "It would simply look like it was missing a part."¶

The meeting came to an end as everyone cleared out except for Mr. Bull, Mr. White, and one of Mr. White's informants. "My colleague here has some interesting news regarding the underground, bare-knuckle fighting league." Mr. Bull closed his meeting folder and stood up. "He can fill me in on the latest developments on the way back to my office." Turning towards the door, Mr. White's informant walked briskly to open the door for the two gentlemen. "Start talking, time is money." Said Mr. Bull. "Well, sir." The informant started in a cautious voice. "Last year a new fighter appeared on the scene and became the bare-knuckle champion in three straight fights, all with knock-outs in the very first round." The three of them walked down the hall towards the elevators.¶

"That's very impressive, but how does that concern Dead-Eye Inc.?" Mr. Bull asked impatiently. "Well, sir. His corner man was the same one who worked for Butch Young and currently owns The Rustic Forge." Mr. Bull stopped walking to face him. "And I'm only being told this now! Where is this person currently?" The informant cringed a little. "The problem is, after he won the championship, he retired. Nobody knows where he is." Mr. Bull started walking again. "What kind of man wins the championship and immediately retires. Doesn't he realize how much more money he could earn if he defended his belt?" The informant continued as he walked alongside Mr. Bull and Mr. White. "My contacts tell me he was only in it for some quick cash. I tried to have him followed on two different occasions, be he simply vanished." Mr. Bull once again became very agitated. "Simply vanished? Is he still in Blackwater?" "Like I said before, sir. No one knows where he is. I used all my resources and contacts over the past year. My colleagues and I just cannot locate this individual. So, my guess is he no longer resides within the Blackwater City limits."¶

The three men finally arrived at the elevators. "You guess? You've been spending all your efforts on finding this person for the twelve months, and you don't know where he is, or if he's still in town? Mr. White... get this piece of shit out of my face!" Mr. Bull pushed the elevator button and waited with his back to both Mr. White and the informant. "But, sir..." Mr. White sucker-punched the man and knocked him to the floor. "Mr. Bull doesn't want to hear anything more from you, worthless scum!" Mr. White took a walkie-talkie from his belt. "Security, I need two guards on the top floor at the main elevators." "Yes, sir. What's the situation?" Came the response. "I need them to dispose some garbage for me." "Yes, sir!"¶

*¶

Dan walked onto Daisy's front porch and knocked on the door. "Just a minute!" Came a shout from inside. Dan peaked in through the screen and could see Rattler doing exercises in the living room. "Hey, Rattler!" He shouted. Rattler finished his push-ups and jumped to his feet. Daisy entered the living room and they both walked to the front door. "Come in." Invited Daisy. "I just finished the last bit of dishes from lunch. I do have some leftovers, care for some roasted chicken?" Dan stepped inside. "Sure, if it's not a hassle." "Have a seat at the table while I get you a plate. We need to talk about our progress on Butch's whereabouts." Daisy said as she returned to the kitchen. Rattler looked down and noticed Dan was carrying a rather large package. "What's in the bag, Dan?" He asked, reaching towards it.¶

"Hands off until I get some food in my stomach." Dan said, whipping the bag behind his back. "Besides, I want to see Daisy's work first." The two friends walked into the dining room and took a seat on one side of the table. "Yes, yes, I finally finished his trench coat this past weekend." Daisy said on her way into the dining room. She placed the plate of chicken and mixed vegetables in front of Dan. "Here you go, I'll be right back. The coat is upstairs." She disappeared down the hall. "I just want the chicken, would you like the veggies?" Asked Dan. "I already had my lunch." "Don't let Daisy find out your pawning your vegetables off on me. Eat 'em, they're good for you."¶

As Dan was finishing the last bite of his food, Daisy came into the room holding Rattler's improved trench coat. "Let me try it on, Daisy, it looks amazing." Rattler said, taking the coat and thrusting his right arm into the sleeve. "It took me quite a while to attach and sew together all of the materials." She explained. "I first covered both the inside and outside of the jacket with the sturdiest buffalo leather. Then I cover the outside with western diamondback rattlesnake skin. Did you remember to use western diamondback, Dan?" "Of course I did. This was a custom job; I wouldn't forget something that important." Dan pulled out the wide-brimmed fedora from the bag sitting on the chair next to him. "Check this beauty out!" Dan said, handing the hat to Rattler. "I also lined it with buffalo leather before adding the snake skin. I added an acetate and rayon blend to the inside so it breathers better and helps with air circulation and sweat." He added.¶

Rattler finished putting the trench coat on and then put on the hat. "How do I look?" He asked. "Dashing." Said Daisy. "Totally bad-ass." Said Dan. "So… dashingly bad-ass!" Rattler said. Daisy and Dan both chuckled a little before Daisy began speaking again. "Let's go over Butch's case file, we haven't reviewed it in over a month." Rattler could hear the anxiousness in her voice. "I know it's been hard, but like they told us; if we comb over the file too often, we'll get burned out." "I know." Said Daisy. "That's why we all agreed we'd only look over the files once a month, and it's been a month." Dan sat down and pulled the case file towards him. "We're ready Daisy, I just hope this time we'll be able to see something new and make some real progress. He was important to all of us." "He *IS* important to all of us, he's still alive." Dan and Rattler supported Daisy with her feelings, but deep down they did not share them. They thought as the police did, Butch was murdered, and there would never be enough evidence to find out who had killed him.¶

They looked over each and every page for nearly two hours, but the outcome was the same; they did not generate any new ideas on what to do next. They were as frustrated and confused as they had been for the last thirteen months. They refreshed themselves with some of Daisy's freshly made lemonade and talked about other matters. "Oh, by the way, I was thinking about building you a new steam-cycle with your bare-knuckle league winnings. I've got ideas for a really awesome concept." Dan was extremely excited about an opportunity to build a unique bike. "I just need to know all the weapons you use." Rattler was too busy checking himself in the mirror again to hear him. "What was that?" He said. "I need to know all the weapons you like to use. I've got an idea for a weapon rack on your steam-cycle that will hold all the weapons you will be using."¶

"That's a good idea, let's see... I use The Snake Blade, two katanas, bow and arrows, a rifle, and hey, speaking of rifles; how's the construction of the new assault rifle coming?" Dan smiled. "I managed to make an improvement on Scotty's design." He said. "Do tell." Replied Daisy. "I'm interested in how you managed to surpass my uncle's version, he was brilliant." Dan unfolded a piece of paper from his pocket. "So, I'm not as brilliant then?" "I didn't mean it as an insult." "I know." Dan countered. "I just stumbled across this improvement by sheer luck." "I knew it." Daisy shot back.¶

He spread out the drawing he had made on the table and pointed to the stock. "By changing the materials to the stock, and fiddling with the firing mechanism just a tad, I was able to reduce kickback by about fifty percent." Daisy and Rattler looked up, and at the same time asked. "How do you know that?" Dan folded his arms in front of his chest. "Because, I have the first one made back in the safe at The Rustic Forge. Come on and I'll show you." The three of them agreed to walk the two miles since it was such a beautiful day.¶

Walking down the sidewalk, Dan brought up an old topic. "Rattler, the league keeps contacting me about your return." "He's done with that underground, bare-knuckle stuff. I was worried sick each time he fought." She turned to Rattler. "I never doubted you'd win, I just didn't want you getting hurt in the process." Dan added his opinion. "But he was only hit once in three fights, and the champ never laid a knuckle on him. "I said no, and I mean no." Daisy said firmly. "Okay, okay." Replied Dan. "They just keep calling me is all." They continued down the sidewalk and arrived at The Rustic Forge in just under forty minutes.¶

Unlocking the front door, Dan let Daisy and Rattler enter before stepping inside and re-locking it. Rattler took off his hat and coat and hung them on the coat rack. "Good job with the clothes." He said. "It doesn't feel that much heavier." "It probably weighs around twelve pounds altogether." Dan replied. "Yes, I could definitely get used to wearing that when I'm sneaking around. And there's barely any noise generated by the interior metal scales. Butch did one hell of a job with it." Rattler said, running his hand down the side of the coat.¶

Daisy spoke up. "I've been doing a lot of thinking about dealing with Dead-Eye Inc. We've been relying on Rattler and Tsume to gather all the intelligence. And although they've found out a great deal of information by sneaking into their headquarters from time to time, I feel that I can be an asset to our, 'quest.'" "No offense, Daisy, but I don't think it would be a good idea to have you accompany me on any recon missions." Rattler quickly replied. "I'm not talking about doing any of that. I was thinking of getting a high-level position within their company. That way I can gather information from the inside." Rattler's eyebrows raised slightly. "I'm not sure…" "I'm a grown woman with a college degree in business, I'm sure I could handle it." "I don't think he meant it that way." Dan said, defending his friend's intentions. "I think he's more concerned with your safety."¶

A man knocked on the door, startling the three of them. Dan walked over to the door and spoke through the glass. "I'm sorry sir, but we're closed." The man pulled a piece of paper from his pocket. "Could I just give you this order form, please." "Yeah, just a second." Dan pulled the keys from his pocket and unlocked the door. The man handed him an order form with a drawing on the back. "I'm looking to have a steam-cycle made for my brother as a birthday gift." He said. "I've heard from several of your customers that you recently started making them, and they have all been top quality." Dan looked at the drawing. "There are a couple of things on this drawing that may need tweaking. Tell you what, come back Monday about one o'clock and we can discuss this further Mr…?" "Oh, I'm sorry, I'm Mr. Bower. I own that little watch and clock store downtown."¶

After a short conversation, Dan locked back up and turned to his friends. "Where were we in our conversation again?" He said. "Oh, yeah. Daisy working for Dead-Eye. I'm a little worried too." "Guys, there's really no need to fret. They don't know who I am. Even if they discover that I'm Scotty's niece, I'm from Mt. Tenino, I didn't actually move to Blackwater until after Uncle Scotty 'moved away.'" "But they might keep a closer eye on you once they learn who you are. You'll need to be very careful." Warned Rattler. "So, you're okay with me going to work there?" She asked. "Yes, I am. You're right, you'll be able to gather much more information on what they're up too then we could. Besides, you're an intelligent, grown woman, like you said."¶

"How about we retire to the back so I can show you the assault rifle. I'm extremely proud of it." Daisy and Rattler followed him to the back of the store as Dan opened his gun safe, took the weapon out, and set it on the work table. "She's a beauty!" Rattler said walking over to the table. "May I?" "Of course." Answered Dan. Rattler picked it up and aimed it at the gun safe. "How many rounds does it hold, and how fast can it shoot?" He asked. "Each clip holds twenty-five rounds and can be emptied in less than five seconds." Rattler whistled. "Man, that's fast. I can barely empty six bullets from a pistol in that time. Where did you field-test it?" "You wouldn't believe me if I told you." "Try me." Said Rattler. "A quarter mile from Dead-Eye's original testing range." "Are you crazy?" Daisy said. "It was three o'clock in the morning, and I was on the other side of a gorge. I was only out there for a few minutes. Besides, there are all kinds of places to hide had anyone came along."¶

"Wait a minute, what about the shop? Whose going to run it if you're working for Dead-Eye?" Rattler said, suddenly remembering. "I've already got that covered. I hired an acting manager who works during the week, and we discuss business on Saturdays, it's been working fine that way for months." "What have you been doing with all of your free time?" Dan inquired. "I've been cooking, cleaning, and helping Rattler and Tsume with their training. And… I've made quite a few contacts with various bounty hunters and networking with Butch's business associates making my own file to go along with the police reports." "Are you reconsidering hiring a bounty hunter then?" Asked Dan. "I've been thinking about it some, yes. I know our lawyer advised against it, but I've heard some encouraging things about a couple of different bounty hunters that charge their fees based on results."¶

"Speaking of Tsume." Dan said. "When are we expecting him back?" "About five or six months if we're lucky. He's fleeing with his daughter, but I don't think that should slow him down much." Stated Rattler. "Why is that? How old is his daughter?" Asked Daisy. "From what he told me, she's about my age, maybe slightly younger. But she's been training to become a ninja since she could walk. So, I'm sure she would be able to keep up with Tsume." "By the way, what's her name?" Daisy asked curiously. "You know, her name never came up in any of our conversations. My guess is Tsume is a very protective father. That's why all he's learned while in Blackwater made him come to his decision to return to Japan and bring her back here." Rattler said, putting the assault rifle back on the work table.¶

"When Tsume does return, do you think you and he could teach us some self-defense?" Asked Daisy. "Self-defense? Like what?" Rattler asked. "You know, in case someone comes after any one of us. We need to be able to defend ourselves against people like those who came after Max, Scotty, Jill, and Butch." Rattler had to agree. "Were you thinking hand-to-hand combat, or did you want to train with weapons?" "I just want to be able to fight off an attacker long enough so I can get to safety." Daisy replied. "Oh, I definitely want to learn how to use a sword." Dan said, excitedly. "Just carrying a sword would be a deterrent. If I saw someone walking down the sidewalk with a sword, I wouldn't mess with that guy." "Or that girl."

Added Daisy. "Fine, I'll train you both the best I can. And when Tsume returns, he'll probably be willing to train you as well."¶

Dan returned the assault rifle to the gun safe and tidied the storage room up a bit. Daisy and Rattler helped their friend by straightening up the showroom. "Hey guys, care to join me for supper? I bought some venison that I've been dying to throw on the grill." Daisy and Rattler looked at each other and nodded. "We'd love too." Said Daisy. "I'll run down to the corner store and buy some fresh produce for a salad." Rattler followed. He knew Dan was big on meat, and not so much with vegetables. But Ronin instilled in him the importance of eating lots of fresh fruits and vegetables for overall health. And Daisy preferred to eat more salad and less meat; she was almost a vegetarian.¶

Dan fired up the grill and tossed three different sizes of venison steak on top. The sizzling sound that immediately began was like music to his ears. Rattler soon returned with lettuce, tomatoes, onion, celery, carrots, and cucumber. "I didn't think to buy salad dressing, do you have some, Dan?" He asked. "I have ranch and thousand island." Dan said as he flipped the venison steaks over, giving off an intoxicating aroma. After Daisy and Rattler finished preparing the salad, they all sat down to enjoy a wonderful dinner under a gorgeous Texas sky.¶

*¶

A steam-cycle pulled up to the entrance of the Blackfoot Indian Village. Several warriors were stationed at the gate to greet the visitor. Hiding his bike in near one of the unoccupied dwellings under a few buffalo hides. Walking to the main hall, he was met by Chief White Cloud. "Hello, my friend. Come, we have much to discuss. Your son, Rattler, has visited me and my people several times over the past year." Max was happy to hear his boy had reconnected with the Blackfoot tribe. "How does he look? Is he doing well?" Max was overwhelmed with emotion with the news. "He towers over most of our warriors. His skills with the bow and arrow is unrivaled. He has even mastered the tomahawk was well as I ever had. I would not want to face him in battle while he wields The Snake Blade for I would surely be defeated."¶

The chief entered the main hall and took a seat near the fire pit that sat in the middle of the building. "He has told me some disturbing things about the company Dead-Eye Inc. They may have already produced a weapon that has surpassed the one you destroyed many years ago." The old man tossed herbs into the smoldering pit so its scent would fill the air with pleasantness. "I'm sorry I haven't visited in such a long time. I'm glad to hear my son is doing well. How has Ronin been?" The smile on the chief's disappeared as he began to speak. "The Great Spirits warned of a stranger that meant to do him harm. Unfortunately for Ronin, The Great Spirits could not tell him under what circumstances he would meet this stranger. Ronin is dead."¶

Max tried his best to deal with this information, but a few tears began to run down his face. "I wish I could see my son. But there are a group of men who constantly try to track all my movements. I have not heard from Scotty, Jill, or Butch since we first fled Blackwater. I fear they might also be dead." Max lowered his head. There was part of him that wished he never came across that stupid prototype. "Don't be discourage my friend. You are a good man. You have spent your entire life helping others. Although things can seem like they will never get better... they will. You need to have Faith in your son and his friends. I have witnessed their determination; they will eventually succeed."¶

They talked for what seemed like hours.

Max wished there was some way that he could help his son, Daisy and Dan. But he feared that if they were spotted together, then a bounty would also be placed on their heads. He handed the Indian chief a letter that he had been carrying for years. "I wrote my son this letter in hopes that one day he would return to your village. Tell him that everything I have written is true, and that I love him very much. I have spent too much time here already. I need to leave before any bounty hunters realize I visited you. I don't want to put you or your people in any danger." "Fear not, my friend. While you are here, nothing will happen to you, me, or my people. We are prepared for such things. But I will give Rattler your letter." "Thank you." Two Blackfoot warriors escorted Max back to his steam-cycle and he rode off into the distance; and as far as he was aware, he had not been followed.

Chapter XVIII -Troubles of the Father¶

Daisy walked into Dead-Eye Inc.'s headquarters and headed directly to her right towards the sign that read "Human Resources." She was only slightly nervous as she approached the main office. Her college education had provided her with plenty of interview preparation classes and workshops, so she was familiar with questions that were typically asked. "Hello, I'm Miss Daniels. I'm here for my one o'clock interview with Mr. Peterson." "If you care to have a seat over there, I'll let him know you are here." The receptionist said, picking up the phone. "Thank-you." Daisy took a seat and starting going over potential interview questions in her head to stay sharp. "What are some of your strengths? What is your biggest weakness? Where do you see yourself in five years?" She thought to herself.¶

"He's ready to see you now." Mr. Peterson's secretary announced as she opened the door. "Wow, ten minutes just flew by." Daisy thought to herself. "Thank you." She said again, as she stood to her feet. The secretary led her down a short hallway and around a corner to Mr. Peterson's office. "Knock-knock" "Come in. Oh,

you must be Miss Daniels, please have a seat."
Mr. Peterson said, standing momentarily and
pointing to the chair directly in front of his desk.
"Here is my resume, sir." Daisy said, handing
him two pages held together with a paperclip.
"Let me just put my reading glasses on and have
a look see."¶

After a couple of minutes, he put her resume
down and looked up. "Everything I see here
looks fine. The position we're hiring for is a
personal assistant for Mr. Lucas, the Head of
Research and Development." Daisy looked a
little confused. "I thought I was applying for a
receptionist in your call center. Shouldn't I
interview with Mr. Lucas if I were to become his
assistant?" Mr. Peterson smiled. "From what I
see on your resume, your actually overqualified
for the call center. Mr. Lucas is looking for an
assistant, but he's way too busy to conduct
interviews himself. He just needs a well-
educated person, such as yourself, to fill the
position. Besides, it pays much better." "So, I'm
hired, just like that?" "Yes, we make decisions
like these rather quickly. And I'm assuming your
references will check out?" "Yes, sir" "Well then,
I'll inform Mr. Lucas that I hired him a new
assistant and to expect you first thing Monday
morning."¶

They shook hands and Daisy walked back to
the lobby to get a drink of water. She had pulled
it off. Despite her confidence, her hands were
shaking a little bit. She decided to go straight
home and tell Rattler the good news; within a
few days, she could potential gain some useful
information for the team. Looking outside, she
saw it had begun to rain. Taking a small
umbrella from her handbag, she stepped outside
and started walking home.¶

*¶

"Mr. White, I have one of your employees
on line two for you. Shall I put him through?"
"Give me his name first, please." There was a
short pause. "He says his name is Burn, shall I
put him through?" "No, Miss Jewel. Tell him to
come to my office right away." "Excuse me, sir.
But you have an appointment with Mr. Cobble in
fifteen minutes." Mr. White looked in his
appointment book. "Call Mr. Cobble and
reschedule him to see me at five o'clock. And
tell him something extremely important has
come up that requires my immediate attention."
"Yes, sir." Mr. White hung up the phone and
made the correction in his appointment book.
Then he poured himself a shot of whiskey,
leaned back in his chair, and waited for Burn's

arrival.¶

*¶

Dan was busy in the forge, shaping four
fenders for Mr. Bower and Rattler's steam-
cycles. Since he was working on two bikes at the
same time, Dan managed to save a little money
by ordering the materials for two builds. He was
confident in his abilities and often wondered
about specializing in custom-made bikes. But he
enjoyed making weapons and felt that he would
let down too many customers by changing the
business that way. It took him nearly two hours
to get the fenders just right, but the results were
well worth it. He set them aside and began what
little work he had left for the week before
closing the shop.¶

*¶

Burn stepped off the elevator and proceeded
down the hall towards Mr. White's office. He
was a little nervous about delivering this piece of
information after what he had heard happened to
the informant. Burn did not know who was
scarier, Mr. White of Mr. Bull. But once he
arrived at his secretary's door, he came to the
conclusion that he was more afraid of Mr. White.

"He's expecting you." Said Miss Jewel. "You can go right in." Burn opened the door and entered Mr. White's office. "You better have something useful for me, I had to reschedule a rather important meeting to see you." Burn sat in the chair facing the desk.¶

"I saw Max leaving the Blackfoot Indian village earlier today." Mr. White turned around and set his now empty shot glass in the middle of his desk. "And do you know where he went. "Well I didn't want to spook him, so I stayed well behind as I followed him for nearly thirty miles." Mr. White took out his bottle of whiskey and poured another glass. "And were you able to find out where he's been living all these years?" This was the question that Burn had been dreading. "I lost him heading towards Bluejacket." Mr. White took a sip of his whiskey. "Well then, things are quite simple then." "Quite simple?" Said Burn, as he swallowed hard, afraid of what he meant by that statement. "Yes, gather several men and search Bluejacket and all the outlying areas. I want this man found."¶

Burn stood up from the chair and cleared his throat. "I'm on it. I know just the men to help me." He was grateful that Mr. White was giving him another chance by allowing a him to continue with his search. "How many men are you planning to take with you?" "I was thinking around seven. We would be able to scour the entire area in just over a week's time." Mr. White nodded in agreement. "Yes, a little over a week. And you know what to do when you find him, don't you?" He took another sip of whiskey. "Absolutely, sir. You can count on me!" A few seconds went by. "What are you standing around here for?" Burn snapped to attention and headed for the door. Once he was out in the hall, both his breathing and pulse returned to normal. It was very stressful meeting with his boss with the stakes being this high.¶

*¶

Daisy walked into her house and hung her jacket and umbrella before putting her purse down on the table near the front door. Walking into the living room, she found Rattler doing sit-ups with his feet underneath the couch. He had placed his gear and some other heavy objects to keep the couch from lifting in the front while he exercised. Rattler was counting his reps out loud as he was nearly finished. He did sit-ups for thirty minutes every day, followed by thirty minutes of push-ups. This kept him in great shape. Daisy could not help but stare at his abs. "935... 936... 937... 938... 939... 940!" Rattler looked up and met her gaze. She blushed and turned her head. But it was too late, Rattler realized that she might have a little crush on him.¶

Jumping up to his feet, he toweled the sweat from his body, took a large drink of water, and started doing push-ups. "1… 2… 3… 4… 5…" Daisy collected herself and addressed Rattler. "I got the job!" Rattler stopped immediately, and stood to his feet. "That's wonderful, when do you start?" "I start on Monday as Mr. Lucas' assistant. And… he's the head of Research and Development." Rattler pulled his shirt over his head. "Even better, you might come across some very important memo or other piece of information. This is good." They both headed into the kitchen; Rattler needed another drink of water, and Daisy began prepping for supper. Rattler returned to the living room and began his thirty minutes of push-ups. "1… 2… 3… 4… 5…"¶

Rattler had just finished his exercise routine and was about to practice with his katanas when Dan knocked on the front door. Coming in from the kitchen, Daisy greeted him. "You know, unless you're coming over in the middle of the night, you don't need to knock anymore." Dan smiled. "I'll keep that in mind. Is Rattler here?"

"He's in the living room, training. Supper will be ready in less than an hour." "What are we having?" Dan asked. "I thought a nice chicken casserole with garden vegetables and freshly baked bread would be a good choice." Dan's eyebrows furled. "Isn't that your favorite dish? What's the occasion?" Daisy couldn't hold her excitement back any longer. "I got the job!" "Congrats, Daisy. I've got some news as well. But we can discuss it further during dinner."¶

Rattler and Dan both helped set the table, and while they were pouring drinks, Daisy brought in the casserole. "Smells amazing." Said Rattler. "If the bread is done, I'll go get it." Said Dan. "It's on the counter, thank-you." They all took a seat and began eating. After several minutes, Dan spoke up. "I was able to complete the weapon saddle from the specifications you gave me. I baked the leather, shaped it, and put a sealant on it. So, it should last you a very long time." Dan took a bite of the casserole. "Delicious!" Rattler swallowed a small mouthful of bread and butter. "Any chance I could test it out tonight." Dan looked a little puzzled. "Test it out?" "I just want to see how well my weapons fit into it. "Oh, no problem, it's hanging on a work bench that's about the same size of a steam-cycle, actually."¶

Finishing their meal, they cleaned up and headed back to the Rustic Forge. Rattler wrapped all his weapons and put them in his knapsack. Daisy carried his bow and quiver of arrows. Dan carried Scotty's shotgun that Daisy had given Rattler. The trio walked down the sidewalk talking in low voices about Daisy's new job, and the possibility of planning another raid on the headquarters. They entered the shop and Rattler placed every weapon into each of the perfectly crafted sheath that it was intended to store. "Awesome, this will serve me well."¶

*¶

Burn and his men arrived at the outskirts of Bluejacket; the men set up camp near a large boulder so the light from their campfire would not shine as bright from a distance. "All right, men. Let's get a good night's sleep and head out at the crack of dawn. I have a map for each of you and we will split up so we can cover more ground." With that they laid down and went to sleep. The morning would bring the first day of their search. Burn was the last to fall asleep because he had a lot on his mind. If he were to fail the Black Bull Society when Max was so close, he would not even bother to return; he would flee Texas for good and head east.¶

*¶

As soon as the sun broke over the horizon, Burn quickly packed up his supplies and woke the other men. They had little time to waste, so he made sure everyone ate breakfast as fast as they could. "Listen up!" Burn said loudly. "Like I told you all last night, I have a small map for each of you. All of them have different areas outlined so we don't overlap in our search. There is a picture of the target attached to the map. Review it often so you know exactly what he looks like. We cannot afford to let him slip through our fingers."¶

Burn passed out the maps, and after a few minutes of planning they all broke up and went separate ways. Hours passed as each man questioned anyone and everyone they came across while showing them pictures. They claimed there was a price on his head and they were professional bounty hunters; but nobody recognized Max from his photo. The search went on for five whole days without any luck. But on the sixth day they struck pay-dirt. "Yeah I've seen this guy. In fact, I've done business with him not too long ago." Said the elderly man. "What kind of business, if you don't mind me asking?" Burn replied. "Well, sir… he mostly does odd and end jobs. He helped me build the fence around my property and fix my chicken coop after that storm. He's a hard worker. Lives somewhere south of town. You sure he's a criminal? Seems like a mighty fine citizen to me." "I can't speak to his character." Said Burn. "I just know what the wanted poster in Blackwater says. Good day to you, sir."¶

Burn had enough information to work with, and so he headed in the direction the old man indicated. He combed the southern outskirts of town for over six hours. After eating lunch and finishing the last of his water, he was about to call it quits for the day and start his search first thing in the morning. But just as he was packing the canteen into his knapsack, he spied something in the distance. Pulling out his binoculars, he took a good long look. It appeared to be some kind of shelter and campfire set-up; but the shelter was very low to the ground. Being that small, it was probably used just for sleeping. That would be perfect for someone who may be in hiding and did not want to bother with a permanent structure. "That's the place!" He thought to himself. He would find a good hiding spot and wait for Max's return.¶

*¶

341

The remaining parts for the steam-cycle that Dan could not manufacture himself was delivered to his store by horse-drawn carriage. With the help of the driver, he brought the packages inside and left them by the door. He would unpack them once the store closed and assemble what he could before bedtime. It had been several days since Dan spent any time with Daisy or Rattler; business had picked up a little and he was focused on his work. It would be nice to go over and have dinner with them within the next couple of days. He would also have the opportunity to fill them in on the progress he was making on Rattler's new bike.¶

*¶

It was nearly dusk when Burn spotted Max pulling up to his campsite. He was driving so slowly, Burn could barely hear the engine. "Very clever." He said to himself as he continued to track Max's movements as he drove up, dismounted his bike, and proceeded to cover it with branches and shrubbery. Within two minutes, Burn could no longer see the bike. And if someone were to get this close, they would not even be aware of it. He wanted to wait at least an hour after Max had climbed into his sleeping structure before approaching. Burn checked his gun to make sure it was loaded and ready for the task.¶

An hour and a half passed before Max finally turned in for the night. Burn was a little tired, but the adrenalin coursing through his body kept him frosty. The next hour seemed to drag on forever, but the time to strike finally arrived. He crept closer and closer, making sure to make as little noise as possible. He occasionally heard the cry of a wolf off in the distance, but Max did not stir from his sleep. Burn was approximately fifty yards from the campsite when he decided to stretch his muscles for a minute before continuing forward.¶

Once he had finished with his quick stretching routine, he took a couple of steps forward. He did not see the tripwire directly in front of him. Triggering it, a medium-size log fell away from him and landed on a small pile of empty glass bottles that were arranged on top of a large, flat rock. "Ttssssshhh!" The bottles all shattered on impact. "Shit!" Burn said as softly as he could, being startled by the loud noise. He looked up just as Max was crawling out of his little sleeping hut. "Who's there?! I'm armed! You best move on, you hear!" Burn ducked into the high grass. Things just got serious.¶

"This is your last warning!" Shouted Max.

"Whatever firepower you're packing, I guarantee
I'm packing more!" Burn would not allow Max
to get away this time, he had to act now. Getting
up onto one knee, he quickly targeted Max in his
sights and fired. "Bang!" The bullet whizzed
past Max's head, putting a hole in a tree behind
him. Max returned fire. "Tt-Tt-Tt-Tt-Tt-Tt-Tt!"
Burn was hit three times, twice in the shoulder
and once in the neck. He fell almost immediately;
he started coughing and spitting up blood. Max
lowered his assault rifle and crouched down,
listening for signs of return fire.¶

After several seconds had gone by, he
checked to see if he hit his target. Walking
cautiously in the direction he was shooting; he
could hear a low gurgling sound. Running
towards it, he came across a disturbing sight.
"Damn you, I gave you plenty of warnings....
why didn't you listen?!" Burn was laying on his
back, clutching his neck with his left hand. His
neck and right shoulder were both spewing
blood all over the place. Knowing the man was
in a great deal of pain with no hope of surviving,
Max decided to end his suffering with a shot to
the head. "Blam!" Burn's arm fell to the ground;
he was dead. Now all Max had to do was give
him a decent burial.¶

It took Max over and hour to dig a hole deep

enough to bury him. Once he was covered with dirt, he looked around and thought to himself. "What do I do now? I should say a few words, but I don't even know who he was." He said a short, generic prayer and returned to his campsite; he definitely needed to relocate to another city. As he destroyed his shelter and covered the campfire pit with dirt, he started thinking more about the situation that had just occurred. "Why was this man after him? Was he sent by Dead-Eye Inc.?" He uncovered his bike and pulled out a map. Looking for another city that was significantly further away, he decided to travel to San Grove. Packing up his things, he gunned it and did not stop until he reached his new, temporary home.¶

*¶

Daisy's first week at Dead-Eye Inc. was uneventful. Her boss, Mr. Lucas, had her checking numbers on spreadsheets regarding various weapons testing. Nothing that she looked over had seemed suspicious. But, she was looking forward to the weekend so she could spend more time with Rattler. She found herself thinking about him often, and was hoping that he was noticing her mild flirtations. "Miss Daniels!" Daisy snapped out of her daydreaming. "Just because it's Friday, doesn't mean we slow down and take things easy." Mr. Lucas had entered her office with some folders, most likely more spreadsheets. "Sorry, Mr. Lucas. I did get those weapons testing numbers finished. I also color-coded each gun by caliber and bullet capacity with tabs on the folder, so if you don't like how I did it, you can just peel them off."¶

Mr. Lucas took the pile of folders and started leafing through them. Daisy wondered if she had overstepped her duties. "This looks like a great system so far. I'll show these to the guys at the lab and see how easy it would be to implement. Great work!" He said. "Look these reports over for spelling and punctuation errors." He said, handing her the papers he was carrying. "And, if I don't see you before five o'clock, have a nice weekend." Mr. Lucas walked out of the office rather briskly, and a memo that had been paper-clipped to a file fell to the floor. "Mr. Lucas…!" Daisy yelled as she got up from her chair. But, as she walked over to the door and looked out, she saw that Mr. Lucas had disappeared down the hallway and around a corner. So instead of chasing after him, she simply picked up the memo and returned to her desk.¶

She finished editing the reports in record time. Remembering why she got a job here in the first place, she decided to read the memo.¶

Mr. Richards, try to increase the magazine capacity by two.¶

-- Mr. Experiment¶

Daisy had never heard of either of these two gentlemen in the week she had been employed. First, she checked the company's directory... no luck. "Well." She thought to herself. "This might just be something." She placed the memo in her purse. She would ask around the secretary pool about the names Richards and Experiment to see if anyone knew these gentlemen. If not, she could at least gauge people's reactions. The memo seemed a little odd with that picture of a bull's head in the middle. As far as she knew, Dead-Eye Inc. did not have a mascot. Punching out for the week at the time clock, Daisy grabbed her jacket and headed towards the front door. She had no idea of the significance of the memo's symbol.¶

*¶

Daisy, Rattler and Dan had just sat down for a dinner of barbecue chicken, rice and steamed carrots. Another month had gone by with little progress. No one at Dead-Eye Inc. had ever heard of a Mr. Richards or a Mr. Experiment. She had even asked her boss, Mr. Lucas, and returned the memo the following Monday. But, all he said was 'Thank-you' and never mentioned it again. The three of them were puzzled; she had Rattler draw a copy of the symbol so they at least had that as a reference.¶

Minutes after they began eating, a knock came from the front door. "Are you expecting anyone, Daisy?" Dan asked. "No. I wonder who it could be." Rattler wiped his mouth. "I'll get it, you two keep eating. Rattler grabbed one of his katanas and carried it behind him as he approached the door. It could be an innocent neighbor or a friend of Daisy's, but with everything that had happened, he would rather be safe than sorry. Peering through the small curtain, he recognized Tsume's face. But he did not recognize the other three ninjas that were standing behind him, their masks completely covered their faces. "It's okay, they're with me." Tsume said through the door. "I also have my daughter."¶

"Daisy... Dan... Tsume's back! And he's brought friends!" Daisy came running to the door. "Well, let them in, quick!" Rattler opened the door and Tsume's daughter stepped inside. When she uncovered her head, they saw she was slightly younger than Rattler. "These were members of our clan." Tsume said. "Were?" Asked Rattler. "Once I returned to get my daughter, I told my three closest friends, and they decided to return to Blackwater with me. This is Yoru, <u>Monsuta</u> (- over the a), and Risu. And this is my daughter, Kana." All four of them bowed to show their respect to Rattler and his friends.¶

"Well, it's a good thing I have a big house. You all are welcome to spend the night. Would your friends care for something to eat?" Asked Daisy. "If we are not intruding on your hospitality." "Of course not. Besides, we're going to need all the help we can get. I'm assuming they're willing to help us?" "When my father told me about Don'yoku's plans for acquiring such a devastating weapon, I decided that my homeland was more important than my clan." Kana explained. "They do not share our views." Daisy was amazed. "How did you learn English so well?" She wondered. "Shortly after my father left on his quest twelve years ago, the clan decided to teach a selected few to learn your language. I was lucky enough to be one of them."¶

Do your friends speak any English?" Asked Rattler. "Unfortunately, no. But I can translate anything you need until they do." "Then we need to get a good night's sleep so we can discuss things after breakfast. A lot has happened since you've been gone." Explained Daisy. After setting up sleeping arrangements, the eight of them went to bed. Rattler knew that the additional ninjas would become a great asset to the team.

Chapter XIX - Starting a New Ninja Clan¶

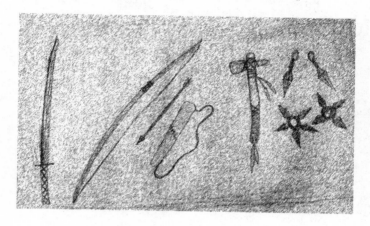

With the dining room table filled to its
capacity of eight people, Daisy wondered how
their plans to take down Dead-Eye Inc. would
change. She was gathering information from the
inside, and Rattler continued his training so he
would be prepared for any confrontations during
his recon missions. Dan had just about finished
Rattler's new steam-cycle. With the addition of
five ninjas, they could possibly gather enough
evidence to take to the sheriff, or better yet, the
Texas Marshall.¶

"How were you all able to get here so fast?
Ronin said it took him over a year to complete
his journey." Rattler asked as they sat around
finishing their orange juice. "Ronin was one man,
he had to sleep. One of us was always awake and

rowing the boat." Tsume answered. "What if it were to rain?" Daisy inquired. "A traditional japanese boat, called a wasen, has a room in the middle with a roof. Only the person rowing would get wet. But, it was a small price to pay for getting here as fast as we did." Kana added. "When we fled Japan." Tsume started. "We left behind some family and a few friends who were not convinced of the impending doom that lay ahead. We tried to warn them of Don'yoku's plans for conquering Japan, but most of my warnings fell on deaf ears. So, there are only five of us here to help."¶

"You are welcome to stay here, but I'm concerned that it might not suit the needs of your… are you still considered a 'clan?'" Daisy was worried about the space restrictions for this many people. Surely they would need much more room for training. Rattler had enough, but with the addition of five more people, she could only picture them doing so outside. That would bring even more problems with neighbors and customers seeing six people fighting with swords and other weapons in her back yard. "I already have a solution for the situation." Rattler spoke up. "Chief White Cloud said we were always welcomed at the village. With the extra land they were able to purchase with the money from the sale of The Golden Snake, he would gladly let us set up residence somewhere. With the eight of us, plus the help of some of the Blackfoot warriors, it would make things much more easy."¶

"So, it's settled then." Said Dan. "Daisy and I will help you with whatever you need this weekend. Things have been so hectic these past few months, I'm thinking about taking on an apprentice." "That would be an excellent idea." Daisy added. "I hired an assistant at the gun shop, and it's been working out quite well." "Speaking of work. How are things going with your job? Do you like your boss?" Rattler asked as he stood up to go to the kitchen with his empty plate and silverware. "Mr. Lucas is a nice enough boss. He definitely needed an assistant. I honestly don't know how he managed without one for so long."¶

"Have you gathered any information we can use?" Rattler rinsed his plate and set it by the sink. "Actually, there is something very odd going on. I found a memo that Mr. Lucas had dropped but it was addressed to a Mr. Richards from a Mr. Experiment." Daisy stated. "But when I asked around the office, nobody had heard of either of them." "Did you return the memo to your boss?" "Yes. But, he just took the note and said thank-you. He didn't mention anything more about it." "Perhaps it was for someone from another company or supplier?" Dan mentioned. "No, it was about improving a weapons test for more ammunition in a clip. Besides, memos are used for inter-office communications. You don't send a 'memo' to another company; you write them a letter." "I didn't know that." Dan said, holding up both hands defensively.¶

"I know what they're up too." Rattler added. "That's some sort of code for their new weapon, think about it. How would you communicate something top secret within a legitimate company…?" Everyone shrugged their shoulders. "You'd use fake names and keep the information short and vague. I suspect your boss is either Mr. Richards, or Mr. Experiment. Mr. Experiment, that's so cloak and dagger." Daisy shook her head a little. "I don't know how I'm going to find out which one Mr. Lucas is, he would probably become very suspicious if I keep poking my nose into the situation. What should I do?" "We'll think of something, Daisy. Right now, we've got to go to the Blackfoot Indian village and speak with Chief White Cloud." Rattler motioned for everyone to take care of dishes so they could get going.¶

Tsume explained to his companions what

the plan was. "Rattler, does Chief White Cloud know about what I've done?" Asked Tsume. Rattler tried to reassure him. "I don't think it would be necessary to tell him, but I think somehow he already knows. He's got a knack for that kind of thing. Chief White Cloud is a very wise man. The Great Spirits tell him a many things; in fact, I think you are the 'stranger' he warned us about before you arrived in Blackwater. But, let's not dwell on the past, we've got more important things to worry about." Kana overheard them while she was sorting her pack in the next room. But, she decided not to say anything and keep the information to herself.¶

Once outside, the six of them started jogging at a brisk pace towards the Blackfoot village; Dan and Daisy had a few things to do before heading out to meet them. On the way, Rattler and Tsume caught each other up on the details of recent events. "So, will they send assassins after you?" Rattler asked. "Their main goal is the recovery of The Snake Blade; if they accomplish that, then they will turn their attention to us. That is another reason my friends are willing to help." As they approached the entrance to the village, Rattler turned to Tsume. "Tell your friends to remove their masks so the

Blackfoot warriors won't see them as possible enemies." Kana said something in Japanese and the three ninjas removed their hoods. "Thank-you, Kana." Said Rattler.¶

Six Blackfoot warriors met them at the gate. "Let me guess... Chief White Cloud is expecting us." Said Rattler. "No, but since your father's recent visit, we've noticed strangers checking out our village with binoculars." The eldest warrior spoke directly to Rattler. "The Chief has put more of us on guard duty until further notice. Who are they?" He asked, pointing to the ninjas. "These are people from Japan who have traveled many miles to help us deal with Dead-Eye Inc." "Why are they helping?" The warrior asked. "Dead-Eye Inc. is manufacturing a weapon that will be bought by Don'yoku, an evil leader in their country, who will use it to take control of more land. Innocent people will die." "Then let's not waste any more time, I will take you to see the chief immediately."¶

Once they were inside, the chief greeted them in his usual fashion. "How can the Blackfoot people be of assistance?" He said smiling and motioning for them to have a seat. "We've come to ask for a piece of land where we can stay until the people at Dead-Eye Inc. are brought to justice." Chief White Cloud seemed to be deep in thought. "We could stay with Daisy, but we need more space to train, without drawing unnecessary attention to ourselves. Dead-Eye has many eyes and ears in Blackwater, we need to be careful." Chief White Cloud finally spoke. "We have dealt with some of these men before during one of your father's visits. We know they would do us harm if they could." Rattler began standing up. "I'm sorry, we do not want to bring your people into all of this. This is our fight." The chief held up his hand to stop Rattler from speaking. "This is our fight as well. We cannot sit here and let those we care about put themselves in harm's way and do nothing. If those people develop such a weapon as you have described, then our people would most surely be in as much danger as everyone else. They only fear us because of our numbers and skills as warriors. But with such a weapon at their disposal, they would fear us no longer."¶

The chief motioned for a handful warriors to step forward. "Let me introduce you to our four most skilled warriors. This is Sahale, he is our most skilled archer; he can help you on your quest. This is Maska, he is our deadliest, close-combat warrior. No one is more adept with a tomahawk; he can help you on your quest. This is Nigan, he is our most skilled hunter and tracker; he can help you on your quest. And this is Sinopa, she is our most skilled cook and healer; she can help you on your quest." Each warrior knelt to the ground as they were introduced. "They know the perfect area for you to set up camp, be it temporary or permanent, our land is your land. The money you shared with our people was a great gift, but you were already our family. Go and train."¶

Nigan led them to the location that they would soon call home for the foreseeable future. Rattler's entire team had now grown to twelve members. Once everyone had been introduced to each other, with Tsume translating when needed, they all learned which part they would play in Dead-Eye Inc.'s downfall. "First thing we need to do is build shelters for us to sleep in." Rattler began. "How many should we build?" Tsume asked. "I'm not sure. Should we each make our own small shelter, or are people willing to share? This is my first time dealing with something like this. Ronin and I had always shared a humble shelter." Tsume consulted with the ninjas, as the Blackfoot warriors went into the forest to collect wood. Rattler felt out of his comfort zone, he had never pictured himself as a leader. "We feel that we should rebuild our own ninja clan here in Blackwater." Said Kana. "We have decided that you, Rattler, will be the head of our clan. But, since you have the most responsibilities and the burden of leadership; Tsume will be in charge of the training. Everyone here needs training in the martial arts, including the Blackfoot warriors, Dan, and Daisy." "Then I will do my best." Said Rattler.¶

Planning the layout of their own little village, Rattler decided that building six living quarters would be the best way. He and Tsume would share a shelter; the two females would share a shelter; and each ninja would share with a Blackfoot warrior. Rattler's shelter would be big enough for Dan to stay when he visited, as well as Kana's shelter being big enough to share with Daisy when she visited. A large fire pit would lay at the center, and two training structures would lay just beyond the living quarters. An outdoor training arena would take little time to arrange. But a dojo would need to be built whenever the weather would not allow outside training and exercising.¶

Once the warriors returned with ample wood, they informed Rattler that they would need to go hunting for wild buffalo. "Doesn't the village have supplies to help us with the construction?" Asked Tsume. Sinopa sat on the ground and started peeling strips of bark off the large branches they had just collected. "The main village will not help us with any construction of our small village." "Why not?" Asked Tsume. "Just as you will be training us, this is part of your training. We will teach you everything we know about hunting, tanning hides, and building structures, as well as our fighting style. I myself will be cooking meals for everyone shortly, so please help the others with building an adequate fire pit." She continued stripping bark and placing it into a pile to use later for attaching the wooden joints before covering it with hide.¶

Finishing the fire pit rather quickly, the Blackfoot warriors started stretching and preparing for the upcoming buffalo hunt. "Have you seen a buffalo before, Yoru?" Asked Sahale. Tsume asked him in Japanese. "He said he has not seen one yet. But, he has seen their hides and know that they are very large." "Well I hope he's good with a bow, because you cannot take one down with only a sword." Tsume translated. "He says that sounds like a challenge." "Not at all. Just advice from one warrior to another, I meant no disrespect." Tsume let them both know that since they are on the same team, they should act like brothers. "It would take more for brothers to get offended than mere words."¶

The Blackfoot warriors, with the help of Tsume, taught the ninjas several words in English so they would be able to coordinate their efforts during the hunt to take down a mighty buffalo. They all needed to be on the same page and understand what each of them was saying to avoid injuries. And in turn, Tsume taught the Blackfoot warriors a few words in Japanese just in case.¶

Kana walked over to Sinopa and knelt down to speak. "Is it your culture for women to do the cooking?" Sinopa looked up after adding a few spices to some boiling water. "It is an honor to make a meal for a fellow warrior. Not only am I providing nutrition for my Indian brother, but there is an amount of trust involved." "Trust?" "They trust that I am providing live-giving food and herbs. I help many warriors heal their injured bodies. Many of the other women in the village seek my guidance concerning cooking. I also have a great knowledge of plants and animals; which are safe to eat; how to cure certain meats. In the Blackfoot tribe, cooking is a very respectful profession. Battles have been avoided with diplomacy and a well-cooked meal." She continued stirring as Kana stood up. "Thank-you, I would much like to learn some cooking skills from you." "You're welcome."

Sinopa replied.¶

    It took them only twenty minutes to locate a small herd of buffalo. The ninjas looked in awe at the large beasts grazing on the Texan plains. Yoru said something in Japanese. "What did he say?" Asked Sahale. "He understands now why he needs a bow." Tsume chuckled. "How many are we going to hunt?" He followed with, more seriously. "One." Said Sahale."Only one?!" Added Kana. "One!" Said Maska. "It will take us a while to consume all of the meat from a single buffalo." "How long will it take us to build the village if we're using hides to keep out the rain?" Tsume asked, turning to face the Blackfoot warriors. "It will take us a while. Building a new village teaches us patience. We will receive no help from the main village. By the time we are done with one structure, any one of you will be able to build one by yourself. Come, let us focus on the hunt."¶

    "I'll let you all take this one down." Said Rattler. Kana did not seem too amused. "You are not going to help us? Then why did you come?" She did not appear to be angry, just curious. It was hard to tell what she was feeling at any given moment; she always spoke with the same voice, with the same tone, and the same volume. "I'm your safety net just in case things become too dangerous. But don't worry, these warriors will help you so you probably won't need me. Besides, I want to see your hunting skills for myself."¶

Sahale, raised his bow and waited. He held his aim for over a minute. "Get out of the way." He said aloud. "Who's he talking too?" Asked Kana. "He's talking to the herd." Answered Rattler. "They cannot hear him." "He knows that, it's just his way. You will learn a lot about your new 'brothers' over the next few months. Let me ask you something, are you always this stand-offish?" "I'm not stand-offish... it's just my way." Kana said forming a little smile.¶

All of a sudden the ninjas started shouting with excitement. Sahale had struck a medium-size buffalo and it had turned towards them and started running at full speed. Thankfully the rest of the herd was running in the opposite direction. Risu and Monsuta raised their bows and fired directly at the buffalo as Yoru drew his katana. Rattler drew The Snake Blade and stood at the ready. As the beast drew closer and closer, the ninjas saw its horns. They shouted in Japanese, some of which the others understood to mean 'RUN!' Yoru managed to jump to one side at the last second and swing along its rib cage; but, instead of slicing into its flesh, it bounced along its tough hide, barely making a nick. It continued charging at Kana and Rattler as the others started firing more arrows after getting clear of the buffalo's path.¶

Time seemed to slow down as Rattler remembered how Ronin had once described stories of various battles. But, instead of an enemy riding atop a large horse, he was facing a rampaging buffalo. He timed the galloping motion of the animal and shuffled aside and took a great swing at its front legs, toppling it to the ground. Then, without any hesitation, ran to the fallen buffalo and plunged The Snake Blade into its skull. It almost immediately ceased its struggling. Rattler had delivered the death blow. The Blackfoot warriors cheered as they ran towards them, it took a great deal of strength to penetrate a buffalo's skull.¶

Rattler and the Indians knelt beside the now motionless animal and began praying. After they had finished, they took out their hunting knives and began carving. "Why did you pray?" Asked Kana. She seemed to be the most curious out of the bunch. "Even though we killed the great buffalo." Maska started explaining. "He is still our brother. We are thanking him for his sacrifice." "His sacrifice… you mean for his life?" She asked. "Yes." Said Rattler, stepping forward. "Although he is an animal, he is still sacred to the Blackfoot people. They give thanks to all the Great Spirits whenever they need to kill one of them." "In our lands, we never kill sacred animals." Said Kana. "Then what do you do?" Asked Rattler. "Well, some pray to them. The Hindus pray to the monkey god, Hanuman." Kana said. "I think you'll come to find the Blackfoot Indian culture very interesting." Rattler said as he took out his knife out and joined his Indian brothers.¶

Within three weeks, two of the residential structures of their small village were completed. The outside training arena was also finished; as well as the set-up for tanning hides. The ninjas were learning some English and were very enthusiastic about improving their archery skills. And the Blackfoot warriors were also enjoying learning how to use katanas. Over the years, Dan had made several swords and had given them to Rattler. The ninjas paid several visits to Dead-Eye Inc.'s headquarters, as well as some of their testing sites. It seemed as though their security had become aware of some investigation, but did not know the source. Nevertheless, additional guards were placed at key locations, making it harder for Rattler and his team to complete each raid.¶

It was dinner time in their little village. They had grown tired of buffalo meat, so they were hunting smaller game for their meals. Most of the cured buffalo meat was given to the main village; but, as was tradition, the main village would only accept the gift, and not give them anything in return. The ninjas enjoyed the dish that Daisy had brought. Rattler always wondered how she had so much time to accomplish what she did. Working a full-time job while running a business; cooking and cleaning; and even learning some martial arts along the way. He was starting to see her in a whole new light. Dan also noticed how Daisy and Rattler had become much closer.¶

"I think it is time to give our ninja clan a name." Tsume announced after swallowing the last bit of BBQ squirrel. "I agree." Said Kana. "We have grown closer with our Indian brothers, and so we should include them in this naming process." Maska stood up near the fire and waited for everyone to stop speaking. "I think there is only one true name that we can give our ninja clan." They all stopped eating and listened to what he had to say. "We owe all of this new land to Rattler and his father, Max. We should honor them by being known as 'The Golden Snake Clan.'" All of the Blackfoot warriors started yelling out, while holding up their tomahawks above their heads. The ninjas tried to fit in as well. They held their katanas above their heads and started screaming. "I think we've decided on a name." Said Daisy.¶

*¶

When Daisy awoke on Saturday morning, she gathered her things and loaded them into her bicycle basket. It would only take her just over half and hour to ride back to town. Pedaling down the road, she thought about Rattler. She missed having him around all of the time. He would typically make sure all dirty dishes were taken into the kitchen and washed. Since he and Tsume moved out to live on the Blackfoot Indian's land, she either made herself a small meal, or stopped at a restaurant on the way home from work.¶

Parking her bike next to the porch, Daisy unlocked the front door and headed upstairs for a shower. Putting on casual business attire, she made herself a light breakfast of bagels, fresh fruit, and a glass of milk. She sat on the living room couch reading the Daily Blackwater and awaited the arrival of her executive assistant, Betty. Flipping through the local news, a headline caught her attention. "Bounty Hunter

Catches Dangerous Criminal" Daisy decided to give the article a quick read. Apparently, this was a rather famous bounty hunter who typically pursued high-profile rapists and murderers. She was so engrossed in the story, the knock at the front door startled her.¶

"Good morning, Miss Daniels." Said Betty. "Good morning, Mrs. Smith. Won't you come in." Daisy said, holding the door open. "Oh, this package was on your front porch." "Thank-you. I'll open it later. Do you have the weekly receipts?" She asked. "Right here, as always. Business was up this week. There's a lot of chatter about Dead-Eye Inc.'s security issues. Apparently there has been a rash of break-ins and they're hiring extra guards for their headquarters, testing ranges, and warehouse." Of course Daisy already knew all of this as she was an employee, but she did not want Betty suspecting she knew a little too much. "My boss thinks Gunz a' Blazin' is trying to sabotage our manufacturing efforts. He's assured me that the culprits will soon be apprehended." Daisy said aloud. "I certainly hope not!" She thought to herself.¶

Betty sat in the comfortable chair in the living room. "All I know is that people in town are spooked by all of this nonsense and gun sales are up. You've made more money in the last month than you did all of last quarter." Daisy looked at the receipts and did a few calculations. "Based on your performance and how well we're doing, I'm giving you a twelve percent raise in your salary." Betty's eyes grew very wide. "I don't know what to say." She gasped. "Simply say thank-you, you've earned it." The two women finished going over business and Betty went home to her husband. Daisy slightly envied her marriage. And, as soon as Betty left, her thoughts once again returned to Rattler. Was she falling for him, or merely infatuated with the strong man he had become. No, it was clear... she was in love.

Chapter XX - The Reveal¶

Daisy woke up fairly early Sunday morning; she showered and got dressed; and after a light breakfast of cereal and a piece of fruit, she headed outside and got on her bicycle. She pedaled as fast as she could towards Rattler's village on the Blackfoot Indian's land. Daisy had devised a plan to find out who Mr.

Richards and Mr. Experiment really are. But, she
needed the help of Kana and Nigan to pull it off.
Cruising down one of the long, downhill roads,
she thought of how she would confess her
feelings to Rattler. If he did not return her
affections, she would be heart-broken. But, deep
down she somehow knew that would not be the
case.¶

After a pleasant ride to the village, she
parked her bicycle by one of the finished living
structures and walked towards her friends. Since
the weather was nice, they were all training in
their outdoor arena. Sahale and Maska were
training Kana and the other ninjas how to use
tomahawks in close-quarter combat. Using
katanas as their main weapon, pulling out a
tomahawk against an enemy from Japan would
confuse them, giving Kana and the other ninjas
the upper hand. Japanese ninjas are used to
fighting with swords, kunai, and shurikins; they
have never seen a tomahawk, and would have a
difficult time defending against a fellow ninja
trained to use one.¶

Rattler was sitting on one of the homemade
benches that surrounded the arena. Daisy walked
over and sat beside him; he seemed to be very
focused on what was taking place in front of him
and did not seem to notice her. "Hello, Daisy."

He said, still watching the fighting going on twenty feet away. She was mistaken, he did notice her. "Hello, Rattler. I was hoping to talk with you alone before I head back to town." She was wondering what was going through his mind at that moment. "Sure." He said. "We can go for a short walk right after supper." She smiled and turned her attention to the training.¶

Once everyone had finished with their fighting exercises, they did a quick workout with some heavy logs. Pulling them around the village as Rattler had done when he lived with Ronin. This exercise was Rattler's favorite, and he always gave it everything he had. The others marveled at he tenacity; he was able to drag his log completely around their village in nearly half the time it took everyone else, even Maska. Once their cardio- and muscle-building exercises were complete, they broke for a late lunch of venison and fresh berries. Since this land was near a small stream, they had a continual supply of fresh drinking water, but the fish that swam by were too small to eat.¶

"I have a very clever plan that should allow us to find out the identity of both Mr. Richards and Mr. Experiment." Daisy stated. "I'm convinced one of them is my boss, Mr. Lucas." Swallowing a hand full of berries, Maska spoke up. "Wouldn't it be dangerous for you to find out?" "I would be completely immune if I can get some help." She said. "How can we be of assistance?" Asked Rattler, finishing his last bite of venison. "I need Nigan to come to Dead-Eye Inc. tomorrow and fill out an application for an entry level position under the alias, Michael Richards. He looks the most similar to Mr. Lucas, which is vital to my plan. And then that's where Kana comes in." Everyone was paying close attention as she continued to lay out her plan.¶

"Mr. Lucas shows up to work at the exact same time every day. So, on Tuesday, Kana waits in the lobby for Mr. Lucas to enter the building. She will follow him down the main hall and call out 'Mr. Richards!' just before they reach the elevator. If he turns around, it means Mr. Lucas is using 'Mr. Richards' as an alias." "And what do I say to him if he turns around?" Asked Kana. "It's simple. You just say, 'Sorry, I thought you were somebody else. My friend Michael Richards filled out an application yesterday and was coming in this morning to follow up. I was hoping to catch him and invite him out for breakfast. Sorry to bother you.'." "But why would I actually need to go in and fill out an application?" Asked Nigan. "That's in case they suspect something. He might actually go down to personnel and check for the application. Sign in at the front desk as Michael Richards and fill out an application; there won't be any loose ends."¶

"Brilliant!" Said Rattler. "I couldn't have thought of a plan like that. It should work." Everyone continued talking about preparations for the plan until it was time to do chores. Sahale was taking Yoru and Monsuta hunting for wild boar; Nigan, Maska and Risu were tanning a buffalo hide for the third living structure; and Sinopa was teaching Kana how to prep and cook supper. Kana was very keen on learning the medicinal aspects of cooking and how to prepare nice meals. Her old ninja clan focused more on combat and work. Their meals tended to be meant only for nourishment and lacked in the tastiness department. She was most interested in all of the spices Sinopa was able to incorporate into each dish.¶

After a filling supper of pork, bread, and various vegetables, Rattler and Daisy went for the walk they had discussed earlier that day. "It's very beautiful out here, away from the city." Daisy commented as they neared the stream. Rattler planned the route they were going to take; it would lead past where the stream entered a large river. "I enjoy the simpleness of it all. It takes me back to my days when I lived with Ronin. Things were much more simple back then. We trained hard every day, and every day I thought of all of the family and friends we left behind." Rattler bent down and picked up a small rock and tossed it in the stream and watched the water ripple for several seconds.¶

"I miss them too." Said Daisy. As they continued walking, she moved in a little closer to Rattler. "I also miss getting to see you every day." She said. "I do as well. Along with your delicious cooking." "You know Sinopa is a much better cook than I am." Daisy quipped. "If you say so, but your pot roast is my absolute favorite." Rattler picked up another rock and tossed it into the stream again. "So, what was it you wanted to talk to me about?" He asked. Daisy started to blush a little. "I don't want to seem too forward, but…" Rattler was about to pick up another rock, but stopped and stood straight up. "Then let me tell you first then. Daisy… I have feelings for you." Daisy did not expect Rattler to be the first to confess his feelings. They both were a little befuddled. They finished their walk without saying much. Each wanted to say more, but they were unsure of *what* to say.¶

Returning to their little village, they helped

straighten things up and Daisy went to get her bicycle. She had about an hour of light left before the sun went down. Rattler followed her and took her hand before she pedaled away. "Let's... just take things slow for now." He said, not really wanting to let go of her hand. "I agree. Let's let things progress naturally." Rattler took her hand and gave it a small kiss before letting go. Daisy had a warm feeling in her heart the entire trip home. Laying in her bed, she closed her eyes and dreamed of how her life was about to change.¶

*¶

Monday morning had arrived and Nigan walked through the front doors of Dead-Eye Inc. wearing a business suit. Sinopa washed his hair the night before and helped him to look presentable. Nigan had never combed his hair before, nor had he ever wore a suit. He tried to act casual as he approached the front desk. "Hello. My name is Michael Richards and I am here to fill out an application please." The guard behind the desk looked him up and down quickly. "Okay. Can you sign in on this visitor's sheet?" He said, pointing to the form attached to a clipboard that lay in front of him. "Don't forget to sign as Michael Richards." Nigan thought to himself. He bent over slightly, picked up the pen next to the sign-in sheet, and signed the name, 'Michael Richards.' "Thank-you. Now just head down that hallway and take a right. Look for the sign that says, 'Human Resources' and ask for an application."¶

He walked down the hall and turned a right. It took him a few seconds to find the sign and entered the office. "May I help you?" Asked a lady behind the desk closest to the doorway. "Yes, I am Michael Richards and I am here to fill out an application, please." The lady took out an application and attached it to a clipboard with a pen and handed it to him. "Have a seat over there and bring it back when you have filled it out completely. Make sure not to leave any blanks. If something does not apply to you, fill the line in with 'NA' instead of leaving it blank." "Thank-you." Said Nigan, as he headed over and took a seat where she had indicated.¶

After completing the application entirely, he returned it to the lady behind the desk. "Thank-you. You can expect a call for an interview within the next two days, Mr." She looked at the application. "Richards." The phone on her desk began to ring. "Have a nice day, sir." She said as she picked up the phone. Nigan smiled and walked back to the lobby. His nerves made him stop to use the restroom. Somehow, filling out a phony application felt more dangerous than taking down a charging wild boar. Walking outside into the fresh air made him fill a whole lot better. His part was finished; he loosened his tie and headed back to the village. Tomorrow was Kana's turn to complete their mission.¶

*¶

Daisy arrived extra early at Dead-Eye Inc., she was waiting for Kana to show. They both agreed to meet twenty minutes before her bosses arrival; luckily for them, he kept a very strict routine. She spotted Kana walking through the parking lot. Daisy went to meet her and go over the plan one more time. "Kana." She called. Kana met her gaze and they stepped over to the sidewalk. "Remember, you sit over on that bench right there. As Mr. Lucas approaches the front doors, I'll walk up and say, 'Good morning, Mr. Lucas. Don't forget your eleven o'clock meeting with Mr. Hughes to go over the packaging designs.' Then, you follow a short distance behind him and wait for him to reach the elevator…" Kana interrupted. "And that's when I call out to him as 'Mr. Richards.'" They finished going over the fine details before they each took their places outside the building and waited.¶

Twenty minutes passed by, and like clockwork, Mr. Lucas rounded the corner of the building and headed for the front doors. "Good morning, Mr. Lucas, don't forget you eleven o'clock meeting with Mr. Hughes to go over the packaging designs." She glanced over his shoulder and saw Kana nod her head as she started walking towards them. "Good morning, Miss Daniels. Do you have the projections ready for that meeting?" He inquired. "Yes, sir. They're in my 'out' box, I'm heading there now to proof-read it one last time before I place it on your desk." "Very good. I'll see you upstairs." He knew she usually took the stairs instead of the elevator, so that part of the plan was already in place. Making sure Mr. Lucas did not see her following him, Kana kept looking around, as if she were looking for someone.¶

After a short walk down the hallway, Mr. Lucas finally arrived at the elevators. "Mr. Richards!" Kana called out. Mr. Lucus, out of habit, turned to see who was calling him by his alias. "I'm sorry, sir. I thought you were someone else." She said nervously. "I was hoping to catch my friend following up on a recent job application and invite him to lunch later today." Mr. Lucas smiled. "Well, young lady. I'm almost sad to say that I'm not this Mr. Richards. I would enjoy having lunch with a woman as lovely as you." Kana felt a little nauseous. This man was obviously at least twenty years her senior. She faked a slight blush. "Thank-you for the compliment. I think I'll go wait in the lobby." She turned and walked away. "I didn't catch your name, Miss…" "I'm Sarah." She said as she kept walking Not wanting to engage in conversation. He must have took the hint because he turned and pushed the button for the elevator.¶

Kana walked through the lobby and out the front doors. She made a quick stop at Daisy's house to change back into her own clothes. They had pulled it off; if Mr. Lucas' alias was indeed Mr. Richards, then it was most likely that Mr. Experiment was the alias of Mr. Boyd. She ran at a steady jog all the way back to the village and delivered the news to the rest of her clan.¶

*¶

As The Golden Snake clan sat around the fire eating pork, vegetables and bread, Rattler described how his plan was going to unfold. "I'm going to Daisy's house and get Boyd's home address. Then, I'm going to pay him a little visit to let him know that there are citizens of Blackwater who are aware of what Dead-Eye is up too." But Tsume did not agree. "You are merely warning them, they will come after us when they find out who we are!" Rattler remained calm, he was not used to anyone questioning him. "I'm not simply informing him that we know what's going on. I'm threatening him to so he has the choice to turn himself into the authorities." "And if he doesn't turn himself in?" Asked Kana. "Then we'll take further measures." He countered.¶

The meal continued as they debated on what their next move should be if Rattler's plan did not work. While he was away on his mission, the Blackfoot warriors were going to learn how to throw a kunai and the ninjas were going to learn how to throw tomahawks. Their clan was eager to cross-train and learn different weapons and fighting styles. Any advantage they could use in battle would be one they wanted to learn. Rattler finished his meal and left for town, the others continued discussing the advantages of various weapons.¶

*¶

Wearing his armored trench coat and hat; and carrying the Snake Blade, two kunai and a few shurikin, Rattler left for Daisy's house. The sun had just about set and he was determined to put a serious damper on Dead-Eye's plans to sell their latest automatic weapon. Even though they were not a hundred percent sure that Mr. Boyd was actually Mr. Experiment, Rattler felt in his heart that he must be. And, if Mr. Boyd was not Mr. Experiment, he was a high enough executive in the company to know who Mr. Richards and Mr. Experiment were. He quickened his jogging pace as he saw the sign on the main road that read, "Blackwater - 8 Miles Ahead."¶

Daisy was waiting on her porch with a pitcher of sun tea and freshly made pecan pie. She was hoping he would stay a while before confronting Mr. Boyd at his house. As Rattler ran up the driveway, she stood up and walked down the front stairs to greet him. "Hello, Daisy. Something smells really good." "It's my homemade pecan pie, plus some freshly brewed sun tea. Come, sit and rest a while." She handed him a glass as he walked up onto the porch and took a seat in one of her rocking chairs. "This is good tea." Rattler said after taking a huge gulp. "Thank-you. I made it especially for you." She blushed only slightly as she offered him a slice of pie.¶

After eating and making small talk, Rattler finally asked. "Can I have Mr. Boyd's address, please." Rattler stood up and stretched his shoulders back and rotated them as he often did to loosen the tension in his chest. "I know this has to be done Rattler, but I'm still a little worried." Rattler tried to reassure her. "I've been training now for over twelve years for missions like this one. Besides, I highly doubt a forty- or fifty-something-year-old executive will be of any threat. Remember why we're doing this. If they succeed with the sale of fully-automatic weapons, hundreds, maybe thousands of innocent people could be killed." Daisy walked over and gave him a long hug. "I know. I'm just worried that he'll remember you somehow. Hey!" She said abruptly. "I have an idea! I'll be right back." She went in the house and disappeared upstairs.¶

Rattler sat back down and rocked slightly in the chair. Although this was a serious mission he was about to take on, he was surprisingly relaxed. Within five minutes, Daisy returned back downstairs. "Come inside for a minute." She called from the sitting room. Rattler got up and went inside. "I really need that address, Daisy." He said, walking into the sitting room. "I'll give it to you in just a second… here, try this on." She handed him a brown bandanna, similar in color to his coat. "What should I do with this?"

He asked. Daisy huffed. "Here, let me." She
folded it from corner to corner. "Turn around."
Rattler did a one-eighty while Daisy stood on a
footstool. She flung it over his head and tied the
two ends in a knot behind him, covering his face
from the nose down. "This will keep him from
seeing your face and being able to identify you
in the future."¶

Rattler looked in the mirror. "This will work.
So are you still worried about me?" He asked.
"A little less." She admitted. "His address is 298
Statehouse Ave. He's still single and has no
children. But, I think he has a dog... a retriever
if I'm not mistaken." Rattler started to leave
when Daisy stopped him. "Wait a minute." She
said walking up to him. "Good luck." She kissed
him on his cheek, but pretty close to his lips.
Rattler wanted to kiss her back, but he did not
want to be distracted. "Thank-you." He said,
turning and jogging back down the driveway.
Rattler had to stay focused on his mission. But
he did enjoy that kiss.¶

*¶

Rattler climbed a tree fifty feet away
from Mr. Boyd's front yard. There were a couple
of lights on in the house. He had already walked
the perimeter and decided on an entry point. He

was waiting for him to go to bed so he could catch him when he was most vulnerable. From what he had observed of his retriever, he was just a pet and not a guard dog. Rattler had some cured buffalo meat in a small pouch tied to his belt. He would offer him a rather large piece and enter through a rear window that he noticed was unlocked when he circled the house earlier. Another light went off, he was probably getting ready for bed. Within twenty minutes, the last light in the house went out. He would wait about ten more minutes before making his move.¶

Knowing the dog was in the back yard in his doghouse, Rattler approached the fence and tossed the cured buffalo meat directly in front of him. The dog immediately started chowing down on the treat as Rattler jumped the fence and made his way to the unlocked window. Once inside, he made his way towards the master bedroom where Mr. Boyd was just about to fall asleep. Slipping inside the room, he looked around. It was extremely dark, but Rattler could see Mr. Boyd's heat signature underneath a very thin blanket. There was a window above the headboard of the bed shedding a tiny amount of moonlight into the room. Beside the bed was a nightstand with a lamp and alarm clock; other than that, the room was spacious with very little furnishings.¶

Rattler spoke in his most intimidating voice. "Wake up, Mr. Experiment!" He said. "I would like a word with you." He made sure he spoke loud enough to rouse him from his sleep without shouting. "What? Who's there?" Mr. Boyd said groggily as he turned onto his back. "I said I would like a word with you... Mr. Experiment!" Mr. Boyd realized the seriousness of the situation. "How do you know my alias?" He asked in a more focused tone. "I know a lot of things about you, your company, and what you've been up too." Rattler stated. He swung the side of his jacket open, preparing himself.¶

Mr. Boyd slowly moved his hand to the nightstand drawer; there was a revolver inside he kept loaded in case of intruders. "I wouldn't do that if I were you!" Rattler warned. Mr. Boyd laid still, but moved his hand more slowly as he spoke. "Do what, exactly?" Rattler's fingers pulled a kunai to his palm; and with one fluid motion, threw it towards the nightstand. *Shhhhewww... thud!* It flew right past Mr. Boyd's hand, slicing through the top fleshy part close to the knuckles and impaled itself into the wood by the lamp. "Aaahhhh!" He shouted. It was not a serious injury, comparable to a paper cut, but it was enough to make him abandon his plans to retrieve his sidearm.¶

"As to who I am." Rattler spoke more softly and calmly. "That is not too important right now. Let's just say I'm a very concerned citizen." "Concerned about what in particular?" Mr. Boyd said, rubbing the small cut on his right hand. "Don't insult me. We both know what's going on at Dead-Eye. And it needs to stop immediately, before someone gets hurt." Rattler unsheathed the Snake Blade and swung it mightily at the foot of Mr. Boyd's bed. It sliced clean through the blanket and into the mattress, missing his toes by mere inches. "Shit, just a minute now!" He shouted, bending his knees and pulling his feet close to his body. He was obviously scared half to death that the stranger who stood before him was about to end his life.¶

"Wait! Wait!" Mr. Boyd shouted, holding both of his hands up in a defensive posture. "What do you want me to do?" Mr. Boyd pleaded. Rattler pointed the sword towards him as he spoke. "You need to put a stop to any further production of your automatic weapons immediately. And you are going to turn yourself in to the Texas Marshall tomorrow afternoon!" Mr. Boyd was shaking uncontrollably. "I cannot do that they'll kill me if I betray them!" He was almost in tears at this point. "Who will kill you?"

Rattler asked. "I thought you knew everything about me." Mr. Boyd said. He seemed to calm down a little bit, but Rattler did not want him to gain any courage. Rattler pulled another kunai from his other pouch and held it to Mr. Boyd's throat. "Who will kill you?!" He shouted into his face. "Tell me!" Rattler demanded. "The Black Bull Society. They'll kill me if I talk, please have mercy…. I just test the weapons, I don't produce them." Mr. Boyd was in full panic mode.¶

The two of them were almost nose to nose. Rattler could see sheer terror in Mr. Boyd's eyes. He needed to drive the point home so he would be taken seriously. "I have people who will be watching you." Rattler stated. "I'll arrange for a Texas Marshall to meet you outside your house at four o'clock on Friday. That gives you five business days to prepare. Turn yourself in to his custody and I can guarantee your safety." "We have a meeting every Friday at five." Mr. Boyd whimpered. "Make up an excuse to leave early then!" Rattler said firmly. "We have eyes everywhere. If you don't turn yourself in by then, someone in our organization will come for you, and kill you!" Mr. Boyd's eyes seemed to roll back in his head as he fainted in Rattler's arms. He laid him back down in his bed gently and checked his breathing. He was still alive; he had just passed out. Rattler retrieved the kunai from the nightstand and climbed back out the window. He even threw a second piece of meat to the dog before climbing the fence and returning home.

Chapter XXI- A Bounty¶

Mr. Boyd paced nervously back and forth outside of Mr. Bull's office, the incident that had just taken place over the weekend had rocked him to the core. He had no idea who the masked man that paid him a visit was, nor did he know how he had found out his code name. He repeatedly checked his watch as the minutes ticked by. "The boss should be here by now." He thought. Mr. Boyd was in a near panic as the elevator around the corner made its ping noise, signaling someone had arrived at this floor. He tried to calm down as the boss approached his office. Pulling out his keys as he neared the door, he finally looked up and saw his employee looking very worried. "I'm very busy this morning." Mr. Bull said. "This better be important. I've got to make rounds for the upcoming inspection."¶

"We need to call an emergency meeting of the Black Bull Society!" Mr. Bull opened his door and shove Mr. Boyd inside, slamming it behind them. "Not so loud, you idiot!" He walked past him to his desk and started pulling files together. "Now why do I need to delay inspection procedures so we can convene an emergency meeting of the B.B.S.?" Mr. Bull huffed as he finally sat down in his chair. "Because, there are people out there who know about our mini-gun project. A masked man with a sword came to my house... MY HOUSE!" He was starting to tremble as he recalled the story. "Calm down. Now, what did this man tell you exactly?" Mr. Boyd took a seat opposite Mr. Bull.¶

"He nearly sliced my feet off when he swung his sword through the foot of my bed, and look at this!" He showed Mr. Bull the cut on the back of his hand. "I tried to go for the revolver I keep in my nightstand, but he threw a knife and it stuck in the hard wood. Oh! And did I mention it was nearly pitch black in my room. There was only a small bit of moonlight shining from behind my headboard." "Well, did you get any look at him?" Mr. Bull asked. Mr. Boyd walked over and filled a cup from the water cooler. "All I could tell you is he was big, over six feet. He was wearing a coat and wide brimmed hat and a mask, like someone about to rob a train. He said if I didn't turn myself into a Texas Marshall by four o'clock this Friday, they're gonna kill me!" He finally took a big drink of water.¶

"And did you believe him?" Mr. Bull asked. "I don't want to find out. He knew me as Mr. Experiment, how would he know that?" He asked. "How did he find out where I live? And why did he single me out?" Mr. Boyd was obviously shaken. "Yes, I'll have my secretary reschedule my practice inspection walk-through for tomorrow, I'll call everyone for an emergency meeting in half an hour." Mr. Bull reassured him. "Try to pull yourself together. This guy doesn't know who he's messing with. The Black Bull Society should not be trifled with."¶

*¶

Daisy had finished her morning report when her boss, Mr. Lucas, entered her office. "Miss Daniels, I have a last-minute meeting with some of the staff; so that project I was going to have you assist me with will have to wait until after lunch." He stated as he looked over the report she had laying in front of her. "This looks good to me. Send it over to accounting right away. I'll be heading to that meeting shortly, I'm just going to retrieve some folders from my office. When you get back, just take messages from anyone who calls for the next hour, hour-and-half, okay." "Yes, sir. I'm on my way now." Daisy took the morning report and headed for the door. "Oh, and Miss Daniels." He added. "I'm very impressed with your efficiency and dedication to the company thus far. Keep it up and there may be a raise in your near future." "Thank-you, sir." She replied as she turned back and exited the office.¶

It took her mere minutes to drop the paperwork off at accounting. On her way back, she spotted Mr. Lucas talking with Mr. Hughes, Head of Ammunition Production. Daisy hung back and followed them down the hallway. "If the testing department was meeting with the ammunition department, it might have something to do with the mini-gun." She thought to herself. They rounded the next corner and headed towards the elevators. Daisy had to be very careful not to be detected; which did not seem likely at this point as the two were completely immersed in their conversation, and were not paying attention to much else. She peered around the corner as they waited for the doors to open. *Ping* As they stepped onto the elevator, Daisy stepped from her hiding spot and approached; she was looking to see which floor they had gone to.¶

After ten seconds had gone by, she noticed it did not stop for other passengers and had gone straight to the twelfth floor. "You need an executive key to access that floor." She thought to herself. "This is not a typical board meeting." In fact, she had never been to that floor, and there was no access from the stairwell. Daisy hurried back to her office and took messages as she continued with her work. It took nearly two hours for Mr. Lucas' return. He entered the office in a very foul mood. "Miss Daniels, could you run down to the cafeteria and bring me my usual lunch?" "Certainly." She answered. "And have them put an extra helping of vegetables and more bread; I'm working through lunch." "Of course. Are we delaying that project, sir?" "Damn it, we won't even have time for that today." "I'm sorry." Daisy offered. "No, it's not your fault, we had an incident… um, I'm going to be delayed for a while; we'll probably pick it up tomorrow morning. My whole day is shot, now!" She did not stick around after that. "Once he got some food in his stomach, his mood may improve." She thought as she headed for the cafeteria.¶

*¶

Rattler awoke the next morning, and after breakfast, a quick workout and some face time with Chief White Cloud on their progress of erecting another village, he asked Sahale to accompany him to town. They grabbed lunch and headed for Daisy's house. Rattler's plan was to wait for her to come home after work to discuss what type of impact his threat had made at the company headquarters. Sahale kept up the same pace as Rattler as they ran their usual path to her house. That was why he asked him to come with him; he was one of the only members of The Golden Snake Clan who could keep up with him at his full pace. Once they arrived at her house, they took a well-deserved rest in the rocking chairs on her front porch. After about twenty minutes of resting, they let themselves into the house and did some sit-ups and push-ups while they waited. Finishing with plenty of time left, Rattler decided to take a trip to the Post Office and look at any new bounties that he and Sahale might be able to take on for some extra spending money for their village supplies. Sahale remained at the house and began prepping vegetables for supper.¶

Walking down Statehouse towards his

destination, Rattler decided to take a small detour and see what had become of the family ranch. He was happy to find out an older couple with children had purchased the property and had begun to incorporate a wide variety of vegetables in the expanded garden. They kept the apple orchard and added a few peach trees. He did not wish to bother the children playing with their dog so he moved on.¶

Arriving at the Post Office, Rattler checked the latest list of people whom had bounties on their head for whatever reason. There were a couple wanted for stealing cattle from various ranches; a few for domestic violence; and then he came upon the most interesting one. Walking over to the window, Rattler asked for a copy from the lady behind the service desk. "Yes, I would like the one for the mysterious stranger who broke into a residential home brandishing a large sword, please."¶

*¶

Daisy clocked out after a long, stressful day. Not only did she have a hunch something important was going on on the twelfth floor, but her boss had acted strangely all afternoon. Sometimes she even heard shouting coming from his office; it was highly probable they had been discussing Rattler's appearance at Mr. Boyd's residence. As she walked outside, gray clouds had gathered overhead and it began to sprinkle ever so slightly. The weather continued getting worse as she walked briskly homeward. Luckily she always brought her umbrella no matter what the weather looked like on her way to work. By the time she saw Rattler and Sahale, it was pouring rain. Walking the rest of the way up the drive, Daisy and Rattler both shouted to each other. "I've got news!"¶

Hanging up her coat and umbrella on the porch, she walked into an aroma-filled house. "What smells so good?" She asked. "Sahale made pork steaks, potatoes, and a huge garden salad." Rattler told her. "I hope everyone is hungry." Sahale said, entering the dining room with a large bowl of salad. "Holy cow! You weren't kidding about it being huge, that could feed six people." Rattler pulled a chair for Daisy, who graciously sat down. "I'm so glad you two are here. And thank-you so much for making dinner. There was definitely something going on at work today." Sahale placed a plate with pork and potatoes in front of her. "Let's eat before we discuss business." He said. "Rattler also has some disturbing news. Stress while eating can give you an upset stomach. Something I learned from Sinopa." They all sat and ate before retiring to the living room.¶

The three of them discussed everything that had happened at Dead-Eye Inc. that day, as well as what should be done about it. "I think two or three of us should break-in and explore that entire floor." Said Rattler. "I also overheard something about a testing demonstration Wednesday night, but I don't know where." Daisy had a disappointed look on her face as she spoke. "That seems like the perfect time to take them down a notch." "Don't worry so much, Daisy." Rattler reassured her. "You can't be expected to get us everything. You're giving us plenty of information. Remember, if you feel that anyone at work suspects you of anything, get outta' there and come tell us." Daisy felt a little better that her 'extended family' had her back. "Perhaps you'll find something about the testing demonstration. But, you have less than forty-eight hours to get that information."¶

*¶

Rattler, Tsume and Maska arrived at Dead-Eye Inc. two hours after sundown; the three of them had gone over their plans all afternoon. "Let's go over what we are each doing one last time." The ninja and the

Blackfoot warrior both nodded in agreement. "Maska, what are you doing?" Asked Rattler. "I'm following you to your entry point; I survey the immediate area and enter only in an emergency." "What else?" Rattler repeated. "I stay hidden as best as I can and only disable a guard if there are no other options." "Good, good. And Tsume?" The ninja spoke softly and steadily. "We climb the drainage pipe to the forth floor of the factory; then to the twelve floor of the office building; enter through the window, and sweep the entire floor for clues." "Right, let's move."¶

Since it was a new moon, there was very little light shining around the building, the parking lot, and the loading docks; it was a perfect night for stealth. Waiting for the guard to round a corner, the trio quickly climbed over the fence and ran between a row of bushes and the outside wall of the factory portion of the main structure. After several minutes, the guard was on the longest route away from where they planned to scale the building. "Let's move!" Said Rattler in a hushed voice. He let Tsume go first as he quickly followed. "Remember Maska, you're our eyes on the ground." "Good luck, my brother." Said Maska. In less than a minute, Rattler and Tsume managed to get on top of the factory; now there was only eight stories to go.¶

The ninja checked the window, fortunately for them it was unlocked; maintenance probably figured no one would ever climb this high to break in. Once inside, Tsume turned and help Rattler inside. "You must add climbing to your training regiment, my friend." "I was right behind you." "If you say so." Tsume said, smiling. Surveying the area, they found that the hallway they were in ran completely around the building without any doors. "I'm guessing the only way into the middle is from the elevator." Rattler pondered. "Elevator?" "I'll explain that later. We either need to get up into the ceiling, or go back out and climb onto the roof."¶

"What about this?" Tsume said, pointing to a vent. "Perfect, but it looks too narrow for me." Rattler observed. "I'll go in, you stay close so we can communicate what I find." Rattler pulled a multipurpose tool from his pocket. "Here, allow me." After several minutes toiling away, Rattler removed the screws and Tsume climbed into the claustrophobic duct work. Five minutes went by before a familiar voice echoed through out to Rattler. "I'm in!"¶

"What do you see?" Asked Rattler. "It's very dark. I'm in one big room, it seems like." Tsume squinted his eyes, straining to see everything. "There's a very large, round table in the middle of the room with ten chairs around it. There seems to be paintings and decorative plants." "Go check out what's on the table." Rattler told him. Tsume walked completely around the table and gathered all the papers and notebooks that were there, mentally remembering where each was placed so he could return every item to its original spot. "I've got everything worth looking at, I'll be right out." Tsume carefully secured the books and documents into his belt and shimmied back out into the hallway.¶

Looking over the documents, most of the writing was in technical jargon and code. Several minutes had gone by, and neither Rattler, nor Tsume found anything useful. "There's got to be something here." Rattler said, frustrated. "Wait a minute, check out this datebook." Tsume whispered. "There's a scribbled address and time for this Wednesday. Maybe you might know where this is." Tsume handed Rattler the open book. "Let's see: 1550, 28th Street, Buckwheat, Texas. This has to be it, but I can't make out the exact time, it's illegible. Looks like we're going to have to camp out there all day to be sure." Tsume reached for the book. "I need to return these to the table so we don't leave any evidence that we were here."¶

Rattler signaled down to where Maska was last hiding; he signaled back that all was clear. Rattler slid down the pipe onto the factory roof; closing the window, Tsume was right behind him. They sneaked to the edge and looked around. Having no guard in sight, they climbed down to the ground and hid behind the row of bushes. After the guard completed his route, he disappeared behind the building and the trio fled the scene and returned to the village as fast as they could. Sharing the news with the rest of their clan, they decided to pass the information along to Chief White Cloud and ask for his guidance first thing after breakfast.¶

*¶

Chief White Cloud sat in the head chair of the council chamber, ready to hear the plight of Rattler and his friends. "We have crucial evidence against Dead-Eye Inc. They are planning a demonstration of their illegal weapon sometime tomorrow for potential buyers." Rattler began his presentation straight to the point. "We want to go to the authorities, but our evidence is not concrete enough to be taken seriously. We are at a crossroad. Tsume and I have seen the plans for this weapon; Daisy has overheard things; Mr. Boyd confessed to me some further details of what is going on within Dead-Eye itself. We do not know how to continue in our quest." Rattler waited for the chief to respond.¶

"I will send a hand-written letter to our local Texas Marshall. Come, bring me my writing quill and a parchment." A young, Blackfoot maiden brought the chief his correspondence supplies and waited for him to write his letter. "If you tell him you have acquired evidence of wrong-doing, he will certainly ask you how you came by it. If I seek an audience with him, he will not question me of such things." Once completed, he handed it to a Blackfoot warrior scout. "Here, take this to Marshal Hamilton Brisco and tell him it is urgent. Most likely he will come later this afternoon. Tell him he is welcome to break bread with us this evening. We are serving a wild boar banquet." The entire Golden Snake Clan thanked Chief White Cloud on their way back to their village; a viable plan was made.¶

*¶

Marshal Brisco arrived shortly after four o'clock later that afternoon, he was greeted by a welcoming committee of Blackfoot villagers.

Hamilton had been here before, and had a good relationship with the chief and his people, that was why he was asked for by name. "Good afternoon." He said to the group that had gathered at the front gates. "Good afternoon." Said one of the villagers. "Chief White Cloud is waiting for you in the great hall, he would like to get business taken care of before the feast. Follow us, please." "Thank-you." Replied Hamilton as he walked behind them. He remembered the last time he had come on such an occasion, they always make wonderful, homemade dishes that incorporate many herbs and spices; some unique to the Blackfoot people.¶

Once inside, he approached the chief, who appeared to be napping in his chair. "Should we wake him?" He whispered. "I am not asleep, merely conversing with the Great Spirits about recent events that have made themselves most dire. Sorry, we cannot call this a social visit, Marshal Brisco." The Marshal took a seat. "That's alright, Chief White Cloud. I go where ever citizens have legal concerns, and from your letter, you have a whopper." The chief sat up straight in his chair. "I have sources that tell me Dead-Eye Inc. is involved with producing weapons that the law prohibits. They want to enable others to have advantages in disputes that could lead to war. Many innocent lives could be lost." The Texas Marshal listened intently as the chief continued. "My sources tell me they will be demonstrating such a weapon tomorrow up in Buckwheat City; but they do not know at what time. I wish I was able to send reinforcements with them should things turn dangerous, but there is not enough time. I would like you, Hamilton Brisco, to accompany Rattler and Maska to see for yourself."¶

Marshal Brisco looked at the address on the letter as he pondered for a moment. "Usually I would like more, concrete evidence to make a move against the largest gun manufacturer in all of Blackwater. But you, Chief White Cloud, do not make such accusations lightly. I will accompany your Blackfoot warriors up to Buckwheat as you have requested. But, this is one situation where I hope you are wrong." "I also wish to be wrong, but I'm afraid this is not the case." The chief stood to his feet. "Now that this has been settled, let us go to the center of the village for some food and fellowship." "After you." Replied Hamilton.¶

*¶

Dan met Rattler and the rest of the clan at

the edge of the village. He was delivering his new steam-cycle just in time for this mission. As he pulled up, Rattler and Maska ran out to meet him. "Hey, Dan!" Maska shouted. He parked the bike and dismounted. "Sorry I'm so late. I just had some last-minuted business to attend to." "That's okay." Said Rattler. "I saved you some of the food they served at the feast. There's plenty of pork, bread, and vegetable stew left for you." Dan did not even bother with a fork. He took a piece of pork with his hands and dug in. "Thank-you, I haven't eaten since breakfast." The juices ran down the side of his face as he wolfed down bite after bite.¶

"So who's the lucky one to be going with you?" Dan asked with a mouth full of food. "It has been settled." Rattler said. "Maska will accompany me on this mission. Hey, but enough of that, tell me all about the bike. It looks awesome!" Rattler approached the steam-cycle. "May I?" "Sure, it's your bike. I put the assault rifle in here." Dan said, pointing to the bike saddle. "You can put your Snake Blade here. You can put two katanas here." Rattler looked more closely. "Two?" "Yes, one goes in here, and the other crosses underneath here. If there are any improvements or additional weapons you want to store, let me know. But don't over do it, or there won't be any more room for a passenger. Go ahead… drive it around a little." Rattler had not driven his own bike before, but he knew enough from watching other people drive. Plus, with a sidecar attached, it was stable enough for the most inexperienced driver. Rattler took a couple of laps before stopping to give rides.¶

After about twenty minutes, Dan stopped him. "Hey, I still need a ride back to town." "Oh, yeah. Come on, let's go…." They took the longer route back to town and talked along the way. Rattler was anxious about confronting whomever he would encounter up in Buckwheat. He remembered his father, Butch, and Scotty discussing plans to take down Dead-Eye Inc., and now it was his chance to finish it. More than anything, he wanted to make his father and Ronin proud of him. Tomorrow would definitely give him that opportunity.¶

*¶

After everyone was about to turn in for the night, Rattler and Maska were making some adjustments to their equipment and supplies. They had eaten plenty of food at the feast and were going to drink only a little water during the next day so when it came time for action, their stomachs would be mostly empty. "A full samurai is a slow samurai." Ronin used to tell him. And, by not packing extra food, it allowed them to travel that much lighter on their trip. After some last minute good-byes and words of encouragement, Rattler and Maska loaded the steam-cycle and headed out. It would take them just over two hours to reach their destination. They wanted to survey every inch of the location so they would be well prepared for anything. Maska was already familiar with the area as he had traveled to another Indian village just outside Buckwheat city limits.¶

They decided to take the fastest route this time. Since Dead-Eye Inc. was not expecting them, and it was the night before, they would not need the element of stealth. Arriving at the address, they spent a couple of hours walking around and finding the best spot to hide and observe the presentation. Afterwards, Rattler and Maska did some vigorous training to tire themselves out before bed. Both men felt relaxed and loose. They needed to stay both focused and well-rested to remain at their peak performance. Marshal Brisco would be there at nine in the morning, that would give them exactly seven hours of sleep before sunrise.

Chapter XXII - The Showdown¶

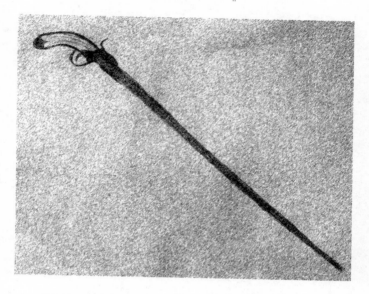

Rattler stood atop a very large boulder, soaking up the sun's rays as they hit his skin from just above the horizon. He had seen many sunrises, but this particular day would prove to be the undoing of Dead-Eye Inc. and so made it extra special. Maska had just finished stowing their gear in the steam-cycle; all they carried were their weapons. "Good morning, Maska. It's a beautiful day." Rattler said, turning around to greet his friend. "Shame the beauty will be wasted on criminals." Replied Maska. "Think of it as a beautiful day for some justice." They both smiled and walked cautiously to the road where Marshal Brisco would be arriving shortly.¶

As they stood there talking for a while, a cloud of dust appeared in the distance, indicating that a vehicle was approaching. Pulling out his binoculars, Maska confirmed that it was the Texas Marshal. His steam-cycle also had a sidecar, which he used to transport people he arrested to the county jail. As he drew nearer, both Rattler and Maska waved to him to let him know they were there waiting. They guided him a quarter mile to where they had hidden their steam-cycle.¶

Once Hamilton's bike was concealed as well, the three of them waited in the spot Rattler and Maska had predetermined was the perfect hiding place in which to observe the weapon demonstration. It was just far enough away to provide them adequate camouflage, but close enough to chase down a fleeing target without the need of a firearm. Now all they needed was somebody to show up. The overall plan was for the Marshal to take whomever Dead-Eye Inc. sent to present the weapon into custody. Maska and Rattler would track down and subdue as many potential clients as possible. That way, they might be able to learn more about the threat from Don'yoku. They would not allow this evil man to get his hands on such a dangerous weapon.¶

Several hours went by without incident. Since this was an out of the way location, not even a single traveler drove past them. They kept going over the plan every twenty minutes or so to keep them alert. It was just about two o'clock in the afternoon when another cloud of dust appeared from the same direction as when the Marshal had arrived hours earlier. Looking through his binoculars again, Maska spoke up. "It's a steam-cycle with a sidecar." Waiting several seconds more, the bike and rider became clearer. "There's something secured in the sidecar." He added. "Could it be a passenger?" Asked Rattler. "Definitely not a passenger; it's covered tightly with a tarp." "Could it be their weapon, then?" Hamilton asked. "It's possible."¶

Mr. Boyd pulled his bike up to the spot where he was going to use to demonstrate the mini-gun. It took him nearly half an hour to assemble the weapon, cover it with a tarp, measure out distances, and place several targets. It took another half an hour before the potential buyers started to arrive. Apparently, the show was scheduled to begin shortly after three o'clock. There were seven clients in all, each with his own body guard, making an audience total of fourteen. They would have to wait until after the demonstration was over and most of the clients left before making their move.¶

Everyone gathered around as Mr. Boyd approached the covered mini-gun. "Gentlemen! We all know why we are here. Nonetheless, are there any questions before I begin with the demonstration?" There was silence for a few seconds. "Most of the questions I have should be answered by the demo. So, let's get to the demo!" Shouted one of the men in a business suit. "Alright, then. Here it is!" Mr. Boyd said as he pulled the tarp off, revealing the mini-gun on its tripod. "Whoa! Now that's what I'm here for!" Shouted another gentleman in the small crowd. There was a little chatter going on between the members of the audience, but nothing that Rattler, Maska, nor the Marshal could understand from that distance.¶

"Let me see the binoculars for a second, please." Said Rattler, holding out his hand. Maska gave them to him. "I don't see any Asians in the group. What are you looking for?" "I thought I saw someone off to the side, behind that boulder." Rattler said, pointing in the direction he was talking about. "Well, there's nobody there now." He stated. "Can you pick up a heat signature?" Asked Maska. "No, that only really works when it's dark." Rattler answered. "What are you talking about?" Hamilton asked. He stopped looking through his binoculars and sighed. "I'll explain all of that later, we need to stay focused. Do you recognize anyone in the crowd?" Rattler asked, handing the binoculars over. "Give me a second." Replied the Marshal.¶

Marshal Brisco scanned over the men very carefully for about a minute. "Yep, I recognize one of them." Passing the binoculars back to Rattler, he continued. "Look for the man who is decked out with lots of jewelry; rings and necklaces." "The guy wearing a hat with a thin beard?" Asked Rattler. "That's him, his name is Victor Turn. He's a major arms dealer from Webbing. I've got you two as witnesses to his attendance at this illegal gathering, so we can pick him and his goon bodyguard up later. Let's see how the demo goes." The three of them continued listening to Mr. Boyd's every word.¶

Once he finished with all of the technical details, such as the rate of fire, reload time, and durability of the weapon, he moved right into a live demonstration. "Who would like to do the honors?" Mr. Boyd asked. Not bothering to wait

to be picked, Mr. Turn simply volunteered by
walking up, shoving others out of his way.
"That's my Victor alright." Said Hamilton.
"He's just digging his own grave deeper."
Rattler passed the binoculars back to Maska.
"Look directly at the mini-gun as it's being fired.
See if there's any part that could possibly
malfunction." "Right." Replied Maska. "Like
what?" Rattler thought for a moment. "I'm not
really sure, just tell me how the gun is reacting
to being fired. If we explain as much detail as
possible, Dan might be able to tell us more
should we not be able to get the gun during the
raid."¶

Before anyone could say anything more,
they heard the gun firing at an unbelievably high
rate. *Pop-pop-pop-pop....* the noise continued
ringing in the air as round after round started
destroying the targets down range. Within
seconds, one of them was almost completely
obliterated, then another, and another. Once the
mini-gun came to the end of its ammunition belt,
all five targets were no more. Everyone
applauded and rushed towards the weapon,
probably to start placing orders.¶

After about twenty more minutes, the crowd
was down to only five people. It looked like Mr.
Boyd was about to pack up the mini-gun as the

two other dealers with their bodyguards started heading towards their transportation.

"Remember what I told you earlier." Said Hamilton. "I'll announce that I'm a Texas Marshal and I'm here to arrest Mr. Boyd. I'm very confident that the other four men will simply flee. But, shoul d they draw their weapons, take cover until the shooting stops." Rattler and Maska both nodded as the Marshal stepped from their hiding spot.¶

"I am Texas Marshal Hamilton Brisco. I am here to place Mr. Boyd under arrest for the manufacturing and possession of an illegal firearm." He said in a booming voice. He also had two pistols aimed directly at Mr. Boyd. The two arms dealers acted just as he predicted and started running. Their bodyguards drew their guns and fired warning shots high above the trio's heads just to say, "we'll kill you if you try to follow us." Mr. Boyd, on the other hand, simply threw his hands up and did not try to resist. Hamilton handcuffed him and led him back to his steam-cycle. Maska chased after one of the fleeing arms dealers. Once he got in range, he would take out the bodyguard with his bow.¶

Rattler approached the mini-gun, already detached from the tripod and sitting on the ground. He slipped a couple of shells in his pocket and went to pick up the main part of the weapon when he felt something. He felt vibrations in his feet; they were slow, steady vibrations, and they seemed to be coming from behind him. He spun around quickly and saw a tall man wearing a white mask pointing a pistol at him from forty feet away. "Impressive. I thought I was rather quiet in my approach." The man said. "I felt... oh, never mind." Said Rattler, standing straight up.¶

The two men stood there, staring each other down for what seemed like five or six minutes before Rattler decided to take action. Spinning in a complete circle, he drew his bow and fired directly at the man's pistol. *Blam!* Rattler was hit in the shoulder while the gun was jarred from the man's hand, leaving a thin cut between his thumb and trigger finger. The stranger seemed shocked to see Rattler still standing. The bullet lay compacted in the grass by his feet.¶

Rattler then pulled the Snake Blade from its sheath. "I will give you only one warning! Surrender and you will not be harmed!" He stated as he walked towards him. That was when he noticed the man's cane. It was dark black topped with what looked like the handle of a six shooter pistol. "Oh, I think it is you who should surrender... boy!" As he spoke, he drew the sword hidden within the cane. "You see, swords don't scare me, and neither do you!" Rattler was ready for this type of fight, he had most likely trained harder than this man. But, Ronin had always warned him about overconfidence. Calling him boy obviously meant he was much older, with more experience. He could not afford to underestimate his opponent.¶

The two men closed on each other, neither showing any signs of fear or hesitation. Their blades clashed again and again as they continued their individualized attacks. Rattler was trying to disarm his opponent, while the stranger was trying for death strikes. "It's no use, boy, I have more experience and will eventually kill you." Rattler knew exactly what he was trying to do, and would not be intimidated by it. "All I do is train, I will simply outlast you, and you will lose. Then you will face justice." Although Rattler was confident with what he was saying, he had no idea who he was talking too.¶

And that split second of confusion allowed the masked man to block the Snake Blade with the sheath-end of the cane and swing his blade at Rattler's face. Fortunately, Rattler was just fast enough to avoid a potentially lethal strike; leaving only a small slit in the bandanna tied around the lower part of his face, concealing his identity. His opponent tried a follow-up attack to the chest, but Rattler instinctively blocked it with a down-swing of his arm, fully utilizing the armored sleeve. He followed through and spun away to regain his composure and raised his sword in defense. "An armored coat… so, that's why my bullet had no effect."¶

They continued their volley of swordplay, trading strike for strike and avoiding the business end of each others' weapon. Nearly five minutes of constant assault seemed to take no toll on either combatant. "You have been trained well." Said the masked stranger. "Who was your teacher?" Rattler shuffled back and blocked another thrust of his opponent's sword. Talking during a fight was an unnecessary distraction, and he would not answer the stranger's questions. "I am not easily manipulated, we all learn from someone, and my teacher's identity is of no importance to you, because you would not even know him." Their swords pushed off each other and they both took a step back to reassess the situation for a moment.¶

"I'm curious as to who you are, and why you're meddling in these affairs." The stranger remained still in a defensive posture while he talked. "It is obvious you are the one who paid my colleague a visit the other night." He said.

Rattler swung his sword around, stretching the muscles in both his shoulders and abdomen to loosen the tension that had been building up. This also kept the blood flowing and helped maintain his cardio while he sized up how to proceed. "It seems someone with your talents and skill should have higher goals than delaying the inevitable." The stranger continued to talk in a desperate attempt to gather information.¶

"And what is the inevitable outcome of all of this?" Rattler said as he advanced, closing the space that had kept a sense of false safety between them. "You know what we are doing here, you are the ones who broke into our headquarters, hoping to find something you can use against us. But, that will no longer be a problem... you will no longer be a problem." He lunged forward, trying to spear Rattler in the face, but that was the area of his body that he defended above all else. He leaned back to avoid the sword, and caught the masked stranger off-guard; he swung upward and away, slashing his left shoulder and making him drop the cane sheath to the ground.¶

"I have my best men looking for you." He said as he stumbled backwards a few feet. He was trying his best to hide the pain and appear unfazed, but Rattler knew better. "You are not going to win this confrontation. And, you mentioned that Mr. Boyd was your colleague, and that me and my friends broke into 'your' headquarters." Rattler's confidence with the situation grew, but he needed to remain focused and not let his guard down. "I know Mr. Experiment is actually Mr. Boyd's alias. We know a lot about your inner workings and that you are planning to do business with Don'yoku." Rattler was hoping to turn the would-be assassin's strategy against him.¶

The masked man kept his sword up in front of him and pondered how anyone outside the Black Bull Society could have this information. Rattler refocused his breathing and moved in to disarm his opponent. "If you know I work for Dead-Eye Inc., then you seem to have a slight edge." The stranger blocked one attack after another as he backed up, piecing bits of information in his mind as he did so. "You mentioned you have a group of 'concerned citizens,' I wonder... perhaps you are working with Max and his friends." Rattler's attack slowed slightly as he tried to clear thoughts of his father and Uncle Butch from disrupting the battle.¶

"You do know of whom I speak. Could you be?" Rattler did not know what the stranger was implying, but he kept attacking. "Could you be Max's boy? We have not seen his son nor the samurai for many years now." He continued talking as he tried his best to mount more offense; the cut in his shoulder began bleeding through his shirt. "You need to save your strength and give up while you can." Rattler said, easily knocking each thrust aside. He knew his opponent would become too weak to continue in a matter of minutes. "It is you! You should know that your father is now dead." The masked man tried to gauge his reactions as he spoke. "You lie!" Rattler said, no longer able to keep his emotions from bubbling to the surface.¶

"Unfortunately he was spotted leaving the Blackfoot Indian village and was discovered heading towards Bluejacket. I sent my best assassin and some of his colleagues to finish what I started with his friend Butch eleven years ago!" He lunged at Rattler, but still could not me contact with anything but the Snake Blade. Rattler finally gave in to his urges. "What do you know about it, anyway?" It took all he had not to kill the stranger outright. "I was there. He was stabbed and thrown off Dead Man's Cliff. Once the bounty on your head includes a name, well... it will only be a matter of time."¶

As Rattler circled around him, the mini-gun

came into view. One of the would-be buyers and
his personal bodyguard were heading right
towards it. They were going to use this moment
to steal the weapon. A light went on in Rattler's
head. "If you know who I am, you must be Mr.
Johnson, the head of security. My father told us
all about you." Seeing that Rattler was looking
past him towards the demonstration area, Mr.
Johnson came clean. "Well, you figured
something out, too bad you won't be able to
prove anything without any evidence." He put
down his sword and held his shoulder, the
trickling blood was now on his hands, and he
was starting to panic.¶

Rattler had a decision to make. But, since
the marshal had not seen this man in a white
mask, he lowered his sword. "Another time
perhaps." The stranger said smugly. Rattler did
not have time to reply as he turned his attention
to the two men attempting to steal the mini-gun.
Since both of them were armed, he needed to
level the playing field. Grabbing the bow from
his back, he drew and let a single arrow fly
through the air. It struck the bodyguard directly
in the knee, sending him howling into the dirt.
The other man drew his pistol and started to
return fire. "I really need to learn how to use a
gun." Rattler thought to himself as he ducked

behind a rock.¶

Since his man was not going to be able to carry the weapon, the would-be thieves made their way back to their steam-cycle and drove away. Rattler ran back to where he and Mr. Johnson had been fighting. There were only a few drops of blood in the dirt where he had once stood. Following the small trail, he wound up behind that large boulder where he thought he had spotted someone right before the demonstration. The blood finally stopped behind some bike tracks. He must have come from a different direction. He really did anticipate them showing up somehow.¶

After about fifteen minutes had gone by, Maska returned from his pursuit. "I am pretty sure those men were heading to Lofty River. Are you okay?" Rattler got to his feet. "Yeah, you just missed the action, that's all. Here, I'll tell you all about it on our way home. I think all of this equipment will fit in the sidecar with you." Rattler retrieved the bike while Maska stood guard over the disassembled weapon. After securing the mini-gun safely, he filled his friend in on all the details of what he missed on their way back to Blackwater.¶

*¶

It was nearly lunch time Thursday morning as Rattler walked into the Rustic Forge. There were no customers, so he locked the door for his friend. "Hey, how did yesterday go? Tell me everything!" Dan tossed the cloth he was cleaning with on the counter and came around. "Marshal Brisco arrested Mr. Boyd shortly after the weapon's demonstration was over. Maska managed to track down our next lead, probably an arm's dealer from Lofty River. We need to make a few phone calls first." The two instinctively walked to the back room as they talked.¶

"I was attacked by none other than Mr. Johnson, head of security over at Dead-Eye Inc." "You mean the CEO's brother, Mr. Johnson?" He asked. "Yeah, he was wearing a weird white mask and had a sword concealed in his walking cane. He got away because a couple of men tried to steal the mini-gun, but we obviously know where to find him. By the way…" Rattler pulled the bandanna from his pocket and showed the slit to Dan. "I came awfully close to needing stitches during that fight. Do you think you can fix me up with an armored version or a mask of some kind?" Dan took the bandanna and whistled. "Damn, awfully close is an understatement." He said, looking at it more closely. "I suppose I can come up with something."¶

There was a rapid knock at the front door. Heading out onto the sales floor, they saw it was Daisy, peering through the window. "Hey guys, come on." Dan opened the door and held it for her. "No, you guys come with me. I got a call from our lawyer and I'm meeting with…, I mean, we're meeting with him for lunch, let's go." "Alright." Dan locked the door behind them and they headed to the diner down the street. Mr. Ace was already seated at a table for four on the restaurant's patio. "Have a seat." He said as he pulled a chair out for Daisy. "Thank you." She replied. "I hope you don't mind, I invited my friends." "That's why I got a table for four, I assumed they would be joining us. Besides, this news should be shared with your friends any way."¶

The waitress stopped at their table and took their orders. After she delivered their drinks, Daisy asked about the important news. "Well, I received a letter from your Uncle Scotty." "I've received letters from Uncle Scotty before, is this about business or something, I could have stopped by your office after work. You shouldn't have to work through your lunch." "It's not a problem, this is a joyous occasion. He wants to set up for a visit." Tom stated. Daisy nearly dropped her glass. "Uncle Scotty and Aunt Jill are coming back to Blackwater?" "No, not that. He's arranging for you to take a train to visit them. The details are in this envelope." He handed her a sealed envelope containing the tickets, itinerary, and some spending money. After their meal, Daisy, Tom and Dan each returned to work; Rattler on the other hand, had some business of his own to tend to.¶

Walking down to the local sheriff's office, he checked in with Texas Marshal Brisco. "The mini-gun is being guarded in the main village square by two dozen Blackfoot warriors, by order of Chief White Cloud. They are expecting you and some local law-enforcement officers to take possession of it some time this afternoon." Hamilton had just finished signing some papers detailing the arrest of a one Mr. Boyd, executive of Dead-Eye Inc. "Blackwater and all of Texas owe you and your friends a debt of gratitude." They shook hands and Rattler headed home. A celebration dinner was being planned by the village, honoring the success of Rattler and the rest of his newly formed ninja clan slash Blackfoot village. Sinopa had already returned to the main village to help with the preparations. The past thirty-six hours had proved to be what everyone involved hoped it would be.¶

*¶

William and Henry Johnson, along with their corporate lawyer, signed the visitor's ledger at the jailhouse. They were then escorted down a hall to the conference room where Mr. Boyd sat, handcuffed to the table. Two guards remained just outside as the lawyer closed the door, giving them privacy to talk with his client. "What did you tell them?" Asked William. "Nothing, sir. I didn't tell them anything. But the Texas Marshal witnessed the weapon demonstration, and he knows we're all involved." The lawyer put his hand up. "No, he knows you're involved." Mr. Boyd seemed a little confused as he looked at his boss. "What was that?" He asked.¶

"Look Jack." Said William. "It's quite simple. Since you were arrested, you take the fall." The lawyer interrupted. "Mr. Boyd, the bottom line is this. Without your collaboration on the witness stand, they've got nothing against any of your fellow executives. Since nobody was hurt, they can only charge you with the attempt of selling an illegal firearm. One which you secretly designed and manufactured at Dead-Eye Inc. unbeknownst to your employer. You will only do three years in a minimum security prison." "Three years?!" Mr. Boyd started shaking his head, seemingly a little worried.¶

"Three extremely comfortable years." Added Henry. "We're not leaving you out to dry here. We take very good care of our own, especially those who fall on the sword, so to speak." "Indeed." Added William. "And your position at the company will be yours as soon as you're released, I personally guarantee it." "There's no other way?" He pleaded. "Trust us, if there was any other way, we'd have found it." They continued going over the details of the upcoming trial for the next hour.¶

"Times up!" Said one of the guards, opening the door. As Mr. Boyd was escorted back to his cell, Mr. Johnson talked with the second guard. "See that he's well taken care of." He slipped two hundred dollar bills into the man's pocket. "If you hear that anyone so much as looks at him cross-eyed, I want to know." "Whatever you say, Mr. Johnson." Henry and William finished with their lawyer and returned to headquarters. Mr. Boyd was served roasted chicken and steamed vegetables for lunch instead of the questionable meatloaf sandwiches the other inmates received. Sitting back in his cell, he felt that his cooperation would be the right decision to make.

Rattler

Nathanial Ghere